This edition of

VERDICT UNSAFE

has been signed by the author

VERDICT UNSAFE

A Fawcett Columbine Book
Published by Ballantine Books

Copyright © 1997 by Jill McGown

All rights reserved under International and Pan-American Copyright Conventions. Published
in the United States by Ballantine Books, a division of Random House, Inc., New York. Originally published in Great Britain by Macmillan Publishers Limited in 1997.

http://www.randomhouse.com

Library of Congress Cataloging-in-Publication Data
McGown, Jill.
    Verdict unsafe / Jill McGown. — 1st American ed.
      p.   cm.
    ISBN 0-449-91067-9
    I. Title.
PR6063.C477V47   1997
823'.914—dc21   97-4949

Manufactured in the United States of America

First American Edition: June 1997

10 9 8 7 6 5 4 3 2 1

Jill McGown

VERDICT UNSAFE

Fawcett Columbine • New York

Book One

THE CROWN
-V-
COLIN ARTHUR DRUMMOND

Barton Crown Court, Monday 6 July

That on the seventh of September of that year you unlawfully and with intent inflicted grievous bodily harm on Rachel Olivia Selina Ashman contrary to Section Eighteen of the Offences against the Person Act eighteen sixty-one. Are you guilty or not guilty?"

"Not guilty."

"Count eight. You are charged that on the seventh of September of that year you raped Rachel Olivia . . ."

Harper sighed, and wished he was defending anyone but Colin Arthur Drummond, as the charges rolled on and on.

"Count eleven. You are charged that on the tenth of September of that year you raped Lucy Mary Rogerson, contrary to . . ."

On the day of his arrest, Drummond had made a full confession to four sexual assaults on women; now that he was on trial, facing eleven charges under the Sexual Offences Act and three under the Offences against the Person Act, he was pleading not guilty to them all.

The fourteenth and final plea was entered and, out of the hearing of the jury, Harper tried to have that confession declared inadmissible, as the interviewing officer had failed to fulfil the conditions demanded by the Police and Criminal Evidence Act; the attempt, as he had expected, failed. But Drummond had also made a statement to Detective Inspector Hill of Stansfield CID concerning another, unreported rape; this time Harper's application that this evidence should not be admitted met with success, since it concerned an incident which had never been the subject of a complaint to the police, and did not therefore concern the court.

The jury filed back, and the prosecuting counsel outlined the case which would be presented to the jury. Next, the sworn statements of those who were not being compelled to give evidence were read, and it was well into the morning before the first witness was sworn in.

In the well of the court, the prosecution barrister—tall, stout, silver-haired beneath his wig and almost as imposing as the wood-panelled courtroom itself—was on his feet, and in the witness box stood the dark-haired, dark-eyed, childlike teenage prostitute who had been the alleged victim of the fourth assault. She was the basket in which Harper was carrying all of Drummond's eggs; it looked to him even more fragile than its cargo.

Harper's adversary was waiting patiently for the slightly shocked buzz of reaction to the witness's profession to die down; the girl herself was edgy, nervous, waiting for her ordeal to begin. Just how much of an ordeal it would be had been brought home to the jury by the fact that Rachel Ashman, the second victim, had taken her own life rather than be forced to give evidence, something which in her acutely depressed state she had felt quite unable to do. Only then had Drummond agreed that the victims of the other assaults could make sworn statements, since the defence was not contesting the facts, but simply the identity of the assailant.

Mrs. Ashman's suicide was being regarded as a direct result of the assault; the charge of grievous bodily harm referred to the mental anguish which had led to it. And to cap it all, thought Harper, Brian Ashman had turned up for the trial. There he sat in the public gallery, a widower at twenty-five, with a two-year-old child to look after, still walking with two sticks after an accident at work a few weeks before the assault. And every time the jury looked at him, Colin Drummond's chances would take a further nosedive; with its usual lack of judicial awareness, the public held the defendant responsible for Mrs. Ashman's suicide and all the other human tragedies that had resulted from the assaults before even one witness had been heard.

And twelve members of that public were sitting on the jury. Harper looked round the courtroom, trying to exude a confidence that he most assuredly did not feel, and saw DI Hill slip into court and make for a seat in the public gallery. He'd seen her around the courts from time to time, but he had never met her. She was more than good in the witness box, from what he'd heard. Juries took to her, they said, and Harper could believe it. She was attractive, well dressed, well groomed, her soft, unfussy, dark hair denoting common sense, her brown eyes honesty. Her word was rarely questioned, and he had been advised that he would have grave difficulty in casting doubt on her integrity. And since that was what he would have had to do, it was just as well he had managed to scupper her evidence.

◊

Judy Hill was officially on leave; she had broken it to give evidence, and now that that evidence was not to be heard, she took a seat in the public gallery.

"Miss Benson, can you tell the court where you were at one-thirty A.M. on Monday, the twenty-eighth of October last year?" Robert Whitehouse asked, his voice gentle, as though he were speaking to a child. She was seventeen now; she looked thirteen.

The girl took a breath, and glanced round the courtroom before she replied, a batsman weighing up the field. "I was . . ." she began, and faltered. She licked her lips, cleared her throat, and carried on in a firm, defiant, voice. "I was in Hosier's Alley."

"This was a hundred-yard-long passageway winding between John Wesley Road and Andwell Street in Malworth, my lord," said Whitehouse. "It was formed by the walls of a derelict shirt factory, an ex-warehouse, and two empty blocks of flats, in one of which the witness was living, with a number of others, as a squatter. The area was awaiting demolition in order to build the bypass now under construction in that area. There was thick fog that night, and the alleyway was unlit." He turned back to the girl. "And could you tell the court, in your own words, what happened to you?" he asked.

"He raped me," she said, with a quick nod towards the dock.

Judy felt irrationally guilty about that; the girl had been a last-minute replacement for Judy herself, as Drummond had lost no time in pointing out to her.

"I know this is distressing for you," Whitehouse said. "But we have to take it step by step. What happened first of all?"

"He grabbed me as I turned into the alley," she said. "He had his hand over my mouth."

"His bare hand?"

"No. He had big gloves on. And he had a knife up to my eye." Her hand unconsciously went to her eye as she spoke. "He sort of pressed his elbows into me, and pulled me down the alley to where it was dark."

"Could you see the knife?"

"Sort of." She went pale when she was shown the knife found on the bank of the Andwell River, which ran parallel to the street bearing its name, and was asked if it was the one she had seen. "It could be," she said, her voice shaking slightly. "The blade looks the same. I couldn't see the handle." The knife was taken away.

"And what happened in the alley?" asked Whitehouse.

"He . . . he pushed me face down and knelt over me," she said. "Then he pulled me up so I was on my knees, and he was behind me. He told me to pull down my leggings and—" She broke off, tried to carry on, failed.

"Take your time," said Whitehouse.

"He—" Her mouth trembled, and she tried to blink away the tears, but she couldn't go on.

"Would the witness like a glass of water?" asked the judge.

Judy was never convinced of the magic properties of a glass of water. Would the witness like a stiff gin, then you'd be talking. The witness shook her head, and took a moment to gather herself.

"He touched me with the knife," she said.

"Where did he touch you?"

She looked hunted, and Judy felt sad; the poor little girl didn't know the socially acceptable word for any part of the anatomy below the waist. "My private parts," she said eventually, her face burning. "He said if I didn't do what he wanted he'd cut me. Down there. And he told me to undo my blouse. Then he pushed my head right down, and he—" She swallowed hard. "He raped me."

"How did he rape you?" Whitehouse asked quietly.

More agony, until the girl thought of an acceptable alternative to the word she habitually used. "He used my back passage," she said.

"Did he say anything to you while this was happening?"

She nodded miserably. "He kept saying something over and over, but I couldn't understand him," she said. "I was dead scared he'd cut me if I made a noise. I was just trying not to cry." She was still trying not to cry. "I'm sorry," she said.

"That's all right," said Whitehouse. "Go on."

"After a bit, these two men came down the alley, and he got off me and ran away. One of them went after him."

When Whitehouse had finished getting as much detail of the assault as he could from the girl, he thanked her. "I know this is very difficult for you," he said, "but you must stay there, please—my learned friend will have some questions to put to you."

The judge looked at the clock, and advised Harper that he was going to wait until after lunch to begin his cross-examination, which didn't, Judy fancied, go down too well with Whitehouse's learned friend. And so it was that afternoon that she got her first proper look at the hotshot lawyer Drummond Senior had retained, as the judge reminded the little girl that she was still under oath, and Harper stood up to cross-examine her.

Slim, blond, early thirties, if that. Quite handsome, in a slim, blond sort of way, but it was a combination that Judy always felt looked better on women. Under his gown his dark court clothes were tailored and sharp. He obviously did well in his chosen profession.

"This morning we heard a very harrowing story," he said. "But that isn't quite how it happened, is it?"

"Yes, it is," she said.

"I suggest that you were walking through the alleyway on your way to your squat, and came across Mr. Drummond as he was returning to his motorbike," he said. "You propositioned him and he paid you for sex. It's as simple as that, isn't it?"

"No." The girl shook her head. "He grabbed me and pulled me in there."

"Did you shout for help when he grabbed you? After all, as it turned out, the police were remarkably close at hand, weren't they? They would have heard a cry for help."

"I couldn't! He had his hand over my mouth!"

"I think you didn't cry for help, not because he had his hand over your mouth, but because you didn't need any help. You needed money, though, didn't you? Had you had many customers that night?"

"Enough."

"But you had spent most of the evening in the police station, hadn't you?"

She lifted her chin a little, her natural defiance beginning to give her the confidence to assert herself. "So what?"

"You had been arrested in a public park for committing a breach of the peace?"

"Yes."

"What had you been doing?"

"A punter," she said guilelessly, to appreciative smiles.

"In other words, you had been committing an indecent act in a public place. And it wasn't the first time, was it?"

"No."

"But you weren't charged, were you? You weren't even cautioned. They simply let you go. Why?"

"I don't know, do I? They just came and said I could go home."

"Very well. But you must have been keen to make up for the time lost at the police station—is that why you approached Mr. Drummond?"

"No! He grabbed me!"

"Is Mr. Drummond known to you?"

She shrugged. "I've seen him up the Ferrari," she said.

"The Ferrari is a drinking club in Malworth, my lord," said Hotshot. "And is known to be frequented by prostitutes."

Judy smiled a little at the description, which made it sound like a Soho vice den. Malworth had once been a large, thriving market town with, Judy was sure, a large, thriving prostitution industry, as prosperous traders had come to do business. But by the turn of the century the Corn Hall had been turned into a concert hall, and Victorian factories had sprouted up to the north of the town, along with workers' cottages and a park. Parkside was where favors were bought and sold; the rest of Malworth had become genteel.

One by one the old factories had closed, and Parkside had been allowed to die with them, leaving it only one industry, and that with only sporadic and uncertain custom. The Ferrari Club was in Parkside, and the odd girl or two trawled for custom there, or hopefully patrolled the park.

"Mr. Drummond used prostitutes from the Ferrari, didn't he?" Hotshot asked.

"I dunno."

"Oh, come on!"

"One," she said sulkily. "Rosa."

The fabled Rosa had been produced by Drummond not long before the case had come to trial, but all efforts to trace her had failed. Judy had doubted her very existence at one point.

"When was the last time you saw her with Mr. Drummond?"

"The last time she was there. I saw her go out of the club with him, then I saw her again after she'd done him, and she said—"

Harper held up a hand. "Don't tell us what anyone said to you. At what time did you see Mr. Drummond with Rosa?"

"He always came in at the same time. About half nine."

"Do you remember what date that was?"

"No. It was September, I know that. And the next day everyone was saying there had been another rape—I think that's why she packed it in."

"And did Mr. Drummond ever use your services after Rosa 'packed it in'?"

"No."

"I think he did, on one occasion. I think that in the early hours of Monday the twenty-eighth of October you turned into Hosier's Alley on your way home, saw Mr. Drummond, and recognized him as a potential 'punter,' didn't you?"

"No. I never saw him! He grabbed me and pulled me in there! He was wearing a mask—I didn't even know it *was* him!"

"I suggest that he paid you for sex, but when you heard people coming down the alleyway, you told Mr. Drummond to go. He wanted his money back, and you shouted, swore at him. That's when he put his hand over your mouth, isn't it, to try to quieten you?"

The girl's head was shaking, all the time. "No," she said. "No. He was raping me—he ran away when he heard these men coming."

"When one of these men ran to detain Mr. Drummond, did you warn him that he had a knife?"

"I couldn't speak—I couldn't stop crying!"

"There was no knife, and no assault, was there? You propositioned Mr. Drummond—isn't that what really happened?"

"No!"

"Why not? That's what you do, isn't it?"

"I don't do it like that, not in the street!"

"Oh, come on," said Harper. "Your activities are a matter of public record, Miss Benson. Of course you do it in the street. In doorways, in alleyways—anywhere anyone pays you to do it, don't you?"

"Not like that! Not like what he made me do! I would never have done it like that!"

Harper allowed a silence to follow the girl's indignant statement, reinforcing it in a way that making her repeat it would not have done.

"Are you putting forward as evidence of your nonconsent the contention that you do not offer anal intercourse as a service?" he asked, after a long moment.

The girl looked blank, not having understood a word of the question, and shook her head. "No," she said.

Whitehouse got to his feet. "My lord, I fail to see the relevance of this line of questioning, and I suspect that the witness did not in any event fully understand the last question put to her by my learned friend."

The judge looked at Whitehouse, and shook his head slightly. "The witness is accusing the defendant of a very serious sexual assault," he said. "His defence is that he paid for her services, and her contention seems to be that she does not offer anal intercourse as a service. I think that is of considerable relevance. However . . ." He turned to Harper. ". . . Mr. Harper, I, too, feel that both the question and its implications should be made clearer to the witness before she answers. The jury will disregard the witness's last reply."

The witness was looking bewildered, and the judge leant over to talk to her. "Anal intercourse is another way of saying that he used your back passage," he said, and her face cleared. "Now," he went on, "you have said that this is something that you would never have agreed to, and if that is the case, it would be an indication that you were indeed sexually assaulted. But if you do sometimes agree to it— even if at that time you did not—you must say so, because you have sworn to tell the truth. Do you understand?"

Wide-eyed, worried, she nodded solemnly.

"Please rephrase the question using words with which the witness is familiar, Mr. Harper."

"I am obliged, my lord," said Harper, and turned back to the girl. "You have said that you would never have agreed to performing sexual intercourse *like that*," he said. "So the question is quite simple. Have you ever allowed a customer to have sex with you like that?"

She looked from Harper, to Whitehouse, to the judge, then back to Harper, a skinny little fox cub trapped by the hounds, trying to work out if she could escape being torn limb from limb. Her only point of reference was that if she told a lie, her case would be strengthened, whereas the truth would damage it, because she had allowed anyone to do anything they wanted with her since before puberty. Judy crossed her fingers, hoping that she had taken her oath seriously. Tell the truth, she silently begged her. Tell the truth.

"I'll repeat the question," said Harper. "Have you ever allowed a customer to have sex with you *like that?*"

"No," she said firmly, shaking her head.

Judy closed her eyes, then opened them again as the girl continued speaking.

"I wouldn't get down on my hands and knees on a muddy street for any bugger!" she said.

The tension which had been generated by her evidence was broken, and the room erupted. Even Harper gave the girl a little smiling nod as the laughter at his expense died away. And the cause of all this merriment stood in the witness box, terminally puzzled.

Then Harper frowned slightly, and looked through the papers in front of him, pulling out a typewritten statement, flicking through it. He looked up from it. "You don't know the word 'anal'?" he asked.

The puzzled frown was back, and she shook her head. "No," she said.

"That's odd," he said. "Because you used it in your statement to the police. Do you know what the word 'subjected' means?"

"No."

"You used it, too. In the same sentence. 'He subjected me to an anal assault,' " he quoted. "Did you say that?"

She shook her head, her mouth opening slightly.

"Can you tell me what the word 'genitalia' means?"

The girl looked quite blank. No embarrassment, which there would have been, had she had the slightest idea of its meaning. She shook her head.

"You used it in your statement, too. 'He touched my genitalia with the blade of the knife.' Did you say that?"

She shook her head, going pink now that she had worked out what it meant.

" 'Straddled'? 'Corroborated'? Do you know what they mean?"

She just stared at him, her face reddening, panic and acute embarrassment at the thought of what they might mean not allowing her even to shake her head.

" 'My head was forced down to the ground and he straddled me, and subjected me to an anal assault. This can be corroborated by the two witnesses, one of whom gave chase.' " He held the statement up. "You didn't use any of these words, did you?"

"No," she said, her voice a whisper, her face stricken.

"But you signed it as a true record of what you had told the police," said Harper.

"I . . . I can't . . . I'm not good at reading and writing and things," she said. "They just asked me questions about what had happened to me, and I signed what they wrote down."

"No further questions," Harper said.

"Mr. Whitehouse, do you wish to re-examine?"

Whitehouse rose, and thought for a moment before he spoke. "Is what you told the court today a true account of what happened to you in the alleyway?" he asked.

"Yes," she said firmly, shooting a look at Drummond as he sat meekly in the dock.

"And is it what you told the police that night?"

"Yes. I can't help what they wrote down!"

Whitehouse smiled. "Did you use the same words to tell them what had happened as you did today in court? For instance, you told the court that the knife had touched your private parts—is that the expression you used to the police?"

The girl blushed ferociously. "No," she said.

"No," said Whitehouse. "Could that be why the police paraphrased what you had said?"

Blank terror.

"I know you don't know what that means," said Whitehouse soothingly. "But I'm sure my learned friend does, and I imagine the jury does. No further questions, my lord."

"The witness may step down," said the judge, and the witness almost fell down from sheer relief.

Now it was the turn of the two men who had found her, and each told substantially the same story. They had entered the alley from John Wesley Road, and had come upon a young woman on all fours on the ground with a man kneeling over her. The man had run away along the alley towards Andwell Street as they had approached. The girl's blouse had been undone, and her leopardskin pants had been round her knees. She had been in considerable distress.

"You didn't call the police, did you?" Harper asked the man who had stayed with her when the other had gone after Drummond. "Did it seem to you that the situation didn't merit the attendance of the police?"

"Of course it did," he said. "But I didn't have to call them—a police car came almost straight away."

"Is that so?" said Harper. "How fortunate."

The area car officer arrived next. He and his colleague had been answering what had turned out to be a bogus nine-double-nine call about youths smoking crack cocaine in one of the empty buildings, when they had heard a commotion further down the road. They had attended the incident at one thirty-six A.M.

Harper rose to cross-examine. "You told my learned friend that the young woman was in some distress, and complained that the defendant had sexually assaulted her," he said. "Can you tell the court her exact words?"

The constable requested leave to consult his notes, and turned to the appropriate page. "I asked what the trouble was, to which she replied, pointing to the defendant, 'That fucking bastard raped me; he did me up the sodding arse.' "

Judy saw the girl colour up as her unladylike words were read out, and smiled.

"More angry than distressed, would you say?"

Whitehouse rose. "While I am obliged to my learned friend for drawing the court's attention to the immediate complaint of sexual assault made subsequent to the incident, and incidentally clarifying the perceived necessity to bowdlerize the victim's statement, I don't think that this witness's opinion as to the victim's emotional state should be sought," he said.

The judge agreed.

"You then used your radio to request CID assistance, is that correct?"

"Yes, my lord."

"And did you use the words 'the Stealth Bomber's been grounded'?"

"Yes, I did, my lord."

It was the duty detective inspector who had been thus summoned who was next to give evidence.

"Did the complainant make mention of a knife?" asked Whitehouse.

"She did, my lord. We couldn't find anything that night, but a knife was found the following morning on the riverbank close to the mouth of the alleyway where it adjoins Andwell Street. The river level had dropped sufficiently for the knife to be revealed."

With that evidence, court was adjourned for the day, and Judy left with the public who had packed the gallery. She had decided how she was going to spend her leave; she was going to see this trial through.

Barton Crown Court, Tuesday 7 July

"All those having business with the Queen's Justices and this court draw near and give attention."

Harper drew near and gave attention, knowing only too well that yesterday had not been one of his finest hours. The assault on the jury's emotions of a little doe-eyed wisp of a girl, barely out of her utterly deprived childhood, describing calculated, deliberate terror being inflicted on her by a six-foot-tall, well-built, privileged youth was all but impossible to combat. When he had scored a point, which had been but rarely, he had looked a bully; when she had, he had looked a fool.

All he could do now was work very hard to rid the jurors' memories of that, and concentrate on cop-bashing, which went down reasonably well even with white-collar middle-class types these days. Not that it would work. But he would try.

꜀

It was the man who had briefly been Judy's boss, the quietly spoken DCI Merrill, who was giving evidence first this morning. He was handed the typewritten transcription of Drummond's statement, and was invited to read it to the court, something to which Judy could tell he had clearly not been looking forward.

He took a deep breath. "Drummond was asked about the assault on Mrs. Carole Jarvis, which occurred in one of a block of garages behind the houses in Austen Street, Stansfield, at ten-thirty in the evening on the fifteenth of August last year," he began. "And stated, 'I saw that one getting into her car in Malworth, and I followed her . . .' "

The crude language employed by Drummond sounded incongruous coming from the prim, God-fearing Chief Inspector, who read the words with as little vocal and facial expression as was possible in the circumstances. The catalogue of increasingly violent assaults carried out on Carole Jarvis, read in a near monotone, produced a more shocked reaction than it would have done if it had been related gleefully by Drummond himself.

Judy sighed. Mrs. Jarvis had not been the only victim of that particular assault; what had happened to her after she had driven her brand-new car into that garage was appalling, but it hadn't ended there. Her marriage must have been severely tested once what she had been doing prior to the attack had come to light. But all that would have to be explained at the appropriate time; right now it was Drummond's version of events that the court was hearing.

Merrill was nearing the end of Drummond's blow-by-blow description of the first assault. " 'When I had finished with her, I cleaned her up. Then I cut the tape off her wrists and ankles. I took it away with me so you lot couldn't trace it.' " Merrill took another breath, and looked at the jury before embarking on the account of the second assault. "Drummond was then asked about the assault on Mrs. Rachel Ashman, which occurred in the ladies' lavatory of the Percy Road Service Station, Malworth, at eleven-fifteen P.M. on Saturday, September seventh, last year," he said. "And stated, 'I pulled her into a toilet at a petrol station. I got her down just like the first one . . .' "

Mrs. Ashman had been in all evening with her husband and baby. Her husband, recovering from a bad accident at work, had been home for the weekend from hospital, still in a wheelchair. She had gone out to get some milk from the all-night petrol station, and he had dozed off. The police had awakened him with the news of what had happened to his wife, who had been found by the next female customer who used the toilet. Mrs. Ashman had committed suicide three months ago; she had been twenty-two years old.

Merrill paused before moving on to the third assault. "When asked about the assault on Lucy Rogerson, which took place at Oakleigh Farm, Malworth, at eight o'clock in the evening on the tenth of September last year," he read doggedly, "Drummond stated, 'I got that one in a barn right after she'd been with some bloke. I did everything the same. I made her take down her own knickers and undo her shirt, and I did her just the same as the others. After, I cleaned her up—everything.' "

Lucy Rogerson had just celebrated her seventeenth birthday; she had been in the barn with a boyfriend who had been kept secret from her parents, because they would have disapproved. He had left her to walk the three hundred yards to the farmhouse; broad daylight, within sight of home, on her own land—what danger could there be?

Merrill cleared his throat, adjusting his stride to take the final hurdle and get to the finishing post. He gave the details of the fourth assault, and turned back to Drummond's statement. "When asked about this assault, the defendant stated, 'I saw her on her own, and I drove past her and took the bike into an alley. I thought I'd be all right because there's never anyone up that end at night, not even your lot because everywhere's being demolished and there's nothing left to nick. I pulled her into the alley. She was wearing these skin-tight leopard-skin pants—I got her to pull them down and unbutton her top—she wasn't wearing anything underneath, the slag. I'd only just started when I heard people coming, so I ran, but someone came after me and pulled me off the bike.' Drummond was asked if he had said anything to the women during these assaults, and he replied, 'I told them not to make a sound, not to make any trouble for me, or I'd cut them open. I told them what to do. And I told them I was the Stealth Bomber, because that's who I am.' The statement ends there, my lord."

"Thank you, Chief Inspector," said the judge.

"Did you have evidence other than the defendant's confession on which to base the charges?" asked Whitehouse.

"Later, a positive DNA match was made with a sample of seminal fluid taken from the clothing of one of the victims of the previous assaults. At the time, there was not only the way he was dressed, but the manner in which the assault on Miss Benson had been carried out, and the specific threats made. Also, surgical tape of the type believed to have been used to bind the hands and feet of the previous victims was found in the first-aid kit on the defendant's motorbike, and he was carrying the sort of wipes used to wash the victims of the other assaults. A search of his bedroom revealed a great deal of literature on the subject of rape and its detection, and several newspaper clippings of the offences with which he was subsequently charged."

When Whitehouse had finished his lengthy questioning of the Chief Inspector, Hotshot Harper made a performance out of sorting out some papers before he rose slowly and looked up at the witness box.

"With regard to the incident on Monday, twenty-eighth October," he said, "was the alleged victim known to you, Chief Inspector?"

"Yes, my lord."

"You knew that she was a prostitute who plied her wares on the street, and frequently also performed sexual services on the street, and that she had been arrested for just such an offence earlier in the evening?"

"I did," said Merrill.

"And yet you had no doubt that her story was true, and that she had been assaulted by the defendant?"

"The forensic medical examiner said that in her opinion the young woman had been the victim of a sexual assault," said Merrill stolidly. "Saliva found on the defendant's glove proved to be that of the victim, supporting her contention that he had held his gloved hand to her mouth to prevent her crying for help. That, taken in conjunction with the eye-witness statements, left me with little doubt that an offence had been committed."

"And—like the arresting officer—you thought you had got your man, the one you were seeking in connection with the other three assaults?"

"Yes," said Merrill. "In view of the circumstances of his arrest."

"That he was dressed in black, and possessed a first-aid kit and the means to clean his hands after working on his bike?"

"I think the face-mask clinched it," said Merrill.

There was muted laughter; the judge immediately silenced it.

"Was he carrying a flick-knife, or any other knife or weapon?"

"No, my lord. But a flick-knife and mask had been found the previous day, which it was reasonable to suppose the rapist had discarded. And in daylight a knife was found close to the scene of the last assault, which could have been the one used to threaten the victim."

"Do you have any forensic or other evidence that either of these knives was ever owned or handled by Mr. Drummond?"

"No, my lord. The knife found by the river had no fingerprints on it, and the flick-knife had been handled by a number of people before it was handed in. But it was found not far from where the defendant had been stopped by the police for reckless driving two nights previously."

"Where he had been stopped and badly beaten by one of the officers while the other stood by and watched," said Harper. "My client was very aware of that during these interviews—were you, Chief Inspector?" said Harper.

Whitehouse rose, and Harper sat down.

"My lord, the officers involved in that assault on Mr. Drummond were not directly concerned with the rape investigation, but in view of the way in which he was dressed, they routinely questioned him about his movements on the dates involved. His replies caused one of them to lose his temper. They have since been convicted of the offence, and dismissed from the police force—there is no justification for suggesting that this behaviour was in any way condoned by their fellow police officers."

Judy, unwittingly instrumental in the downfall of her two ex-colleagues, felt guilty about that too. Her inadvertent whistle-blowing had created hostility at Malworth; she had been transferred back to Stansfield, to work on a murder investigation. But Colin Drummond had turned out to have vital information about that murder; she had found herself interviewing him, an experience she had no desire to repeat.

They shouldn't have beaten him up, but Judy knew that the quiet, handsome young man in the dock was not at all the Colin Arthur Drummond they had had to deal with. He had been taunting them with being unable to catch him; she had understood their actions from the moment that Drummond had told her how narrowly she had avoided being his fifth victim, and had promised her that she would be his sixth.

The judge looked a query at Harper, who stood up.

"My lord, I shall be calling one of the police officers involved in that assault on Mr. Drummond to give evidence. My client maintains that no mention of the rapes was made during this incident; he believes that he was beaten up because of a previous encounter with these two officers in which he had come off the better, and that he was being targeted by the police. The next morning he was taken to Stansfield police station on another matter altogether, and was questioned—for the first time—about his movements on the dates and at the times of these rapes. He was released only when he made a formal complaint about the officers who had assaulted him, and that night was visited by the police at his home. The following night he was arrested and taken to Malworth police station, where he was questioned all night about the rapes. He is quite prepared to admit that he admired the exploits of the rapist, and that his mode of dress could have led the police genuinely to believe that he *was* the rapist, but his contention is that *he* at no time led them to believe this, and that he eventually confessed to these horrendous crimes in the belief—mistaken or otherwise—that he would be hounded until he did, and quite possibly once again be physically harmed if he did not."

The judge nodded. "I agree that the incident is relevant," he said, glancing up at the gallery, quietening the disbelieving whispers.

Harper turned back to the witness box. "Mr. Drummond agreed to take part in a voice identification procedure, didn't he?"

"Yes, my lord."

"Each of a number of male speakers spoke the words 'I am the Stealth Bomber,' including Mr. Drummond?"

"Yes."

"With the exception of the alleged assault on the twenty-eighth of October, which lasted an estimated five minutes, and during which the alleged victim is unable to confirm that she heard these words spoken, the assaults went on for some time, didn't they?"

"The assaults lasted from twenty to thirty minutes," said Merrill.

"And in addition to the threats and instructions issued, that phrase was used incessantly by the rapist to his victims throughout, wasn't it?"

"It was."

"How many of the victims picked out my client's voice as that of their assailant?"

"None, my lord."

Harper looked astonished. "None? Didn't that surprise you?"

"No. The rapist was in a state of violent sexual stimulation during the assaults, and his voice might well sound very different in other circumstances."

Voice identity had always been a long shot, and an unnecessary trauma for the victims, in Judy's opinion. Now Harper was trying to make something of it.

"But the evidence we have been given of the assaults describes a man frighteningly in control of his actions, doesn't it? A man who commits the same acts in the same order on each of his victims, a man who removes every scrap of evidence that is capable of removal before he leaves the scene—that is not someone in a sexual frenzy, Chief Inspector. That is deliberate, calculated violence perpetrated on victims whom he has first rendered helpless."

"He was highly sexually aroused during these assaults, nevertheless, and it is reasonable to suppose that the character of his voice would alter when he was not."

"One wonders why you attempted such a distressing procedure, in that case," said Harper.

Damn the man. Judy didn't want to think that she agreed with him about anything.

"If that is your last question on that topic, Mr. Harper," said the judge, "I think this might be a convenient time to adjourn for lunch."

The court rose, once again at a point that did not suit Harper, who had had the upper hand for once. But in the afternoon, DCI Merrill once again faced Harper across the courtroom, and Judy knew that this wasn't going to be easy.

"Now we come to Mr. Drummond's statement itself," Harper said. "It is perfectly possible, isn't it, Chief Inspector, that this statement was a fabrication from beginning to end?"

Judy gasped as loudly as anyone at the sheer nerve of the man.

"No," said Merrill. "It is not. Drummond's statement is very explicit. The only details made public were the descriptions of the assailant's clothing, and the fact that he carried a knife, in order that the public might be warned."

"But while I have no wish to take up the court's time by asking them to listen to the seven hours of taped interviews, the statement read by you was given by Mr. Drummond after he had been questioned several times, but had said nothing in reply, wasn't it?"

"It is normal practice only to transcribe relevant information given by the interviewee," said Merrill.

"Quite. But during the earlier interviews, it was indicated, wasn't it," said Harper, "by way of various questions and remarks, that the victims had been forced to remove their own clothing, that the same assaults had been carried out in the same order on each victim, including anal and oral assault? That the victims had been bound hand and foot, and repeatedly raped and assaulted?"

"I would have been surprised if these things hadn't been put to him," said Merrill. "Leading questions are often very efficacious in eliciting a response."

"I'm sure they are. They also supply information that the interviewee might not otherwise have had, as we lawyers are only too well aware."

Merrill shook his head. "The interview was conducted in several sessions over seven hours, as you've said—the information wasn't given in one lump and in the correct order, as you've just done."

"But it was given, nonetheless. My client will say that he merely used the information he had gleaned from the newspapers and from your officers," said Harper. "That after several weeks of what can only be described as hero-worship of this rapist, of reading avidly where and when each assault took place, and a sleepless night during most of which he was told over and over again of what he was supposed to have done, he, afraid of more physical retribution if he did not admit his guilt, simply told you what you wanted to hear. This is entirely possible, isn't it?"

Amid growing and audible scepticism which the judge did not try to quieten, Merrill shook his head. "No, it is not," he said firmly. "The defendant's statement indicates the precise modus operandi, and the increasing violence of the assaults. And while mention was made by the investigating officers of the victims having been bound hand and foot, those were the words that were used, and not 'taped,' which is the word the defendant used in his statement."

Judy nodded vigorously. Merrill had been doing his homework on the interview tapes as well. Not that any of it mattered very much, really. The DNA evidence placed Drummond at the scene of the second assault, and he had been caught in the act of committing the fourth. Hotshot Harper must be on a good retainer to be working this hard for a lost cause.

But he wasn't giving up. "You had questioned Mr. Drummond very closely as to the contents of the first-aid kit on his motor-bike, hadn't you?" he asked. "About the roll of adhesive bandage in particular?"

"Yes. The victims had described material of that sort being used to bind them."

"It wouldn't need too great a leap of imagination to work out to what use you thought this adhesive bandage had been put, would it?"

The muttering had grown into open expression of disbelief, and was at last disapproved of by the judge; the courtroom went quiet again.

"Let us look for a moment at the assault on Miss Rogerson," said Harper, not allowing a reply to his previous question. "In his state-ment, Mr. Drummond says 'I made her . . . undo her shirt,' whereas Miss Rogerson says that she was wearing a light summer top designed to go on and off over the head. Doesn't this suggest that Mr. Drummond might in fact have been inventing the details of this incident?"

The cat-calls were loud enough for the judge to threaten to remove the women who were making them.

"No. It simply means he got confused about what his victims were wearing," Merrill replied. "There are details in the defendant's state-ment that he did not get from any of the interviews, or any news-paper, and which he could neither have invented nor surmised. The specific threats uttered, the cleaning-up of the victims, the cutting away and removal of the tape at the cessation of the assault, the fact that the assailant called himself the 'Stealth Bomber'—none of that was made known to him by any agency whatever."

"One of them was, Chief Inspector," said Harper. "One of the offi-cers at the scene of the alleged assault on Miss Benson said, in Mr. Drummond's hearing, that the Stealth Bomber had been grounded."

"I wasn't aware of that," said Merrill.

"Evidently not." Harper turned a sheet of paper over on the desk and looked up. "And we have no way of knowing how many other remarks were made off the record, so to speak, have we?"

Merrill didn't feel obliged to give an answer, and Harper didn't seek one. "But what we do know," he went on, "is that this statement was made after Mr. Drummond had been held at Malworth police station from one forty-five A.M. for over ten hours with no more than refreshment breaks—isn't that right, Chief Inspector?"

"It was necessary to interview the suspect immediately after the assault complained of, and to question him about the previous assaults."

"The Police and Criminal Evidence Act provides for eight hours' uninterrupted rest from questioning, does it not?"

"Eight hours in twenty-four," said Merrill. "He got that."

"Isn't this eight hours intended to be at night?"

"If possible. In this case, it wasn't. He had several refreshment breaks, and a breakfast break."

"Where?"

"In a cell."

"I think the spirit of the Act was being stretched to its limit, Chief Inspector, but let us move on. After the breakfast break, you yourself conducted the resumed interview, I believe. Did you remind Mr. Drummond that he was not obliged to answer your questions, as required by the Act?"

"Not at that time, my lord," said Merrill. "It was an oversight—he should have been reminded."

"Was he reminded of his right to free legal advice?"

"No."

"Another oversight, Chief Inspector?"

"The same oversight, my lord."

Judy wished that Merrill had had a little more time for what he regarded as new-fangled molly-coddling. Malworth wasn't exactly coming out of this too well.

"And it was during this interview, conducted with a young man who had had no sleep, and who had spent the breaks from questioning locked in a cell, that you brought up the subject of DNA, wasn't it? And told Mr. Drummond that you could prove that he had raped these women?"

"I explained how DNA profiling worked," said Merrill. "And I believe my exact words were that *if* he had raped those women, we could prove it. The tape will bear me out, I think. I certainly meant to say 'if.' "

"I'm sure you did say it, Chief Inspector," said Harper. "Perhaps its significance escaped Mr. Drummond. And when you said you could prove it, you meant that you had collected samples for DNA typing from all three assaults, and had already obtained a DNA profile from the first assault which was just waiting for a match, didn't you?"

"Yes."

"But it wasn't a match for my client, was it, Chief Inspector?"

"No."

There was a puzzled murmur in the courtroom, and Judy sighed. They had known that the defence would have a field day with this.

"So you had misled him?"

"Not deliberately."

"But the fact is that you got three different profiles from the three different samples, isn't that correct?"

The murmuring grew; the judge quietened it.

They had thought that they had more physical evidence than they needed, when traces of seminal fluid had been found on the under-skirt of the second victim, and the other two vaginal swabs had proved positive, but gradually they had become aware of why Drummond had called himself the Stealth Bomber. Stealth planes, she had been informed by her more knowledgeable colleagues, produced controlled emissions, and could not therefore be easily detected by tracking systems.

"We did." Merrill turned to the judge. "If I may explain to the court, my lord?" On receiving consent, he faced the jury. "The first victim, Mrs. Jarvis, was unsure whether or not there had been any emission during the assault, but when the vaginal swab taken as a matter of course proved positive, we assumed that there had, and since there was no match, the defendant was charged only with the assault on Miss Benson, and held in custody pending trial for that offence.

"The victim of the second assault, Mrs. Ashman, had stated that her assailant had ejaculated into a tissue, but seminal fluid was found to be present on her underclothing, and when the DNA profile obtained from this second sample *did* match that of the defendant, he was then charged with that offence.

"In view of these findings, and information given in the defendant's statement, we questioned Mrs. Jarvis again, and found that she had not, as she had originally stated, been returning from visiting a female friend in Stansfield, but had in fact been with a male friend in Malworth, with whom she had had unprotected sexual relations. Mrs. Jarvis then gave us details of the gentleman concerned, a blood sample was obtained, and he was eliminated from the inquiry."

The Jarvises were somehow still together, sitting in front of Judy in the gallery, listening to their private lives being discussed in open court. She looked pale, even less well than she had yesterday, her fair colouring making her seem almost transparent; he looked angry, as he had yesterday, as he had since he had been brought home from his tour of duty in Northern Ireland to his wife's hospital bed. He would listen intently, then his head would drop down, colour creeping up the back of his neck to his short, sandy-red hair, and even from where she sat, Judy could see the muscle working in his cheek as he controlled his anger.

"But the third profile didn't match either, did it?" said Harper.

"In the third case, we knew from the start that Miss Rogerson had had sexual relations immediately prior to the assault," said Merrill. "Both from her own statement and that of the defendant. We had expected a mixed sample, but we got only one. Miss Rogerson was unwilling to give us the name of her boyfriend, and in the light of medical advice, we felt it both unwise and unnecessary to persist with our enquiries, especially when it was revealed that the assailant had ejaculated into a tissue as with the second assault, and that the vaginal sample was of no further interest to our investigation. The defendant was subsequently charged with all four assaults."

"Did you ask Miss Rogerson why she hadn't told you that her assailant had ejaculated in this manner in the first place?" asked Harper.

"It is not at all unusual for such details only to emerge after a considerable time has elapsed," said Merrill. "It is very difficult for badly hurt and severely traumatized victims of violent assaults—particularly sexual assaults—to recount or even sometimes to recall the details of their ordeal."

"Yes, I'm sure that is very true," said Harper. "We can only guess at what these young women went through. No further questions, my lord."

"Mr. Whitehouse, do you wish to re-examine?"

"No, thank you, my lord."

And with that, the court adjourned until the following day.

Barton Crown Court, Wednesday 8 July

Most cases engendered very little public interest, especially in Barton, a not very well-known county town that had sought and failed to acquire city status almost all century. But Colin Drummond, son of the third generation of one of the county's oldest established retailers, was being accused of terrorizing two neighbouring Bartonshire towns for over two months, and more people wanted a ringside seat at his trial than the court could accommodate.

Now the medical evidence was being presented, and this was where Whitehouse could ram home to the jury—and the judge, come to that—the sheer brutality of the assaults. This judge was anything but soft on sex offenders at the best of times, and Harper was uncomfortably aware of the life sentence at his disposal should Drummond be found guilty.

The forensic medical examiner was in the witness box now, giving details of her more or less immediate postassault medical examinations of the victims. Harper asked no questions; he had to try to divorce his client from the horror of the first three assaults, and concentrate on the fourth.

◊

"And Miss Benson?" Whitehouse was asking, as Judy took her place in the public gallery.

"There was some minor bruising of the anus, and pressure bruising to the buttocks consistent with their having been held apart to facilitate anal penetration," she said.

"In your medical opinion," asked Whitehouse, "having examined the other victims after they had been assaulted, was there any similarity with those previous assaults?"

"Similar bruising was found on the other three victims."

"Did you also examine Mr. Drummond after the alleged assault?"

"I did. There was slight chafing to the penis, and his knees were quite badly grazed."

"Thank you, Doctor," said Mr. Whitehouse.

Harper stood up, and looked at the doctor. "Surely minor bruising and 'slight chafing' could occur during consenting anal intercourse?" he asked.

"It might."

"These minor injuries bear no relation to those found on the other victims, do they?"

"To the extent that I mentioned, they do. The anal assault in the first three cases was markedly less violent than the ones which followed, being apparently intended to establish the assailant's dominance over his victims, and to facilitate the binding of his victims' hands and feet."

"Did you find any evidence during your examination of Miss Benson of the tearing injuries that might be expected to result from forcible insertion into an orifice not intended for the purpose?"

"No," said the doctor. "But despite her years, this victim was, unlike the others, very sexually experienced. Insertion in this instance would have been achieved with comparative ease."

"May I ask then what led you to the belief that this was an assault?"

"The grazing of the defendant's knees indicated the level of force used, in my opinion," said the doctor.

"The grazing on his knees," repeated Harper. "Did you not consider—given the supposed ease of insertion, and the low level of bruising—that the grazing on the defendant's knees might have had another cause altogether?"

"I did, but the defendant offered no other explanation," she said.

"He is now offering an explanation," said Harper. "Mr. Drummond is a motorcyclist, and you may have seen motorcycle races where the rider bends into the corners with his knee almost touching the ground. My client will state that he was at the disused Malworth airfield, practising just such a high-speed manoeuvre, without the usual protection of leathers, a matter of ten minutes or so before this incident. Isn't such a manoeuvre, attempted by a non-professional, *more* likely to explain the grazing than the carrying-out of this alleged assault?"

The doctor frowned a little. "Yes," she said, a little reluctantly.

"I will be producing a witness to the fact that carrying out this and other high-speed manoeuvres on his motorbike is indeed how my client spent that evening, my lord," said Harper.

"Thank you," muttered the judge.

Harper smiled at the doctor. "Given that information, would you, on the medical evidence alone, have come so readily to the conclusion that this young woman had been violently assaulted by the defendant?"

"Possibly not," she said, after a moment's thought.

My God, thought Judy. He wants him found not guilty because he hadn't had the chance to tear her open like he had his other victims.

"I understand that you have made a particular study of both the victims and perpetrators of rape and sexual assault, is that right?"

"Yes, I have."

"Mr. Drummond was eighteen years old at the time of these offences, and yet this court has heard of someone who washes his victims, and removes the materials used to bind their hands and feet, in order to foil the forensic procedures—does that seem likely to you?"

"It isn't as unusual as you might think for rapists to wash their victims," said the doctor. "Or to remove other evidence."

"You were of the opinion, weren't you, that the assailant was likely to be a previous sex offender who had been through the mill of a forensic examination, and knew to some extent what would or would not incriminate him? But now you are happy to accept that it was an eighteen-year-old boy with no experience of such a police investigation?"

"There is a great deal of literature on the subject of both rape and its forensic detection," she said. "And literature of this sort was found in the defendant's possession. This is again not unusual."

"And does this literature contain references to *coitus interruptus,* which the assailant apparently practises with the ease of a considerate Victorian husband?"

The doctor smiled. "No," she said. "But I don't imagine it was *coitus interruptus* as such. I think it much more likely that the assailant suffers from ejaculatory inhibition whereby penile erection can be maintained for long periods, but emission during coitus cannot be achieved. Self-stimulation may be an alternative to the eventual loss of penile erection without emission."

"Is this condition common in eighteen-year-old boys?"

"It's not common at all, but less uncommon amongst sex offenders than the rest of the male population. Offenders have a marked tendency to sexual dysfunction, and since dysfunction is almost always psychological, eighteen-year-olds are as likely to have the condition as anyone else."

"The court has heard that Mr. Drummond was in the habit of visiting a prostitute," said Harper. "If she were to give evidence to the effect that Mr. Drummond functions quite normally in this regard, would that preclude his being the assailant?"

"Mr. Harper," said the judge. "Is it your intention to produce this witness to the court?"

"Not at the moment, my lord. As the court has heard, the lady in question gave up the profession, or at least gave up practising it in this area, alarmed by these very rapes. We have unfortunately so far been unable to trace her."

"Then unless and until this witness is located, such evidence as she might present cannot be evaluated. Please confine your questions to the evidence which has been or will be presented to the jury."

"I beg your lordship's pardon," said Harper, having achieved what he wanted to achieve merely by asking the question. Judy shook her head slightly.

The courtroom emptied almost as rapidly that afternoon as it had filled up that morning as the scientist who had carried out the DNA tests explained at considerable, and to Judy at least, virtually incomprehensible, length how a DNA profile was arrived at. She wasn't convinced that any of the jury was still awake; she was having to work hard at keeping her own eyes open.

"DNA analysis is as accurate and as reliable a means of identification as a fingerprint," he said, in what she sincerely hoped was a winding-up tone, "hence its popular name. No two people have the same DNA profile, except identical twins."

But it seemed he had only just started. The first lecture had been on the nature of DNA, and the reasons why it was such a powerful tool of identification; now, he was explaining exactly how this specific test had been carried out, with illustrations which necessitated the bringing in to court of an overhead projector, which at least caused sufficient diversion to waken everyone up, if only for a moment. At last, the result of this test was being shown.

Judy looked at the two profiles; one, with the DNA fragments showing as bold black bands, was Drummond's DNA profile, while the other, with paler but clearly matching lines, was the profile obtained from what the man called, rather coyly, "the scene."

What had happened to Rachel Ashman had been reduced to lines on a piece of paper, as impersonal and untraumatic as a supermarket bar code. Her life had been shattered to the extent that it had seemed to her no longer worth living, but science was there to come along and tidy everything up for the investigators, for the judge and jury. It had yet to come up with a similarly painless treatment for the victims.

"Forensic DNA testing is done, not on the whole DNA code, but on the four genetic markers in which the core differences can be seen, where individuals differ most widely," he finished. "In theory, there is a chance of an accidental match, which is capable of being computed."

Judy had a strong suspicion that Whitehouse had begun nodding off again as the expert launched into an even more wordy explanation of how one strand gave you a one-in-a-thousand chance of an accidental match, the next one in a hundred, and those multiplied to give one in a hundred thousand, and the next . . .

"In this case there is one chance in three million that this could be an accidental match," he concluded.

He *concluded*. The few who had remained throughout shifted in their seats; Whitehouse looked up, smiled at his expert, and stood.

"While I am sure that the jury is grateful to you for your detailed explanation of the process," he said, "they are going to be asked to judge a man's guilt or innocence in respect of a series of exceptionally serious crimes, and your analysis will form a very large part of that judgement. I imagine that they would like to know what conclusion you, as an expert, draw from that analysis."

"That the seminal fluids found on the underclothing of the second victim, Mrs. Rachel Ashman, originated from the defendant," he said.

"And you have no doubt of that?"

"None at all."

"Thank you," said Whitehouse, with an audible sigh of relief. "No further questions, my lord."

"Mr. Harper, do you wish to cross-examine?"

"No, my lord," said Hotshot, who at least knew when to fold his cards, thought Judy.

Whitehouse rose again. "That is the case for the prosecution, my lord."

Barton Crown Court, Thursday 9 July

The jury filed in, conscious that they were merely dressing the set. The excited murmur of anticipation from the gallery began only as the stage filled up with the players.

And in they came, the black-gowned court officials, the bewigged barristers. Amid the muted hubbub, Harper and Whitehouse talked seriously to their instructing solicitors about nothing whatever, aware of their more substantial roles in the drama, and trying to look as though they were not.

The public gallery which had emptied yesterday during the DNA expert's dissertation on his infant discipline was full once more, and Harper was beginning to recognize a few of the faces; whether their interest was personal, professional, prudent or prurient, he had no way of knowing. DI Hill was there, as she had been every day; her interest, he presumed, was professional. His interest in her was rather more personal. He'd found out so far that she was a Londoner, whose father was some sort of academic. He wondered what he thought of his daughter's choice of career.

The murmur fell away to nothing as the houselights metaphorically dimmed, and the entrance of the judge, solemn and stern, brought those who had business with the Queen's Justices to silence, and their feet. But even he was to be upstaged, for the packed house awaited the appearance of only one man: the accused.

The first witness for the defence was to be Colin Arthur Drummond himself; he was going to attempt to account for both the circumstances in which he had been arrested and his subsequent confession, in the hope that he would somehow be found not guilty.

Harper had had one last go at dissuading his client from entering the witness box, but had failed. Before that, he had failed to persuade him to plead guilty in the light of the DNA evidence, he had failed to persuade him to change the story to which he obstinately clung, and he had failed to get out of taking the case at all.

Drummond's solicitor was an old friend of Harper's father; he had sent the young Harper a lot of good work when he had been starting out, and he had called in all the favours he had ever done him when he had asked Harper to represent Drummond.

Now, assuming his pessimism as to the outcome of the trial was justified, Harper knew that he was simply going to fail. Period.

ò

"... and nothing but the truth." Drummond handed back the testament, and slightly loosened the tie which his mother had doubtless insisted that he wear. Judy sat slightly forward in her seat.

"Mr. Drummond," Harper began. "The night you were arrested, you were wearing black Doc Marten boots, black jeans, a black sweater, black leather jacket, black PVC gauntlets, and a full facemask. Why were you thus attired?"

"I always dress like that." Drummond looked down at his brand-new suit. "Usually," he added.

"And do you always wear a mask?"

"No. I got it to look like him," muttered Drummond.

"To look like whom?" asked Harper.

"The bloke that was raping women."

"Why?" Harper asked.

Drummond looked down at his feet. "I wanted women to be scared of me," he mumbled.

"Why?"

"Because they scare me."

It was all Judy could do not to join in the cat-calling that the judge quietened with a look. There was a whole gang of women in the gallery of the rapists-should-be-castrated school; she would doubtless be regarded as being among their number by some of her colleagues.

"And did you also carry a knife?"

"No."

Knives scare them witless, that was what he had told Judy. She glanced at the jury, tried to gauge what they were thinking, but they sat listening, their faces not giving anything away.

"*He* carried a knife," said Harper.

"Yeah, but . . . I didn't *do* anything to them. I just wanted to scare them a bit. I didn't need a knife to do what I did."

"And what did you do?"

"I'd follow them, if I saw them on their own. I'd follow them real slow on the bike. They'd start to walk faster, and then run. They'd see me and think I was the rapist. It put the wind up them. And sometimes I'd watch them, in parked cars and that. With men. You know."

He had had to admit to that, of course, thought Judy, because the police were aware of his Peeping Tom activities. Hotshot would have advised him to bring it up himself rather than let Whitehouse do it.

"Why did you do that?"

"So I could follow them after, when they got dropped off. They usually got out a bit of a way from home if they'd been—you know, with other men. Men they shouldn't have been with. But I didn't ever do anything. Just like . . . you know. Imagined I was him. What I'd do to them if I was."

"Did that excite you?"

"Yeah."

"So what did you do about that?"

"I'd go to Rosa."

"Rosa was the prostitute whom you were in the habit of visiting?"

Drummond flushed. "Yeah," he said.

"When was the last time you saw Rosa?"

"It was September seventh. I remember, 'cos it was my mum's birthday, and she was mad when I came home late and missed the barbecue."

"September seventh. What time were you with Rosa?"

"About half nine."

"How long were you with her?"

He shrugged. "Twenty minutes, half an hour."

"And then what did you do?"

"I drove round for a bit—took the bike along the dual carriageway and that. Fast. You know. Then I went home."

"What time did you get home?"

"Just after eleven."

"So, on September seventh from half past nine until a few minutes to ten you were with Rosa, and from a few minutes after eleven you were with your parents and several other relatives and friends?"

"Yes."

Rosa, of course, could not be found to confirm this, and oddly enough, only Drummond's blood relations could recall at what precise time he had arrived home that night. The other party guests had thought that it might have been closer to midnight when Drummond had come home. The earlier time would, of course, have made it impossible for him to be raping Rachel Ashman, as Hotshot was busy pointing out. Whitehouse had felt that determined cross-examination would have got the other guests to revise their opinion of when Drummond had come home; they had all been half-cut anyway, and their memory of something entirely unmemorable was best left alone. It had seemed better just to let their nonappearance on Drummond's behalf speak for itself, he had said. Judy wasn't so sure.

"Would you tell the court what happened the night the police stopped you for reckless driving?" Harper said, moving on.

"I'd been at the football match. It was this special match with celebrities and that. But it was too foggy, so it was abandoned. And I drove around in the fog for a bit. I was going fast—I didn't have my lights on."

"Why were you doing that?"

"I like it. And they stopped me and said they'd seen me before. That I'd got away from them that time, but I wouldn't this time."

"Did you know what they meant?"

"Yes. One of the times I took the bike on the dual carriageway I was speeding, and they couldn't catch me, and they couldn't get the bike's number, because I didn't have the lights on. But this time they caught me, and they knew it was me, because I was doing the same thing. They kept me there an hour and a half. Then when they couldn't find anything wrong with the bike, and they couldn't get me for drink or drugs or anything, one of them punched me in the face."

"Did you retaliate?"

"No. I was too dizzy. Then he hit me a few more times, and punched me in the stomach. I fell, and he gave me a kicking until the other one got him off me, and they drove off."

"Did either of these officers question you about the assaults?"

"No."

"What happened the following day?"

"More cops came to the house and took me to Stansfield police station."

He was trying to make it sound like harassment, thought Judy, but it had just been straightforward police work. Motorcycle tyre impressions had been found at the scene of Stansfield's murder, so when they had heard about a motorcyclist who had been apprehended for speeding out of Stansfield and into Malworth, without lights, in the fog . . . naturally, they had been anxious to interview him. Colin Drummond had been brought in for questioning about the murder, but his resemblance to what description they had of the rapist had pushed the questioning on to a different tack. Because murder wasn't the only thing that Bartonshire Constabulary had had to deal with that night. That was the night that Bobbie Chalmers had been raped. She had told Judy about it off the record; she had refused to make an official complaint.

But what Drummond had seen as he had watched and waited in the shadows had turned out to be relevant to the murder inquiry; when he had described that rape in minute and abhorrent detail to Judy, he had been making a witness statement, not a confession. It had convicted a murderer, but it couldn't even be heard at Drummond's own trial, because officially there had been no rape.

No matter, Judy thought, bringing her attention back to the here and now. We have enough to nail you without that, Drummond. More than enough.

"I got asked about the rapes," Drummond was saying. "And they said they wanted a blood sample, so I said all right."

"You freely offered a sample of blood?"

"Yes. I was there for hours. They only let me go when I made a complaint about the ones that had stopped me the night before."

"Which brings us to the night you were arrested," said Harper. "At what time did you leave the house that night?"

"Late. I'd been in all evening, and I was bored, so I thought I'd give the bike a workout."

He had been out all evening, waiting for Judy to come home, according to what he had told her. But she had had company when she had come home; Drummond had had to pick on someone else. That poor little girl.

"Where do you take your bike for a workout?" Harper was asking.

"I go up the airfield. I'd never gone there at night, and I wanted to try it in the dark."

"Try what?"

"Stunts and that. It would be more dangerous in the dark. No lights. Like bombers during the war."

There was a muttering in the public gallery as the word bomber was mentioned.

"What time did you arrive there?"

"About half eleven."

"And how long were you there?"

"A couple of hours. Then I packed it in and went home."

"And why did you stop in the town?"

"I needed a slash, so I took the bike up an alley."

Harper turned to the judge. "What Mr. Drummond means is—"

"I know what Mr. Drummond means, thank you, Mr. Harper," said the judge testily, and turned to Drummond. "Do you always relieve yourself in alleys?" he asked.

"No, sir, but they close the toilets at half seven, and I was desperate. I couldn't even wait until I got home."

"Carry on, Mr. Harper," sighed the judge.

"Can you tell the court in your own words what happened in the alley?"

"I was on my way back to the bike when I saw this girl."

"You are referring to Miss Benson?"

"Yeah. I'd seen her hanging around the Ferarri. She's a hooker. She said did I want a . . ." His voice trailed off, as though he were too gently nurtured to quote her. He looked at the judge, then back at

Harper. "To have sex," he said. "Only that wasn't how she put it. So I said OK, and paid her, and we . . . you know. Only the next thing I know she's telling me to—" He broke off, and looked at the judge again. "To go away," he said. "I said I wanted my money back, but she starts . . . you know, effing and blinding, and I put my hand over her mouth to stop her yelling, because these guys were coming. But she wouldn't stop, so I gave up and went back to the bike. And I've got on the bike, and I've tried to start it, when someone's pulled me off, and next thing I know there are cops everywhere, and she's saying I raped her."

"Why didn't you tell the police that you had paid her for sex?"

Drummond looked down at his feet as he spoke in a low voice. "I didn't want them knowing I had to pay for it," he said.

"But she was saying you had raped her—surely you didn't want them to believe that?"

"Well, he didn't pay for it, did he? He just made them do everything he wanted, everything he told them to do." He looked up then, directly at Judy, the suspicion of a smile on his lips, and for a moment he was once again the alarming young man that she had interviewed. But the jury couldn't see the look on his face. He looked back at Harper. "They said I was him. They said I'd done all those things."

"Did *you* say that you had?"

"No. I never said anything."

"But you did make a confession in the end. Why?"

He had told Judy why. He had made the statement because he had wanted everyone to know what he had done. He had clearly thought that he would get a couple of years at most—it was only rape, he had said, not murder or anything. He hadn't even used the knife. And he was only eighteen. He'd be out in twelve months, and then it would be her turn. Judy hadn't disabused him of his idea of the sentence, but someone else had.

"They said I'd raped that little whore. That she would swear to it in court, and they said they were going to prove I'd done them all. And I thought they would give me another going-over if I didn't . . . "

He shrugged, shook his head. "I was scared," he said, his voice no more than a whisper.

The scepticism was audible, almost tangible where Judy was sitting. A relative of one of the victims called something out; the judge warned him as to his future conduct, and the courtroom fell silent.

"You thought you were in physical danger?"

"Yes. I'd complained about their mates, hadn't I? They were telling me all these things that I was supposed to have done to these women, and they said it would be better if I confessed. And the Chief Inspector, he said he was going to prove I'd done them with this DNA. He said I should make a statement, and I thought I'd get another kicking if I didn't. So I said OK, and told them all that stuff. But I didn't do it."

"What made you retract the statement?"

After he had made his statement to Judy about assaulting Bobbie Chalmers, Drummond had been put in the cell with a regular who would steal the paint off a door, but who had a deep distaste for violence of any kind and against women in particular; he had reported the conversation that had taken place. Drummond had boasted about his exploits, and had been told, quite rightly, that he could get life for what he'd done. Lifers weren't fussy, Drummond had been assured, and a good-looking lad like him would soon get a taste of his own medicine. That was why Drummond had changed his statement.

"I told the solicitor that I got at the magistrates' court that I hadn't really done anything—I wasn't so scared once I was away from the police station. He said if that was true I should plead not guilty. So I did."

"Did you rape any of these women, Mr. Drummond?"

"No. I just . . . I just wanted women to be scared of me. But I was scared they'd have me done over again, so I said I'd done all those things. But I didn't. Honest, I didn't."

Judy half-expected applause for his performance. It deserved applause; she just hoped the jury could see through it.

"Thank you. No further questions."

Drummond made to leave the witness box, and was called back. At first, Judy thought that he wasn't going to be afforded the chance to recharge his batteries, but true to form, the judge's stomach was telling him it was lunchtime.

When the court reconvened that afternoon, Drummond back in the witness box, Whitehouse standing looking at him, it was, for a few moments, like a tableau. Like one of those old paintings. No one spoke, no one moved, until Drummond began to shift a little uncomfortably.

"What we heard this morning," Whitehouse said at last, "was a complete fiction, wasn't it, Mr. Drummond?" He left his place, and walked over to the witness box, sweeping his gown behind him, and clasping his hands behind his back. "And not even very good fiction at that," he went on. "Because it depends so much on coincidence, doesn't it?"

Drummond's head went back a little.

"Let us start with the premise for your fiction," Whitehouse said. "You aren't the rapist. You just wanted to be like him. You wanted to commit repeated acts of sexual violence, like any normal lad."

Drummond didn't speak.

Whitehouse looked at the jury, at the gallery, and spread his arms wide, his suitably frayed gown falling back round his legs. "Which of us here can say that he has not also dressed in black, pulled on a mask and stared into parked cars to watch courting couples copulate? Which of us has not also followed women in the street until they ran in panic, while we conjured up visions of committing brutal acts of sexual abuse on them?"

"Mr. Whitehouse," said the judge. "Is there a question for the witness on its way in the near future?"

"I do beg your lordship's pardon," said Whitehouse. "I was quite carried away with memories of carefree youth." He turned sharply to look at Drummond. "Is that a fair description of your hobby, Mr. Drummond?"

"No! It wasn't like that."

"You have told us it was like that. You have admitted following women in the street, and watching courting couples in cars, haven't you?"

"I didn't watch *them*. I just . . . watched the cars. Then followed them."

"Ah. I see. Followed them until—with luck—the female was dropped off a little way from home. And then you would follow her until she would run in panic—yes?"

Drummond swallowed. "Yes," he said.

"Well, that's the scenario," said Whitehouse. "Young man hero-worships rapist, dresses like him, rides a bike like his, and wants to 'put the wind up' women. So to this end, you purchased a mask. So—tell me, where do you buy a face-mask?"

"I got it in a sports-goods place in Malworth. It's for protecting your skin, really. Mountaineers and skiers and people use them."

"You'll have a receipt then, won't you? A receipt for this item, dated after the date of the newspaper report on the first assault."

"No, sir. I didn't keep it."

"I don't imagine you did. You got this mask long before the first rape, didn't you?"

"No, sir. I got it because I'd read about the rape in the paper."

"Very well. That brings us to the first coincidence. And it *was* a coincidence, was it, that just such a mask, together with a flick-knife, was found on the very road where you had been stopped by the police the evening before?"

"Yes."

"Did the newspaper report describe the sort of mask the rapist wore?"

"No, sir."

"No. It could have been a balaclava, or a stocking, or a Halloween mask, couldn't it? But it wasn't. It was a ski-mask. And so was the one you purchased. A coincidence?"

"Yes, sir."

"And yet you didn't have *your* mask with you when they stopped you, did you? Sounds horribly like another coincidence to me, Mr. Drummond."

"No," said Drummond. "I didn't *always* have it with me."

"Only if you were going to 'put the wind up' women?"

"Yes."

"You led these officers to believe that you were the rapist, didn't you?"

"No, sir. They never said anything about the rapes, and neither did I. I was just standing there while they went over the bike, and checked me for drugs and all that. I didn't say anything. One of them just started hitting me."

"Very well. Let's turn to the night of your arrest. You took your bike to the airfield in order to do stunts in the dark, and that was how you grazed your knees. My learned friend said that this was because you were doing this stunt driving 'without the protection of leathers.' Do you have leathers?"

"Yes, sir."

"Motorcycle leathers are a sort of all-in-one with reinforcement at the knees for just such a manoeuvre as high-speed cornering, aren't they?"

"Yes, sir."

"Then why weren't you wearing them, if that was your sole reason for going out that night?"

Drummond shrugged.

"I'll tell you, shall I? Because it would be less than easy to rape someone while you were wearing them, wouldn't it?"

Drummond shook his head.

"Oh," said Whitehouse. "You mean it *is* easy to rape someone while you're wearing them?"

"Mr. Whitehouse," said the judge, sounding like an infant school teacher at the end of a long morning.

"I withdraw the question, my lord," said Whitehouse, and turned back to Drummond. "Let's put it another way, Mr. Drummond. I don't really want to know why you weren't wearing your leathers so much as why you *were* wearing your rapist's outfit, complete with mask. Why was that?"

Drummond shrugged again.

"Because you went out looking for someone to 'put the wind up'?"

"No, sir."

"But you've just told the court that that was the only reason you would have had the mask with you."

"Yes, well," said Drummond. "I did think about that, but there was no one around. It was Sunday evening—the town was dead. I got bored just riding round, so I went up to the airfield."

"But on your way home you found someone, didn't you? And you sexually assaulted her, as you had sexually assaulted and raped three others before her."

"No, sir. I was in the alley, and she came up to me and said did I want to . . . you know. So I said OK."

Whitehouse drew in a long, slow breath and released it. "You had just relieved yourself," he said. "Did you keep your gloves on while you were doing that?"

Drummond frowned a little. "No," he said suspiciously.

"Where were they?"

"In my helmet, on the bike."

"Oh—you had removed your helmet, too?"

"Yeah, well . . . I do that automatically when I get off the bike."

"And where was the bike?"

"Up at the entrance to the alley."

"Why were you wearing your mask?"

"I'd just never taken it off."

"And yet you say Miss Benson approached you? Didn't it 'put the wind up' her?"

"No. She knew it was me."

"Not much of a disguise, then, was it?"

"She'd seen the bike!" said Drummond, his voice rising, his patience wearing thin. "She came along the alley, asked if I wanted a fuck, I gave her a tenner, and we did it. It was as simple as that."

"Simple? But it brings us to another coincidence, doesn't it? That you have the same dubious—and dangerous—taste in sexual positions as the rapist?"

"It was her idea to do it that way, not mine."

The silver eyebrows shot up, disappearing right under his wig. "*Her* idea?" Whitehouse paused for a moment. "Did that surprise you?"

Drummond frowned. "No," he said. "She's a whore. She asks more money for doing it that way."

"But it was a foggy, damp night, and as she memorably told the court, the ground was wet and muddy, wasn't it?"

Drummond shrugged. "She didn't seem to mind that," he said. "She wanted the tenner."

"Do go on," said Whitehouse.

"She heard these men coming, and told me to eff off. I wanted my money back, and she starts screaming at me, effing and blinding. So I put my hand over her mouth to keep her quiet."

"My learned friend has said that that was how her saliva came to be on your glove," said Whitehouse. "Is that right?"

"Yes," said Drummond.

"But you weren't wearing your gloves, were you?"

Drummond's eyes widened a little at his elementary mistake. "I'd put them back on by then," he said.

"But they were in your helmet, on your bike, at the end of the alleyway, weren't they?"

"Yeah—but I'd been back at the bike. I was going, like she'd said. But then I thought how I hadn't had my money's worth, and I wanted my tenner back. So I went back and asked her for it."

"And she was still there? Still hanging about in the middle of the alleyway?"

"Yes," said Drummond.

"Still on all fours?" asked Whitehouse.

"No," said Drummond, through his teeth. "She got up when she told me to fuck off, all right?"

"But the gentlemen who apprehended you saw her face down on the ground, her leopard-skin leggings round her knees, with you kneeling over her, and then you ran away. How come?"

"That was after."

"After what?"

"After I asked for my money back. She tried to run, but she fell over, and I tried to get my money from her when she was on the floor—that's what they saw."

"I'm not surprised she fell over," said Whitehouse. "Women," he said, smiling indulgently, shaking his head. "You would think with all that standing around while you walked fifty yards to your bike and put your gloves on, then walked fifty yards back again, she would have thought to pull up her leggings, wouldn't you?"

"I don't know or care what she did with her leggings," said Drummond, stepping dangerously out of character.

"No—quite. Why should you?" said Whitehouse, still smiling. "And all this toing-and-froing and putting on of gloves and falling over happened *between* her hearing footsteps approaching and these two gentlemen arriving at the scene?"

"She must have heard them when they were a long way away," said Drummond. "Sounds travel in the fog."

"But not the sound of her 'effing and blinding,' which you were so anxious to quieten? No one but you heard that, Mr. Drummond. The two witnesses said nothing about anyone shouting, swearing—don't you think that that would have been what caught their attention rather than the silent tableau they described?"

Drummond shrugged.

"Ah, well," said Whitehouse. "Fiction is quite difficult—I know. I've tried my hand at it. So many things to think about at once, aren't there? Do go on."

"I left her to go back to the bike, and next thing I know I'm being dragged off it and she's yelling that I raped her."

"So it was yet another coincidence that you, who so admired this rapist, should go with a prostitute who takes your money and then just happens to accuse you of sexually assaulting her for some inscrutable reason of her own?"

"The cops put her up to it," said Drummond.

"And it was merely a combination of circumstances that caused two independent witnesses to see her sprawled face down on the ground, her clothing pulled down, with you kneeling over her? Sheer coincidence that it should look exactly like someone sexually assaulting his victim in the grim silence which had been enforced by the threat of mutilation with a knife?"

"I never had a knife."

"No. It was just another coincidence that a knife was found exactly where you would have thrown it on returning to your bike, wasn't it?"

"You'd have to ask the cops about that too."

"Ah, yes. And this statement that you gave the police after you had been arrested—did they manufacture that? We can have it played to the court, if you wish, Mr. Drummond, if you are saying it's a fake. Are you saying that?"

"No. But they told me all those things I was supposed to have done."

"And you pieced them all together and came up with a blow-by-blow account of what was done to these young women, and in what order, and with what degree of violence?"

"I must have."

"Another coincidence, no doubt. But—perhaps you can explain one thing about your statement, if you would?" Whitehouse picked up some papers, and put on his glasses. "It's concerning the assault on Mrs. Carole Jarvis," he said. "You began your statement thus: 'I saw that one getting into her car in Malworth, and I followed her.' " He looked up, removing his glasses again. "Who told you that?" he asked.

Drummond frowned. "I don't know what you mean," he said.

"Who told you that she had been in Malworth? The police didn't know that that was where she had been until some considerable time after you made this statement. Only *she* knew that. She, her gentleman friend, and the person who followed her, of course."

"I just said it."

"Why?"

"Because . . . I live in Malworth, don't I? I wouldn't be hanging round Stansfield. But I knew the first one had been in Stansfield. So I just said I'd followed her there."

Whitehouse threw the papers back down onto the desk. "What a remarkable coincidence, then, that she had *indeed* been in Malworth," he said. "And did you just 'say' that you had threatened to mutilate your victims if they made a sound? Did you just 'say' that you had cleaned them up, then cut away and removed the tape? More coincidence, Mr. Drummond?"

"I heard the cops talking," said Drummond. "I heard them saying that was what he'd done."

"And it was a coincidence, was it, that you should have about your person adhesive bandages of the type described by the victims as having been used to bind them? Or are you also saying that the police planted them?"

"They were in the first-aid kit—it comes with the bike."

"And moist tissues of the sort used to wash the victims after the assaults?"

"They come with the first-aid kit."

"And best of all—that you have the same DNA profile as the rapist," said Whitehouse. "The odds, Mr. Drummond, are three million to one against that single coincidence alone—one shudders to think *what* giddy odds your version of events reaches." He turned to the judge. "No further questions, my lord."

"Do you wish to reexamine, Mr. Harper?"

Harper shook his head, and the court rose for the day.

Barton Crown Court, Friday 10 July

So far Harper had called a couple of people to confirm that Colin Drummond had always dressed in black since leaving school, and a motorbike salesman to confirm that the bike came with a first-aid box which included moist tissues—evidence which hardly cleared his client of involvement, but which at least confirmed that he was telling the truth. Now, his father was about to go into the box.

Harper had had considerable doubt about including the alibi evidence; the Drummonds had insisted that they knew for a fact that

Colin had been at home, stripping down his bike or whatever it was he did with the thing, on the occasion of the first and third rapes, and belatedly attending his mother's birthday party when the second took place. The party was one thing, but there was no way the Drummonds could remember off-hand what Colin was or was not doing eight months ago on two otherwise unremarkable nights; Harper knew that they had devised the alibi evidence between them, and so would everyone else who heard it.

But in the end he had gone with it, since he had nothing much else to offer. Not even a character witness. Drummond's total lack of friends made Harper feel almost sorry for him. He had never had a relationship, sexual or otherwise, with any female other than his mother and Rosa. And that wasn't just sad. It was hampering his defence. Harper had had people scouring the county for sight or sound of Rosa once the police had established that she wasn't after all a figment of Drummond's imagination, but she had gone to ground and was staying there. Drummond was now very anxious that she should be found, given the supposed sexual dysfunction of the assailant; Rosa, he said, could tell them that he didn't have any problem at all in that regard. He hadn't given anyone much of a chance to look for her; he hadn't even mentioned her until eight weeks ago. He hadn't, he had explained to Harper, wanted people knowing that he had had to pay for it on a regular basis.

Rosa had turned up at the Ferrari, worked it for a few weeks, then had left, probably to go somewhere that didn't have a rapist on the loose. She hadn't had premises, hadn't even had a surname that anyone knew. Drummond thought she had had a pimp; he'd seen a man approach her once or twice after he had left her, but he only saw him in the dark, couldn't describe him, and didn't know his name.

So the other little prostitute remained his only hope; there were facets to the police version of that drama in the alleyway that Harper had so far merely hinted at, and which didn't entirely ring true. But they would have to wait for his closing address, because he had no evidence to back up his doubts. He could voice them; he could give the jury something to think about.

For now, iffy alibi evidence, the irate resident who had seen Drummond at the airfield, one of the officers involved in the assault on Drummond, and a psychologist who would say that he was a harmless Peeping Tom comprised, God help him, the remainder of Drummond's defence.

¿

Judy had watched Drummond's father lying his head off about how Colin was at home with him and his mother on three of the four occasions in question. Whitehouse had made mincemeat of him, and now he was doing the same to Mrs. Drummond, showing how their answers had been rehearsed, right down to their using the same words as one another.

Retired Major Harold Masterman was called next. He had been arriving home from an evening out when he had seen Drummond drive up to the old airfield, on to which the major's house backed. He had put up with the screaming of the engine and the squealing of the tyres for about an hour, but then he had phoned the police. Much good that had done him, he said. The noise went on for almost another hour, with no sign of the police doing anything about it. Almost half past one before he finally drove off, and never a policeman to be seen.

In the afternoon, Barry Turner was first on. Ex–Police Constable Barry Turner. He and PC Matthew Burbidge had stopped Drummond for reckless driving at thirty-two minutes after nine P.M. on Friday, October twenty-fifth last year. Drummond had been riding his bike at almost eighty miles an hour in thick fog with no lights; they had stopped him, and questioned him about his movements on the nights the rapes had taken place. He had laughed at them, said they would never catch the rapist. PC Burbidge had lost his temper. Turner had at first turned a blind eye, but then had stopped it before it got out of hand.

"Why didn't you take him in for questioning if he had admitted assaulting these women?" asked Harper.

"Well . . . that was just it, really. He didn't say he had. I mean—he wasn't saying anything, not really. Just hints, and remarks. I thought

Matt was just going to . . . you know, rough him up a bit. But he . . . well, I stopped it before he did too much damage."

"Mr. Drummond had previously eluded you in a chase, hadn't he?"

"Yes."

"And you had been frustrated in your attempts to find evidence of drink or drugs with which you could charge him?"

"Yes."

"Could that perhaps have been why your colleague assaulted him?"

"It might have been partly why."

"Not because he believed Mr. Drummond to be the rapist?"

Whitehouse was on his feet, objecting on the grounds that the witness could not know what Mr. Burbidge had or had not believed.

"Did *you* believe him to be the rapist?" asked Harper.

"No."

The psychologist was wheeled on next, and was asked for his personal assessment of Drummond.

"Colin Drummond is a young man of surprisingly high IQ," he started off, "given that the persona he projects most of the time is one of mumbling, inarticulate immaturity."

Judy's eyebrows rose in surprise. She couldn't have given a fairer assessment herself.

"He reads little; he learned little at school. He is not particularly interested in anything except motorcycles, but he has a quick, receptive mind, and a capacity for learning about those things which do interest him."

Like rape and its detection. Judy sneaked a look at Drummond, who looked appalled. Good. Sometimes even *your* mummy and daddy can't buy you out of trouble, you little sod, she thought.

"Colin knows that he is capable of much more than serving in his father's shop, and he knows that his hang-ups—to use a colloquial term—about relationships with other people resulted in his being turned down by the RAF."

Better and better. Drummond was a frustrated bomber pilot.

"To avoid the contact with other people which he finds so difficult, he retreats into a world where Colin Drummond barely exists; he pulls on the figurative mask of inarticulate stupidity that he almost invariably shows to the rest of the world, and becomes in his mind almost anyone *but* Colin Drummond. A mask to disguise his very real feelings of resentment towards his father, whom he regards as weak and submissive, and towards his mother, whom he sees as domineering and superior. A mask to hide his own feelings of inadequacy, his own submissiveness to his mother's rule, his own fear of all women. And he harboured these feelings, these thoughts, under his mask. He dressed in black so that not even his choice of colours and patterns could give him away."

Judy didn't usually have much time for psychologists. She could make an exception in this one's case. Harper didn't seem worried; he was listening gravely, his face betraying nothing. Perhaps he had just given up. If your own witnesses turn against you, what else could you do?

"Then he read of a man who really did wear a mask, whose dark and undetected presence was inspiring fear in an entire community. In women. Women, whom Colin finds unfathomable, frightening creatures, were being subdued and controlled by this man. A man who dressed as he did, in black. A man who rode a motorbike. And that appealed to him. If he, too, wore a mask—a real mask—he would truly cease to be Colin Drummond; he would become this man, and he could experience by proxy the same control, the same power. He could frighten those who most frightened him.

"And that was what he did. He watched women, followed them, made them run from him. But he made no contact with them; he is a voyeur, and voyeurs are by nature passive. He admits to fantasizing about these women, but his only physical outlet for those fantasies was increasingly frequent use of a prostitute. And that makes sense; that was his safety valve, the bridge between fantasy and reality. In my opinion, Colin Drummond never lost sight of which was which. He knows he is Colin Drummond; he just wishes he wasn't. And to that end, he play-acted. He pretended to be the rapist, just as he has pretended to be a hundred different things, a hundred different people. Perhaps without even being aware of it, he did cause the police to believe that he was the rapist by his reactions, and his body language, but not, I wouldn't think, by saying so openly. A mask, real or figurative, does not imply openness of any sort."

Harper started asking questions then, designed, of course, to make Drummond appear to be nothing more than a sad inadequate whose innocent fantasies had got him into hot water.

When it was over, Whitehouse got to his feet. "Wouldn't such a man as you describe—one who has a fear of women, one who is dominated by his mother, one who retreats into fantasy—be capable of rape?" he asked.

The psychologist smiled. "There is a school of thought which says that all men are capable of rape," he said.

There was a muted cheer from the women who sat across from Judy.

"Isn't one who follows women in the street and watches them make love in parked cars just a touch more likely to put that capability to use?" Whitehouse asked.

"Possibly. But in this case the safety valve was there in Rosa, the prostitute with whom Drummond could find release for these fantasies."

"But not for long," said Whitehouse. "The safety valve seems to have left town after people started being raped."

"I think," the psychologist said, "that the important part of that sentence is '*after* people started being raped.' Not before. Two people had been raped before Rosa left. So there is little reason to connect Mr. Drummond to the rapes on those grounds."

"No further questions," said Whitehouse.

Harper stood. "That is the case for the defence, my lord," he said, almost apologetically.

The judge looked at his watch, and disappointed the gallery, who had been hoping for a verdict, and Judy, whose leave was up. "I think this will be a convenient time to adjourn," he said. "I will hear the closing speeches on Monday."

"All rise. Let all those having business . . . "

Barton Crown Court, Monday 13 July

Colin was brought up for the last time. Whitehouse and Harper were going to make their closing addresses to the jury, and the judge would sum up, Harper had told him. They were almost bound to get a verdict today. Harper had said that it was his duty to warn him that he believed it would be a guilty verdict, at least on the first three.

Colin looked round the courtroom, watching it fill up. Those dykes in the gallery would take the roof off the building if he got sent down. Detective Inspector Hill wasn't there today; she'd been there all last week, sitting with that lot. But she wasn't a dyke. She was Lloyd's girlfriend.

Detective Chief Inspector Lloyd had come to see him, come into the garage when he was working on the bike, walked in without so much as asking. The garage was his place, where he could work on the bike, and think. His dad parked his car there, but that was all. Even his mum didn't come in when Colin was working on the bike. But Lloyd had walked in, calling him "Colin," as if he owned the place. Next morning, Colin had taken the bike out, had seen Lloyd leave a flat with a woman. Detective Inspector Hill. Lloyd had trespassed on his property, and Colin had made up his mind then to trespass on Lloyd's. He'd waited for her outside her flat that night, but Lloyd had come home with her, and he'd had to let it go. But he'd get her. One day. He'd get her.

At last, Whitehouse stood up, and faced the jury. "Ladies and gentlemen," he began. "Colin Drummond was arrested within moments of having sexually assaulted a sixteen-year-old girl in an attack which had begun as three previous attacks had begun; someone had pushed her down to the ground, and subjected her to an anal assault, after having held a knife to her genitals and uttered a specific threat to 'cut her open' if she did not do as she was told. On each of the three previous occasions, the victim had then been bound hand and foot and subjected to further horrific abuse, leaving physical and emotional scars, which in one tragic instance led to suicide.

"Colin Drummond's attire at the time of his arrest—black clothing, and a full face-mask—and his means of transport—a black motorbike—matched that of the assailant in the previous assaults; he carried on him materials of the sort used in each of these previous assaults, and in daylight, a knife was found at the scene of this final assault which matched what description the victim was able to give of it. That same morning Drummond made, as you have heard, a full, boastful, and foul-mouthed confession to all four of these assaults. There can be little doubt of what Miss Benson's fate was to have been, had there been no interruption of that final assault.

"But he would have you believe, ladies and gentlemen, that this confession was fabricated by him, pieced together from fragments of information, because he was afraid of being physically harmed. It is true that he had been beaten by a police officer, and you may accept that he was understandably alarmed when he was arrested. But this was just one man losing his temper, and, as a result, his job, and his liberty. Both officers involved were immediately suspended from duty. One was subsequently imprisoned, the other fined, and both were dismissed from the service. In what way could the police be thought to be condoning what they had done, even by a frightened suspect?

"And then there are the coincidences attendant upon his two brushes with Malworth police," Whitehouse went on.

Colin sat in the dock, watching the jury's faces as Whitehouse drew attention to the parts of his statement which couldn't be accounted for by anything he had learned during the interviews, and his responses when questioned about them, then took them through the coincidences, one by one. Then he reminded them again of the DNA evidence, the most damning evidence of all. Harper hadn't even asked the DNA bloke any questions, useless bastard. And you would have thought he could have found out about Rosa, with all the money that was being thrown at him to do just that.

"No evidence has been offered to back up the veiled suggestion by the defence that the police in some way engineered what went on in Hosier's Alley that night, or that the statement given by Miss Benson was anything other than a—possibly misguided—translation into standard English of her spoken word. An emergency call was received which resulted in a police car being on the spot, and two independent witnesses have told you what they saw and heard.

"In light of all the evidence presented, you must find the defendant guilty on all counts," Whitehouse finished.

Now. Colin held his breath as Harper got up. Earn your money, you lazy sod.

"Ladies and gentlemen of the jury," he said. "You have heard much over the last three days of the appalling experiences of three young women at the hands of a brutal and methodical assailant. But please don't allow your very natural revulsion at the disgusting and damaging acts of violence that they endured to cloud the issue, or your judgement of it.

"That these attacks took place is beyond doubt, and not in dispute; what you are judging here is who was responsible for them, and I believe I have demonstrated to you that despite the understandable conviction of the police that they had apprehended the right man, there is in fact very little evidence to support this contention.

"These three young women, the victims, have no personal knowledge of the identity of their assailant. The rapist took great care, as you have heard, to keep his identity well hidden. He covered himself from head to foot, and none of his victims is able to offer anything in the way of a description of the man himself beyond his approximate height and build, and in one instance, the colour of his eyes—blue, like my client's. But no hair colour, no skin tone, no distinguishing features.

"There was, however, one way in which his victims might have identified him: they heard a voice. A voice that gave them instructions, that threatened them, that warned them of the consequences of defying him, of making a sound. A voice which told them that their assailant was 'the Stealth Bomber.' This voice must have burned itself into the victims' memories, but not one of them— not one—recognized Mr. Drummond's voice as the voice of her assailant.

"No real, tangible connection has been made between my client and these crimes. No one has been brought before this court who witnessed Mr. Drummond anywhere near the locations of the first three assaults, and indeed his parents have sworn on oath that he was at home with them on all three occasions."

Colin listened, shaking his head slightly. His mother and father's evidence had done more harm than good. Why hadn't his father just said he was out raping women? He might as well have done. She would have told him to perjure himself, of course; Colin didn't suppose he had wanted to, but her word was law. His father was a spineless prick. He turned his attention back to Harper. He was another prick. And that doctor. They were all pricks.

"No one has given evidence that he or she has ever sold Mr. Drummond a flick-knife, or even seen him *with* a flick-knife. No one has been brought before you to say that he or she sold Mr. Drummond a ski-mask prior to the first of these rapes, or a replacement mask after he is alleged to have thrown away the first one. In short, nothing has been put before you to identify my client as the perpetrator of these crimes except one piece of evidence. The DNA profile."

There was a murmur then, and Colin glanced up at the gallery as it grew louder, and Harper had to raise his voice slightly as he continued to address the jury.

"Yes, my client's DNA profile is a match for the one found, but you have heard that there *is* a possibility of an accidental match, and this possibility must not be cast aside. And yes, he admired this rapist, something that you and I might find incomprehensible, but which the psychologist who spent many hours with Mr. Drummond has told you is quite in keeping with his admitted actions. Because yes, he occasionally wore a mask, and yes, he occasionally followed solitary females in the hope that he might induce fear in those who induced fear in him. But you have heard that he, to quote the psychologist, lives 'in a Walter Mitty world,' and was entirely capable of fantasizing about being this rapist without ever doing anything other than that, because inducing fear was an end in itself.

"You have heard from a prosecution witness that Mr. Drummond was in the habit of visiting a prostitute, and indeed had visited her less than two hours before one of these assaults with which he is charged. Why would he be moved to rape, when his needs had so recently been met?"

More cat-calls. A warning from the judge. Silence.

"And yes, he made a statement confessing to these crimes, but only after having been beaten up by one police officer while another stood by and did nothing, only after being taken in for questioning to another police station altogether, on another matter altogether, from which no charges arose. Only after being visited at home by the police, then arrested again and taken to Malworth police station where he was questioned for many hours with no sleep, all in the space of a weekend.

"It is entirely possible that the investigating officers, in the belief that they had got 'their man,' and in their understandable eagerness to rid the streets of a very real menace, prompted some of the assertions made in that statement, either inadvertently or otherwise. And—mistakenly or otherwise—Colin Drummond, so recently a victim of brutality at the hands of the police, believed that he would put himself in further physical peril if he did not do as they wished, and made a confession which was retracted as soon as he was beyond the walls of Malworth police station.

"He maintained then, and has ever since, that he has no knowledge whatever of the first three assaults with which he is charged, and that the fourth charge is malicious. We must therefore look at the night of his arrest, and ask ourselves what really happened in that alleyway.

"The medical evidence of the grazing of my client's knees, intended to support the prosecution's case, has been shown to be no more than a jumped-to conclusion, and the very minor bruising caused to the alleged victim no more than she would expect from an evening's work."

Howls of protest. A threat to clear the court if there were any more disturbances. Drummond didn't look at the women who bayed for his blood, who thought that little whore was worth their sympathy. He had passed her in Andwell Street, but he hadn't recognized her, not then. He had when he had seen her close to. He'd seen her with Rosa.

"There is, therefore, no physical evidence of an assault. But what of the circumstantial evidence? The prosecution has made much of coincidence in this trial, but the coincidences are not confined to the defence. It was something of a coincidence, wasn't it, that the alleged victim of this assault had been held by Malworth police for some hours that evening, arrested in the act of committing an offence for which she had many previous convictions, and was then released without charge in the early hours of the morning and allowed to walk home when a rapist was at large? Something of a coincidence that a police car was waiting just a few hundred yards up the road, and arrived on the scene of the alleged assault less than five minutes after it had begun? Something of a coincidence that the knife which was searched for that night should turn up next morning, but without any fingerprints on it? That it had been apparently immersed in water, which would have removed any other possible evidence of the use to which it had allegedly been put?

"It is clear from the evidence given by the alleged victim herself that the police gave her statement regarding the incident something of a rewrite; words and phrases which she demonstrably does not comprehend, never mind use, were to be found in that statement. And it is that same statement which contains the words and phrases alleged to have been used by Mr. Drummond to her. So how reliable is it? How much of what she says happened *did* happen, and how much was suggested to her by the questions she was asked? How many of her answers were improved upon as they were written down? She doesn't know—she just 'signed what they wrote down.' The police are very well acquainted with Miss Benson—is it unfair to assume that they knew of her admitted illiteracy, knew that she would not be able to read what had been written, chose not to read it aloud to her? Or is their apparent lack of knowledge of her difficulty with reading and writing just another coincidence?

"Perhaps you will feel that these coincidences could explain some of those objected to by the prosecution. Perhaps, if you examine Mr. Drummond's account of that incident in the light of the possible explanation to *these* coincidences, you will find that it is Miss Benson's behaviour which seems odd, rather than my client's. After all, if it was her intention all along to say that she had been sexually assaulted, to alert the police whom she knew to be close at hand, and to be found in circumstances which lent credence to allegations of sexual assault, then she wouldn't 'think to pull up her leggings,' however much time she had had in which to do so, would she? And my client's account of what passed between them begins to make much more sense.

"The police have *not* proved that the knife found at the scene was used in the alleged assault, and have not offered any other evidence to indicate that the defendant was carrying a knife or any other weapon at the time. The doctor who attended the alleged victim has agreed that what she took to be indications of violent sexual activity during her examination of the defendant were *more* likely to have been caused by the motorbike stunt riding that he had been performing earlier in the evening than by committing the sexual offence complained of. No evidence, therefore, has been offered which points to the minor injuries sustained by the two people involved as being the result of sexual violence, or which bears out the allegation of the use or threatened use of a knife.

"The prosecution must prove their case beyond a reasonable doubt, and I believe that now you have heard all the evidence you will agree with me that a reasonable doubt as to Mr. Drummond's guilt does exist, and must be taken into consideration in your deliberations. I ask you to find Mr. Drummond not guilty of these charges."

The judge looked up gravely at the jury when Harper had sat down, then sorted through his papers, referring to them now and then as he spoke to the jury, explaining the law with regard to rape, sexual assault, grievous bodily harm, the lot. They were even blaming him for that stupid bitch topping herself.

"Rape trials are often attended by doubt," he said. "In a great many cases, the doubt is as to whether or not the act *was* rape. A woman accuses a man of rape, the man says she consented, and the jury has to decide whether or not the prosecution has proved beyond a reasonable doubt that she did not. And that question, in essence, is indeed something to which you will have to address yourselves with regard to the alleged assault on Miss Benson on October twenty-eighth last year.

"But first, you must consider the charges arising from the first three assaults. In these instances, no doubt whatever exists as to the offences themselves. As learned counsel have said, your job is to decide whether or not the prosecution has proved beyond a reasonable doubt that it was the defendant, Colin Drummond, who committed them. And such a doubt may have presented considerable problems once upon a time, with no eye-witness identification, a failed attempt at voice identification, and what is little more than circumstantial evidence, albeit *strong* circumstantial evidence, to indicate the defendant's guilt.

"Juries are, quite rightly, loath to convict on circumstantial evidence alone, however strong, and the defendant has offered an explanation for the circumstances of his arrest, for his attire, for his possession of these materials. You have heard evidence that Mr. Drummond habitually wore what he was wearing that night, with the exception of the mask. His explanation for wearing the mask, though bizarre, has been backed up by very distinguished medical opinion as to his emotional state. It is for you to decide whether or not you accept this evidence.

"But whether or not you accept it, it would not of itself point to his guilt or innocence, and that is where this powerful identification tool comes in. DNA profiling is, as you have heard, as certain a method of identification as we have ever had. More certain than voice identification or even than eye-witness identification. As certain, and more compelling, than fingerprint identification, DNA profiling removes the doubt that often presented itself in cases where identification was an issue. You have heard from an expert witness that the odds are three million to one against the seminal fluid found at the scene of the second assault having originated from anyone other than the defendant; such odds surely take us well out of the realms of possibility, and even of probability; such odds amount to virtual certainty.

"It is true that the defendant had been assaulted by a police officer, and was treated with less regard than the law expects after his arrest, so you may accept that his confession was obtained in less than ideal circumstances. You may hear the tape of the confession, if you think that this will help in your deliberations. And if you feel that the defendant's explanation of the detail contained in that confession is believable, that he was capable of piecing together the snippets of information given to him by detectives and gleaned from newspapers in order to produce an entirely accurate account of three assaults of which he had no personal knowledge, that the wording of the confession was such as would have been used by someone making it in fear of physical retribution, that you can safely ignore the overwhelming odds against the DNA belonging to anyone else, and that this represents a *reasonable* doubt, then you must find him not guilty.

"If, however, you feel that the prosecution has produced compelling circumstantial evidence in the form of the detail surrounding the defendant's arrest, backed up by a full confession which bears out all three victims' evidence of the modus operandi, plus almost unassailable corroborating identification evidence in the form of a DNA match, and no such doubt exists in your minds, then you must find him guilty of all the charges pertaining to these three assaults.

"But whatever decisions you come to regarding the charges arising from the first three assaults, you must consider the charges arising from the fourth in the light of the facts concerning it, and the evidence presented on it, and it alone.

"The allegation by the prosecution is that Miss Benson was sexually assaulted at knife-point, and that a threat was issued to ensure that she would comply with the defendant's wishes. You have heard evidence that the young woman made an immediate complaint of anal assault, and that her subsequent medical examination revealed bruising which indicated recent sexual activity of this specific nature. The fact that her injuries were not serious is of no moment; it is not necessary to cause injury to be guilty of serious sexual assault. You have heard that the defendant was apprehended running away from the scene, and that he was wearing a full face-mask and clothing which matched the description given by recent victims of rape, and riding a motorbike which also matched the description given by one victim. You have also heard the defendant's confession to this assault.

"The defence maintains that Miss Benson was merely plying her trade, and that she maliciously accused the defendant of sexual assault. You have heard that the alleged victim lived as a squatter in an empty flat, the entrance to which was reached by the very alleyway into which she alleges she was manhandled. You have been told by the alleged victim herself that she knew the defendant, and knew him to be what she calls a 'punter,' in other words a possible customer for her services. And you have heard medical evidence which states that the particular sexual activity which took place was one to which the alleged victim was not unaccustomed. It has been demonstrated that the statement given by her to the police was not entirely verbatim, and she has admitted that she is not a fluent reader, and merely signed what she was given to sign.

"The decision must be yours. You are the sole judge of the facts, and you may feel that the prosecution have brought a case against the defendant which the defence has failed to answer, in which case you must find him guilty. But you may feel that these facts, taken together, constitute a reasonable doubt as to what exactly went on that night, and if you do, then the benefit of that doubt must be given to the defendant, and you must acquit."

Colin stopped listening when he got to that bit, and started telling the jury what they had to do. Unless he had the most perverse jury in the history of the legal system, he was going to be found guilty on the first three, whatever they did about the last one. And he couldn't see that it mattered.

It took the jury less than two hours. Guilty, on the first twelve counts, not guilty on the last three. Harper was pleased with that; Colin couldn't see why.

The judge called him an evil predator, an outrage to society, a public menace that had to be removed from the path of civilized people, and Colin was sentenced to life imprisonment, with a recommendation that he serve at least ten years before being considered for parole. The women in the gallery cheered, as he had predicted, and he gave them the finger.

è

The DNA had sunk them, Harper had said, but he had told Colin not to despair, that he would go on looking for Rosa. Colin hadn't been able to believe that Rosa was still eluding everyone, but she was, and for months he lived in hope of a breakthrough.

But the months had moved agonizingly slowly, and imprisonment, even in a Youth Detention Centre, had gone from being frightening and alien to humiliating and soul-destroying as he had learned that he must survive it at any price; the price had been his submission to it and those who ran it, on either side of the locked doors. Then, it had become the bleak, unending norm. The visits from his parents had gone from dreaded interludes to welcome, even vital, breaks from routine, and his hopes of Rosa had dwindled.

Then one day, Harper had come to see him. He had grounds for an appeal, he had said. Not Rosa. Something about the presentation of evidence, about the DNA. He had read something that had made him realize that the prosecution had made mistakes that could turn things Colin's way without Rosa.

Various experts had had to be lined up, but Harper had lodged an appeal. And twelve months later, which Harper had assured Colin was good going, though it didn't seem like it when you were celebrating your twenty-first birthday in a prison cell, the case had reached the Court of Appeal, amid huge publicity. Colin hadn't dared hope. He had just watched.

Harper had appealed on four grounds. The first was that the DNA scientist had usurped the jury's function when he had said that the semen originated from Colin. He should only have said that the DNA profile matched Colin's; it was up to the jury to decide if that meant the semen was his. As it was they had been told categorically that it was, by an expert witness.

The second was that the judge had compounded that error, giving the jury little choice but to find him guilty when he repeated this statement in his summing-up.

Thirdly, Harper had found other experts to point out that the likelihood of an accidental match of three million to one was not "unassailable," and did not "amount to virtual certainty," which was what the judge had said. Ten other men from a population of thirty million could have produced that profile, and they were more, not less, likely to originate in the same area, because of blood relation-ships going back beyond anyone's memory. And that DNA profiling in general, far from being infallible, was capable of error. How the tests were conducted was important, and how the comparisons were made. And there was evidence to suggest that accidental matches were much more frequent than previously thought.

And fourth, the method of arriving at three million to one was not universally accepted as accurate. More experts had given evidence, showing how if you added up the sums differently, you came out with something more like three hundred thousand to one. That way, a hundred other men could have produced the same profile.

Colin hadn't entirely followed everything that had been said in the Appeal Court, as it had all become too technical for him on the DNA side, and a bit academic for him on the legal side. But the judges had said that the DNA evidence had been given much too much weight with the jury, that the DNA scientist had been wrong to say what he did, and that the judge had made serious errors throughout his summing-up.

They had declared themselves quite happy with the method of testing, but had agreed that the odds arrived at were to some extent dependent on the method of calculation, which had not been made clear to the jury.

They had said that even if uncontested, odds of three million to one were not sufficient to convict without corroborating evidence, and that since the corroborating evidence had all arisen from the challenged and dubious circumstances surrounding his arrest for an offence of which he had been found not guilty, it was impossible to say what the jury's verdict would have been had they been given the true picture with regard to the DNA evidence.

Accordingly all the guilty verdicts delivered in the Crown versus Colin Arthur Drummond had been adjudged to be unsafe and unsatisfactory. And fifteen months after his conviction, just over two years after his arrest in Hosier's Alley, Colin Arthur Drummond had walked from court a free man.

He hadn't gone home straightaway. He had spent a few days in London, and his first purchase—before he had looked for anywhere to stay, even—had been a mobile phone. It was a symbol; a symbol of his right to contact anyone, anywhere, any time he chose. They had said he would be connected within twenty-four hours, and he had been. His first phone call had been to his mother, and his mother had made sure that there was money at his disposal. He wouldn't always be dependent on her for money, because he was taking Bartonshire Constabulary to court, and ten percent of someone's life didn't come cheap.

But it was on his mother's money that for four days and four nights Colin had lived the high life in a way he had never done before, or would again. Until this morning, Wednesday morning, when his lawyer would be making an official complaint about the conduct of the Bartonshire police, and had said that Colin would have to be available for interviews and so on.

He had left a gambling club in the small hours, having lost the last of his ready cash, with nothing but a rail ticket in his pocket. He had found himself alone except for a hooker, well past her sell-by date, who had attached herself to him at the tables and had seen the wad of money he had started out with. She had thought that there was more where that had come from, and that he was wet behind the ears. He had used her, since there was nothing better on offer, then had lain naked on her bed and watched through half-closed eyes as she had gone through his pockets. He had given her the beating she had been asking for, then had dressed and left her lying unconscious in her squalid little room. He had walked to the station and had caught the milk train to Stansfield.

Colin Drummond was going home.

Book Two

Chapter One

Wednesday 3 November

What time's the train?" asked Rob Jarvis, as he swung the black cab round in the quiet predawn street, his muscular arms bare in his heated cab, his fair skin still tanned from the summer.

"Six thirty-five," said the man, with an anxious look at his watch as they went under a streetlamp. "I suppose the next one would do—they always tell you to check in hours before the flight. But this one would be better."

"Everything went wrong this morning," said the woman. "Sorry you had to wait so long for us."

"Oh, don't worry about that," said Rob, negotiating one of the mini-roundabouts which dotted the length of the road. "We should make it. There's no traffic about at this time in the morning." He looked at them in the mirror. "Going anywhere nice?" he asked.

"Spain," said the man. "Who needs November in England?"

It was a very pleasant month, in Rob's opinion; he liked November, when the weather became crisper and the nights clear and frosty, when the trees dressed themselves in flamboyant, defiant colours before masochistically stripping themselves naked to face winter. "Do you go for the whole month?" he asked.

"Three weeks," said the woman. "It's a timeshare."

"And it works out all right, does it? Only you hear all these stories."

"We've never had any trouble. We go most years, but if we can't, we can always swap."

Rob kept up a flow of conversation as he made his way to Stansfield railway station, and picked up the luggage when they got there, outrunning his passengers despite the handicap of three suitcases. They followed him onto the platform, out of breath, as the train rounded the curve, and drew in.

"Thanks ever so much," said the woman, giving him a handsome tip as the train slowed and stopped, and the man opened the door, letting a passenger out.

Rob's smile of thanks faded when he saw the young man who stepped off the train and walked briskly away. He handed up the suitcases, and walked slowly back over the bridge to his cab, his hand absently smoothing down his sand-coloured hair as the breeze ruffled it.

The young man was standing beside Rob's cab, using a portable phone. "I'm just getting a taxi now," he said. He pressed a button to terminate the call, and looked at Rob. "Malworth?" he asked.

Rob's instinct was to refuse, but he didn't. "Sure," he said, as though he hadn't recognized him. Drummond, he was certain, knew who he was, was enjoying this, but he needn't rise to the bait.

They drove in silence out of the new town, past the light industrial estates which had replaced the heavy industry that had brought it into being, out to the much more venerable market town of Malworth, along its shop-lined High Street, where he was instructed by his passenger to stop outside a greengrocer's shop, closed and shuttered like all the others. Across the brickwork a banner had been attached: JUDY HILL IS FORTY TODAY, it read.

Drummond told him to wait, got out, crossed the road, and stood in the doorway of one of the buildings opposite, his mobile phone in his hand, looking up at one of the flats.

¿

Matt Burbidge rubbed his eyes, ran his fingers through his dark, longish hair, and packed away his stuff to keep himself awake. His flask, empty now; his sandwich tin. Ten to seven—another two hours before the staff arrived, and his shift would be over. The screens in front of him showed five scenes: the vaults; the rear of the premises; the roof; the doorway; and High Street. Northstead Securities took no chances with the stuff they held as surety, nor with the safety-deposit boxes that they rented to people who didn't want their considerable assets known to the Inland Revenue, or the police, or anyone else who might be interested.

Thus it was that he had seen two men come and erect the banner for Judy Hill's birthday. She was two years younger than him, and if life began at forty, he hoped hers went the same way as his had. He had seen the taxi arrive, and had thought she was getting a surprise visitor, but whoever it was had got out and crossed over to this side of the street. And the odd thing was that the taxi hadn't left. It still sat there, engine rattling. So where had its passenger gone? There weren't any flats on this side of High Street, and none of the shops and offices were open. He manouevred the High Street camera to take in less of the street and more of the pavement immediately outside, and his eyes widened.

Colin Drummond was standing right outside the bank. Matt had thought that he would stay away from Malworth, but there he was, standing right outside the building, and he was holding something—what? A gun? Had he done a bank robbing course in prison? No, no. Nothing so sinister. A phone. So what the hell was he up to? He was watching something across the road. A flat, presumably, unless a row of closed shops held some fascination for him.

Judy Hill's flat, of course. Drummond had had a thing about her, hadn't he? Said he was going to get her? He'd had one go before, or so they said, but her boyfriend had turned up, and Drummond had

had to change his plans; that was how come he'd got caught with the little whore.

Not just any old boyfriend, of course. Detective Chief Inspector Lloyd. That bit of gossip had cleared a lot of things up for Matt. It was Lloyd, of course, who had pulled strings to get her out of Malworth once she'd shopped him and Baz.

Well, well, well. It looked as though Drummond hadn't forgiven and forgotten any more than he had. Matt stood up and went to the box on the wall, opening it, killing the alarm, then crossed to the window in whose painted glass he could see his own oval, heavy-featured, defeated face until he snapped the light out. He silently slid the window open. If Drummond intended using that phone, he wanted to hear what was said.

ò

Judy's hand reached out and felt for the button that would stop the repeated buzzing in her ear. She switched on the bedside lamp, and a moment later the phone rang as if to underline the fact that the working day had begun.

"Hello—Judy Hill," she said.

"Happy birthday, Detective Inspector Hill."

Oh, yes. It was her birthday. She hadn't got round to remembering that. "Thank you," she replied, with an uncertain smile. "Who's that?"

"Don't you recognize my voice?"

"No," she said. "Who is it?"

"You'll work it out, Detective Inspector," he said, and hung up.

She looked at the phone, and hit the keys to get the number of the caller, but no number had been stored. She shrugged, replacing the receiver and walking with a shiver across the corridor to the bathroom. It was an ordinary sort of voice, local accent; young, she thought. Someone from work? Probably. It was her fortieth birthday; her colleagues were possibly planning some sort of horrible surprise.

She had a bath, rather than a shower. She would pamper herself. And, she thought, allow herself a sausage with her breakfast. She always ate breakfast: bacon, eggs, tomato. She quite often didn't really eat anything else. Lloyd found this life-style inexplicable.

She towelled her short hair vigorously, then put on her bathrobe and headed for the kitchen as a key turned in the lock. She jumped, though there was only one person to whom she had ever given the keys to the flat.

"Happy birthday," Lloyd said, bringing cold morning air in with him, pecking her on the cheek. He smoothed down the obstinate strip of hair that still grew in the middle of his otherwise smooth scalp, and smiled at her, his blue eyes bright from the chill air.

"What's going on?" she asked suspiciously, trying not to look as though she had been given a start. Lloyd never got up before he had to, and she had thought that he must have lost her key, so rarely did he use it.

"Nothing. I've brought you your present." He handed her a small gift-wrapped box.

She took it. "Who did you get to ring me?" she asked, going into the sitting room, snapping on the light.

"What?" he said, closing the door, joining her.

She looked uncertainly at him. He looked innocent enough, but she had long ago learned not to be fooled by how he looked. "Someone rang me," she said. "Wished me happy birthday. Anonymously."

He shook his head. "Nothing to do with me," he said. "Aren't you going to open your present?"

She smiled, sat down, carefully undid the wrapping, then opened the box to see car keys. She looked up at him, her eyes wide, her mouth slightly open. "You haven't," she said.

"Go and look," he said, nodding towards the window.

She went slowly to the window, pulled open the curtains, and looked down at the road to see, parked under the orange glow of a streetlamp, a silver Renault Clio. "That's Freddie's wife's car," was what she said, idiotically.

"It's not," said Lloyd. "It's yours."

Lloyd was always trying to make her buy what he called a proper car, and to that ostensible end he had dragged her round to Freddie's one evening, where they had "discovered" that his wife wanted to sell her car. Freddie, their friendly neighbourhood pathologist, worked such odd hours and in such unlovely surroundings and with such unpleasant materials that his wife had threatened to leave him if he didn't remove his name from the Home Office books. He, however, was deeply enamoured of suddenly deceased corpses found in suspicious circumstances, and for a while his marriage had been touch and go. But a compromise had been reached which had involved the bribe of a new car, hence the sale of one silver two-year-old Renault Clio with a burst of speed that would turn what was left of Lloyd's hair grey. But she hadn't really been able to afford the asking price.

Lloyd joined her at the window. "You were going to buy it, weren't you?" he asked. "Freddie said it was just the price that was holding you back."

"But that's just it!" she said. "You can't afford to give me it as a present!"

"I live very simply," he said, with a grin, in his RSC Welsh accent. "I have a good salary, and I don't spend very much. My children are grown up, my ex-wife has remarried—I have very few outgoings." He expanded on the theme. "I am what is known as a good catch," he said. "Or at least I was, until I began buying my fancy woman expensive presents."

She nodded, still bemused, taking the keys from their box.

"Is it all right?" he asked anxiously. "Only Freddie was certain that you were going to buy it."

She looked at the car, and then at him, shaking her head a little. "It's beautiful," she said, dropping the keys into her pocket.

"So are you," he said, kissing her, his hands slipping under her bathrobe as the kiss grew more and more amorous.

"Oh, your hands are cold," she complained. "Anyway—I thought you didn't go much for this sort of thing first thing in the morning."

"No, but you do," he said, smiling. "Anyway, it isn't first thing in the morning. I've been up for hours—I couldn't very well park the car at the flat, could I? You might have seen it. Freddie and I had to organize all this." He released her only to steer her out into the hallway, sharp right into the bedroom.

"You'll have to move the car first," she said, aware of her lack of romance, but unable to abandon her practical nature. "The traffic wardens start massing for attack at five to eight."

"Don't go away," Lloyd said, fishing the keys from her pocket.

He had been gone two minutes when the phone rang.

"Doesn't hang about, does he?" said the voice. "That's what I call a quickie."

Judy swallowed. "Who is this?" she demanded.

"Still don't recognize my voice? A lot of women have that trouble."

She dropped the phone and ran to the window. The dark street was empty as far as she could see in both directions. Slowly, she walked back and picked up the receiver again, but he had hung up. She replaced it and sat on the edge of the bed, her hand pressed to her lips.

Lloyd came back, and she went out into the hallway. "Did you see anyone on the street just now?" she asked.

"No." He took off his jacket. "Why?" He frowned slightly. "What's the matter?"

"He called again," she said.

"Your anonymous well-wisher?"

She looked up at him. "I don't think he wishes me well." She told him what he'd said.

"Oh, forget it. It's just someone's idea of a joke." He tried to cuddle her, but she pushed him away.

She shook her head. "Sorry," she said. "I'm not in the mood anymore."

"Judy," he said, putting his arm round her. "Don't let it worry you—it's just someone trying to be clever, that's all."

"He's watching the flat," she said.

Lloyd shook his head. "No one's watching the flat."

"Lloyd, he's been out there since before seven! Watching, waiting for the light to come on so he could ring me. I'm not going to—" She broke off, feeling embarrassed, not something she often felt. "Not while he's out there, watching."

"Oh, come on, Jude—this is silly. Who do you imagine would want to watch your flat?" he asked.

Judy knew who it was. Perhaps she hadn't recognized the voice, but she knew who it was, all right. She looked at Lloyd. "Colin Drummond," she said.

"Well—even if he is. He can't see in. Just forget about it," he said.

"No. I'm sorry, Lloyd. I just—" She shook her head. "Please. Not now."

Lloyd sighed. "All right," he said, philosophically. "What do you want for breakfast?" he asked, walking towards the kitchen.

"Nothing." Judy went back into the bedroom, and selected clothes from the wardrobe. "How could he know it's my birthday?" she called through, only to find when she emerged from the wardrobe that Lloyd was in the room with her.

"No mystery about that," he said. "There's a huge banner up outside. I expect you've got Tom and Bob to blame for that. Did I hear you say you didn't want *breakfast?*"

"Not now," she said. "I'm sorry. I just . . . I can't help it. I think about what he did to those girls, and—"

"If it affects you like this, you're in the wrong job."

Judy's apologetic air vanished at that, and she went on the attack. "You didn't see the victims!" She pulled on a crisp white blouse, tucking it into her skirt. "One of them *killed* herself, Lloyd! And I'm next, or had you forgotten?" She pushed past him, out of the bedroom. "He's ringing me up because I'm still a target," she said, going into the kitchen, putting the kettle on for coffee. "He's watching me, and he wants me to know it."

They drank the coffee in silence. Lloyd waited until she had finished hers, then looked at his watch. "Eight o'clock on a Monday morning," he said. "Since there isn't a good hanging to go to, what do we do now?"

She shrugged.

"The Ford place opens at eight, doesn't it?"

"The Ford place?"

"We could take your old car. See what you can get for it."

It sounded spontaneous, but Judy knew that it had been plotted, rehearsed, refined, all through the silent coffee drinking. And it had the desired effect, as she blushed with guilt. She had forgotten all about his present, and he knew it.

ₒ

At the other end of Malworth, Ginny Fredericks cancelled the alarm, and swung her thin legs out from under the warmth of the duvet, sitting on the edge of the bed, her eyes still closed, and began dozing off again.

"Get up, you lazy cow," Lennie muttered, the words accompanied by a gentle push in the small of her back.

"Who are you calling lazy?" she demanded, standing up and smiling down at her husband's pleasing face as he lay sprawled on the bed, already taking up her half too. Lennie was thirty—twelve years older than she was, but when he was sleepy he looked about five years old. "You never get up first."

He grinned back at her, his soft brown hair falling over his forehead. "I don't start work as early as you," he said. "Bring us up a cup of tea, doll." He was asleep again practically before he had finished the sentence.

She went into the bathroom for a quick shower, pulling a shower cap over her dark shoulder-length hair, tucking it in. She would have a proper bath and wash her hair later. She smiled as she thought that, as she always did; she didn't believe she would ever get used to the luxury of being able to have a bath any time she liked. Lennie had made that possible. She went back into the bedroom and pulled on the flimsy negligee and fluffy slippers that he had given her last Christmas and smiled at him again.

Downstairs, she made tea, and poured a big mug for Lennie, taking it up to him as requested. He was a devil for tea, was Lennie. She put it down beside the bed, and shook him. "Tea," she said. "Lazy sod. What did your last slave die of?"

He opened blue eyes and pulled himself up on to his elbow, pushing his thick straight hair back, stretching. "Great," he said, and rubbed his eyes as he reached for an open packet of cigarettes, removing with his lips the one that stuck out of it, and picking up his lighter.

"Aw, Lennie—don't smoke in here," she said.

He lit it, giving her a V-sign with his other hand, then blew the smoke at her with a smile. She gave up, and went downstairs again to make breakfast.

Lennie came down, dressed, his hair wet and brushed back, as she was dishing up.

"Great," he said, planting a kiss on her neck, squeezing her bottom through the thin material.

"Bugger off." She elbowed him out of her way as she opened the cupboard to get the teabags for a fresh pot of tea. A fitted kitchen. A built-in hob. The house had come like that. Lennie had got her a real house to live in, and she still couldn't get over it. She'd made it really nice for him, though. He deserved that. She made a pot of tea and took it to the table. She had a slice of toast and some flakes for breakfast, but she liked cooking for him. She liked watching him eat.

Lennie pushed away his empty plate, and drank down his tea as Ginny got up and cleared away. She heard the diesel engine arriving outside as she finished washing up, heard it cut and shudder to silence. "Rob," she said, over her shoulder.

Lennie got up from the table, arriving at the door as the doorbell rang, and opened it to Rob, who looked, if anything, even less happy than usual. Rob nodded silently to Lennie, and didn't look at Ginny at all as he went upstairs. Downstairs was open-plan—she liked that, too. It was nice, opening the door and coming straight in to the kitchen.

She dried her hands, and threw Lennie the tea towel as he went back to the table. "You can dry," she said. "And shave, Lennie."

"Stop nagging, you bitch," he said, and flicked her on the bottom with the tea-towel as she passed him, hard enough to make her yelp.

She laughed.

ỳ

Nine o'clock, and Lloyd and Judy walked into the CID room as it began filling up with keen-eyed, razor-sharp detectives yawning and complaining about the nip in the air. She hadn't mentioned Drummond at all, and was accepting their various birthday greetings with a good grace. They had taken her old car into the dealers; the man had said he would see what he could get for it. He seemed to think they'd be lucky if he got anything.

"What headway are we making on the burglaries?" Lloyd asked Detective Sergeant Sandwell.

"There's been another one," he said. "They got back this morning, found the place had been done. Exactly the same MO. The uniforms took all the details. And still the only factor in common is that the householders were all on holiday when they were burgled. And before you ask, sir, no—they didn't all use the same travel agent, or the same airline or coach company, nor were they all going to the same destination, nor did they all have the same tour company, or tour guide. Not all of them had burglar alarms, and those who had, or who had ever made enquiries about one, did not go to the same place. They don't get their papers or their milk from the same source, they don't all have animals in the same kennels, and they don't all have the same postman."

Lloyd laughed. "You should have saved that for the new Chief Super," he said. "It's going to be the first thing he asks about."

All serious crime in South Bartonshire was now being dealt with by Stansfield, and as a result, Lloyd's second brief tenure as head of Stansfield CID had been brought to an end, a higher rank being thought necessary. The new DCS wasn't going to get too favourable an impression if they couldn't clear up burglaries on their own doorstep. Their burglar—just one, they were sure—did a beautiful job, and left the house looking untouched, so the householders only found out when they got back. He'd been at it all summer, and they were no further forward than they had been in June. Good God, they were actually being asked to *detect*, something detectives very rarely did.

"What else do you *do* when you go on holiday?" DC Marshall asked, his slow Scottish delivery making the question sound like an earnest plea.

Lloyd thought. "Get travellers' cheques?" he suggested. "Perhaps they all went to the same bank."

"They didn't all go abroad," said Sandwell.

Marshall sighed, and made a note. "It's worth a try, Sarge," he said. "They might all use the same bank, or post office or something. The clerk gets them talking maybe, and . . ." He didn't exactly look overconfident, and looked at Lloyd. "It seems unlikely, sir," he said. "They aren't anywhere near one another. Just all in Stansfield, so far. But no particular area."

Judy's phone was ringing; Lloyd followed her into her office as she picked it up. The room had been decorated with balloons and cartoons, and a wrapped present sat on the desk; Lloyd wondered if she had even noticed.

"Judy Hill," she said crisply, then said nothing else until she hung up, and looked at him. "That was to remind me that I'm number six," she said. "And to indicate that he knows where I am. Now do you believe he's watching me?"

Lloyd had never thought otherwise. He had hoped he might make *her* think otherwise, or at least think of something else for five minutes. "That does it," he said. "As soon as the new Chief Super arrives, we're going to see him."

"Sorry," she said, getting up, throwing her bag over her shoulder, and picking up the present. "I'm in court in Barton at ten. I have to go."

"Oh, right. Don't drive too—"

She was gone, throwing her thanks for her present over her shoulder as she walked through CID. He picked up her phone and rang the front desk to see when Detective Chief Superintendent Case was expected, to be told that he had come in at eight. New brooms. They gave Lloyd the creeps.

His knock was answered by a peremptory "Come," and at ten past nine Lloyd went in, introducing himself to the large, grey-haired, bluff man behind the desk, a man roughly his own age, but, as ever, a good three inches taller than him when he stood up.

"Len Case," he said, shaking hands, and sitting down again. "Take a pew."

At first, Lloyd was relieved to discover that DCS Case was not twelve, and that he had hung his jacket over the back of the chair and was working in shirtsleeves. He filled him in on the happenings of the morning, and suggested that they ask for uniforms to be made available to keep an eye on Judy's flat.

"You're joking," said Case.

Lloyd frowned. "No," he said, his voice light, something that Case would come to recognize as a danger sign.

"You'd better bloody be, if you think I'm pandering to some woman's fantasy," he said. "She's a police officer, whether she likes it or not."

Lloyd had learned, mostly from Judy, that giving vent to his anger at the moment it swept over him was not the best policy; with Judy herself, it meant saying things he didn't mean and couldn't call back. It meant losing more of what little time he had with her, and feeling guilty until he had apologized, and sometimes even after that. With Chief Superintendents, it could mean losing his job for gross insubordination at a time when hanging on to it for dear life was required, if redundancy was in the offing. He ran a hand over what he still thought of as his hair, and held his tongue.

"We should never have had bloody women in the job, never mind making them bloody detective inspectors," Case went on. "Christ—protection? How long for? The rest of her life? I'm not about to ask for men to be taken off normal duties to protect an hysterical female who can't stand the heat, and neither are you."

"I think," said Lloyd, slowly and Welshly, "that you should reserve judgement on Inspector Hill until you've met her."

"I don't need to meet her! I know the type. His next victim, my arse! This kid's twenty-one years old, and she thinks he's after her? She should be so lucky."

Lloyd knew then and there that this was going to be just the first of many unpleasant interviews. Redundancy couldn't come fast enough.

ò

Carole Jarvis glanced at the clock; Rob would be home in about an hour, she supposed. If he wasn't home just after nine, it was usually an hour later.

His earnings had gone way down when he had started working

nights; that had been the impetus she had needed to look for another job, but he had wanted her there in the morning to make him something to eat before he went to bed. They had compromised, and she had got an afternoon job. Things were a lot easier; he wasn't doing so badly now that he had someone driving the cab during the day.

She had had to give up her real job, of course. They had kept it open for months, but she couldn't have expected them to do that indefinitely, and with her being unable to drive the car she hadn't been able to go back, even when she had recovered. Somehow she blamed the car, blamed the garage. Rob would take her car for runs, keep it in good working order, against the day when she could face it. She had told him to sell it, when they were so hard up that they were counting every penny, but he hadn't wanted to. He thought it was important that she drive *it* again, not some other car. She couldn't bear even to look at it.

The last time she had got out of that car, the garage door had slammed shut, someone had grabbed her, and she had been plunged into a nightmare of pain and terror. She sighed. Would there ever come a day when she didn't think about it?

But life was a bit easier now than it had been back then, without so many money troubles to add to the tension that had existed between them for over two years. She had offered to leave, offered to let him go, and start again with someone else, but he didn't want that.

She had some hotpot that she could heat up in the microwave; he preferred an evening meal after his night's work.

≀

Lennie dried the dishes and the pots and pans, putting them away neatly, all except his mug. He put his hands round the teapot to test the temperature; hot enough, he decided, pouring himself another, spooning in sugar, splashing in milk, stirring it soundly, remembering to put the spoon on the little dish that Ginny used for the purpose, and not on the worktop. She was a good girl, Ginny. She looked after him and the house like they would wither away and die if she didn't tend them daily.

He lit his second cigarette of the day, picked up his mug, and turned the paper to the back page, contentedly drinking his tea and reading the football reports as the bedsprings creaked rhythmically and unmistakably above his head.

Chapter Two

She's overreacting, like all bloody women," said Case. "I'll tell you who his next bloody victim's going to be. It's going to be us. Do you know how much he's suing us for?"

Lloyd didn't know, and didn't care.

"Drummond's lawyers have lodged an official complaint," said Case. "The Police Complaints Authority are going to order a second enquiry into the circumstances of his arrest. They don't think the internal enquiry after his trial was conducted vigorously enough."

"Neither do I," said Lloyd.

"Quite. Some very slimy stones are going to get turned over, believe me. Why do you think the CID function was headed up here as soon as Drummond's appeal was allowed? Because your lads are the Baron von Richthofens of criminal investigation?"

Lloyd opened his mouth, but he didn't get the chance to speak, not a situation in which he often found himself.

"No," continued Case. "It was because the last thing the top brass needed was Malworth investigating anything worth a damn when it all hits the headlines."

Lloyd knew exactly why Crime Detection had come to Stansfield, why both Malworth's Superintendent and DCI had decided on early retirement, why its small CID complement and several uniformed officers had been transferred, scattered throughout the county. He had had his doubts about how Malworth was being run long before the first lukewarm enquiry into the circumstances of Drummond's arrest.

"I take it you will see DI Hill when she comes back from court?" he said. "Before deciding on your course of action with regard to protection?"

"I'll see her, all right," said Case. "Put her wise about a few things. If she wants to play boys' games, she can't come running for help when she gets out of her depth."

"And you have no objection to my being present?"

"Suit yourself. You can give her all the protection you like. Just don't expect me to."

Judy wouldn't need protection from any male chauvinist dinosaur, Lloyd was sure. But he wanted to be there, all the same.

"If that's all?" said Case. "I have to attend a meeting at HQ."

At half past nine, Lloyd left the Chief Superintendent's office, wondering if he would waken up soon, and be able to consign Case to the oblivion of other long-forgotten nightmares. But he had a nagging suspicion that he was, after all, awake, and that Chief Superintendent Len Case was *real*.

ò

Rob Jarvis threw the condom in the bin and sat on the edge of the bed in his white tee shirt, feeling dirty, like he always did.

"Drummond's back," he said, twisting round to look at the skinny little prostitute who sat cross-legged on the bed.

"Yeah?" said Ginny.

"Doesn't that worry you?" he asked. She had stood up to Drummond in court. If she hadn't, he might not be here; he could never have gone looking for a whore. But he had picked her up one night, and he had remembered her from when she'd given evidence. He hadn't had any money, but he'd had her for the price of the post-midnight fare to Malworth, and things had developed from there.

"Why should it worry me?" she asked. "I never set him up."

"I just think you should watch yourself, that's all," he said.

Ginny shrugged. "Yeah, well," she said. "I've got protection this time."

Rob gave a sour laugh as he picked up his underpants. "Lennie?" he said.

"Better than Lennie."

"Oh?" He turned to face her again.

She hesitated for just a moment before getting off the bed and crossing the room, pulling open the drawer of the dressing table.

Rob walked over, shaking his head slightly as she rummaged through the collection of handcuffs and whips and studded leather G-strings. "Do people actually use these things?" he asked.

"Some," she said.

"So what's this protection?"

"This," she said, drawing out the gun, turning to face him, pointing it towards him.

His eyes widened, and he automatically turned her hand so that the gun was pointing elsewhere. She did have protection more lethal than Lennie, then. "Where the hell did you get that?" he asked.

"Someone give it me."

"People don't just *give* you semiautomatic pistols."

"Well, I've got it, and it's loaded. I can protect myself now. Only—don't tell Lennie I've still got it. He gave me a hiding for taking it."

"Why?"

"He was like you," she said. "He said no one gave something like that away. He said I was a stupid cow for taking it. He reckons it was used in a job, and they were dumping it on me. He told me to give it back."

"He's probably right," said Rob. "Why didn't you give it back?"

"I feel safe with it," she said.

"Is that right?" he said, and he put one hand round her small neck, slowly increasing his grip. "How safe do you feel now?" he asked.

"Stop," she said, her voice distorted by the pressure of his fingers on her throat. "I can't breathe."

"That's the idea," he said. "I'm strangling you. You've got a gun—use it. Because I'm not going to stop. You're going to have to stop me."

She really couldn't breathe now, and she began to panic, trying to pull away, but he tightened his grip further. She held the gun up to his face, her hand shaking, her other hand pulling vainly at his wrist, as she gasped for air, her struggles growing weaker. The gun waved in his face, and he smiled at her, his hold on her throat not slackening for an instant. She was trying to scratch him, unable to summon up the strength to do any damage.

Pull the trigger, you stupid little bitch. Can't you see I'm not going to stop?

She was barely struggling now.

Pull the trigger, for Christ's sake. Pull the bloody trigger!

◊

Lennie jumped as a firework exploded in the street, echoing through the alleyway. Jesus, they got louder every year, these things. He smiled at himself, and lit his third cigarette. Maybe he just got older every year, he thought. He used to put them through people's letterboxes, throw them at cats. Now they were a loud, dangerous nuisance. He looked at his watch, and sighed. He was shaved, ready to go when Jarvis was, but Jarvis was showing no sign of leaving. He was usually cruising by now.

The deal was that Rob had Ginny for as long as he wanted, any morning he wanted, which was usually a couple of times a week. In return, Lennie drove his cab during the day, keeping one third of the takings. Rob paid for the cab's upkeep, diesel, insurance, all the rest. At first, he'd wanted Ginny in the evenings, but Lennie had put his foot down about that. Evening was her busy time; he wasn't having her lose custom over the deal.

Mornings, he'd said, or no deal. Ginny could have killed him, but it was business, and he'd told her to stay out of it.

Now, though, it was the waste of his own time that he resented;

Rob's cab was a goldmine. He got a third of everything on the clock, and all of everything that wasn't. You could do deals all the time—people got a bargain, and he got the cash. Stansfield people took taxis everywhere—they reckoned there were more taxis per head there than anywhere outside London.

There were other perks, too. The punters liked having a cab to pick them up, and Ginny had a small but growing regular clientele. And Stansfield had a big new conference centre and hotel—visiting businessmen got cabs all the time after their high-powered lunches—often boozed up, always flush, and sometimes looking for a bit of action to while away the afternoon. Lennie knew where all the illicit gambling went on, and the other sort of action he could provide for them, with a door-to-door service into the bargain.

Ginny was the best move he'd ever made. He'd got talking to her after that business with Drummond, and he'd taken her in hand. Her main asset had been that she looked way below the age of consent, and that effect had been lost when she had slapped on makeup and wiggled about on high heels with her matchstick legs, so he'd put a stop to that. She was skin and bone, and the usual tarty clobber didn't make her look any better. Small, skinny—he could still pass her off as fourteen in a curtained room, and charge through the nose for her, which was what he did, when he got a customer that wanted that sort of thing. And she was experienced, unlike Rosa, who had taken the huff, and jacked it in after a couple of months.

He'd married Ginny six months ago when they'd moved into this place. That still surprised him a bit; he'd told his mates down the snooker club that it was so they couldn't make her give evidence against him. It got a laugh. But she'd wanted all that. The Mr. and Mrs. bit. So why not?

She was a good kid. She kept him in food and cigarettes, and he kept her out of trouble. And she had got him the cab, which was worth its weight in gold. So it wouldn't do to upset Rob, but it was after ten, and he'd been up there an hour.

Jarvis was paying as much for her, if he did but know it, as he would for a high-class call girl, but not if Lennie couldn't get the cab on the road. He wished the bastard would hurry up with her.

ò

Ginny was on the floor, dizzy, gulping precious air, and from somewhere far away, she could hear Rob's voice.

"If you're going to use a pistol for protection, you should learn how it works," he said, sounding as though nothing had happened at all.

She lay breathing heavily, her eyes closed, the blood singing in her ears, her heart pounding so hard it hurt. "Bloody thing *doesn't* work," she gasped, her voice hoarse. "That's why they gave it away."

"Sit up," he said.

She opened her eyes and saw him crouching beside her, holding the gun loosely in his hand. Reluctantly, she sat up.

He pointed to something on the left of the gun. "This," he said, "is the safety catch. It was on." He slid it away from him, and pointed the gun up at the dressing table. "If I were to pull the trigger now, it would work, believe me," he said. "That mirror would be history." He slid the catch back again, and got to his feet. "Stand up," he said.

"I can't." Her knees were still like jelly; her chest was still heaving. She shook her head. "I can't."

"You can," he said.

He still had the gun, so once again she did as she was told, and stood on shaking legs.

"Hold it in both hands, with your finger on the trigger," he said, handing it to her. "Go on," he urged, when she hesitated. "It's quite safe as long as the catch is on."

She looked at him. "What if the catch had been broken or something?" she said. "When you made me pull the trigger?"

"The way that gun was waving about, you'd have been lucky to hit the ceiling."

Ginny didn't say anything. She tried to do what he'd said with the gun, but there seemed to be too much hand and too little gun.

"Like this," he said, standing behind her, putting his arms round her, down her arms, his hands over hers, directing their position on the gun. "You always hold it with both hands. That steadies it, helps you cope with the kick. Hold it away from you and towards your target," he said.

He extended her arms further than they wanted to go, his own being longer, pointing the gun at their entwined reflection in the mirror. "And remember two things," he said. "One—if you're not used to handguns, never try to hit anyone or anything that's any more than three feet away from you, or you'll miss, and two—never point a gun at anyone unless you intend to use it."

"You would have done it," she said. "Wouldn't you? If I hadn't tried to pull the trigger. You would have strangled me."

"You wouldn't have let me," he said. He looked back at her reflection. "Self-preservation, Ginny—it's the strongest instinct there is. You learn that much in the army, if nothing else."

"You were in the army?" He had never talked to her about himself; never talked to her at all, really. Had never called her Ginny before. But if she had thought that that moment of friendliness had changed the way he felt about her, she was wrong.

"Whores don't ask questions," he said. And then he just stood there, not looking at her, not looking at anything. Forever.

"Let me go, Rob," she said eventually, when her arms had started to quiver. She looked at him in the mirror, at his eyes, far away, and she knew he hadn't even heard her. And they stayed like that, like a double statue, his arms bent, but hers outstretched. "My arms hurt," she said, after a while, but he ignored her. Then, in desperation, almost in tears, as her arms ached for relief, "Let me go, Rob, please." But he still stayed there, for so long that she would have sworn he'd forgotten she was there, except that something was making him hard again.

A firework cracked outside the house, and his eyes snapped back to hers. He released her arms, and turned her to face him as the gun fell from her hands, throwing her back against the dressing table, scattering the stuff on top of it as he pushed into her.

"I'm not supposed to do it without a condom," she said belatedly, anxiously, convinced that Lennie could practically *hear* it if she did. "Don't tell Lennie." He'd skin her alive if he found out.

Ginny didn't like having sex with anyone but Lennie—and even then, it was the time before and after the sex that she really enjoyed, the bits you missed out on with the punters. But she hated it with Rob, because he hated doing it with her. He couldn't do it with his wife, so he did it with her, but he hated it, and so did she. Twice a week, first thing in the morning. She had tried to argue about that, but Lennie had agreed to it, and she was stuck with it, because Lennie reckoned they made more out of his deal with Rob than they did out of all the other punters put together.

She closed her eyes like a child, so it wasn't really happening. But it was hard to convince herself of that as the back of her head was being bumped regularly and uncomfortably against the mirror.

He didn't speak when he'd finished. He pulled on his pants and jeans, and at last, he had left, and taken Lennie with him.

Ginny tidied up the dressing table, putting everything back where it had been. Rob had taken up two hours of her precious morning. She only had the mornings to herself, truly to herself. Thursday afternoon and Friday lunchtime she had regulars, and Lennie sometimes brought punters in the afternoon. And he always brought some from the Ferrari in the evening. Mornings were her time off—the only time she knew she wouldn't be working. That was why she'd argued with Lennie about Rob, but it had been no good.

Two hours, and most of that spent being half throttled, or cold and miserable with him making her hold that stupid gun out like that. She picked it up from the floor, tentatively slid the safety catch off, and extended her arms of her own accord, something she had thought she might never do again. As he had done, she pointed it at the mirror. She had only kept it to scare anyone who tried anything, really. It was all right for Lennie saying take it back, but you never knew what was going to come through the door, and Lennie wasn't always there.

And she knew how to use it now, so that was even better. She pushed the safety catch back on again, and put the gun back in the drawer. Lennie never came in here much, and if he did, he never looked in the drawer. So it was safe to keep it there.

She left the room and ran the bath she had promised herself, letting herself into its delicious warmth with a sigh of relief.

ℓ

In Austen Street, Stansfield, Carole Jarvis listened as Rob showered away the cheap perfume in the fond notion that she didn't know where he'd been and what he'd been doing. It hadn't taken a genius to work out why he had teamed up with Lennie Fredericks, someone he wouldn't even let into the house, why most days he was home at nine o'clock in the morning, after the office runs, but now and then he wasn't. And why those were the days he felt the need to shower before he even saw her.

It had started three or four months ago; to begin with, she had just been pleased that he had got the cab on the road during the day, and that money was less tight. She had thought that the days when he was late home were just good days, days when he'd been busier than usual. But then a court case had come up in which Lennie Fredericks had been involved, and she had realized that Mr. and Mrs. Fredericks weren't at all how she had visualized them. Then she had worked out that Mrs. Fredericks was the little prostitute who had been Drummond's last victim, and put two and two together about Rob's mysterious late home-comings.

That was when she had said she would go, but he wouldn't even discuss it.

ℓ

Matt Burbidge couldn't sleep; it was seeing Drummond again like that, he supposed. He had thought—hoped—he would stay away. He smiled briefly as he thought of the nuisance calls he had overheard Drummond making to Judy Hill, then got up, automatically switching on the television on his way through to the kitchen. The lunchtime news came on, and he went back into the living room at the mention of Drummond's name. The Police Complaints Authority had announced a full enquiry into the circumstances of

Drummond's arrest and detention, to be headed by senior officers from another force.

Oh, well, perhaps there was a bright side to having been dismissed already; the axe had fallen in his case. Some of his ex-colleagues would be shitting themselves, not least, as he understood it, Judy Hill herself. They had thought they'd got away with it, but perhaps not. Matt had never been privy to the details, but he knew they had pulled something off that they had all thought was very clever. Not so clever now, maybe.

But they had done it for him, in a way, and if he could help them out, he should, even if it did mean keeping Judy Hill out of trouble, something he had no desire to do. But the others were his mates, and he didn't want to see them go down. He wasn't sure there was much he could do, but little Ginny would get a visit from the investigating team for sure; there would be some pressure brought to bear there, naturally. Perhaps he could get in first.

She had married Lennie Fredericks since, but needless to say Lennie still had her on the game. He doubted that Lennie knew anything about the business in Hosier's Alley—Ginny didn't work for him then. Best that he stayed ignorant; Lennie hated cops, and he wouldn't take too kindly to Ginny's involvement. He didn't want to get the kid into trouble. He supposed he could just about afford the going rate, whatever it was these days. Lennie wouldn't have to know a thing about it.

ò

There was no way Judy could avoid the meeting, not without being very rude to Freddie, who, she gathered, had been up since before dawn helping to organize her birthday present. Everyone she knew seemed to have been up and about in the middle of the night, including Drummond. Freddie had seen her; she could hardly walk the other way. But he was walking along the corridor with Hotshot Harper, of all people.

Harper was a high-flyer; Barton was rarely graced with his presence, and on the odd occasion Judy had glimpsed him, she had avoided him. Not this time.

"Ah, Judy," Freddie said, beaming in the unexpected way he had, turning his perfect pathologist's face into something altogether more welcoming. "Happy birthday."

"Thank you," she said.

"I don't believe you've met Detective Inspector Hill," Freddie said, turning to Harper. "Judy, this is—" he began.

"I know who this is," Judy said, interrupting him. "I've seen Mr. Harper in action."

"Ah," said Freddie. "Good."

"And what I'd like to know," Judy went on, "is how you sleep at night, Mr. Harper."

"Very well," said Harper, with a little smile. "Thank you for your concern."

Freddie looked interestedly from Judy to Harper, then at his watch. "Oh, sorry," he said. "I must dash, I'm afraid."

Judy could tell that he really was sorry to leave; there was nothing Freddie would like better than to witness an unseemly brawl.

Harper smiled at her. "Are you going anywhere decent for lunch, by any chance?" he asked.

"The police canteen," said Judy.

She didn't know why she'd said that; she wasn't going anywhere for lunch. She didn't often eat lunch, her court case was finished, and she was supposed to be going back to Stansfield. Besides, she should be taking her colleagues out for a drink, and thanking them for the electronic organizer that she had found, rather to her surprise, when she had unwrapped her present. She had thought it would be some sort of joke present, which was why she had opened it elsewhere.

"Do you mind if I join you?"

"If you like," she said. She hadn't had breakfast, and her stomach had been in danger of keeping the judge awake. Otherwise, she wouldn't be taking Hotshot to lunch in the police canteen. Would she?

"Why should I have trouble sleeping?" he asked, when they were settled at a table with their food.

"Because you know as well as I do that Colin Drummond

raped five women, and you've just put him back on the street," said Judy.

He shook his head. "I don't know that he raped anyone at all," he said. "And I didn't put him back on the street. The court did."

"That's splitting hairs," said Judy. "But then—that's what you do, isn't it?"

He considered that, then nodded, smiling agreement.

"Don't you have any conscience about defending someone like Drummond?" she demanded.

"What's someone like Drummond?"

"A serial rapist," said Judy, angrily stabbing a piece of cheese from her salad.

"He was *accused* of being a rapist," said Harper. "He maintained that he was innocent of the charges. And my job is to defend him, to put his case—or are you saying that people charged with very serious crimes should have no defence?"

Judy flushed a little. "No, of course not," she said. "But I don't think that Hotshot Harper should come along and manufacture a doubt that doesn't exist!"

He was smiling again. "Hotshot Harper," he said. "I like that."

"It's not a compliment." Judy looked at him coldly.

"I still like it."

"What if he rapes again?" she asked. "Will your conscience prick you then?"

"No." He ate for a few moments before speaking again. "My job," he said slowly, "was to defend Drummond to the best of my ability. That resulted, in the end, in a not guilty verdict. I succeeded in doing my job. If he *is* a serial rapist, then the prosecution failed to do theirs. Why should that be on my conscience?"

"I didn't fail to do *my* job," Judy said immediately. "You stopped me. You got my evidence disallowed. Drummond gave me a blow-by-blow account of a rape that he couldn't possibly have invented, but the jury never got to hear about that, did they?"

"No," he said. "But if they had, I would have put it to you that you wrote that account, and told Drummond to sign it with the implied threat of violence if he did not."

Judy gasped. "And is that what you believe?" she asked.

He smiled again. He really had a very charming smile, Judy thought. It was difficult to loathe someone who could smile like that. She'd never seen him up close. He was younger than she had thought. He would be . . . what? Ten years younger than she was? She felt her face flush a little. She didn't usually compute the age of her fellow diners in comparison with her own.

"What I believe is of no consequence," he said. "It's what Drummond says happened. I didn't fancy my chances of making the jury believe that, because I've seen *you* in action too."

"So you found some more legal hairs to split."

"Yes."

"He told me I would be his next victim."

"He denied that."

"What do you *really* believe?"

"I believe that Drummond was convicted on DNA evidence on which too much emphasis was laid," he said. "Plus circumstantial evidence for which he had an explanation, and a very dubious allegation of sexual assault for which he had apparently been caught in the act, but which the jury did not accept."

"Dubious?" Judy looked up. "You saw that little girl giving evidence," she said. "You *know* she was telling the truth. You just gambled on the jury having forgotten her by the time they came to deliver their verdict."

"True. But I don't know she was telling the truth," he said. "And neither do you. She was very compelling, I agree. But on paper, that whole incident looks very, very iffy."

Judy smiled for the first time. "Now there's a word you wouldn't use in court," she said. "You'd be explaining to the judge what it meant."

He laughed. "I like irritating judges," he said. "It's harmless."

"You haven't answered my question," said Judy. "Do you—you, not his defence lawyer—do you believe Drummond raped those girls or not?"

He took a deep breath, and let it out slowly. "What I believe," he said, "is that it simply doesn't matter what I believe. The courts found him not guilty. That's all that matters."

"Doesn't the truth matter? Why don't the courts seem interested in the truth anymore?"

"British criminal justice doesn't concern itself with discovering the truth."

"It did once!"

"No. Inquisitions attempt to discover the truth. A coroner's inquest attempts to discover the truth. But the British criminal court is adversarial, one side versus the other. People swear to *tell* the truth, but that's not the same thing as trying to discover it. No one does that, not in a British criminal court."

"Then we should have a different system."

"I disagree."

"You would."

He smiled again, seriously this time. "We do it that way because it's impossible for a third party who wasn't present to *know* the truth. In Drummond's case, not even the victims knew the truth."

"Ginny did."

"She did. And Drummond did. But no one else did, and no one else ever can. All anyone else can do is listen to the arguments, and give the victory to the one who pleads the better case."

Judy pushed her empty plate away. "That's fine," she said. "That's just fine, if you live in a virtual reality chamber where everyone gets up and walks away. But we don't. We live in a world with murderers, and rapists, and burglars, and drug dealers, and the courts are supposed to be there to protect us against them."

"Wrong. The courts are there to protect them against us."

She stirred the little carton of milk into her tea, recognizing the start of a lecture. Why did she like men who lectured her? Why did she like this man at all?

"The courts are there to keep people like Drummond out of the clutches of the lynch mob," he said. "The whole system is loaded in favour of the defendant, because it has to be. When someone is arrested, charged, held in custody, and accused in court, everyone already has him down as guilty. Someone has to be on his side—someone has to put his case, his version of events."

"I hadn't realized it was such a noble gesture," she said.

"It can be. Defending someone accused of sex crimes is anything but career-enhancing." He smiled. "But I can't claim that it was a noble cause on my part," he said. "I just couldn't get out of it."

"Then did you have to work so hard to get him off?"

"Yes. Because once you've agreed to defend someone, that is what you must do."

"Even when the odds are three million to one against its being anyone else?"

"Especially when they are. No one must ever be allowed to think that DNA is some sort of magic formula that means you can do away with trials altogether. I have a book at home," he said, his face growing serious for the first time, "which says in words of one syllable—or thereabouts—that either the DNA doesn't match, in which case the suspect is not guilty, or it does, in which case he is." He sat back, and looked at Judy. "That is fallacious, and dangerous, and it's gaining credence, which is frightening."

Judy sighed. "All right," she said. "But did you have to ride your hobbyhorse for Drummond?"

"I was *defending* Drummond," he said, with a little shrug. "It only became my hobbyhorse because of him. Because that's my job, Inspector Hill, and I'm far from ashamed of it."

"Judy," she said, a little grudgingly.

"Hotshot," he said seriously, extending his hand.

This time she shook hands with him, and smiled. "I'm sorry I was so rude to you," she said. "I'm not usually rude to anyone."

"No problem."

"But I believe he raped those women," said Judy. "And what I do know to be true is that he gave me that statement of his own free will, that he threatened me, and that he's back, and he's still threatening me."

Harper nodded seriously. "But I don't know it to be true," he said. "Forgive me. But I don't. I only know which of you I believe, and what I believe is of no importance at all."

"And if I do become his sixth victim?" asked Judy. "What would you feel like then?"

"I'd be very distressed indeed."

"Would you feel guilty?"

"No."

"Would you defend him?"

There was a pause. "No," he said.

"Why not?"

He looked at her. "I imagine you know why not," he said, with a smile.

Judy looked back at him. He had grey eyes. Grey eyes that were looking amused; looking into hers. She didn't speak.

"I don't suppose you'd consider making it dinner next time?" he asked.

"No," she said softly. But firmly.

"Why not?" he asked, in a deliberate echo of her last question to him.

"Well ... since you obviously know Freddie, and Freddie is a gossip, I imagine *you* know why not," she said, in an equally deliberate echo of his answer. This wasn't right. This was all wrong, this minueting with Hotshot Harper.

"Yes," he said. "But perhaps you'll take my card, anyway." He put it on the table between them.

She looked at it, smiling. *Harper, Harper, Singleton and Streete, Barristers at Law*, it read. "Why should I want your card?" she asked.

"I'm hoping you'll change your mind. It could be fun." He got up. "I have to get back into court," he said apologetically. "I'm delighted to have met you at last, and I enjoyed lunch very much."

Judy looked up at him. "So did I," she said.

"Then do please take the card," he said. "You never know when you might need a good lawyer."

He left. Judy watched his back view making its way through the tables, had an argument with herself, then picked up the card, and she too made her way out.

Chapter Three

The Chief Super was back from HQ, and Lloyd and Judy had been summoned. Lloyd affected introductions, and they all sat down, eyeing one another suspiciously.

"The rape inquiry is to be reopened," said Case. "We're to have an incident room—the lot. And we're using the service-station's security camera picture of Rachel Ashman on a poster."

"A poster?" said Judy. "What for?"

"To jog people's memories."

"It was over two years ago, sir," she said.

"The Assistant Chief Constable doesn't care if it was over twenty years ago. This is window dressing. No one's expecting an early arrest—just a nice, high-profile, reopened inquiry, so Drummond can't say we aren't looking for anyone else. We are not, of course, looking for anyone else, and neither are you, Inspector. This is damage limitation, nothing more. Don't make waves."

"What about the victim's anonymity?"

Case reached for a bundle of files, opening the top one, glancing at it as he spoke. "Rachel Ashman's dead," he said, not looking up. "Anonymity doesn't come into it anymore. Anyway—the husband's agreed, so that's that. Her face is going to be on posters all over Malworth and Stansfield whether you like it or not." He marked something off on the file, closed it, and picked up another. "And your being given protection is out of the question—you'll just have to avoid dark alleys if you think he's going to come after you next."

Judy shot a less than kind look at Lloyd. He'd be in trouble for that.

"I don't want protection!" she said. "I want the little creep to have a go! I'll go down every dark alley in Malworth until he tries something. And we'll be watching him, so when he does, we'll have him on something he can't wriggle out of. Then I might be able to persuade Bobbie Chalmers to bring charges, and his statement to me about her rape would be admissible this time."

"Absolutely not."

"It's out of the question."

Lloyd and Case spoke in unison, and in total agreement. Lloyd had a feeling that it might be the first and last time.

"I can handle myself," Judy argued. "I teach self-defence classes twice a week—I should be able to."

Did she? Lloyd frowned a little. He didn't know that. Why had she never told him? How long had she been doing it? But all that was, for the moment, beside the point.

"He carries a knife, Judy," he said. "I can't let you put yourself at risk even if you can do jujitsu or whatever."

"More to the point—having Drummond watched is a nonstarter," said Case. "His legal team would put another nought on the claim."

"You mean we're not going to be keeping an eye on him?" said Judy.

"No," he said. "He's been acquitted. He'd do us for harassment. And since he already seems to have been beaten up, set up, and fitted up once, who could blame him?"

"With respect, sir," said Judy. "That's—"

Case held up a hand. "I believe I outrank you, Inspector, so you will *always* regard me with respect, and you won't need to draw my attention to the fact unless you intend being disrespectful. And if you do, you'll keep your mouth shut. Got it? You can go now—I want to talk to your boss."

Judy looked as though she was going to say more, but she evidently decided against it. "Sir," she said, icily, and left.

"I'll say this for her," Case said, as the door closed. "She's got spunk."

Spunk. Now there was a word Lloyd had thought he would never hear again. It was nicer than its modern equivalent.

"Which is more than I can say for the rest of the department," said Case. "Or this burglar wouldn't still be giving us the slip."

Lloyd groaned. Not out loud, of course. At least—he hoped it wasn't out loud.

ė

Carole waited for the bus, feeling cold, though it wasn't really a cold day. An autumnal chill in the air, that was all. But she was cold. Rob had come downstairs as she was getting ready for work, and had told her that Drummond had come back.

The little bus came up the hill to the stop, and she got on, making her way to where she could sit on her own. She didn't want to make conversation with her fellow passengers, all on their way to the same industrial estate. She wanted to come to terms with what Rob had told her.

She supposed she should be afraid. But she wasn't. It was other women who should be afraid. Other, unsuspecting women who parked in their own garages, who walked in sunlit meadows. She was bewildered, she was confused; she couldn't understand why they had let him out. But she wasn't afraid. She was angry, as her mind kept dragging her back to the blind terror of the garage.

She had thought it was all over when the painful anal thrusts had stopped, but the thought, the prayer, had barely formed when her hands had been whipped away from under her, her head had hit the floor with a sickening, dizzying blow, and her hands and feet had been bound.

What had followed she consciously refused to think about. She had never known she could do that; had never known anyone could. But she could; she could force her mind past that.

When it was over, she had been on all fours, sobbing with pain and fear, when the garage door had swung noisily open, and light from the courtyard had invaded her private hell. She had turned to see a dark figure mount a motorbike, and drive off. She could have got the number of the motorbike, and she hadn't. She hadn't. And because of that, it had happened to more women.

What had happened to her might happen to someone else tonight, tomorrow night. And it would be her fault.

◊

Judy went into the CID room when she saw Tom Finch come in, his curly fair hair in need of a trim that she was sure would be advisable before he met DCS Case, though he looked even more like a cherub with the halo effect. It might be nice to have Case discover the hard way that Tom was as tough as they came, despite his looks. He was alone, so she could get it off her chest.

"That man is insufferable," she said.

Sergeant Finch smiled. "So I've heard," he said, not having to ask which man.

"He actually believes that Drummond was set up—can you beat it? He must know that someone like Ginny wouldn't lift a finger to help us out, never mind tangle with a rapist."

"Well . . ." said Tom, looking uncomfortable. "There's something you maybe ought to know before you go shouting the odds with senior officers."

Judy looked at him, her mouth slightly open. "You're not going to tell me Drummond was set up," she said.

"No," said Tom.

Judy expelled her breath. "Good," she said.

"Ginny was."

She stared at him.

Tom sat down at his desk, looking up at her. "I didn't tell you any of this at the time, because . . . well, because—"

Judy pulled a chair across and sat down. "Never mind why," she said. "Tell me now."

"Right," said Tom, running his hands down his face, taking a breath, letting it out. "Drummond gave us a blood sample on the Saturday morning that we brought him in for questioning over the murder," he said. "There was blood on the jeans he'd been wearing the night before, and we wanted to know whose—he said it was his. We got his sample tested for the blood group."

Judy hadn't known about his jeans. She was very interested in that blood, but she let Tom carry on.

"And it turned out that his blood group was the same as whoever had raped Mrs. Ashman," he said. "That was when it got sent for DNA profiling. When they heard that, Malworth CID were convinced that Drummond was the rapist. But they had been told hands-off, because he'd made this complaint about Burbidge and Turner doing him over, and everyone was a bit jumpy about harassment. So . . . some of them and the uniforms arranged a little off-duty surveillance from a van. They watched him, kept in touch with the on-duty ones with mobiles."

He paused; Judy didn't speak.

"And they were watching him the night Drummond was waiting for you outside your flat," he said. "You were never in danger," he added quickly. "If he'd tried anything—"

"Oh, sure," said Judy, wondering just how long it would have taken her hostile ex-colleagues to come to the rescue.

"But you came home with Lloyd, and . . ."

Judy flushed slightly. She had been in Lloyd's car, trying to persuade him to spend the night with her, and they had been *watching*? No prizes for guessing what the canteen gossip would have been the following day. Tom had obviously been given an account, and he hadn't even worked there.

"That's one reason I never told you," Tom said.

"Go on."

"Well, when Lloyd went into the flats with you, Drummond left, and they followed him. He cruised around, then went up to the airfield and did wheelies and things. Meanwhile, Ginny was caught giving some old guy a blow-job on a park bench, and was brought in.

They didn't know if she was to be cautioned or charged, and the inspector was busy, so they stuck her in a cell, and then someone—I'm not telling you who—someone realized that Ginny had to go along Andwell Street to get home, and so did Drummond. They figured if the guys at the airfield let them know when Drummond left, and they let Ginny go at the same time . . ."

Judy's eyes widened. "A tethered lamb?" she said.

"Pretty much," said Tom. "They knew he was up for it, because he'd been waiting for you," he said. "Reckoned he'd have a go at Ginny if he saw her on her own."

"They sent that little girl on a collision course with a *rapist?*"

"Yes, well. But someone was right behind her all the way," he added. "Anyway, the retired Major nearly ruined it all when he rang in complaining about Drummond, but they managed to head the patrol car off at the pass. And when they got the word that Drummond had left the airfield, they let Ginny go."

More like badger-baiting, thought Judy, angry beyond words. She just listened.

"The guys with Drummond made the bogus nine-double-nine to get the area car in position. Then they followed him from the airfield, saw him pass Ginny, then turn into Hosier's Alley, and they drove off. The guy following Ginny was supposed to wait until he taped her hands, then *he* had to ring nine-double-nine, say someone was being attacked, give the location, and melt away. The area car would have been there in seconds, and they would have got him, with all the evidence they needed. But these two guys from the factory rescued her before it got to that stage, so he just made himself scarce and let it take its course."

Judy couldn't believe she was hearing this. "Are you telling me someone stood and *watched* that happening to Ginny?" she said, her voice quiet.

Tom nodded. "But in fairness, Judy—Drummond didn't do anything before he taped them up that hasn't happened to Ginny a hundred times. They knew she wouldn't get hurt."

"Wouldn't get hurt? She had a knife held—" Judy broke off, still too angry to speak. After a moment, she shook her head. "That's really why you didn't tell me," she said. "Isn't it? I'd have reported the lot of them."

"I know," he said. "I only found out after the event, or I might have done something to stop it. As it was . . ." He shrugged. "It was easier to let it lie," he said.

"She went through all that in court just to hear the jury find him not guilty—and there was a witness all along!"

Tom nodded again. "It didn't work," he said. "But no one who was in on it had anything to do with the arrest. The area lads knew nothing, the duty CID inspector knew nothing—he was at home when it was all going down. Everyone in that courtroom was telling the truth about what happened, except Drummond. He wasn't set up. But . . . well, word got round that events had been . . . orchestrated, so now everyone thinks he was."

"Great." Judy shook her head. "And the knife?" she said. "The one they found on the riverbank?"

"It was kosher."

"How dared they?" Judy said angrily. "How dared they treat anyone like that? She was sixteen years old!"

"I know. But they figured the end would justify the means."

"Well, it didn't! It never does."

"No. But DNA results took weeks to come through then, and they thought that was the only way they could get him behind bars before he raped anyone else. Anyway," said Tom. "I thought you ought to know. I expect this investigation will bring it all out in the open." He waited for a moment before he spoke again. "Are you going to tell Lloyd I knew about it?"

"No." She stood up. "The blood on his jeans," she said, drawing a line under the discussion. "*Was* it his?"

"No."

"Did it go for profiling?"

"No. Once we'd established it wasn't the murder victim's, we had no further interest in it."

"I have," said Judy. "They'll still have that sample, won't they?"

"They should have," said Tom slowly, realizing why she wanted it.

"Of course . . . Bobbie Chalmers was raped that same night, wasn't she?"

"I want it analysed," said Judy. "He's still a suspect in an outstanding rape, even if it wasn't an official complaint. Bobbie's flatmate reported that there had been an assault. If anyone queries it, refer them to me. I'll see if I can persuade Bobbie to give us a sample for comparison. She might, now that the circumstances have changed."

"Will do, guv."

Bobbie Chalmers lived on Parkside. The road that had relieved Malworth of much of its choking traffic had devoured most of that area except for a few narrow streets lined with workmen's cottages, which had somehow got themselves listed by British Heritage, and in one of which Ginny Fredericks lived; two low-level blocks facing one another, where Bobbie Chalmers had her flat—still sharing with her friend; an unlovely high-rise, and a scattering of shops and small businesses. Malworth had finally managed to cut Parkside off from the rest of the town completely; the bypass had severed it even from the desolate park which had given it its name, and in which Ginny had once plied her trade.

For motorists, it meant that getting from one side of Malworth to the other actually took longer than it had, because of the volume of traffic on the bypass which had priority over that turning into Parkside, and for pedestrians it meant using the underpass, which now, less than a year after its completion, few people used after dark except street girls and muggers. It had been designed for them; it was supported all along its length by buttresses behind which the girls could do business, and the muggers could wait unseen for the foolhardy or the unwary. Occasionally, the two joined forces; that sort of crime was rarely reported. The lights were constantly vandalized, and even when working produced pools of light beyond which the dark was even more impenetrable than it would have been without them. Those going for an evening at the pub, on the other side of the by-pass, preferred, as a rule, to risk the traffic. There was talk of a bridge to replace it, already.

Thus isolated, Parkside had become more and more run down,

until the council had been forced at least to look as though they were doing something about it. The Parkside Regeneration Programme had caused a great many more unsafe buildings to be demolished, and large expanses of uneven ground lay waiting for some enterprising, not to say dotty, speculative builder to snap them up.

One such, not far from the cavernous opening of the underpass, in the shade of the high-rise, was being put to good use at the moment; someone had had the idea of piling up the combustible debris from the demolition and making a huge bonfire of it, and the council had entered into the spirit of the thing. They were laying on hot-dog stands and baked potato vendors, a professional firework display, and, Judy understood, recorded entertainment in the form of the *Music for the Royal Fireworks,* no less; the flattened ground all around was to become a car park for the evening.

To prove that Parkside really was being regenerated, the Malworth bonfire was going to be something special. If no one set it alight before Friday, of course. To this end a posse of guards had been formed, mostly from the area's long-term unemployed, and it was being guarded twenty-four hours a day. Bobbie's block of flats was within sight of the towering pile of wooden windowframes and floorboards.

Bobbie was auburn haired now rather than blonde, but as immovable as ever, though her original reason for being so no longer mattered. No, she would not give them a blood sample, she said, and whatever argument Judy used, that was her answer.

Judy looked at her steadily. "He'll rape again," she said. No ifs or buts. He would, and Bobbie ought to think about that. "He'll do that to someone else," she said.

Bobbie tilted her head back slightly, looking up. Tears weren't that far away. The iron control with which she had refused to cooperate before was slipping, deserting her just a little, as it had immediately after the rape. That was when she had told Judy about it, only to refuse to make it official when her resolve had returned moments later. Judy knew she could work on that slight weakness, but she was puzzled; something other than Drummond's reappearance was bothering the girl.

"If you give me a sample of blood and it's the same as the blood on his jeans, then he'll go back to prison and he'll stay there," said Judy.

She shook her head. "I'm not making myself a target," she said.

"It's your blood on his jeans—I know it is, and so do you. As soon as we have confirmation, he'll be arrested again. That, your evidence, and his statement to me will convict him, Bobbie."

"No!" she shouted, almost sobbed. "It's been two years! I was just beginning to get over it. I was making some sort of life again—I was even seeing someone! I was putting that whole business—all of it—behind me. Marilyn thought she might even be getting rid of me at last," she said, with a half laugh, half sob. "She's been great. She went through it all with me. She put her own life on hold. I don't know what I'd have done without her."

Judy nodded.

"And then as soon as things start getting better, this happens. And I'm getting calls from him all the time."

Judy's eyebrows shot up. "Drummond's ringing you up?"

Bobbie closed her eyes, took a short breath. "Whoever raped me is ringing me up," she said carefully. "And I didn't tell you that much—got it?"

Judy sighed. "Is it the same ground rules as before?" she asked. "You'll deny this conversation if I try to make it an official complaint?"

"Yes."

Judy rose. "All right," she said. "But he can't get to you, Bobbie, not if he's inside. And that's where he'd be."

"Sure," said Bobbie, scornfully. "I was a hostess in a nightclub—that's one step up from prostitution in their book. They'd treat me just like they did Ginny and you know it. Look where it got her. Not guilty."

Judy didn't want to think about that. "Do you know Ginny?" she asked.

"Yes," she said. "I work at the Ferrari. So did she, in a manner of speaking. I don't see much of her now, though."

"Why? Has she given it up?"

"I doubt if her husband would let her. I see him, flashing a card round. I expect it's hers."

"What do you do at the Ferrari?"

"I work behind the bar. At night. It was a long time before I could face going out in the evening at all, and then . . . well, I made up my mind that I wasn't going to let it rule my life."

The phone rang, and the two women looked at one another. Bobbie picked it up, listened, and held it out to Judy. "It's him," she said, her voice scared. "He wants to know if you're still here." She pressed the privacy button as Judy took the phone. "Don't tell him I told you he's been ringing me," she begged.

Judy shook her head, then nodded to Bobbie to press the button again. "DI Hill," she said.

"I just thought I'd let you know I've changed my mind about you," he said.

"Drummond, if you think you can get away with following me round, and ringing me every—"

"There are other ways of screwing you, Detective Inspector," he went on, talking through her. "Better ways. And I've got some unfinished business to attend to."

He hung up, and Judy tried to trace the call, just in case, but it was the waste of time she had thought it would be. She replaced the receiver, and looked at Bobbie. As Hotshot would doubtless point out, she didn't *know* who was ringing her either, but the odds were three million to one against its being anyone else. "I have to go," she said. "If you change your mind, you know where to get me."

She drove the short distance to where Ginny now lived with Lennie; she hadn't liked Drummond's reference to unfinished business, and Ginny should know that he was back. Ginny's house was at the end of a small terrace of shops; an inevitable alleyway ran alongside it, joining it to the street behind. The front door was practically for show; the side door in the alleyway was the one in constant use. People didn't want to be seen coming and going.

"I know," said Ginny, when she told her. "Someone saw him. I'm not bothered—Lennie'll look after me."

He certainly seemed to be looking after her. Judy looked round the cosy little kitchen, at the washer-drier, the fridge-freezer. "Very nice," she said.

Ginny beamed, and waved a hand at the door into the sitting room, following Judy in, inviting her to sit down. State-of-the-art hi-fi, TV, and video gleamed in the soft light from the table lamps. "Would you like a cup of tea or something?" she asked.

Judy shouldn't really. She was supposed to be at Lloyd's flat, enjoying a pre-birthday dinner drink. But Ginny had come so far up in the world that she must be finding it hard to breathe the thin air; she was intrigued, and wanted to know more. "That would be lovely," she said.

Ginny busied herself in the kitchen, and Judy still looked round, slightly openmouthed, at the sparkling glass shelves on which vases of flowers and little ornaments were grouped, at the fitted carpet without a strand of pile out of place.

"This is a bit of an improvement on your last place," she said, when Ginny came in with a tray which she set down on the coffee table.

"Lennie got it," she said. "He knew the guy who said who could have one of them."

Judy worked on that. The allocations manager, she presumed. And Ginny had doubtless got to know him pretty well too. She plunged in—there was no such thing as subtlety where Ginny was concerned. "Lennie must be getting you a better class of client," she said.

"Lennie's not my pimp," Ginny said.

She wasn't in the least offended; the denial was automatic, as was Judy's disbelieving acceptance of it.

"He's not! He's got a job. A proper job."

Judy smiled. "Lennie? A proper job?"

"Yes," she said stoutly. "He's driving a taxi."

That Judy simply couldn't believe.

ℓ

At five o'clock Lennie was sitting outside a house, opulent by anyone's standards, in Malworth. His passenger wore an expensive suit over a muscled body, smoked cigars, and now, it seemed, had a deep interest in Lennie's affairs.

"I'll have what you've got, then," he said.

Lennie handed his passenger a bundle of notes. The man counted it, and nodded.

"Pick me up the same time, same place, Friday," he said. "And bring the rest."

"Friday?" Lennie repeated, twisting round in his seat. "I can't get it for Friday, not all of it!"

"That's all right," he said pleasantly. "If you haven't got it all, I'll settle up with you some other time."

Lennie knew what that meant. "Friday," he agreed.

Short of robbing a bank, he didn't know how he was supposed to comply. His passenger got out, failing to pay the substantial fare that had been clocked up on the meter, and which would be coming out of whatever he managed to take over the next couple of hours. Lennie lit a cigarette, and headed back to Stansfield. There might, with luck, be a randy businessman looking for a bit of relaxation while he was attending the conference, he thought, and made his way out to the new hotel complex with fear-driven optimism. He could sometimes get customers for her when a conference was on. Especially an international one like this one—men away from home liked to try the local delicacies. He hoped he got something, because if things were bad before, they were critical now. He'd put Ginny's card in the phone boxes, but the phone had been cut off, so there would be nothing from that source. The gas and electric would be next. But none of that mattered now.

Until he'd picked up his cigar-smoking passenger, he'd been happy in the knowledge that things would get better, because they would. They did. These things went in cycles. But now he had no time left to let them get better. He had to make them get better. Now.

ℓ

The rape enquiry was being reopened. Matt stared at the television, where Drummond was leading off the news as if he was some sort of celebrity, and licked his lips, which had gone dry. Surely to God they didn't *really* think Drummond wasn't guilty? It was just some technicality, some clever lawyer's trick that had got him off; there couldn't be any more real doubt than there had been in the first place. Except that they were reopening the enquiry

"In an unusual move, Bartonshire police intend producing a photograph of one of the victims," said the reporter. *"Her name will not be released, but a spokesman for Bartonshire Constabulary said that it was hoped that people's memories would be jogged. Mrs. A, as she is known, was caught on security cameras as she entered the all-night service station where she was later assaulted, and, tragically, took her own life three months before the case came to trial. Her husband's permission was sought and granted for the publication of her photograph. He was unavailable for comment this afternoon."*

Back to the newsreader. *"Colin Drummond was cleared of all charges of rape and sexual assault . . ."*

Matt switched off the television. Bloody hell. Had they nothing better to report? No wars? No famines? Wasn't that what was on the news every other night? Tonight, it was Colin Drummond. It was the rapes. It was the police corruption, the miscarriage of justice story. Sex, violence, and dodgy cops—you couldn't beat it. All that statement-falsifying and evidence-rigging wasn't confined to big metropolitan forces. Here was a cosy little county force doing the same thing. The story was big.

And now he too was waiting for the axe to fall.

ₐ

God, was she never going to leave? Ginny answered her questions without ever wondering if she had any right to be asking them; police asked questions, and if it wouldn't get you into trouble, you answered. If it would get you into trouble, you said no comment.

"I can charge a lot more," she said. "Now they can come to me."

DI Hill looked impressed. "You don't go out looking for them any more?" she asked.

"No."

It wasn't against the law, doing it like this, Lennie said. Sometimes they rang up—well, not at the moment, because the phone wasn't working—but they had, for a while. And Lennie brought the others.

She had her fingers crossed that she didn't hear the double hoot of the taxi horn that meant he had one with him, and she should go upstairs and get ready. Because that *was* against the law. Him getting them for her. Ginny had never understood why some things were and some weren't against the law, but she knew which was which.

"You must be charging a great deal more to have all this," said DI Hill.

"Yeah. And there's Lennie's money from the taxi."

"Oh, yes." She looked as though she found that funny. "How on earth did Lennie get into taxi driving?" she asked.

"It belongs to a—" Ginny stopped, and thought, unable to assess whether or not the deal with Rob was against the law. Better not say, just in case. "A mate of his," she said.

"Oh." Inspector Hill smiled again. "How many taxis does this mate of his have?"

"Just the one."

"Maybe I should take it up," she said. "It must be a very lucrative business."

Ginny frowned. "A what?" she asked.

"It must pay."

"Yeah."

Ginny felt slightly more at ease as seven o'clock came and went; Lennie never brought anyone after that, because the taxi had to be back at eight, and Rob got mad if it wasn't. But she was beginning to worry that DI Hill might still be here when Lennie got home; he would go ballistic if he found a cop in the house, and he'd blame her. She told the inspector that.

"So he would," she said, getting up. "I'm on my way. Just—you know. Watch yourself."

"Yeah," said Ginny. "Right."

Her free time had been taken up by an unwelcome visitor once again; Ginny sighed with relief when the inspector had gone, and set about making Lennie's tea. It would have to be another fry-up—she didn't have time to do anything else. She didn't like giving him too much fried stuff, though he would live on it given half a chance. But they said it was bad for you. Men in particular. And she didn't want anything happening to Lennie.

She was chipping the potatoes when she heard the taxi drawing up.

ℓ

Rob got out of the backseat, and slid in behind the wheel, catching sight of Lennie's wallet lying on the floor. He picked it up, flipping it open: two fivers, that was all. He had thought it would have a lot more in it than that, in view of the way Lennie was ripping him off.

"Hang on, mate!" he shouted to Lennie's retreating figure, and got out, taking him the wallet. "You must have dropped this," he said.

Lennie took it, nodded his morose thanks, then let himself into the house. Funny—Lennie was usually talkative, almost like a real cabdriver, giving a running commentary on his day, and his life. He wasn't usually down, but he was tonight. He hadn't said a word on the way home.

Rob drove back into Stansfield, being hailed almost as soon as he was within its boundaries. He drove past to a V-sign, switching off the FOR HIRE sign, and cutting the radio.

He had more important things to do.

Chapter Four

"You could have rung," Lloyd grumbled.

"I tried to—Ginny's phone was out of order." She looked penitent. "It's not as though anything spoiled," she said.

"You didn't know that!" Lloyd poured himself a drink, then remembered that it was after all supposed to be her birthday celebration. "What do you want?" he asked.

"A G and T will be fine," she said. "I knew you weren't likely to be doing a soufflé when you didn't even know when to expect me," she said.

"I did expect you some time before seven forty-five. I intended to eat at eight."

"So how long's it going to take? Does it matter when we eat?"

"Not to you, obviously." He handed her her drink as churlishly as one could hand someone else a drink. In truth, the birthday dinner was one which would take as long as it took the tiny late new potatoes to cook; there had never been a problem about that. He had been worried, that was the problem. Worried because she was gone so long, and that nutcase was ringing her up. But he wasn't going to tell her that. She was already far too personally affected by Drummond without his adding to it.

She sighed. "I'm sorry," she said. "I just got worried about Ginny after that phone call."

"Perhaps you could give her some lessons in self-defence," Lloyd said.

Judy sat down, too. "Is that what this is all about?" she asked.

"Well, no, since you ask. It isn't what it's about. It's what brought it home to me, though."

"Brought what home to you?"

He looked at her for a moment before he spoke. "This is your fortieth birthday," he said slowly. "I have known you since before your twenty-first, and I don't believe I know you any better now than I did then."

"Don't be silly."

He and Judy had met in London, when he had been trying to make it in the Met, and she had been a probationer. He had been married then; she had been single. They had met again in Stansfield ten years later, when he was no longer married, but she was. Despite that, they had embarked upon the love affair for which he had always known they were destined, and her marriage had ended in divorce. But it was still a love affair, not a relationship. He told her that.

"That's nonsense."

"Is it?" he asked. "Is it?" His voice rose. "You teach self-defence, apparently—now that's something I would have thought most people might know about their partners, but me? No. Why not, Judy? Why don't I know?"

She shrugged a little. "No reason," she said. "It just ... never came up."

"Oh, for God's sake! It isn't something you just find yourself doing! You must have thought about it, arranged it, publicized it—and you never said a word. Something must have made you think of doing it—what?"

She flushed a little, and put her drink down on the table. "Drummond," she said, looking at him at last. "I made enquiries with the college the day after my interview with him. And you already thought I was obsessed with him—what do you suppose would have happened if I'd told you?"

"What?" he said, feigning a lack of comprehension. "What would have happened?"

The air of innocence wasn't cutting much ice with Judy. "You wouldn't exactly have approved, would you?"

He would not. He had given her many lectures on fear-mongering, on press-promoted hysteria, which was what he thought it was. Drummonds were few and far between. He sipped his whisky, trying to make himself change the subject, to stop the row that he was quite deliberately starting, but he couldn't. "That won't wash," he said. "Because that's just one thing. I see you at the weekends, and high days and holidays, like this. What about all the rest of the time?"

She shook her head slightly. "What about it?"

"I don't know what you *do*! You have a life I know nothing about, Judy!"

"Well, I don't know what you do." She picked up her drink again.

"Yes, you do," he said. "You know all there is to know about me. You know what I do to relax, you know who my friends are, you know which pub I go to, and when you're likely to find me there. You do, Judy. You know. I don't. What do you do when you're not teaching self-defence?"

"This is silly."

"Tell me!"

"I don't know! I—I do normal things. Visit friends, stay at home and do things that need doing, like ironing or washing . . . I'm going to have a go at putting some tiles up in the bathroom—I don't know! Oh—" She looked a little sheepish. "I do some stuff for MADS," she said.

"Who?"

"Malworth Amateur Dramatic Society."

"Oh—you act. I'm sorry I didn't catch your *Hedda Gabler*."

"I don't act! I do their admin—their books."

He stared at her, shaking his head slightly. "How did you get involved with something like that?" he asked.

"You're making it sound like a pedophile ring."

"I just want to know how you got involved! I didn't know you had the slightest interest in amateur dramatics."

"I don't. A friend of mine was in it—"

"Which friend? Anyone I know, by any remote chance?"

"I don't think so."

"No, I don't imagine I do. What sort of friend?"

"What *sort* of friend?" she repeated, puzzled, then her brown eyes widened a little. "Not the sort I sleep with, if that's what's bothering you," she said, tight-lipped.

"I wasn't suggesting that you—"

"Oh, yes, you were."

"Well? Why not? How am I supposed to know what you're getting up to?"

"Getting *up* to?"

"You know what I mean."

"Yes," she said. "I know what you mean. And I don't like it."

He didn't think she was getting up to anything. But he felt as though she was a stranger, sometimes. Once, he'd thought it was because she was locked into a dead marriage that she had kept a part of her life to herself. Out of loyalty to her husband, or consideration of his own feelings, even. Now that marriage had long since ended in divorce, and he knew that her motives were, as ever, selfish. She didn't want him to be part of her life, not her whole life. She just wanted him to be there when she needed him, or wanted him. Damn it, it wasn't right, and it wasn't fair, and he hit back sometimes, despite himself.

"I don't like it, either!" he shouted. "You could be doing anything, for all I know! You shut me out, Judy! You go home to that damn flat and shut me out!"

"You've got a key, Lloyd," she said, maddeningly reasonable. "You're welcome to use it morning, afternoon, evening—in the middle of the night, if you like. But you don't, do you? I thought I had burglars this morning—that's how often I get a visit from you."

"That's because I don't *want* to visit you!" he shouted. "I want you with me."

"Where you can keep an eye on me? See what I'm getting up to? Well, tough." She put down her untouched drink, and stood up. "And I'm going," she said.

"Oh, for God's sake, Judy—" He got to his feet in a halfhearted attempt to stop her, but she brushed him aside.

"This isn't going to get any better, and I'm not going to let it get any worse," she said, going out to the hall, shrugging on her jacket. "Good night."

The door closed, quietly, and she was gone. She didn't even slam doors. She didn't shout. She didn't let rows run their natural course. She just walked out on them, left them up in the air, unfinished, unresolved. Always. If she stayed, he hurt her, with his wicked tongue. Always. She knew that, so she didn't stay. And who could blame her?

Oh, to hell. At least it was a good night on the telly. He switched on the television, got himself a beer, and sat down as the programme started. Within fifteen minutes the policeman hero was bedding yet another desirable woman in his ceaseless search for whodunit.

Life wasn't really like that, he thought, then amended that. It sometimes was. But not if you couldn't stop yourself saying things you didn't mean, and buggering everything up. All the same, it couldn't always be his fault. She did shut him out. She did hang on to that flat and her independence because that was how *she* wanted it, and to hell with what he wanted. Oh, he could force the issue— make her do things his way, give her an ultimatum to move in with him or else. In an uncharacteristic moment she had shown that she needed him enough for that to work.

But that would make him feel guiltier than ever, and she knew it.

ℓ

Lennie's good humour of the morning had entirely vanished. He had eaten in silence, drunk his tea, and now he was watching television. When the credits went up, he switched off the TV and shrugged on his jacket. "Get your coat," he said.

Ginny went upstairs and got the fake fur jacket that he'd bought her for her birthday. Once, she had dreamed of real fur, but now it was cruel, so she'd got fake. "Where are we going?" she asked, as she came down.

"You'll have to work the park," he said.

"The park?" she said, dismayed. "Why, Lennie?"

"Because I'm telling you to."

"But it takes too long for them to bring me here with the bypass."

"They won't be bringing you here."

She frowned. "Where, then?"

"You can work out of the van," said Lennie.

"Aw, Lenny—you said I wouldn't have to do that anymore!"

"Well, now I'm saying different." He opened the door. "Out," he said.

"No!" she said. "It'll be bloody freezing in the back of that van! And you can't charge as much as you can if they come here, so it's stupid!"

"You can do more punters," said Lennie.

That didn't sound like at all a good idea to Ginny. "Not if I don't go!" she shouted.

He caught her by the arm, and his other hand delivered a stinging backhanded slap to her face. "You're going!" he said, pushing her out.

"I won't get any punters at all if I'm covered in sodding bruises!" she shouted, as she stumbled on to the pavement.

&

Matt walked round the corner to see Lennie pull his side door shut, and manhandle Ginny towards the Transit.

"Get in the fucking van!" he said, delivering a blow to the back of her head. "Now!"

Matt strolled into the alley. "Can't get the staff these days, can you, Lennie?" he said.

Lennie let go of Ginny and turned, looking Matt up and down. "Joined the Foreign Legion, have you?" he asked.

Matt hated the uniform, aping as it did a police uniform except that it was black. He felt like some sort of fascist soldier. "Watch your lip, Lennie," he said.

Lennie smiled. "What do you want?" he asked.

"Half an hour of your wife's time."

"Yeah? It'll cost you thirty."

Matt shook his head. "You must be joking," he said.

"That's what she charges. Take it or leave it."

What *she* charged. The money went straight to Lennie, useless parasite, and God help Ginny if she tried to hang on to a couple of quid. "It wasn't too long ago she thought a fiver was big time," said Matt.

"Times have changed."

Hadn't they just. Matt looked at Ginny, sullen and silent, leaning against the van. He'd just seen Lennie in action—he didn't want to let the kid in for any more of that. Trouble was, he couldn't pay thirty quid for her; he hadn't got that sort of money. But there was something desperate about Lennie's air that made him think that he could beat him down without too much difficulty. "Ten," he said.

"Twenty."

"Ten," he repeated. "That's more than she's worth."

"Fifteen."

Matt gave him the money; Lennie unlocked the door and went into the house, jerking his head at Ginny, who pushed herself away from the van and brushed past him, taking off her jacket and hanging it over the stair post as she went up ahead of Matt. She started taking off the rest as she got into the room.

"You can keep your clothes on," Matt said, closing the door. "I just want to talk."

"Aw—I'm no good at that sort of thing," she said from inside the thin, sleeveless top she was pulling off over her head.

Matt frowned, then his brow cleared. "No," he said. "Talk. As in I want a word with you."

She pulled her top back down. "Why'd you pay fifteen quid for it, then?" she asked, her voice heavy with suspicion, her eyes alarmed.

Matt sighed. "Because I don't suppose Lennie knows about your part in that little charade with Drummond," he said. "I don't want you on my conscience."

"You what?" Her eyebrows drew together in a total lack of comprehension.

"As far as Lennie's concerned, I'm here for a screw, and you don't tell him any different or he'll knock your head off. Understand?"

She nodded uncertainly, her brows still meeting.

"Now. They're holding an inquiry into Drummond's arrest. You're going to get policemen asking you what happened that night in Hosier's Alley."

She understood one word, at least. "Cops? Here? Lennie'll go spare!"

"Well, I can't do anything about that. They'll ask about what happened in Hosier's Alley with Drummond. They'll go on about perjury and perverting the course of justice, but they can't prove a thing."

"What?"

Dear God. This was the hardest fifteen quid he'd ever spent. "They'll tell you that you can go to prison," he said. "But don't let them scare you. They can't prove anything if you just stick to your story."

"What story?"

Matt sank down on the bed, and prepared to start again. Maybe Lennie did earn his money after all.

ò

The ten o'clock news was all Drummond, as the six o'clock had been. Carole watched despite herself; she longed to switch it off, to stop listening, but she couldn't.

She had finally left the garage, and knocked on a neighbour's door. She had vague memories of ambulance men and urgency. Then she had opened her eyes to find Rob, still in uniform, at one side of the hospital bed, and a policewoman, not in uniform, at the other.

She had had to lie to the police about where she had been, and she had been relieved, so relieved when the spotlight had moved on to someone else. Relieved, she had eventually realized, that someone else had gone through that hell. She had gone to counselling more because of the guilt she felt about that than because of the attack itself.

But her lies had come back to haunt her, and she had had to tell the truth in the end. Rob hadn't done any of the things she had imagined he would do, and that had just made her feel guiltier than ever. He hadn't flown into a rage, hadn't hit her, hadn't called her names. He had understood, had confessed to the odd infidelity of his own in Ireland. Separated, lonely . . . it happened, he had said. He had truly understood.

They had had a happy marriage, once. But he was right; she had been lonely, with him away so often and for so long. And she had met someone. It had got more serious than she had intended. Even so, she would probably have finished it when Rob had come home from Ireland. But that wasn't how things had worked out.

When the police had come back, almost three months later, wanting to know where she had been, she had been so scared. Drummond's statement said that he'd followed her from Malworth, they had said. *Had* she been in Malworth? The DNA wasn't Drummond's. Did she know whose it was? On and on, until she had had to tell them, and then poor Stephen had had to get involved and have his private life investigated until they eliminated him as a suspect. His marriage had broken up; he'd given his wife the house, and now the Child Support Agency were taking more money from him. He was living in a flat in a high-rise, all because of Drummond.

Rob had come out of the forces, and had bought a secondhand taxi with his money from the army and a loan from the bank. Her physical injuries had healed, and the strong-mindedness which allowed her to reject the memory of the rape had eventually made it possible for her to want to resume relations with Rob. But that was when it had all gone wrong.

Rob couldn't. Not wouldn't—couldn't. He had tried. He had wanted to, naturally, after months of being patient. But he just couldn't. Nothing happened when he tried to make love to her. She had been raped. Defiled. And he couldn't handle that. To start with, they had kept trying, but after six months of it Rob had started working at night so that he didn't have to share her bed, didn't have to face it. He had changed, become cold and hard and uncommunicative.

And a few months after that, he had apparently discovered that he *could* do it with Ginny. When Carole had finally realized that, she had reasoned that if he was all right with someone else, then she could leave, let him find someone else. She didn't tell him she knew about Ginny, but she had suggested that they divorce, so he could find someone else. He had said that she was his wife, that he didn't want someone else, and that was an end to it.

Ginny was a stopgap, obviously. He still thought things would be all right between them. But they wouldn't. Not now. Not now she didn't love him anymore.

ò

Rob glanced at his watch as he indicated the right turn into Parkside across the six-lane carriageway, and waited at the break in the central reservation. On his left was the turnoff that took you into Malworth proper, and in between sat the park, a dark, cold and dismal no man's land. He could see a couple of hookers hanging round on the far side, leaning on the railings, waiting for customers. He had to wait long minutes for oncoming traffic, even at this time of night, his fingers tapping impatiently on the steering wheel. At last, the road was clear, and he went down the B-road that now took you into what was left of Parkside, past the dark tower of the bonfire, to the squat block of flats. He left the engine running, and got out of the cab.

ò

Lennie sat smoking at the kitchen table, waiting until Matt came down and let himself out, then he crushed out his cigarette, picked up her jacket, and took the stairs two at a time to hurry Ginny up. She would be wasting as much time as she could up there to delay going out.

He frowned. She was sitting on the bed, fully dressed. The bed was made. And nothing about the room suggested that anything had ever been any different. "What did Burbidge want, if he didn't want to get laid?" he asked, intrigued to know what Matt Burbidge's sexual preferences were.

She looked at him, the big dark eyes a little in awe of his powers of observation, a little scared, a little puzzled, then resigned. "Don't hit me, Lennie," she said.

There was something surreal about living with Ginny. "Why would I hit you?" he asked.

"Matt said you would."

"I won't hit you," he said, totally bamboozled, but taking the line of least resistance. "What did he want?"

"He said I had to stick to my story."

Lennie frowned. "What story?"

"That's what I said," Ginny replied, her face perplexed.

Sensing that this would be a long job, Lennie put out a hand and pulled her up from the bed. "Tell me in the van," he said, thrusting her coat into her hands. "We're wasting time."

ò

Judy switched off the news, which had had Drummond all over it, which hadn't helped. The rest hadn't exactly been a barrel of laughs, and then the local news had had nothing *but* Drummond. He would be in his element with all this attention. Wasn't that why he had done it? Why he had confessed? They were giving him exactly what he wanted, and a cash bonus into the bargain.

No one had set the vicious little bastard up. He had assaulted Ginny, and now he was threatening to finish the job, and there was damn all she could do about it until he did. Hotshot Harper had a lot to answer for.

But she had enjoyed his company. And sitting there, listening to him explain his point of view, it had even seemed reasonable. But sitting in Ginny's house, looking at her, knowing what Drummond had in mind for her . . . no.

She thought again of Ginny's house, bristling with mod cons and soft furnishings, and shook her head. There was no way Ginny was making enough for all that, not in Malworth. And Lennie? Driving a taxi? It was hard enough to believe that he was turning an honest penny doing anything, but he certainly wouldn't be making very much out of it if it wasn't his taxi. She tried to work out what Ginny would be making a week, given what she knew of Malworth's over-staffed red light district, and what she would be likely to command now that she had a room to offer rather than the back of Lennie's Transit. Not enough.

It had been partly a desire to find out why their circumstances had taken such a turn for the better that had made her stay at Ginny's, and partly, she knew, a desire not to go to Lloyd's. She had seen his face when she'd told the Chief Super about the self-defence classes; she had known there would be a row. She had thought it would be about Drummond, about her so-called overreaction. But Lloyd could always take her by surprise.

Hotshot had taken her by surprise, too. She wished he hadn't been so easy to be with. She wished she wasn't thinking about him. She wished she could be sure that he had had nothing to do with her reaction to Lloyd's fairly run-of-the-mill wild accusation of infidelity. He did that sort of thing all the time when he was angry. But it had hit home.

She had only had lunch with the man in the police canteen, for God's sake. It wasn't exactly a candlelit dinner for two.

She would go to bed. No she wouldn't, because the phone was ringing. Lloyd, to apologize. Poor Lloyd. He always ended up apologizing, and that wasn't really very fair.

"Hello," she said.

"Judy?" Her guess had been right, but she hadn't guessed what he was going to say. "There's been another rape," he said. "And . . ." He paused. "There isn't an easy way to say this," he said. "It was Bobbie's flatmate. And she's dead. I don't have details—just that it happened in the flat."

Marilyn. Who had called them out two years ago when Bobbie had arrived home to that very flat and had passed out from the carbon monoxide that had poisoned her as she had been raped in the exhaust stream of her car. Otherwise they might never have heard about Bobbie's assault. And they might not have the slender thread they did have with which to link Drummond to the rapes. Marilyn, who had helped Bobbie through it, who had been great, who had put her own life on hold, was dead.

"I'll see you there," she said, finding her voice at last.

Flat two, Balfour House, was swarming with uniforms, scenes-of-crime officers, detectives, photographers, all the dismal circus that attended a suspicious death, when Judy got there. In the room itself, Tom was telling the photographer what he wanted; Lloyd was talking to the FME outside the door, and he acknowledged Judy's presence with a slight nod.

Judy looked into the neat room, at the young woman who lay sprawled on the bed, at the injuries that she had seen five times before, and looked away, first at Tom, then at the rest of the room. One drawer was open; the fingerprint man was dusting it for prints. No chance, she thought. Drummond isn't that stupid. Had he been looking for something?

She had a look round the rest of the flat: the other bedroom, also tidy; the bathroom; kitchen; living room. Nothing disturbed, except for the telephone table in the corridor, knocked over, and the telephone smashed, stamped on, probably. There had been no break-in; he must have come to the door. Marilyn had in all probability opened the door to a masked man and, unable to pass him, had picked up the phone and been overpowered as she had tried to ring for help. Then she had been dragged, ordered, whatever, to the bedroom.

"Mm," said Lloyd, when he joined her, and she gave him her initial thoughts on what had happened. "Why would he take her into the bedroom?" he asked. "Why not do it here, in the corridor? No windows. Further away from the neighbours—less likelihood of the sound travelling—which it did, at some point, or the neighbour wouldn't have got suspicious. All he had to do was put out the light and he would have had his preferred environment of total darkness."

"She might have got away from him, briefly," Judy said. She tried to visualize the scene though her entire being wanted not to. "While he was disabling the phone, probably. He would be between her and the door, so she couldn't get out. But she ran along to her bedroom, and tried to shut herself in. He was too quick for her." She looked at Lloyd. "And he raped and murdered her on her own bed," she added bitterly. "Will Case take Drummond seriously now, do you suppose?"

Lloyd nodded. "Yes," he said. "I think so." He looked down the corridor. "But why did she run into the bedroom?" he asked, and went into the bathroom, shutting the door, locking it. He came out again, and looked at her. "Why not the bathroom? It's right here, it has a lock that might have kept him out. If she got away from him at all—why not run in there?"

Judy thought about that, and shook her head. "I don't know," she said.

"It's a little puzzle," Lloyd said.

Lloyd thought the answers to little puzzles solved the big one. Judy had learned to believe it. But there was no big puzzle about who had murdered Marilyn—what they had to do was prove it. "I'll work on it," she said, and sighed. "Meanwhile, someone's got to tell Bobbie, and it had better be me."

"I'll come with you," Lloyd said. "There's not much I can do here that Tom can't do."

He was giving her moral support. He did it all the time, automatically. He was always there when she needed him. And she'd walked out on her birthday dinner.

In the car, she apologized for that.

"It'll keep," he said. "Until we're more in the mood."

Telling Bobbie what had happened was the hardest thing she had ever had to do. The landlord of the Ferrari got Bobbie a brandy; the landlady got them all a cup of tea, and went off to make up a bed for Bobbie. She had to stay with them for as long as she wanted, she said.

"Someone will have to tell her boyfriend," Bobbie said dully.

"Where does he live?" asked Lloyd.

"Stansfield." She was staring straight ahead, her eyes wide and blank with grief. "But . . . he works away. On the gas-rigs. Two weeks on, two weeks off—" She broke off, and took a long time before she spoke again. "He only left last night," she whispered. "I don't know which one he's on, just that it's off the Essex coast. His name's Des Hewitt. Someone has to—"

"We'll deal with that," said Lloyd. "We'll find him. Don't worry."

Judy looked at the shattered girl and knew that she was right back where she had been two years ago, after the rape. And she knew that she would never have a better chance. "Bobbie," she said quietly. "We've *got* to stop Drummond. Please, please give us a blood sample."

Bobbie Chalmers turned her eyes painfully to Judy's. "What for?" she asked, her voice just audible.

"To compare with the blood found on Drummond's jeans," said Judy. "I told you this afternoon, remember? It's yours, Bobbie, and we can prove it."

She shook her head slightly. "No," she said. "It can't be mine."

The defences were torn and ragged, but they were still in place. Judy had met her match in Bobbie before; she was meeting it still. Because Bobbie was a survivor, and Drummond had just made it clear to her what she had to do to stay alive.

"I wasn't raped," she went on. "And I never said I was."

Chapter Five

Thursday 4 November

Midnight. Lennie sat in the front of the Transit, elbows on the steering wheel, chin in his hands, an eye open for the cops, an ear open for Ginny, in the back with a punter. He had counted every penny he had; it would have been more if that randy bugger hadn't kept the cab off the road all morning. Please God, let it be a busy night.

The john emerged, and drove off. After a minute Ginny came out, and Lennie opened the door.

She got in, pulling the fur jacket round her as she shivered. Lennie took the money from her, and he drove off, back to the pitch.

"Lennie—let's pack it in. I was there for hours before I got him— there aren't enough punters."

"The other two are doing all right."

"Well, it's their pitch, isn't it? They've got regulars."

He pulled up, and leant across her, opening the door. "Out," he said. "And try looking as if you want to fuck them, for Christ's sake."

"I *don't* want to! I want to go home!"

He raised his hand, and she scuttled back to the pavement as a car inched its way along. It picked up one of the others, and Lennie swore, and drove back to the discreet parking place that hid the van from the road. Half an hour passed, and she arrived with one on foot. And as soon as she was on her way back to the pitch, she was complaining again, and didn't stop when they got there.

Business at last became reasonably brisk, but she was still complaining all the time, and started saying she wanted to go home as soon as the cars began to thin out, and the rush hour was over. But he made her work until the trickle of cars dried up altogether. She'd got a regular tomorrow and one Friday lunchtime, and whatever he could skim off the taxi takings. He was well short of what he needed, but there would be no more trade tonight, and Ginny finally got her wish.

"I'm fucking freezing," she announced, as she got in, slamming the door, huddling into her jacket. "It isn't fair. You said I wouldn't have to do this any—"

"Shut it, Ginny," he said. "Just *shut it*, all right?"

Ginny lapsed into silence, and Lennie drove her home.

~

Lloyd caught sight of Freddie as he made his way through to the sealed-off room where white-suited people looked for, and hopefully gathered, evidence.

"The FME pronounced life extinct at eleven-twenty," Lloyd said. "She's left notes about temperature readings and so on. She said the girl was very recently deceased when she saw her."

"Good." Freddie looked at his watch. "One-fifteen," he said. "Two hours since she examined the body. Anything else?"

"The emergency call was made at ten forty-five—one of the neighbours. She heard noises that worried her a bit, but when it went quiet she didn't think any more about it. Then she heard the front door slam and saw someone leave. Wearing black—she just saw his back view, but it worried her, in view of recent events. That's when she tried to raise Marilyn, and when she couldn't, she called us."

Freddie nodded, and went into the room at the end of the corridor to begin his task. Lloyd knew that he was secretly delighted to be about to get his hands on a fresh corpse, but Freddie had attended sex-crime scenes with Lloyd before, and knew now that it was politic to disguise his pleasure.

Tom came back from the neighbours, all awake now, and coming out of their flats to see what was going on. For once, they had some information. Someone had heard a diesel engine running outside for about twenty minutes, and had looked out to see a black cab parked over by Lloyd George House, the block of flats on the opposite side of the street. She couldn't be sure of the time, but she knew it was after ten and before eleven. She couldn't say whether or not there had been anyone in it. Black cabs were from Stansfield; Malworth didn't have them.

"I'll get Marshall to check on cabs in the morning," said Tom. "The driver might have seen something."

A man on his way back from the pub, crossing the busy road in preference to using the underpass, had almost been run over by someone on a motorbike, going too fast, at about quarter to eleven, he thought. No description of the bike, no vehicle registration number. The rider was wearing black, and a crash helmet that entirely covered his face.

Judy had found a couple from the neighbouring block who had been out walking their dog, and had seen someone in dark clothes running towards the underpass. About ten twenty-five, they decided, so they doubted if he had had much to do with it.

"The wife of the couple said she thought she recognized the man running to the underpass," said Judy. "He works as a night security guard at Northstead Securities—you know? The bank across the road from my flat?"

Lloyd didn't know the bank opposite her flat, but he didn't really want to draw attention to his lack of knowledge of her flat and its environs. "Oh, yes," he said. "Right."

"Sir?" A constable came over. "Drummond's been picked up," he said. "He was seen in Stansfield, on his bike—he said he hadn't been anywhere, just riding round."

Judy detailed Tom to talk to the security guard, find out if he had seen a motorcyclist. Lloyd then allowed her to drive him to the station, trying not to peer over at the speedometer as she pulled out on to the bypass and gathered speed. He wanted to get there just as much as she did.

Drummond had cooperated fully, they were told. Had agreed to help with their enquiries, had come to the station without a murmur. He had asked if he could ring his parents, and had done so from a mobile phone.

That explained how he could follow Judy and call her up wherever she was, Lloyd thought, as they settled themselves down in the interview room, and he looked at the young man. He looked different, in an indefinable way. He was two years older, of course, but there was something else. Something his time behind bars had perhaps produced. The cockiness had been replaced by confidence. Drummond wasn't afraid, wasn't alarmed, not this time. He could handle himself now. He smiled at Judy as she spoke to him.

"Mr. Drummond, you're not under arrest," said Judy briskly, after she had gone through the preliminaries with the tape, and cautioned him. No mistakes got made when Judy conducted the interview. "You are free to leave at any time, and to have free legal representation during questioning if you wish."

"No, thanks."

"I would like to ask you some questions concerning a rape and murder which took place in the Parkside area of Malworth late yesterday evening," she said. "A motorcyclist answering your description was seen leaving the area. Can you tell us where you were between ten and eleven o'clock?"

"I took the bike up and down the bypass for a bit," he said. "It's a new one. I wanted to take it out, see what it could do. Then I went up the airfield. When I left, I just carried on into Stansfield, and I was riding about here for a while until I got stopped." He smiled. "They didn't beat me up this time," he said. "Do you want my clothes again?"

He was, as ever, dressed in black, but this time his clothes were manifestly free of any incriminating stains.

"Yes," said Judy.

Drummond still smiled. "Do you want me to take them off now?" he asked.

"It'll wait until you get home," Lloyd said. "Thank you for being so cooperative, Mr. Drummond."

Drummond hadn't taken his eyes off Judy. "Is there anything else I can do for you before I go?" he asked.

There was something else he could do for them, thought Lloyd. He wanted a sample for DNA. He decided to go for it. "We would like a saliva sample," he said. "Are you prepared to let us have one?"

Drummond's eyes left Judy, and snapped over to him. "What for?" he asked.

"So that we may extract a DNA profile," Lloyd said steadily.

"You've already got one. It didn't do you a lot of good, but you've got it anyway."

"No," said Lloyd. "We're only allowed to keep the profiles of people who have been convicted of violent offences. And you haven't been, Mr. Drummond. Besides—that legislation is of very recent origin. It wasn't in place when you *were* convicted."

"And that means you didn't keep it? I wasn't born yesterday, Chief Inspector."

"Oh, I'm sure we kept it. But a comparison made with it might well be inadmissible as evidence."

Drummond was thrown by this frankness—so, Lloyd could feel, was Judy. It was a gamble. They might, just *might* find something; Drummond must be out of practice. And if they did, then there was no way they were going to compare it with the previous DNA profile which they shouldn't still have, because Hotshot, as Judy called him, would be on to that like a flash. But a freely given *new* sample . . . He just hoped he had judged the young man's overweening conceit correctly, or he had handed him his defence on a plate.

Drummond sat back. "If it's like the others, you won't find anything," he said. "The rapist's very thorough, isn't he?" He looked at Judy again, and smiled again. "You said this one was murdered," he said. "How did he do it? Hadn't you better tell me? Otherwise I won't know what to say in my confession, will I?"

Lloyd hoped that Judy's professionalism was going to see her through this, and that Drummond's baiting wouldn't produce a reaction. But he should have known better than to worry; Judy sat, her face expressionless, her pen poised over the inevitable notebook in which she was noting everything down, despite the tape.

"So, Mr. Drummond," Lloyd said. "Would you be prepared to allow us to take a saliva sample? It's entirely painless, and it might enable us to eliminate you from our enquiry."

"Sure," said Drummond, still talking to Judy, still smiling. "Why not?"

After the sample had been taken, Drummond was taken home; the officers with him—two, at Judy's insistence, in view of Drummond's tactics—would collect the clothes he was wearing, and they would go to forensic. But no one held out any hope at all about that, not in view of the eagerness with which he had offered them.

Lloyd explained his thinking about the DNA to Judy; she was impressed at his beating Hotshot at his own game before Hotshot even knew he was playing.

Tom came back to report that the night security man at Northstead Securities was none other than Matt Burbidge; Judy positively winced when his name was spoken.

"It wasn't your fault," Lloyd said, for the umpteenth time.

"He got the sack because of me, Lloyd! And why? Because he gave that little ar—" She pursed her lips together, not swearing, because she knew he didn't like her to, and she was trying not to give any more offence than she already had tonight. "Because he did what every one of us wants to do right now," she said.

"He assaulted a suspect instead of bringing him in for questioning," Lloyd said. "I don't want to do that."

"Well, anyway," said Tom. "He was visiting friends, lost track of the time, and had to run, literally. He remembers seeing the couple, but he didn't see anyone on a motorbike. He assures me that if he had, he would have remembered."

"He would. Let's call it a day," said Lloyd.

Judy drove him home; she stopped at the entrance to the garages behind his flats, engine running, a signal that she wasn't coming in with him.

"I'm too tired," she said.

He smiled. "So am I." He pecked her on the cheek. "See you tomorrow."

He watched her drive off too fast, and wished he had got her something more sedate.

ϙ

Carole Jarvis had woken from the nightmares that the evening news and her memories had reawakened, when her unconscious mind would go over and over what she had banished from her conscious mind, and she couldn't get back to sleep.

The whole thing was a mess. They couldn't go on like this forever—Rob working nights so as to avoid her, her pretending that she didn't know about Ginny. Rob . . . well, he had found some sort of release with Ginny, and he would be prepared to go on like this for another two years; forever. But she wasn't. Their life together was a sham. Rob wouldn't leave her, wouldn't let her leave, wouldn't discuss their problems, wouldn't try to make it work, wouldn't admit that it was finished.

She had to do something. Anything. Just whatever it took to shake them out of this dreadful impasse. She got up, eventually, when she realized that it was almost seven o'clock, and she might as well.

ϙ

Light fell on the pavement across the road, catching Matt's attention, and he looked out of the high window at the pale yellow rectangle in the building opposite. Judy Hill was rising, with a proper job to go to. A job with pension rights and a decent salary. With prospects. Especially if you were prepared to sleep with whoever you needed to in order to get ahead, and grass up your colleagues as soon as look at them. Bitch.

Yesterday, she had had Drummond ringing her up to wish her happy birthday. Matt had watched and listened as he had made his call; Drummond had walked over to the taxi when he'd finished, and Matt had thought he was leaving, but he had just paid off the driver and come back to the bank doorway. Then Lloyd had arrived. Drummond had stepped into the recess of the doorway, waited, watched, and so had Matt. A few minutes later, Lloyd had come out again, got into the car and driven off. Matt knew why; he was shifting the car before the traffic warden booked him, but Drummond, not aware of Malworth's new traffic systems, had thought he'd gone; he'd rung her up again.

Drummond had been too deep in shadow for Judy Hill to see him when she came to the window, for Lloyd to see him when he walked back. In his black clothes, Drummond could make himself invisible. If Matt had turned his head from the opened window he would have seen him on the screen, caught on the camera that would record any in-and-out holdup, the one that took in the recess of the doorway, and enhanced the picture until it looked like underwater daylight.

This shift had been livened up by a visit from Sergeant Finch. Where was Matt, he had wanted to know, between ten and eleven o'clock? There had been another rape, Finch had said. The girl was dead, and they were questioning everyone who had been in the area. Matt had spun him a yarn; Tom Finch knew him, was happy to accept what he had told him, and hadn't asked for detail. Yes, he had said, he had been running into the underpass at about that time. That couple had seen him, recognized him, for God's sake. How come they knew who he was? She works in the off-licence next door, Tom had said; she sees you arrive here when she's on lates.

All very friendly. Nothing to worry about. Matt stretched, yawned, and turned his attention back to the screens, where no one was tunnelling into the vaults or abseiling down the roof. At ten to nine, the staff began to arrive, and Matt was released from bondage for another day.

૭

Ginny watched the cab arrive; Rob hooted for Lennie, and sat behind the Transit, engine running, in the alley.

She turned from the sink. "That's Rob," she said.

Lennie was sitting at the table, smoking, lost in thought. He looked at her when she spoke, but it was as if she wasn't there.

She was wearing an old grey polo-neck sweater of Lennie's and nothing else; Lennie usually liked that, usually couldn't resist pinching her bum where the sweater just covered it, but he hadn't done that, hadn't even spoken to her this morning. He didn't now; he just got up from the table and went out, getting into the back of the taxi. Rob backed the taxi out, and they were gone.

Lennie was still in the same rotten mood as he'd been in last night; Ginny was quite relieved to see the back of him.

◊

"I think we should pay Baz Turner a visit, guv," said Tom, knocking, entering and speaking all at once.

Judy looked up from the files she had pulled on the rapes, and had been reading all morning, in an effort to find something the original enquiry had missed. "Why?" she asked.

"I want to know why he gave evidence in Drummond's defence," he said. "When I spoke to him at the time, he said he thought Drummond was the rapist. I want to know what made him change his mind."

Judy thought about it. "Do you think Drummond might have got to him?" she asked.

"It hadn't occurred to me before, but it's possible. If he can do what he did last night to scare Bobbie Chalmers off, he could do anything."

Getting him for seeking to pervert the course of justice was better than nothing. Judy agreed that they should talk to Baz, and she and Tom drove to Barry Turner's house.

"Won't he be at work?" Judy asked.

"Unemployed," said Tom.

Judy sighed. The only two police officers in Malworth who had done something worthwhile, and they were the ones that had got the sack.

Turner didn't look overjoyed to see them, but he invited them in, and Tom asked his question.

"Well, I just . . ." Turner began, and floundered immediately. "Is it true?" he asked. "Has someone been murdered this time?"

"Yes," said Tom. "And we think it was a warning."

Turner sat down. "A warning?"

"To Bobbie Chalmers. To keep her mouth shut. It was her flatmate."

Turner went pale, and Tom sat opposite him. "Come on, Baz," he said. "What haven't you told us?"

Turner looked at him, and then up at Judy. "You . . . you'd better sit down, too," he said. He looked at her, then at Tom, then at his hands. "When Matt Burbidge beat that kid up," he said, "he hadn't mentioned the rapes. No one had."

"But you said he'd been taunting you—" Judy began.

"I know," said Turner. "That was Matt's idea. But it was like the defence bloke said. Matt was just getting him back for giving us the runaround before. We told him he'd be getting a summons, and I walked back to the car. Next thing, I hear Matt saying that Drummond would remember us, and I turned round just in time to see him throw a punch at the kid, right in the mouth. I yelled to Matt, but he said it was private, and hit him again."

"Private?" said Judy.

"Yeah, well—you know. Stay out of it. So I did. But then he punched him full in the stomach and the kid went down like a stone. I thought he'd leave it then, but next thing, he's trying to kick the shit out of him. It took me all my time to get him off him. I made him go back to the car, and checked that Drummond could stand up. Then I went back to the car and took off like the clappers."

"Did you ask him why he'd done it?"

"Sure. He just said he'd felt like it, and not to worry, Drummond wouldn't make trouble. Then a little while later, we got sent to a minor RTA—no one badly hurt, but one of them needed patching up. So I go to the car for the first-aid box. Only the roll of adhesive bandage is gone."

Judy could feel Tom's eyes on her; she wouldn't look at him.

"I never thought anything of it, not at the time. It was back in the tin next morning. But then I heard about the Chalmers girl—how there had been a rape just before we'd stopped Drummond. And . . .

well, the thing is . . ." He looked away. "Matt wasn't in the car when that happened," he said.

"Not in the car? For how long?"

"About half an hour," said Turner, miserably. "We'd been on duty at the football ground. That celebrity match. They'd thought there might be a lot of traffic, but with the fog and everything . . ." He looked up again, then, at Judy. "The match was abandoned at half time," he said. "We were told to go down to the lay-by on the Malworth Road. Matt lived right across the road from the ground—still does. And he said he wanted to sort something out at home, and would I cover for him. He got back to the car about a minute before Drummond passed us."

"And you didn't tell anyone about this?" asked Judy.

"Well—no. I mean, you can't go shopping your mates . . ." He looked away from her, and appealed to Tom, who was less given to shopping his mates. "I mean, you can't, can you?" he said. "Anyway, there had been no official report of the rape. And I'd only just started to think about it all when the next thing I know we're on the carpet, being suspended—I didn't know what had hit me." He looked at Judy. "I know Matt blames you," he said. "But it was his fault, not yours. The inspector reckoned you were just trying to stick up for us."

Judy nodded. Her helpful intervention had got them the sack. She had happened to witness the incident on her way home from Lloyd's flat; she had seen Drummond all in one piece, proudly reported that fact to her boss when Drummond had said the police had assaulted him. Trouble was, they had said he was in his battered condition *when* they had stopped him, so she had landed them in it instead of getting them out of it.

"That was Matt's idea, too," said Turner. "Saying he was in that state when we stopped him. Then after that got blown out, he said we should go for provocation, to lessen the sentence, and he came up with the rape business. Then things got worse. Because I heard on the grapevine that the lads were going to get Drummond back, and next night he's nicked for assaulting a prostitute. And—well, Matt knew the little tom, didn't he? And he knew the one called Rosa, too."

"He what?" said Tom, his voice flat.

"Definitely. He was the beat man in Parkside for months. He knew all those girls—he nicked them all the time. He told me stories about it, you know, like you do—and he told me about one called Rosa. He said he hadn't ever nicked her because he felt sorry for her. She wasn't cut out for it. And just before the trial, everyone was looking for her, weren't they? And he never said he knew her—he couldn't have, because everyone thought Drummond had made her up until the other one said she'd seen him with her. And it might have got Drummond off, if she'd given evidence."

It might not have. "And you still said nothing?" said Judy.

"I couldn't. But now someone's been murdered. I can't live with that."

He could live with the rapes, though. Judy wondered how many more times in the course of this enquiry she was going to have to sit and listen to tales of police corruption and cover-ups, and began to wonder if she was the only straight police officer in the job. But there was Lloyd. Lloyd was straight. She made herself look at it rationally. Corruption had obviously become rife at Malworth—that was why serious crime had been taken away from them. It didn't mean that it had set in anywhere else.

"So that's why I gave evidence in his defence," Turner said. "He was being fitted up. I had to stick to the story about provocation— that was what I'd used in mitigation. But the rapes never crossed my mind—it had been six weeks since the last one. I never thought he'd raped anyone, so that was what I said." He looked at Judy. "And I still don't think he raped anyone," he said. "Do you know why Matt Burbidge was taken off the beat at Parkside?"

Judy was certain she didn't want to know.

"They needed him for undercover work," said Turner. "He was doing that most of July, and then he came into Traffic. He was working at Oakleigh farm."

Judy and Tom left Barry Turner's house shell-shocked; neither of them spoke on the journey back to the station, which was where Judy was going, despite Tom's urging her to go to see Matt Burbidge. She suggested that Tom have lunch first, and spent her lunch hour setting up the incident room. Whatever Case thought, though, she was no window dresser.

"When *are* we going to see Matt Burbidge?" Tom asked, as she came back through the CID room, where Alan Marshall was engaged on his mammoth task of ringing round Stansfield's many taxi firms, trying to find out which taxis had had trips into Malworth yesterday.

"My office," Judy said to Tom, who followed her in, and closed the door. "I don't want this to become public knowledge," she said. "Not if it doesn't have to."

"No. Right. But he *was* working undercover at Oakleigh farm," Tom said. "And it was the school holidays. He must have known Lucy Rogerson—seen her around, at least. He never told anyone that, Judy. Why not?"

"It's all circumstantial," said Judy. "And irrelevant. Matt didn't rape these girls, Tom! Drummond did."

"We have to talk to him. He would know all about forensic procedure, he was out of the car when Bobbie was raped and in Parkside when Marilyn was—and that's a very long way from where he lives or where he works. He knew that farm, and Lucy. It was his idea to say Drummond was boasting about raping these women, he kept quiet about Rosa— Guv, you can't ignore all that!"

"You told me yesterday that someone watched Drummond raping Ginny," said Judy. "Are you saying we've got two rapists with exactly the same MO?"

"Well, I said I was *told* Drummond had raped Ginny. There's a difference. There's a big difference when you're talking about that lot in Malworth, obviously. I mean, they wouldn't tell me, would they? Not if they really did set him up, pay Ginny to approach him—"

"Pay her to approach a rapist? Ginny might not be bright, but she isn't stupid!"

"She didn't know he was a rapist, or that anyone even thought he was. She knew him as a punter. All she'd need to know was that they wanted him fitted up and they'd pay her to do it—she was living off scraps, guv, and she'd been banged up all evening! If they offered her enough money, she'd have bitten their hands off."

"It was Drummond who was waiting for me," she reminded Tom. "Not Matt Burbidge."

"But we don't know why, do we? He never got the chance to do anything. We don't know he was going to rape you. He might have just wanted to put the wind up you, like he said. Maybe that was all he ever did."

No. No, she wouldn't believe that, not for one moment. And for one good reason. Colin Drummond had given her a statement about a rape which had contained information known only to the victim, herself, and the rapist. "Tom—how could it have been Matt?" She said. "He was in uniform when Bobbie was raped! Who rapes anyone when he's wearing a police uniform?"

"He would be wearing a sweater," said Tom. "Take off the epaulettes, pull on a mask—what have you got? Someone wearing dark clothing. Blue, black—who's going to know the difference on a foggy night? Not someone being raped over and over again! And what was he wearing last night? As near as damn it the same gear! And the mask and knife were found on that road—if Drummond could have ditched them, so could Burbidge." Tom leant on the desk. "Judy," he said urgently, "we have *got* to talk to him."

ò

Rob had found himself awake by lunchtime; he had tried to get back to sleep, but it hadn't worked. He came down as Carole was getting ready to go to work.

"Rob," she said, almost as soon as he had hit the bottom step, before he had even sat down. "I want us to stop pretending."

"What?" Rob picked up the paper, sat down. Why now, out of the blue, like this? She had her coat on, for God's sake. You didn't expect people to have meaningful discussions on their way out of the door.

"Oh, for God's sake, Rob! I know about you and Ginny Fredericks. It's been going on for months, and I won't pretend anymore!"

"I—I just . . ." he began, then abandoned apologies or excuses. "All right," he said. "So you know."

"Drummond raped her, too," said Carole. "Doesn't that matter?"

Maybe. He wasn't sure that Drummond had raped Ginny. *He* raped her, technically, every time he had her. She had never agreed to the arrangement; Lennie had, and Ginny's protests had been silenced by the back of his hand, as ever. And she still thought the sun shone out of his backside. But even if Drummond had raped her, it had never been a problem.

Rob had waited for Carole to recover from her ordeal, only to find that he was impotent. For over a year, he had thought that Drummond had made him impotent. Until the night that Ginny had got into his cab and he had seen her in the mirror as she crossed her legs in her little short leather skirt, and he had discovered that he wasn't. He had pulled into a lay-by and had taken her in the back of the cab to prove it. He had had her again when he had got her home.

He'd had no money for the second time; Lennie had been less than pleased. That was when he had done the deal about the cab, which suited everyone but Ginny. Rob didn't give a toss about that, or about whether she had been raped. All he wanted with her was to keep proving to himself that Drummond hadn't damaged him beyond repair.

"She's a whore," he said. "Everyone rapes whores. That's what they're for. No—it doesn't matter, not with her."

"But it means you're all right with someone else," she said. "So . . . you could have a proper relationship with someone. Surely you would rather have that?"

"I'm married," he said.

"Rob—we can't go on like this. I should leave, let you find someone else. We're finished . . . our marriage is over. You must see that."

"So we should split up? Let that bastard win?"

"I doubt if he even knows who we are!" she said.

"He knows, all right. And he's never going to know the damage he did me. Never. I am not leaving you, and you are not leaving me."

"Rob—I think I must."

He got up, walked out past her, and turned at the bottom of the stair. "I'd kill you first," he said. "I swear to God, Carole. I'd kill you first."

Chapter Six

Carole sat down on the arm of the sofa as Rob went upstairs to the bedroom, slamming the door.

Drummond. That was why she was trapped in this sham marriage. It was because of Drummond that it had become a sham, and it was because of Drummond that she wasn't allowed to leave it. She had thought that it was because Rob wanted it to work again, because he still loved her, and that had made her feel guilty, because she no longer loved him. But it wasn't that at all. She had thought that his inability to make love to her was because she had been raped; it wasn't. It was because *Rob* had been raped, and he had never got over it.

And their marriage had disintegrated. So would she, if she couldn't break free from it. She got up and went to the job that she had no business doing, when she was capable of so much more.

Drummond wasn't going to rule her life any longer.

ġ

Freddie catalogued the injuries, depressingly familiar. "... and there has clearly been very violent penetration, but swabs are negative," he said. "In addition, there are marks on her wrists and ankles which indicate that some sort of adhesive tape was used to restrain her. Death was caused by asphyxia resulting from the restriction of the air passages and pressure on the chest and abdomen, preventing breathing."

"Could death have been accidental?"

"No," said Freddie, with unusual emphasis. "It was murder, Lloyd. And a particularly cold-blooded murder at that. There's pressure bruising on either side of her nose, and along her right cheekbone and chin, which corresponds to a hand being held over her mouth with considerable downward pressure, and for some considerable time, at the same time as the nasal passages were being obstructed. The three marks here were made by the third, fourth, and fifth fingers of a right hand, and the ones on the nose presumably by the forefinger and thumb."

"Is there the remotest chance of fingerprints?"

"No. The chances of lifting prints from skin are remote enough at the best of times, but I imagine the assailant was wearing one of these." He held up his own hand, in its surgical glove. "Or something very like it." He motioned for the body to be taken away. "Death occurred between ten and eleven," he added. "But you already knew that."

"Is there anything on the body to help us?" Lloyd asked.

"No. She was washed with something impregnated with a perfumed cleansing agent—the lab will be able to tell you what sort, but that's all. There's no saliva, no seminal fluids, no hairs, no fibres—not on the body."

Lloyd hadn't expected to hear anything else. He looked down at his shoes, and sighed.

"But."

Lloyd looked up again, and wondered if other people had to put up with dramatic pathologists.

"A pubic hair was found on the bedding which does not belong to the deceased, and which had its root intact. We can get a DNA profile from it."

Lloyd's sigh of relief was checked when he remembered about the boyfriend. He had only left the night before, according to Bobbie. They'd have to check it against his. But there was just a possibility, a faint possibility, that it was Drummond's. "It's probably her boyfriend's," he said. "But if it is Drummond's, what's the position about the DNA? I mean, if that's all the evidence we've got? Are they going to say it could have been ten other men this time, too?"

"Oh, you'd be far better off this time," said Freddie. "The hair itself can narrow down the possible suspects. That *plus* a DNA match—which might well be a more definite one this time—would increase the odds against to astronomical levels that no court would overturn."

Except that it would be her boyfriend's, thought Lloyd morosely. "What about his clothing?" he asked. "What sort of state would it be in?"

"It's quite likely that her blood would get on to his clothing," said Freddie. "Particularly anything round his lower body. Trousers, underpants, whatever."

As Lloyd was leaving, Freddie made a rare off-the-record remark. "Get him this time, Lloyd," he said quietly. "I don't want to see another one like this."

It was Judy that Freddie was fearful for; he wasn't the only one.

Lloyd drove back to the station where he had a message to telephone the forensic lab. There were, surprise, surprise, no transferred fibres on the girl's clothing. There hadn't been with any of the others, either. And, said the lab, the clothes he had given them bore no signs of sexual activity. And there were no transferred fibres from *her* clothing, which they would have expected to find if these clothes had been worn during any sort of prolonged close encounter. But they hadn't been, of course; that was why he'd offered them up for examination.

Lloyd had asked Essex to trace Marilyn's boyfriend; now he would have to ask them to get the sample of hair that he needed for comparison with the one Freddie had found. They might be lucky. Surely they were entitled to some luck?

He had barely formed the thought when he was told that someone had come in wanting to speak to whoever was dealing with the rape. He was in the interview room, a carrier bag on the floor beside him. He lived in one of the houses by the boating lake, where Stansfield had its official bonfire; he had been coming home from an evening out when he had noticed someone there, and had thought that it might be vandals going to set it alight before the due day. He had shouted, and the person had run away. Too far away for a description, but wearing dark trousers and a jacket. He had gone down to check that he hadn't actually started it burning, and had found a carrier bag pushed under the wood.

He placed the bag he had been carrying on the table. "It's got clothes in it," he said. "At the time, I just thought it was a shame to burn good clothes—you'd only need to give them a spin in the washing machine and Oxfam or someone could use them."

But then he'd heard about the rape, and had wondered about the clothes, so that was why he was here. Lloyd looked into the bag, and saw black jeans, black sweater, black gloves. The little sod had taken a change of clothing with him. And had intended for them to be burned up in a bonfire. He couldn't dump them in Malworth's great bonfire, because of the vigilantes, so he had taken them into Stansfield, and its more run-of-the-mill edifice. That was why he had been in such a hurry that he had almost run someone over.

Lloyd looked at his informant, and nodded. "This is most useful," he said. "I don't suppose you noticed if he had transport of any kind?"

"Got away in a bloody taxi, of all things," he said.

ò

Matt Burbidge had been brought to consciousness by an incessant ringing and knocking that only police officers had the nerve to keep up. He pulled on trousers and a shirt, and went downstairs.

Judy Hill stood on his doorstep with Tom Finch.

"Well, if it isn't the bitch copper from hell," he said.

"Can we come in, Matt?" she asked.

Matt stood aside, and his visitors walked into his tiny hallway. He

motioned them through the door to the sitting room, and followed
them in, running a hand over his unshaven face. He would have preferred it if he could have been washed and dressed before having to
face Judy Hill. As it was, three o'clock in the afternoon was like three
in the morning to him.

"Can you give me the name and address of the friends you were
visiting last night?" Tom asked.

"Not friends, exactly," Matt said, unsurprised that his vague answer hadn't been good enough. "And I expect you know the address.
I was with Ginny Fredericks from ten o'clock to about twenty-five
past, for the usual reason that men are with Ginny Fredericks. You
know where I was after that."

"I didn't think you approved of that," said Tom.

"My wife's left me. I work nights. I earn next to nothing. I can't
even afford to run my car except for journeys I can't do on foot. It
doesn't exactly do much for your sex life."

"You didn't do the journey from Stansfield to Malworth on foot,"
Tom said. "But you were running into the underpass. Where was
your car?"

"I parked on the other side of the bypass," said Matt. "You can
wait fifteen minutes to make the turn off for Parkside. It's quicker
just to leave the car inside the park gates and use the underpass. And
I didn't want my car parked outside that house."

"No," said Tom. "Did you ever go with Rosa?"

This time Matt was surprised; he hadn't expected them to home
in on that so soon. "No," he said.

"But you knew her."

Chickens were coming home to roost already, but perhaps they
didn't know too much yet. "Yes, I knew her," said Matt. "Lennie
Fredericks ran her before he took up with Ginny."

"Why didn't you tell anyone that when the rape team were
looking for her pimp?" asked Tom.

"Why should I? I was suspended from duty." He smiled. "So who
have you been talking to?" he asked.

"Baz Turner."

"Why?"

"The rape enquiry has been reopened," Judy Hill said. "And whether she admits it or not, Bobbie Chalmers was raped the night you and Baz stopped Drummond. We wanted to talk to him about that. The other things just came up in the conversation."

Matt pushed his hair back from his face and went into the kitchen, picking up the kettle, shaking it, switching it on. "Other things?" he said.

"I'm interested in what Drummond really said," she said.

"And the problem is," said Tom, "Baz says he didn't mention the rapes at all."

Matt sighed, got a mug from the cupboard, and spooned in coffee and sugar. "Baz reckons I lost him his job," he said, and turned to look at Judy Hill. "But it's you he's got to thank for that," he said.

"Are you saying Baz is lying?" asked Tom.

"No. Baz just didn't hear him, that's all." The kettle boiled; he poured water on the coffee, and carried it back through to the sitting room, passing between his visitors. "He said he heard him to back me up. But he was too far away. He didn't hear him. And now he's telling it like it is, because he blames me for what happened."

"Baz also said that you went AWOL that night," Tom said.

They were both still standing; he hadn't invited them to sit down, and he wasn't going to. Baz had been busy putting the boot in, obviously. Because Matt had finally got a job, and he hadn't.

"I was on duty over at the football ground," he said, jerking a thumb towards the window. "I could see Isabelle loading up the car, getting ready to leave me. Yes, I went AWOL. I was trying to stop her going away and taking the kids with her. But I failed."

"Where's your wife now?" asked Tom.

"Somewhere in France," he said. "That's where she comes from."

Finch looked surprised. People always did, as though France wasn't less than thirty miles away.

"She came here to teach French," he explained. "Took up with some guy who left her with two kids. But I married her—and I brought those kids up like they were my own. Just never got round to—you know—adoption. But now she's back home in La Belle France. Avec les kids. If you find her, let me know."

"You don't know where she is?" said Tom.

"No. I knew that's what she was going to do, and I couldn't stop her. I got back to the car, we chased Drummond, and when he started mouthing off about the rapes, that was the last straw."

"What did Drummond say?"

"I couldn't catch the rapist if he was standing right in front of me, maybe my wife needed a seeing-to from him—all the stuff I told the court. Nothing we could get him on. Just hints."

"He didn't have time to say much while Baz was walking back to the car," said Tom. "And that's the only time he could have been out of earshot."

"I maybe embellished it a bit. I was trying to stay out of jail." He looked up at Judy Hill. "Without success."

"Why did you hit him?" she asked.

"Christ, woman, I've just told you why!"

"No," she said. "You've told me why you should have brought him in for questioning. There's more to it than that. Why did you hit him?"

"Was it because you knew Lucy Rogerson?" asked Tom.

The pincer movement threw him. He masked his discomfort by blowing steam from his coffee, and looked at Tom. "I'd met her," he said. "I'd worked undercover on her dad's farm. I worked on a farm for years before I joined the police. Expensive kit was going missing, and they put me in because I knew one end of a tractor from the other. I worked there for a month. Lucy was seventeen—full of life, happy—she was a nice kid. And then I read her statement about what some vicious bastard had done to her. And when Drummond started going on about the rapes, I thought we were never going to get him for them. He didn't even have to give a blood sample if he didn't want to— What was the point of bringing him in for questioning? I just saw red—all right?"

"Why didn't you tell the court you had known one of the victims?" she asked.

"Because the last thing I wanted was that kid thinking she was the cause of my going to prison, on top of everything else," he said. "She didn't know me. I was just one of the temporary farmhands. She didn't know my name, didn't know I was a copper. So there was no reason for her to know it had anything to do with her. I wanted to keep it that way."

She didn't believe him; you could see it in her eyes.

"You don't have the monopoly on compassion for rape victims!" he shouted.

She raised her eyebrows a fraction. "It might have kept you out of prison," she said. "That's what I call compassion above and beyond the call of duty."

"Well, you should know. You're very hot on duty."

"Baz told us something else," said Tom. "He says a roll of adhesive bandage went missing from the first-aid kit that night and was replaced next morning. Do you know anything about that?"

"Yes," said Matt. "I know about that. I cut myself on the little sod's belt buckle when I punched him in the stomach. I used some of the bandage and forgot to put it back until the next day. What of it?"

"Would you be prepared to give us a saliva sample for DNA testing?"

Matt stared at him, then turned his hostile gaze on Judy.

ę

Judy was sick with disappointment. Matt had cut himself on Drummond's buckle. The blood on Drummond's jeans was Matt's. It was only Matt's. Her one hope, her one piece of tangible evidence, had vanished.

"You bitch," Matt was saying, getting to his feet. "You *bitch.*"

"Calm down, Matt," said Tom, his hands held up in front of him.

"Calm down? Calm *down*? Do you think I don't know what all this is about? She's not content with grassing me up—now the slag's accusing me of rape!"

"I'm not accusing you of rape," Judy said, unmoved by the description of herself. "These things were brought to our attention, and had to be investigated. You've given us an explanation—that's fine."

Matt shook his head. "Oh, you're so cool, aren't you, Detective Inspector? So cool and calm and collected that it hurts." He looked at her with sheer loathing, and walked towards her. "What have I ever done to you?" he said, pushing her, making her stumble backwards.

Tom was there instantly. "No," said Judy, holding up a hand. "It's all right."

"Well?" Matt repeated, his heavy face close to hers, pushing her again. This time she stood her ground, prepared for it. "What have I ever done to you, that you come here accusing me of rape?"

"I'm not accusing you of anything," she said, a little surprised that her voice wasn't shaking like her legs were. "Bobbie Chalmers can still bring charges against Drummond, and you saw him ten minutes after he had raped her. I believe you hit him because he said something that made you *know* he'd just raped someone. Not hints and jibes. Something much more. Something you couldn't admit to, not after you'd lost your temper and beaten him up."

"Sorry," said Matt. "You'll have to solve your own cases, Detective Inspector. I can't help you." His face was still thrust into hers. "Still, you don't need to solve cases, do you? You can make Superintendent the same way you made Inspector—on your back."

"That's enough," said Tom.

"It's nowhere near enough. She knows what I'm talking about."

"I just need something I can give my boss to persuade him that it's worth pursuing," Judy said.

Matt gave a forced laugh. "Your boss?" he said. "Just keep shagging him, sweetheart, and you'll persuade him. He'll swallow anything you say, like he did the last time."

"I don't mean Lloyd," Judy said steadily. "I've got to convince DCI Case now. Do you know him?"

Matt nodded, his eyes still six inches from hers. "The Hard Case, they call him. You'll have your work cut out with him, darling—he hates women."

"He's all for letting sleeping dogs lie," Judy said. "So if Drummond said anything at all about Bobbie, I need to know what. He's murdered her flatmate, Matt. I *need* to know."

Matt's eyes widened slightly, then dropped from hers, and he sat down.

Judy wished that she could. But dearly gained advantages had to be held. She didn't speak, offered up a silent prayer that Tom wouldn't, either. There was a long silence, but Matt did speak again. It wasn't what she had wanted to hear.

"I really *can't* help you," Matt said heavily. "Drummond didn't say anything about the rapes. Baz told you the truth."

"Would you be prepared to let us take a saliva sample for DNA testing?" asked Tom again.

"No," said Matt.

"Will you come to the station to answer further questions?"

"No. You'll have to arrest me if you want me to do that."

"Right," said Judy. "Let's go, Tom."

Tom frowned, clearly unhappy, but he left with her. He didn't speak until they were back in the car, when he sat at the wheel, making no attempt to drive off. "Judy," he began. "Ma'am," he amended. "We should be taking him in for questioning."

"Why?" said Judy.

"You know why! His wife's whereabouts are conveniently unknown, so we can't check his alibi for the night Bobbie was raped. And why was she leaving him, anyway? He lied about what Drummond said that night—all he did was get up Matt Burbidge's nose, but he tied him in with the rapes. And his alibi for last night is Ginny Fredericks, who helped set Drummond up in the first place! He knew about Rosa, he won't cooperate with the enquiry—you can't walk away from all of that."

"I can."

"Guv." Tom ran a frustrated hand through blond curls. "Inspector," he tried. "Judy. You *can't*."

She looked at him. "The issue's quite simple, Tom," she said. "Either you believe that Drummond gave me a description of raping Bobbie Chalmers that will stay with me for the rest of my life, or you believe that he was innocently bombing around in the fog without lights, and I wrote it all down for him and told him to sign it or I'd have him beaten up. That's his version. If you believe it, by all means, go and arrest Matt."

Tom's shoulders sagged. "Oh, this isn't fair, guv," he said.

"I know."

She knew. But she had done enough to Matt Burbidge, and she certainly wasn't going to arrest him on suspicion of committing rapes she knew damn well Colin Drummond had carried out.

Tom reluctantly started the engine, and she could feel the waves of perfectly understandable resentment as he looked at her. "Can we at least check with Ginny and Lennie about a couple of things?" he asked, through his teeth. "Or are they off-limits, too?"

"No," she said. "We'll talk to Ginny first."

◊

Ginny, too, had to get out of bed to answer the door to the police, but she hadn't been sleeping. She pulled the negligee round her slight body, and ran downstairs as the knocking echoed through the house. She opened the door on the chain.

"What the hell do you want?" she said through the crack to the man with the fair curly hair who stood on her doorstep, and then saw Detective Inspector Hill. She wasn't too bad, for a copper. Not as bad as some. "Oh—it's you," she said, and closed the door over, releasing the chain, opening it again more fully.

"Did you see Matt Burbidge last night?" the man asked.

"What's it to you?"

"Just answer the question."

"Yeah."

"When? How long for?"

She looked at DI Hill. "About ten," she said. "For half an hour."

DI Hill smiled. "Thank you," she said. "Is Lennie here?"

"No," said Ginny. "He drives a cab—I told you."

"Whose cab? We need to speak to him."

Oh, Jesus. She couldn't very well not tell them. They'd find out anyway. But Lennie would skin her if he knew she'd sent them. Still—Inspector Hill was all right. She would keep it to herself. "ABC

Cabs, they're called," she said. "But there's only the one cab really. Don't tell Lennie you got it from me. I've got to go," she said, closing the door, putting the chain back on, and shivering as she ran back upstairs to the by now quite worried man who lay handcuffed to the bed.

δ

Rob was also being visited by the police, which wasn't something he really wanted right now. Detective Constable Marshall was an amiable Scot with a slow delivery who explained that he was checking up on Stansfield cabs which had had runs into Malworth yesterday evening. Would he be right in thinking that Mr. Jarvis had had one?

"Last night? Yes," said Rob. "I was there twice. I took a fare there early in the evening, and was asked to go back to pick her up at ten-thirty."

"Whereabouts in Malworth, sir?"

"Parkside. Lloyd George House."

"And . . . how long were you there?"

"Forever. I arrived, went to the door. Some bloke asked me to wait, so I waited, then I went to the door again, he asked me to wait again, and then he came out, gave me a fiver for my trouble, and said the lady wouldn't be leaving after all. I was there about twenty minutes."

He gave Marshall the flat number.

"And did you see anything while you were waiting? Anyone else around? Any other traffic?"

"No." Rob shook his head.

"About ten minutes after that, a taxi was seen in the vicinity of Stansfield boating lake," said Marshall. "Would that have been you, by any chance?"

"Might have been," said Rob. "I come in from Malworth on that road, and turn left for the rank."

"Did you see anyone in the vicinity of the bonfire?"

"No, sorry. But I wasn't looking at it."

"No. Well—thank you for your time, Mr. Jarvis."

"That's all right," said Rob, seeing him out, closing the door.

Most of what he'd told him wasn't true, but Marshall wasn't to know that.

ò

"Can you pick up at the rear entrance to . . ."

Lennie listened to his instructions, and acknowledged that he was on his way. Jarvis was in some sort of cooperative where individual cabdrivers clubbed together to pay for a radio control. Whatever number people dialled, they came through to it, and the appropriate cab was sent. But if it couldn't go, one of the others did, so you hardly ever had to tell a customer you were booked up. It was a pretty good system, really, because you got bookings as well as being hailed, and they were sometimes long-haul, on which Lennie could make a lot of money.

He pulled up and saw a couple walking towards him. They were in the back before he recognized them; they had looked like real people, at a distance. "Bloody hell," he said.

"And a very good afternoon to you, too," said Finch. "We want to ask you a few questions, Lennie."

"Is it going to take long? Only I've got a job to do."

"I know," said Inspector Hill. "I still can't get over it. What do you know about a prostitute called Rosa, Lennie?" She sat down directly behind him, on one of the folding seats.

"Never heard of her."

Finch smiled. "This can take a very few minutes in your cab, or a very long time at the station," he said.

"OK, I've heard of her. She worked up the Ferrari for a while a couple of years back."

"What was her surname?"

"I never knew."

Inspector Hill tapped him on the shoulder, and he twisted further round to look at her.

"Lennie," she said. "We're very short staffed at the station. We've got a murder on our hands, and it could take simply *hours* to get round to interviewing you. We know you pimped for her, we know you denied all knowledge of her before, and we don't care. Just tell us all about her now, there's a good boy."

"I don't *know* all about her! I saw her one night, walking up and down by the park railings, and she had no idea. I mean, she just didn't know how to go about it. So, I had a word. Took her to the Ferrari, showed her off a bit, told her the do's and don'ts—I looked after her."

"You're an example to us all, Lennie," said Finch. "*What was her surname?*"

"I don't *know*. She told me to call her Rosa, and I don't suppose that was her real name. And that was all I ever knew about her. I don't know where she lived, I don't know zip. She'd see me at the Ferrari, and I'd keep an eye on her when she was with the johns. She was only on the game a few weeks—she wasn't a pro."

"Did she give up because of the rapes?"

"Maybe. Or maybe because of me. One night she tells me she's done a punter without a condom because she'd run out. Well—I had to give her a talking-to, didn't I?"

"Your usual conversational style?" asked Inspector Hill.

He twisted round again to look at her. "I smacked her, yes. And told her to get a pack of three from the toilets in the Ferrari. She tried to sponge some off Ginny—said I was making a fuss about nothing, because he couldn't make her pregnant anyway. They think if they're on the pill, they're laughing. Christ, they'd all be HIV positive in five minutes if you let them."

Finch shook his head, smiling. "The world would be a poorer place without you, Lennie," he said.

"Anyway, she was mad at me because I'd clouted her, and that was the last time I saw her."

"All right," said Inspector Hill, opening the door. "You can get on with your work now, Lennie."

"Hang on," Lennie said. Very few people knew about him and Rosa. Ginny. Rosa herself. And Matt Burbidge. He'd grassed him up, the sod. Well, two could play at that game. "Matt Burbidge," he said. "He used to be one of your lot. The one who gave Drummond a kicking?"

"What about him?"

"He came to see Ginny last night," he said. "And told her to stick to her story. He seemed to think that she'd set Drummond up for the cops, and he didn't want her telling anyone any different." He looked at Inspector Hill. "And it was worth fifteen quid to him to tell her that in private," he said.

It was the first time in his life Lennie had volunteered information to the police. Serve the bastard right for shopping him. He drove to Rob's, picked him up and drove home, told Ginny she would be working the park again.

She knew better than to argue with him, but she complained. Just as loud, just as long. There was more custom tonight; he was working her even harder than he had last night. And she complained even harder. All bloody night.

Chapter Seven

Friday 5 November

Matt finished work at nine o'clock in the morning, and drove home to his empty house and his empty life. He had spent all night thinking about his visit from the police, wondering how much they knew, how much was guesswork. She was the last person he had expected to be on the reopened enquiry. He had assumed that she would be under investigation like all the others.

He had had no time to prepare, no ready answers, hadn't even realized that that was why they were there until it was too late. The truth had had to do once or twice when Finch had fired the bullets that woman had made for him.

He read for a while; the morning paper, full of Drummond still because of the rape and murder. He tried to sleep, but the sunshine was distracting, and anyway every time he even looked like drifting off, someone would let off a firework. And his head was swimming with questions and answers and memories and regrets, and he just kept waking up again.

Finally, he got up and made himself some lunch. He wished Isabelle was here, and the kids. He remembered her horrified face when she found out; he had tried to explain, but it had been no use.

He was supposed to be sleeping. He had a long night ahead, and an even longer day tomorrow.

◊

Rob waited until he heard the front door shut before he got up, not wanting to find himself having yet another discussion with Carole.

He hadn't really slept; he was always a bit hyper if he had anything planned. In the army, they had laughed at him because he got so worked up before they went out on border patrol, or even manoeuvres. At first, they had thought he was scared, but they had found out that it wasn't that. It was anticipation, like a child on Christmas Eve. The mere fact that something was planned for a particular time made him want that time to come round.

He had thought that his visit to Ginny might relax him, but it hadn't. And now he could feel the familiar restlessness; he wanted the day to hurry up and leave the sky to the darkness that he had grown accustomed to. He liked the night; he liked the solitude.

He made himself coffee, which would just make him more hyper, he knew, put on a CD, and plugged in the headphones. He would listen to loud music. That usually helped.

◊

Lloyd read the reports of the morning's endeavours. The house-to-house had turned up nothing more, but they hadn't really expected it to; they had already got a great deal more from the residents than they usually did. But, as he moved through the reports, he discovered that none of it had been of much use. The taxi driver had turned out to be the husband of Mrs. Jarvis, the first of the previous rape victims, which had caused a bit of a stir. They had checked out the unlikely possibility of his having raped his own wife and everyone else, but it had proved to be an *impossibility*, much to everyone's relief. He had been guarding some fortified police station in Northern Ireland when the first three rapes had been committed, sleeping, eating, and patrolling with a dozen other people twenty-four hours a day. And Marshall said that his story about his fare had checked out—his intended passenger had indeed been persuaded to stay the night by her host.

Unlike Judy, Lloyd thought. And last night, she had taken the department out for a birthday drink; he had left early, the company of drunken police officers having never appealed. He had thought she might come up to the flat afterwards, but she hadn't.

And it could, of course, have been any of Stansfield's many taxis which had been seen near the boating lake; it seemed possible to Marshall that Lloyd's informant had merely seen the taxi leaving, and had thought mistakenly that the person leaving the clothes had got into it. Lloyd wasn't so sure about that. He might have a word himself with Mr. Jarvis.

Judy had been to see Matt Burbidge, who had furnished them with details of where he had been between ten and eleven o'clock, which had been checked. He had been with Ginny Fredericks, and though Lennie Fredericks had indicated that this was not for the usual purposes, but rather to tell her to "stick to her story," Judy was satisfied that he *was* there, and she was taking no further action. She had made a note to the effect that Burbidge had known of the prostitute Rosa's existence, and had not made this known, due to resentment over his suspension and dismissal. This knowledge would not have helped trace her.

They were going through the motions, of course. No one seriously thought that Jarvis or Burbidge or anyone else had raped and murdered Marilyn Taylor. Drummond had, and Lloyd just had to keep his fingers firmly crossed about that one tiny piece of evidence that they might, just might, have found. The clothes that he had hoped to burn had indeed been worn during the assault on Marilyn Taylor, but forensics couldn't tie them into Drummond; Lloyd was trying to trace their origins, but he had grave doubts about that yielding anything worthwhile.

The summons to Detective Chief Superintendent Case was one

he could have done without; he went upstairs slowly, wishing for the first time ever that his senior officer was a thirty-year-old whiz kid with a degree in corporate strategy.

"Come!"

Lloyd went in; Case was writing something in one of the files he always seemed to have on his desk, and didn't look up. Lloyd sat down, without being invited to. He just let Case make something of it.

He looked up. "A bit of a bombshell from HQ," he said.

"Oh?"

"It's about DI Hill," said Case. "She can't be involved in either the murder or the reopened rape inquiry, at least for the moment."

He didn't look too cut up about it. Lloyd frowned. "Why?"

"It seems that Drummond's made an official complaint about her conduct following his arrest."

"But Judy wasn't *at* Malworth when Drummond was arrested," said Lloyd.

"She took a statement from him some hours afterwards, though, didn't she? That's what his complaint concerns. I don't know all the details, but I gather that she'll be getting a visit from the complaints investigation team. They don't seem too worried about it at HQ. They expect her to come out of it smelling of roses, apparently."

Lloyd didn't like the implication of that phrase, but he let that pass.

"In the meantime, as the subject of an official complaint, Inspector Hill can't deal with anything touching on that same inquiry. I suggest that she replaces DS Sandwell on the burglaries, and frees him up for the murder team." Case picked up another of his inevitable files.

"Right." Lloyd sighed, getting up.

"You should have told me that DI Hill was ex-Malworth."

Lloyd shrugged a little. "She was there for a few months," he said. "Why should I have told you?"

"Because then I would have been forewarned. I wouldn't have had her on the reopened enquiry in the first place, nor the murder.

We've got to be whiter than white, if we're going to get Drummond this time. Not give him the opportunity to cry foul again."

Forewarned. Cry foul. The man was a moron. "Judy Hill is as straight as a die," Lloyd said. "You have no cause for concern."

"Oh, dear," said Case. "Have you got a soft spot for her?"

"I know her," said Lloyd. "You don't."

"No, I don't," said Case. "Which means that *I'm* not wearing blinkers. Practically every station in the county has got one of Malworth's rotten apples—why should we be the exception?"

It was too ludicrous for Lloyd to get angry with him. It was really quite funny. "I can assure you that Judy Hill is not one of Malworth's rotten apples," he said, with a smile.

"Don't be too sure, Lloyd. The jungle drums are beating. There's a lot of rumour—a lot of speculation. One or two of the Malworth Mafia are choosing to cooperate with the enquiry, and her name's come up more than once, I gather."

Lloyd gave up. "If that's all, sir," he said.

"Oh—you do know the word, then?" Case opened the file. "Yes," he said. "That's all."

Judy was back in her office; Lloyd relayed in its entirety what Case had said. She didn't seem as startled as he had been. It was almost as though she had expected something like that.

"You don't seem surprised," he said.

"Drummond said there were better ways of screwing me," she said. "I presume this is it."

"Yes—but how can he? You did do everything by the book, didn't you?" Judy was meticulous about procedure, except when she chose *not* to follow it to the letter, of course. "Did you call him names or something?"

The only other time Judy had been the subject of a complaint— that time informal—it had been because she had told someone who made an unwelcome pass what, in mainly Anglo-Saxon, she thought of his suggestion as to how she should spend her evening.

She sat back and looked at him for a moment, then spoke slowly and carefully. "I went to Malworth police station," she said. "I took a statement, someone typed it up, I took it back to Drummond, who read it, and signed it. I barely spoke to him. It was bad enough having to sit and listen to the little creep."

"Then, as they say in all the best old British B movies, you've nothing to worry about, have you, sir?" said Lloyd. He smiled. "That means you're guilty, of course."

"As charged," said Judy, with a little smile. "Perhaps I should get up to date on the burglaries," she said.

"How do you want me to handle this with Bob and Alan?"

"Tell them."

"Right. We'll tell them now, shall we? They were both there last time I looked. Besides, I'd like to brief Bob on the murder enquiry."

They walked into the CID room, where Bob Sandwell was using a computer with an expertise that Lloyd found baffling, and Alan Marshall was on the phone. When they completed their respective tasks, Lloyd told them the situation, and they laughed.

"Quite," said Lloyd. "So let's ignore that and get on with our work, shall we?"

"I had a thought about the burglaries just now," said Marshall, pointing to the phone that he had just put down. He looked at Judy. "It was when I was checking up on the cabs," he said. "It got me wondering how the burglary victims actually got to where they were leaving from, if you see what I mean. Coach stations, airports, whatever. So I did a bit of ringing round—I've only managed to contact two of them, but they did take cabs. Two different cab companies, but it seems they both belong to a sort of collective, and you can ring one number and get a cab belonging to someone else. So, in theory, they could all have got the same cab."

"And I know which one," said Judy, suddenly brightening up. "ABC Cabs."

"Could you not have swapped her and the sergeant before, sir?"

Lloyd laughed. "Go on, then," he said to Judy. "Amaze us."

"Lennie Fredericks has suddenly got rich," she said. "The house is bristling with things I don't see how he can afford. And guess what he's doing these days?" She smiled. "Driving for some outfit called ABC Cabs." She picked up a pen. "Right, DC Marshall, off you go and get a search warrant for this address." She wrote it down on a piece of paper and handed it to him.

"A search warrant, ma'am? Will we get one, just on that?"

"Yes. Go to Peabody. He's always available, and he signs anything. List everything from the three most recent burglaries, and tell him we have reason to believe that some of the items could be on these premises."

Lloyd frowned a little. "Are you sure about this, Judy?" he asked.

"Yes. Lennie's never worked a day in his life—I couldn't imagine why he was driving a taxi. He's also got a record of breaking and entering—and he was pretty neat and tidy, just like the current one."

"I'm not convinced that constitutes reason to believe that there are stolen goods on the premises," said Lloyd. This was exactly the sort of thing he meant. "You don't want to give anyone else reason to complain."

"Lennie would die sooner than complain. And he acquired his taxi-driving job last June," said Judy. "He acquired the house about the same time. It's full of exactly the sort of things that have been stolen. Lennie probably kept the best ones for himself—that's how he got caught last time."

Lloyd nodded. "All right," he said. "It just about scrapes by. Though I doubt if anyone but Peabody would sign it," he added.

Marshall went off in search of Mr. Peabody, and Lloyd and Sandwell went to what was now the murder room, for Lloyd to brief the nightshift. It would seem very strange working without Judy, but Tom Finch was a reasonable substitute, and Sandwell could take over the murder room duties. Sandwell stood aside to let Lloyd go in first, and ducked automatically as he went through the door himself. That was Sandwell's drawback, of course. He made Lloyd feel shorter than ever.

ò

Drummond seemed to be controlling Carole's entire life. She wanted to go somewhere. Tonight. And she was regarding it as practically impossible, because the buses were so slow and infrequent in the evening as to be virtually unusable. But she had a car. It was a ten-, fifteen-minute drive. The bus took in every village, and three-quarters of an hour.

Except that even before she could make herself get into the car, she had to make herself get into the garage, and she didn't think she could do that. Her knees grew weak at the very thought. She could ask Rob to bring the car round to the front, she thought briefly. But no. That would involve explanations—she wouldn't even let him leave it where she might see it, so the request would hardly go unnoticed. And besides, she couldn't involve Rob, not in this. That really wouldn't be right. She had to do this on her own.

If she was going to go through with it, she would just have to go and get the car out when she needed it like she would have done before. Exactly like she had done before.

And she would do it, she thought, actually putting her hands on her knees to stop them shaking. She would.

◊

"It's still short. I said it had to be paid back today."

They were parked outside the opulent house.

Lennie played his last card. "You . . . you wouldn't be interested in payment in kind, would you?"

"What sort of payment in kind?"

Lennie explained what sort. "She'd give you a good time," he said. "We could come to some arrangement."

"No, thanks." He opened the door.

"Come on, mate, give me a break," said Lennie.

He got out. "All right," he said. "You have until eight-thirty tonight. Come straight here. Wait in your cab until I come out. I might be delayed—don't come to the door. And I want the money this time. No excuses—no deals. The money, or I make an example of you—I don't mind much which."

Lennie couldn't believe he had wriggled off the hook. "Right," he said, before his passenger changed his mind. "But I won't be in the cab. It'll be a Transit."

"Whatever." He got out. "Be here," he said. "I don't give second chances."

Lennie drove back into Stansfield, without the faintest idea of how he was to get hold of the rest of the money.

"*ABC Cabs?*" crackled the radio.

Lennie picked up the mike, grateful for anything. He had to pick up someone with an unpronounceable name at an address in Stansfield he knew to be a gambling club of which the law was unaware, which had some hefty wins and losses. It was usually the winners who took taxis home, he thought philosophically. Maybe home was a long way away. You could do good deals on long trips.

Home was indeed a long way away, obviously, but his destination was predictably and disappointingly the conference hotel, a two-quid run away. His passenger, a small, olive-skinned man with a mustache, spoke little English; Lennie wondered if they had simultaneous translations, or did he just sit there and wonder what they were all conferring about?

He pulled up on the concourse, and made to switch off the meter, at which his passenger was peering. "All right?" he asked, his hand hovering.

"Is twenty—yes?" he said, and handed Lennie a twenty-pound note, which he peeled off a role of twenties, then fished in his pocket for a fiver, and gave him that, too. "For you—yes?" he said. "Tip, right?"

Lennie stared at the money, at the misread meter, and at the man. "Oh, yes," he said. "Tip. Thanks." He switched off the meter, and went into his routine for visiting businessmen, in an effort to find out if he was a likely punter. "Is there some sort of do tonight?" he asked. "Last night and all that?"

The man frowned in concentration, and shook his head. "Say again, please?"

"Have you got a conference function tonight?" They nearly always spoke jargon.

"Ah. No. Finished. I go home tomorrow."

Lennie felt his mouth go dry. He had in the back of his cab a man with money to burn, nothing to do, and the belief that a four-minute taxi ride cost twenty quid. That's what happened when all you did was sign your name and room number on bar bills. You didn't use the currency, get to know it. He wondered what the jargon for at a loose end was. "Are you going to be spending some of that?" he asked, speaking clearly and slowly and loudly.

"This?" The man shrugged. "Only in bar," he said. "There is no . . ." He shrugged again. "Disco, or . . . fun," he said eventually.

"You looking for fun?"

"Fun? Yes."

"Do you like girls?" Lennie asked.

The man laughed. "I like," he said. "But no girls. All businessmen."

Lennie could hardly speak now, but he managed. "I could get you a girl," he said.

The man shook his head, and a little bit of Lennie died.

"Is not . . ." He shook his head again. "I have colleague. Here. Knows my . . . er . . . wife, yes?"

Lennie smiled broadly. "I can take you to a girl," he said. "Now. Your colleague would never know."

"Yes?"

"Yes."

"How much?"

At last, the jargon that he also spoke. All he had to do was multiply by ten. Could it work? Could it honestly work? His lips could hardly form the words, but he had given him twenty pounds for the taxi, so . . . "Three hundred," he said.

"Yes?" he pulled out another roll, this time of fifties. "Is young girl?"

"Yes, young." Lennie watched him count out six fifties, and fold them in two. He didn't know if he dared, but it was worth a try, surely. "You like them young?" he asked.

"Young."

"How young?"

"Not child," he said.

"Fourteen too young?"

"No. Fourteen. That's OK."

"It'll cost you more. She's under age."

"How much?"

"Another hundred." Lennie watched as he extracted two more fifties, and folded them with the six. "All right?" he said.

"I see girl first," he said, holding back the money.

"Yeah, mate. Sure." Lennie turned the cab. "Pinch me, some-one," he said, as he roared off into the early evening traffic. "I'm dreaming."

"Say again, please?"

"Get you there in no time," said Lennie. Four hundred quid. Four hundred—over twice as much as he needed. He had died and gone to heaven. He had won the pools. Oh, he wished his passenger wasn't going home tomorrow. This was better than the lottery.

He pulled up in the alley outside the lit, curtained house, hitting the horn twice in positive triumph. The cavalry was here. He didn't release the back doors for a moment, to give Ginny time to go up.

"Right," he said, getting out, opening the back door. "Come with me. I'll take you up, you can see Ginny—that's her name. Then you give me the money, and she's yours for half an hour, and I'll take you back to your hotel."

"Yes."

Lennie's heart was pounding as he put the key in the lock, and opened the door. His face fell when he saw Ginny still downstairs, still wearing the old sweater of his which swamped her, and a pair of jogging pants. And then, coming out of the sitting room, the cop. Plain clothes, but Lennie could smell them. He froze in the doorway.

"Lennie Fredericks, is it?" said the cop, coming towards him, showing him his ID card. "DC Marshall, Stansfield CID. We have a search warrant—your wife has seen it."

"I go," said the punter, heading back out.

Lennie watched, dismayed, as his four hundred pounds disap-peared down the road. He stood, blinking a little, watching it leave. It took him a moment to comprehend his loss. Then he came in, stared at Marshall. "You could have shown her a take-away menu for all she'd know!" he yelled at him. "She can't bloody read!" He turned on Ginny. "What the hell's going on?" he roared, slapping her. "What have you done now, you stupid bitch?" He raised his hand again.

"You can cut that out!" said Marshall.

Lennie turned, and saw DI Hill at the top of the stairs. "What are you doing up there?" he demanded.

"Looking for stolen goods," she said, as she came down.

"Have you found any?"

"No."

"Then get out," he said, striding to the open door.

She and Marshall went out into the alley, and she turned back to him. "I read Ginny the warrant," she said. "And don't blame her. It's got nothing to do with her."

Lennie slammed the door shut, and Ginny started gabbling at him as soon as he turned round.

"I'm sorry, Lennie," she said. "But it's all right, they didn't find it. Rob must have taken it. Maybe he told them—I'm sorry. It must have been stolen— Do you think that's why she gave me it? They must have thought there were more."

Lennie stared at her. He didn't have the energy to unravel what she was saying. He didn't care what she was saying. He didn't give a stuff anymore. He didn't know anyone who could lend him two hundred quid, and he didn't know anyone who could buy anything for two hundred quid. He sank down on the sofa. There was sod all he could do about it, and he was no worse off than he'd been before he picked the dream punter up. He wouldn't be meeting his newfound friend at eight-thirty; he would just have to watch his back. But they'd get him. Sooner rather than later, they'd get him. One night, he'd leave the snooker club and walk into a couple of heavies.

"Put the kettle on, doll," he said.

ℓ

"Well, now you know why he's driving a taxi," said Marshall, as he drove back to Stansfield.

Judy smiled at his tone of voice, despite the day she was having. "Do I gather you disapprove of Lennie?" she asked.

"Don't you, ma'am?"

She thought about that. "No," she said. "I don't think I do."

"I never thought I'd hear you stick up for someone like him."

She frowned. "Why not?"

"He knocks her about, for one thing," said Marshall. "You saw him."

"Oh, that. Ginny's used to that—I doubt if she even noticed."

"We should do him for living off immoral earnings."

"Mm. The problem is that he's living *beyond* his immoral earnings," said Judy. "And I want to know how."

"How can you joke about it? He's a parasite. He hires his wife out. He brings men home to her."

"I know. But he's probably the best thing that ever happened to Ginny, all the same," she said.

"Oh, yes?"

"Yes. She was a drifter. She would hang about motorway service stations and go with the truck drivers for a meal and a lift to the next one. Somehow, she fetched up in Malworth. She was virtually vagrant—some people in a squat took her in when the weather turned cold, like a stray cat. She let anyone do what they wanted with her for a bag of chips."

"And being exploited is better?"

"Of course it's better! Lennie got her to charge a reasonable amount—gave her three meals a day and a bed to sleep in. He stopped her having unprotected sex with the customers. He makes her go to the clinic for regular checkups. I know he looks as though he couldn't give a damn, but he does."

"He just doesn't want to catch anything."

"Maybe, but the result's the same. Ginny's clean. And he kept her off drugs. Left to her own devices, she would have been shooting up with used needles and been dead in a ditch by now. He knew she was going that way, so he didn't let her keep any money, and clouted her if she tried to, so she never got the chance to graduate to that."

"Well, that's the charitable point of view," said Alan. "Other people might say he's just greedy."

"Most pimps like their girls to be dependent on drugs," said Judy.

"But he's never taught her to read, has he? That might mean she'd find out she could manage without him. That's as good as drugs, without the drawbacks."

Judy smiled. "True," she said. "But I don't think teaching people to read would be Lennie's forte. This is. Thanks to an arrangement with the allocation manager, and, I imagine, the rent officer, she's got a house to live in, and a room to work in, and she doesn't even have to walk the streets, because Lennie gets her clients for her. She adores him."

Marshall snorted.

"Oh, Lennie's all right," said Judy. "If he's burgling houses, I'll nick him, but we'd never prove immoral earnings. I'm not even convinced it is immoral—he's done a lot more good than harm with Ginny."

"I'm sure he speaks very highly of you," said Marshall.

"I've met so many people this last two days who hate the sight of me that I practically regard Lennie as an old and valued friend," said Judy.

Marshall smiled at last. "I suppose he's not so bad," he said. "I didn't know her background. It makes more sense of that business with Drummond. I mean—if she was living the way you say, you can understand her taking money to set him up, can't you?"

Yes. She could.

⟩

Ginny wasn't sure how she had escaped a hiding, but she had, and she was grateful for that, as she made Lennie's tea.

"Four hundred quid," he said, the first words he'd spoken since he'd asked her to put the kettle on.

"What?"

"Four hundred quid," he repeated. "That's what these cops cost me. Four hundred quid."

Ginny frowned. "How do you make that out?" she said.

He looked up at her. "He had it in his hand," he said, making a fist of his own. "He was going to give it to me, Ginny. He just wanted to check that you weren't an old boiler. Four hundred quid." He shook his head. "It's almost funny."

Ginny's eyes grew wide. "What the fuck was I supposed to do for four hundred quid?" she asked.

"Nothing!" He got up to get himself a mug. "He didn't understand English money. I just multiplied by ten."

"What does that make?"

Lennie smiled. He looked tired, Ginny thought. "He thought it was forty quid," he explained.

"But I don't get forty quid, either," Ginny pointed out.

"I told him you were fourteen."

"Aw, Lennie! You can't get away with that for much longer."

"I don't know," said Lennie. He caught hold of her, and ran his hands up inside the sweater, feeling her breasts. "You've still got no tits to speak of," he said.

"It's not just tits! You'll have to stop sooner or later, Lennie." She put her arms round his neck. "They'll guess when I get wrinkles."

He laughed, then looked at her seriously, his hands still holding her sides, his thumbs brushing her nipples. It was a nice feeling. "Don't stop," she said, when his hands fell still, and she felt the gentle brushing start again. She smiled.

"If anything ever happens to me, you'll remember what I've told you, won't you?" he said.

Ginny thought furiously. "What about?" she said, anxious not to annoy him.

"About taking care," he said. "Looking after yourself."

"What's going to happen to you?" she asked.

"I don't know," he said. "If I did, I'd go in for fortune-telling."

"Yeah, but what made you say it?"

"Nothing." He crouched down, pulling the jogging pants down, getting her to step out of them. "That's better," he said, standing up and squeezing her bottom, like she'd known he would. "You've got no bum, either," he said, pulling her close and kissing her again, for a long time.

"You're supposed to be working," said Ginny.

"No," he said. "I'm supposed to be having a ciggy and a read of the paper. *You're* supposed to be working." He drew back, looked her up and down. "Four hundred quid's worth," he said. "It's a shame to waste it."

"Don't you want your tea?"

"Later." And he hooked one arm round her shoulders, the other round her knees, and carried her upstairs.

Chapter Eight

When Judy got back to the station, it was to find the complaints investigation team waiting for her. She was taken to an interview room; the proceedings were taped. A Superintendent and a Chief Inspector from an outside force were conducting the interview; a member of the Police Complaints Authority sat in, observing.

The preliminaries over, the DCI told her Colin Drummond had alleged that she had taken a statement from him in which he had made it clear that he knew nothing about a rape, that he had not been in that particular place at that particular time, and that he could not be of assistance in her enquiries. She had apparently written down what he was saying, but that she had then left the room, and had returned with a typewritten statement describing a rape that he was supposed to have carried out, and indicating that he was a witness to certain things which he had not seen. She had asked him to sign it and had pointed out that he had little to lose by helping her out in this way; charges would not be brought in respect of that assault, and that since he had confessed to four, he might as well throw in a fifth. It had been intimated that if he did not, there could be repercussions.

Judy listened, shaking her head slightly. "I'm not sure what I'm supposed to say in reply," she said. "What else can I say but that he did give me the statement that he signed, that I did not in any way interfere with it, and that he can't possibly produce any evidence to indicate that I did?"

The DCI nodded. "That would have been our reaction," he said. "Your word against his, and all that. But it isn't, because he appears to have given you a statement about a rape that quite simply *never happened*."

"Of course it happened," said Judy. "Everyone knows she was raped, and why she refused to make a complaint. It's all on record," she added. "She was unwilling to go to court. But her flatmate reported the assault, and she was admitted to hospital—"

"Suffering from carbon monoxide poisoning," interrupted the Superintendent. "Hardly the usual result of a sexual assault, Inspector."

"She was raped at the rear of her car, which was pumping exhaust fumes into her face!" said Judy.

"It was the result of a faulty gas boiler, according to her statement to us," he said. "She maintains that she was never raped, and that she at no time indicated to you that she had been."

I wasn't raped. And I never said I was. Judy sighed. She hadn't realized the implication of that last sentence, not when Bobbie had said it. She did now.

"You went to see Miss Chalmers on Wednesday, didn't you? Why?"

"To ask her to let us have a blood sample," said Judy. "There was blood on Drummond's jeans when Stansfield brought him in for questioning—I thought it might be Bobbie's. I now know that it was Matt Burbidge's—the officer who assaulted him that night."

"So there was little point in asking Miss Chalmers for a blood sample, was there?"

"I didn't know that at the time," said Judy. "I believed it to be her blood."

"Miss Chalmers maintains that you went there to ask her to change her story—to say that she *had* been raped. Is that untrue?"

"No," said Judy. "Of course I asked her to admit it. She told me that Drummond had been intimidating her. What he did to Marilyn Taylor was part of that intimidation process, and it has obviously worked. He has a mobile phone—I suggest you look at the calls he's been making. He's been ringing me, too. His last call more or less advised me that something like this was going to happen." She took out her cigarettes, and lit one.

"Oh, we have checked," said the DCI. "Chief Superintendent Case informed us that he had been making nuisance calls to you, and we investigated that. He says he was indeed warning you that he intended taking action."

Judy crushed out her barely smoked cigarette. "Then why didn't he take it before now?" she asked. "Why didn't he take it at the time? I'll tell you why—because until now he had no way of getting to Bobbie Chalmers. He has been ringing her up—hasn't he?"

"He has rung the club where Miss Chalmers works several times. He says he was attempting to get information on a prostitute who used to pick up custom there, and whom he is anxious to trace. Miss Chalmers maintains that was all that passed between them."

"Where does all this leave me?" asked Judy.

The Superintendent smiled. "At the moment, the hospital is unwilling to release information about Miss Chalmers's admission that night," he said. "But clearly, if an attempt is being made to pervert the course of justice, they will have to. So, providing Miss Chalmers *was* raped, you'll be in the clear. You know better than I do where that leaves you."

The interview was terminated, and Judy was left to wonder just how much Drummond had cost, was costing, and would cost Bartonshire police before he'd finished. It was late, but through the glass of his door, Judy could see Lloyd still at his desk. She gave him the gist of her interview.

"So it's all a matter of injunctions and legal moves," said Lloyd.

She nodded. "In the meantime I'm stuck with the burglaries," she said.

Lloyd smiled. "How did you get on spinning Fredericks's drum, as Tom would have it?"

"It was no go." She sighed. "I still think it'll be him, though. But none of the stuff in the house is stolen—Ginny showed me a whole sheaf of receipts. The trouble is, no one finds out about the burglaries until at least two weeks after they've been done—getting the goods before they've disappeared isn't going to be easy."

Lloyd gave her an I-told-you-so look, then smiled. "I thought you could do with cheering up," he said. "So I stayed to invite you to dinner. Assuming you have nothing else on," he added.

"No. I'd love dinner," she said, trying to sound enthusiastic, though in truth she was rather dreading this celebration now. The continuation of the row was hovering, despite appearances.

Out of the corner of her eye, she saw DCS Case appear in the corridor. He knocked, and popped his head round the door. "My office," he said to Lloyd, and glanced at Judy. "When you're finished," he said.

"Yes, sir," said Lloyd. "I'll be right there." He watched Case's figure retreat. "Bloody glass doors," he said. "You go to the flat. I don't know how long this is likely to take. I'll be there as soon as I can."

Judy drove to Lloyd's, trying not to think about the further complication to their already complex relationship. She could have told him why she hadn't been taken by surprise by Drummond's allegations—Hotshot had told her that had been his intention all along. She wondered a little about him inviting himself to lunch with her; had he been spying on her? Or warning her? Either way, it was a little unethical. But she hadn't told Lloyd about having lunch with him at all, and telling him now would just start another row. And thinking about that just made her start wondering *why* she hadn't told him about it, and . . .

It was easier to think instead about what Marshall had said. She did rather seem to be marching the opposite way from everyone else. Case, Harper, Tom Finch, Marshall, Matt Burbidge—even Lloyd, probably, though he hadn't said so—all seemed convinced that Ginny really had set Drummond up. And Tom and Alan had both pointed out that Ginny's stray-cat existence would have made a cash payment irresistible. But Judy still couldn't believe that Ginny had been lying in the witness box.

She couldn't be that wrong about her.

ঽ

Matt Burbidge didn't bother with an evening meal. He had slept badly; the whisky he had drunk instead of eating had made him wake up with a hangover, and he felt nauseous at the thought of food.

It was all her fault, like every other miserable thing that had happened to him since that night. Well—she wasn't to blame for his wife leaving him. But everything else. Losing his job, going to prison. He hadn't been able to find a job when he had come out. Eventually he had got this one, despite his record, or maybe because of it. They liked people who could use their fists, and only crimes of dishonesty were regarded as barring you from service with Wainwright Watch and Ward. He had thought it was three people, when he'd answered the ad. It turned out that "Watch and Ward" was what Wainwright did. The logo was three double-yous interlocking to form a barrier round a fort. So if gun-wielding commando-style raiders came crashing through to the Northstead vaults from the cellars of the liquor store next door, Matt would fight them off single-handed, presumably, in view of his excellent criminal record. They paid just over subsistence level for a forty-two-hour week; the system was four days on, three days off. He'd never met his opposite number—WWW didn't go in for staff parties.

But when he'd found out where Northstead Securities was, he had almost turned it down. Right across the street from her flat, where she could gloat to her heart's content every time she looked at the fascia, with its three brass balls. Discreetly stylized, but there. He was nothing more nor less than a night watchman at a pawnbroker's. It might be one which only dealt with very large sums of money, but it was still a pawnbroker's. And he was still a night watchman.

And it was all her fault.

ọ

"You'll understand if I prefer to take Inspector Hill's word for it without waiting for the hospital to release its records," said Lloyd.

"Yes," said Case. "But it might not be a good idea to be too obviously in her corner. In case those records reveal that Bobbie Chalmers was *not* the victim of a sexual assault."

Lloyd leant forward a little, and spoke quietly. "As I mentioned before, sir, you don't know Inspector Hill. I can assure you that anyone who does would give no credence whatever to the ramblings of a very unstable young man—you told me yourself that the ACC had no doubt that she would be exonerated if Drummond insists on pushing this to the limits."

Case shook his head. "Lloyd," he said. "You're not listening to me. I've also told you that her name is being bandied about by those of the Malworth Mafia who are cooperating with the investigation. They seem to admire what she did."

"I'm listening," said Lloyd. "But all you've told me is rumour and gossip, and I'm telling you to ignore it."

Case inclined his head a little. "But it isn't rumour or gossip that she was transferred out of Malworth the day before that arrest took place," he said. "And that was more than a little convenient, don't you think?"

Lloyd controlled his temper with considerable effort. When he spoke, his voice was low, Welsh, and angry. "Judy Hill was transferred out of Malworth because of the hostility of a group of officers—presumably those you call the Malworth Mafia—who held her responsible for two of their number being suspended and subsequently dismissed," he said. "In what way do you find that suspect?"

"They were 'suspended and subsequently dismissed' for beating up Drummond," said Case. "Who was then arrested in as blatant a piece of stage management as you could imagine."

"What had that to do with Judy? She was here, working on a murder investigation by then!"

"I know. And once Drummond had been arrested, he confessed to four rapes, and then to a fifth that just happened to clear up that murder investigation."

Lloyd realized his mouth was open. "What are you suggesting?" he asked.

"I'm not suggesting anything. But the Mafia is. They're saying the whole thing was invented to net her an arrest."

Lloyd shook his head. "I don't believe I'm having this conversation," he said.

"Believe it."

"I don't know the extent of the corruption at Malworth," Lloyd said. "But it didn't extend to Judy Hill. If she says she took that statement, then she did."

"You've spoken to the alleged victim of this rape once or twice, I believe—has she ever told *you* she was raped?"

"No, but—"

"Has she told you she *wasn't* raped?"

Lloyd opened his mouth, and closed it again.

"I see she has."

"She had reasons of her own for denying it," Lloyd said. "But you don't just have DI Hill's word for it. Bobbie Chalmers managed to get home and take a bath before she passed out. Her flatmate saw the injuries when she found her unconscious on the bathroom floor, and she reported that her friend had been the victim of a sexual assault."

"Reported it to whom? Malworth, naturally. And we can't go and ask her if she really did report an assault, can we? Because she's lying in the bloody morgue!"

Lloyd blinked at him. "What are you saying?"

"I'm saying that I believe Drummond was fitted up. That whoever really raped those women knew that Marilyn Taylor could prove the extent of the corruption at Malworth, and removed her before she could be asked any questions. I'm saying that he has a thorough knowledge of the rape investigation, and that he was in a position to lay the blame at Drummond's door."

"You're saying it's a police officer," said Lloyd. "And that the others are covering up for him?" he said, incredulously.

"They weren't then," said Case. "Good cause corruption, they call it. Bang the bad guys up any way you can. They believed it was Drummond, so they gave the investigation a helping hand. But they're covering up for him now. Because if he goes down, they go down with him."

"And you are suggesting that Judy is involved in this cover-up?" Lloyd said. "I've never heard anything so ridiculous!"

"Is it ridiculous? I've been holding a glass to a couple of walls, and what I am telling you is this—you should distance yourself as fast and as far as you can from DI Hill, because it's not all over yet."

Lloyd gasped. "What?" he said, almost laughing, it was so ludicrous. "Why on earth should I do that?"

Case sighed. "The words shit and fan come to mind," he said.

"What shit?" demanded Lloyd. He spread his hands. "What fan?"

"I don't know yet," said Case. "But I'll recognize it when I see it."

"Perhaps you've been overworking," said Lloyd. He laughed. "If you knew DI Hill, you wouldn't—"

Case threw his pen down on the desk in a gesture of frustration. "I'm trying to do you a favour here!" he shouted.

"May I ask why you should *want* to do me a favour?"

"Good God, man, why do you think? Because shit goes in all directions, including up! I'm asked to conduct a damage-limitation exercise on a claim visited on us by a load of bent coppers, and what do I find? My second in command is humping one of them! She's using you, man! She used you to get her out of Malworth before that arrest went down, she used you to get a quick arrest on the murder, and she's using you now that she's trying to cover her arse! This whole thing is going to blow, sooner or later. Is it worth risking your pension for the sake of an occasional leg-over?"

Lloyd leapt to his feet. He did not obey the order to sit down. And he wasn't laughing anymore.

ꝗ

Ginny woke up, momentarily confused, thinking that she had to get up and get Lennie his breakfast, then realized that she was wearing the sweater, and remembered why she was in bed, with a smile.

It was too hot in here with the duvet and the central heating and Lennie *and* the sweater. She sat up and peeled it off, shivering a little as perspiration dried on her skin. He hadn't let her take it off. She snuggled up to him, skin against skin, and kissed his cheek as he slept. Then she saw the time, and reluctantly nudged him.

"It's ten to eight," she said. "You've got to get the taxi back to Rob."

Lennie opened an eye. "Fuck the taxi," he mumbled.

"Aw, Lennie, he gets mad if you don't take it back on time, and you're going to be late as it is. He might take it off you."

He was asleep again. She leant over him and switched on the bed-side light, shaking his shoulder. "Lennie," she said.

He pulled her down on top of him, kissing her, then held her in his arms, his eyes still closed.

"Do I have to go down the park again tonight?" she asked.

"No," he said.

"The Ferrari?" she said.

"No." He cuddled her. "We'll have a night off," he said.

Ginny burrowed herself in to the crook of his arm. "Can we have a take-away?" she asked.

"Yeah," he said. "A take-away and a couple of videos—how's that sound?"

"Great. But Lennie—"

"I know," he said, opening his eyes at last. "I've got to take the taxi back first." He made to kiss her, then frowned, touching her neck. "What are those marks?" he asked.

Ginny giggled. "You should know," she said.

"They're not love bites! They're bruises."

His fingers touched them; it didn't hurt. The bruises had come out that morning; she'd seen them in the mirror. That was why she'd put on the polo neck, so Lennie wouldn't see them and ask about them; she'd forgotten.

"Someone's had you by the throat," he said.

"Must've been one of the punters at the park," she said.

He shook his head. "I'd have heard all about it if one of them had done it," he said, sitting up, kneeling beside her. "You never stopped complaining. Who was it, Ginny?"

"The one this afternoon," she said.

"You wouldn't be able to see the bruises yet." He pushed her chin up so she had to look at him. "Don't tell lies. It was Jarvis, wasn't it?"

"No," she said, twisting away, looking down at the duvet. It matched the curtains. She loved their bedroom.

"It was Jarvis—why did he do that?" He caught her shoulders, made her look at him again. "Why, Ginny?"

"No reason. He just gets mad sometimes. 'Cos he can't do it with his wife and he doesn't want to do it with me, not really. Don't make a fuss, Lennie—it was last time. He was all right this morning."

"I don't give a stuff when it was," said Lennie, pulling on his clothes. "I'll make a fuss, all right. That bastard isn't going to do that to you and get away with it." He was out of the door, in seconds, rattling down the stairs.

"Lennie—" She scrambled out of bed, running after him, trying to think of some way of stopping him. The front door slammed, and she sat down on the top step. She couldn't have stopped him, anyway.

She went back into the room and pulled on the sweater, then went downstairs, picked up the jogging bottoms, and pulled them on.

Then she sat at the kitchen table, her head in her arms, dreading Lennie coming back.

ↄ

Where was the bloody cab? Tonight of all nights, he has to be late with it, Rob thought, pacing up and down the living room, looking out of the window every time he reached it, taking the same measured strides, the same length of time, for each trip.

If there was one thing Lennie Fredericks knew, it was that the cab had to be back here at eight o'clock. My God, didn't he skim off enough money in the time he had it, that he had to run into overtime?

He picked up the phone, and punched Lennie's number, but the line was out of order, or something.

Finally, on one of his trips, when he was at the other end of the room to the window, he heard the mournful squeal of the brakes, and ran through the room, out into the hallway, out of the front door, to where Lennie had pulled up.

¿

Carole heard the brakes, too, and looked out of the bedroom window to see Rob pull open the back door and get into the cab, and the cab turning in the road and roaring off in a great puff of exhaust smoke.

Lennie would have to be late tonight, when she had been sitting on the edge of the bed, a pillow clasped to her stomach, as she had when she was a child, and was being expected to perform in some school production. The pillow seemed to help fill the terrible empty pit of fear. She had longed for Lennie to come, and prayed that he wasn't going to, that she could legitimately cancel her plans.

But she had got the worst of both worlds; Lennie, late. They had gone now, she told herself, forcing herself to remove the pillow, put it back where it belonged. Now, she had to stand up, walk downstairs, open the front door, and walk round to the garage and get the car.

Her knees still shook, but she was walking, she was going downstairs.

¿

"Where the hell were you?" Rob demanded, raising his voice against the protesting engine as Lennie drove too fast through Stansfield, out to the dual carriageway. "Don't get us a ticket!" he shouted. "There's a speed trap along here!"

"There were cops all over the house," Lennie said, slowing down.

"Why?"

"Looking for stolen property," said Lennie, approaching the first of the big new roundabouts, the one that took him on to the bypass. "Ginny might have nicked something."

"What?"

"I don't know. I couldn't make head nor tail of what she said. I don't know, I don't want to know, and I don't care."

Rob shut up then, but he started going at him again when he had to wait for ages at the turning for Parkside. At last, he was on his way, driving past the still unlit bonfire which was beginning to gather a crowd while everything was being set up for it to start at eight-thirty. The smell of hot dogs wafted in through his half-open window; he was reminded about the take-away. He couldn't stop at the Indian, Rob wouldn't hear of it. He had a booking, and Lennie had made him late. Oh, dear, what a pity.

He'd go out later, get a Chinese, maybe. She liked that better than Indian, anyway.

He pulled up outside the house, pulling on the hand brake, getting out as Rob did, taking him by surprise, grabbing *him* by the throat and pushing him hard against the shuddering cab, holding him there as Rob tried to pull his hand away.

"You lay a finger on Ginny again and you're a dead man," he said, and released him.

Rob rubbed his neck, cleared his throat a little. "I was just giving her a lesson in self-preservation," he said. "There's no point in keeping a gun if you don't know how to use it."

A what? Lennie couldn't believe what he'd heard. She still had it? He had told her to take it back where she'd got it. Shit! She hadn't taken it back at all. And that's what all that nonsense had been about. All that business about the police not finding it, about Rob maybe having told them. What if they had found it? They'd have done him for having it, and quite likely done him for whatever job it had been used for.

"She keeps it in the drawer with S and M stuff," said Rob. "I think she reckons it's better protection than you, Lennie." He got into the cab, and closed the door. "So do I," he added, through the open window.

Lennie wasn't listening. "Just wait till I get my hands on her," he said, as Rob reversed out.

She didn't know the first thing about guns—the stupid little bitch, the *stupid* little bitch. She would blow her head off with the bloody thing. And if she thought she'd avoided a hiding with that rigamarole this evening, she was wrong. She was going to get the hiding of her life for this.

Chapter Nine

Carole stood in the courtyard, looking at the row of garages. Each door had been painted a different colour now; theirs was maroon. The Council must have used vandal-proof paint, she thought; there was no graffiti. She stood still on the pavement, her foot unwilling to step onto the tarmac. She kept turning at every sound, looking along the little exit road, thinking she could see someone in the shadows, but there was no one there. And the dark skies were lit by flares and sparks, the night full of loud, comforting noises.

She tried to walk forward, towards the maroon door. She had the key. She just had to open it. Once she had done it, it would be all right. Once she had walked in there, the worst part would be over. Getting into her car wouldn't seem so impossible anymore. Somehow, she moved to the door, and crouched down to the low lock. Her hand was shaking too much to insert the key, and she couldn't stop the memories.

Of lying on her face, her hands taped behind her back, her ankles crossed and taped together. Of being pulled up by her hair, onto her knees, the knife touching her neck, the ungloved hand lifting her head, forcing open her mouth; of the voice telling her what she must do, of retching when it was over. Of being pushed down onto her back while she was still on her knees, of lying there, exposed and vulnerable, unable to move, her feet trapped beneath her body, her thighs splayed painfully wide. Of being penetrated over and over again with sudden, savage thrusts, of being viciously stretched and squeezed and bitten and sucked, her involuntary sobs of pain and fear stifled by a gloved hand stuffed into her mouth. Of being told all the time that he was the Stealth Bomber, he was the Stealth Bomber. Of the terrifying silence that had followed the ferocity, of listening in the darkness to his breathing growing fast and shallow, not knowing what was happening, what was going to happen. Of lying rigid with fear as she had been washed with some sort of baby wipe.

She could still smell it, a strange, alien, innocent smell in amongst the sweat and the blood and the dust and the degradation. He had worked carefully, silently, wiping her, combing her, cleaning up her bleeding, bruised and torn body as methodically as he had violated it.

Then he had pulled her back up onto her knees, and she had heard the scrape of metal as he had picked up the knife once more, heard the swish as its blade flicked out. *Don't kill me, don't kill me. Please, please. Don't kill me.* She hadn't spoken the words aloud; he hadn't killed her. The tape had been cut from her wrists and ankles, and it had been over.

It *was* over. Tears were streaming down her face, but the key was in the lock. Behind that door, there was no horror. It had been twenty minutes of her life; it had been twenty-seven months ago. It mustn't rule her life, not anymore. She wiped the tears, turned the handle, pulled it up. He had dominated her then, but she had been helpless to prevent him; she wasn't helpless now, and he must *not* be allowed to dominate her now. She had to get past this; she had to move on, and there was only one way. The door opened with a rush, and Carole looked into her garage for the first time since that night.

And her eyes widened at what she saw.

៖

Eight twenty-five, and still no sign of Lloyd. Judy wanted to talk to Ginny; she wanted to know what had happened in Hosier's Alley. She could have gone to see her from work, if she had known that Case was going to keep Lloyd this late. Another ten minutes passed; she left a note for Lloyd to the effect that she would be back at about nine, and went to set her mind at rest.

The traffic at the turnoff held her up; she wouldn't be back for nine, which had been a silly thing to think in the first place, since Ginny might be entertaining a client, and she would have to wait. Lennie would probably be out looking for the next one, though, so that was one hurdle she shouldn't have to clear.

She would be late back, and there would be another row. But she had seen Ginny in court, and none of the people who were so certain they knew what had happened that night had seen her give evidence, except Hotshot, and even he said she had been compelling. She just wanted to know. It was personal. It was a test of her instincts.

The lights were on, so at least someone was in, but the Transit was in the alley, so she would have to negotiate Lennie after all. Judy knocked on the door, and waited, but there was no reply. Maybe Lennie was still out with the cab. Ginny must be with a client. Unlike Tom, she did not keep knocking on the door in order to bring her down from her labours. She would wait in the car until she saw the punter leave.

She had been waiting about five minutes when she saw Drummond approach; the number of that bike was one that she had firmly committed to her less than reliable memory. He drove past; she checked her watch. Five to nine. Oh, well, she might as well be hung for a sheep and all that. She wanted to know where Drummond was going, in view of his unfinished business. She did a three-point turn, which surprised her with its efficiency; she wasn't the world's greatest manoeuvrer of a car. A car that obeyed her was a plus. She followed his rear light through the cobbled streets, the traffic moving slowly as people made their way to the bonfire, stepping out into the road with no regard for safety. And as the flames of the bonfire lit the black shiny surface of his bike, Drummond rode across the rough ground, behind the crowds of people, heading towards the underpass.

Judy couldn't follow in the car; she ran down the window and watched Drummond as he arrived at the underpass and dismounted, hoisting the bike onto its stand. He removed his helmet, and walked down the ramp. She parked as soon as she found a space, and jumped out. He had a three-minute start on her, but she might as well see if she could find out where he was going. She walked quickly through the onlookers, feeling the heat from the huge crackling fire as she passed, seeing the Guy Fawkes perched on top begin to catch, smelling the onions from the hot dogs. She was hungry; she was supposed to be having dinner.

But if, as she suspected, she had lost Drummond, she might just come back and have a hot dog and watch the real fireworks, rather than go back to Lloyd's emotional ones. The music began, and a *whoosh* of flame rose and burst, raining colour against the black sky as she reached the underpass. The firework display had begun.

◊

Her lip swelling, blood pouring down her face, down her neck, soaking into Lennie's sweater, Ginny had cowered into the corner of a buttress, trying to make herself invisible; the footsteps had passed, and with the relief, she had felt herself drift away.

Now her head was swimming, her eyes were throbbing, and there was a dull ache down the side of her face. She closed her eyes; it hurt too much to keep them open. There was a lot of noise. Bangs and cracks, and something that sounded like a machine gun. Music. More bangs and sizzles. She screamed as someone touched her, covering her head to shield it from further blows. But the hands were gentle, the voice female.

"Ginny?" An arm was round her shoulders. "Oh, my God, Ginny— What's happened to you?"

She looked up, but she couldn't see very well. Her eyes hurt, and anyway it was growing very dark . . .

She opened her eyes again. Her eyes still hurt, and the left one wouldn't open. She was lying on her side, her face on the damp paving, her legs drawn up.

"Ginny—just lie still till you feel better."

It was Inspector Hill. She was feeling her pulse, moving her hands over her ribs, moving her arms and legs.

"I'm all right," Ginny said.

"You're not. I've got to get you to casualty, Ginny. Do you think you can get up?"

She didn't want to get up. Why did she always have to get up first? Couldn't someone bring her a cup of tea in bed sometimes?

A voice from very far away. "Ginny—don't think there's anything broken. I'll be back in a minute. Don't move."

She'd gone. Good. Ginny wanted to go back to sleep . . .

She opened her eyes again, and she was sick. She sat up, her back against the wall, and closed her throbbing eyes. She heard more footsteps, and opened them again. Inspector Hill crouched down beside her.

"Good girl. How do you feel?"

"Terrible. Sick."

"Do you still feel faint?"

"No."

"Do you think you can get to the car? I've brought it right to the underpass."

She was being lifted up. Not like Lennie lifted her up, not swept up into someone's arms. Just lifted, the inspector's hands under her armpits, like you lifted a baby.

"Ginny, if you lean on me, can you walk a few steps to the car?"

Oh, yes. She walked two, three, four steps, and they were out where the fireworks were louder and brighter, hurting her head, going up the ramp towards a car. She was lowered down into the car seat, her arms slipping away from the inspector, who tipped the seat back gently.

It was better, once Inspector Hill had closed the door, and the noise had gone. But her face hurt.

ℒ

Matt wrestled with the nonsnarl hose of the air pipe, which had somehow tied itself into a reef knot, and persuaded it to stretch to the other side of his car where he checked the tyre pressure.

He went through his mental list of what he still had to do. Oil. Water. Antifreeze. Windscreen washer. What else were you supposed to check when you were going on a long trip? Lights.

It would save time tomorrow, because he would have to fit in sleeping at some point before he set out, if he didn't want to end up a statistic.

ℒ

Bangs and flashes were all around him; the smoke from someone's bonfire drifted across Rob's line of vision as he crouched down below the level of the bush that spilled over the unfenced frontage of the garden onto the pathway. He watched as a youthful policeman crossed the road and walked along the side of the house towards the people round the bonfire.

Kids were gathered round, their parents shouting warnings about not getting too close. Dad was getting ready to light some goodie that had cost the earth and would rise and burst into life and die in seconds. *Daddy, Daddy, can we go in the garden and play with explosive devices and naked flames? Of course, dearest.*

The noise, the smell, the flames . . . They didn't seem like fun to Rob. They seemed like a particularly bad night in Belfast, when he had watched as a car bomb had gone up. They had had a warning of a bomb; they had evacuated the area. He hadn't been hurt; no one had.

But it was the first time Rob had seen a Semtex explosion in the flesh. TV gave you a miniature of it. You saw a street, a car. You saw a flash. You heard a dull thud and saw the camera shake. When the picture cleared, you saw smoke and buildings without glass.

You couldn't feel the breathless instant between the seeing the flash and hearing the explosion; you didn't feel the air shake and the earth vibrate with the blast. You were given no conception of what it was like to see a complete and sturdy car there one minute, and its tangled innards the next; the twisted metal that fell from the sky, the shattered glass that sprayed into the air like lethal, lacerating champagne. You couldn't smell the air afterwards. But November the fifth was full of similar sights and sounds and smells; playing with fire seemed an odd way to Rob to want to spend your leisure time.

The policeman was in conversation with the man; he pointed towards the house across the road. Rob took his chance when he turned away again, and stood up, strolling to the cab. He was unlocking the door when the policeman thanked the neighbours and walked back down the path, crossing the road towards him.

"Excuse me!"

Rob turned from the cab.

"Can you tell me when you parked here, sir?"

"About twenty to nine, I think," Rob said. "About half an hour ago or so."

"Did you see anyone round here? Hanging about—showing an interest in this house, maybe?"

He pointed to the house again.

"No," said Rob. "Sorry."

"Well, thanks anyway."

Rob got into the cab and rolled down the window, watching as the man across the road lit the blue touch paper and took long, backwards strides to where his children stood.

A jet of flame shot down and the rocket took off, soaring up through the air with a piercing whistle before its short, violent life ended with a bang.

ò

Lennie backed the Transit out of the alleyway. A constant stream of people were walking past, on their way to the bonfire. There were dozens of ways to get to the sodding bonfire—couldn't they take a different one from this?

A flashing blue light caught his eye, and he held his breath as he heard the siren. A fire engine, going the same way as the crowds. Perhaps they could give some of these people a lift. A police car, too. Oh, no, groaned Lennie. No more cops. Please, no more cops.

He drove the Transit back into the alley, as close to the door as he could get.

҉

Case had remained seated throughout Lloyd's off-the-cuff analysis of his character, his motives, his competence, his politics, and, for good measure, his honesty, credibility, and integrity.

Lloyd, breathless, and perhaps beginning already to reflect on what he had said, as he did when he thus castigated Judy, fell silent. But his blue eyes still shone with anger, and there was no guilt attached to this reflection. He was reflecting that, unlike Judy, Case had not got up and left before the tirade had become wounding. And—also unlike Judy—Case did not appear to have been wounded. So it had been a bit of a waste of breath, really. If Judy failed to leave in time, something would hit home, something would really hurt her. And he would have a moment's satisfaction, and feel guilty for weeks. But this had been like trying to land a telling punch on a man in full medieval armour.

"Chief Inspector Lloyd," said Case. "You are aware that I could have you up on at least three if not four different disciplinary charges?"

"You can do as you please," said Lloyd. "I have to work with you, but that doesn't mean that I have to like you, or respect you or your judgment. And it certainly doesn't mean that I have to listen to you speak of a friend of mine in insulting and abusive terms."

"A friend of yours? That's a very coy way of putting it."

"There's nothing coy about it. Judy Hill is a friend of mine. A trusted friend, whom I will continue to trust, regardless of this great favour you have done me."

Case shook his head. "Then you're a fool."

Lloyd sat down. "You might be right that Drummond was someone else's fall guy," he said. "You might be right that the Malworth Mafia is trying to cover it up. But I think there's something your jungle drums have failed to communicate to you. I've known Judy Hill for twenty years."

"Then I'm sorry," Case said. "I thought your relationship was of more recent origin. But I strongly advise you to put an end to it. Look—I don't doubt that she sincerely believed Drummond was the rapist. I don't doubt that you had got your murderer, and just needed the proof. I can see how tempting it would be to use one of the bastards to nail the other. But good cause or no, corruption is still corruption in my book."

"And in mine."

"Not from where I'm sitting. You're standing too close to it."

"I'll offer you a wager," said Lloyd.

Case's eyebrows rose.

"My flat, my car, my bank balance, to a penny piece—when we get to the bottom of this, Judy Hill will be proved to have had no part in any of Malworth's shenanigans."

Case smiled. "I've never been much of a one for women," he said. "Never felt the urge, really. A confirmed bachelor. And when I see someone who has got it as bad as you, I'm glad."

"It's a serious bet," said Lloyd. "Are you taking it?"

The phone rang, and Case picked it up. "Case. Yes, he's here."

Lloyd waited to be handed the phone, but Case continued to hold on to it, listening without speaking. "He's on his way," he said, eventually, and replaced the receiver. "That was Inspector Bell," he said. "His men had to go chasing after an anonymous nine-double-nine. Caller didn't speak, but didn't hang up. The emergency operator recognized Handel's *Fireworks* music, reckoned the phone must be at the Malworth bonfire, sent a fire engine, and informed us. We found Colin Drummond's body in the Parkside underpass."

Lloyd stood up. He was disconcerted to find that his first reaction to this second murder—his very first reaction—had been relief. His second was that if Case always took that long to send officers to a murder, the bodies must often be mouldering by the time they got to them. He went to the door, and was called back.

"Oh—and Lloyd."

Lloyd turned. "Sir?" he said. Unofficially he could call him a bigoted, deluded incompetent. Officially, now and then, he would call him sir. It might be nice to hang on to his job.

"That bet?" he said. "You're on."

Chapter Ten

Carole's hands were still shaking as she got back in, put on the television, and the kettle.

Twenty-five minutes to ten. One hour and ten minutes ago she had left the house, barely able to put one foot in front of the other. She had done the hardest thing she had ever had to do in order to do what she must do. And she had done it. She had done it.

So why didn't she feel different? Why didn't she feel free? Why did it feel as though nothing at all had changed?

Surely, surely, it was over *now*.

ò

The firework display was taking a breather before its finale; pop music had replaced Handel for the moment, the fire was blazing, and the vendors were vending.

Lloyd had tried to ring Judy, to explain why he wasn't there, and that they had yet another enquiry from which she would doubtless find herself barred, but she hadn't been there. She had probably got tired of waiting for him, and had gone to visit some friend he knew nothing about, he had thought, irritated with her again. It was as if she were deliberately avoiding him.

He picked his way through spent rockets and Catherine wheels, breathing in wood smoke, sulphur, and potassium nitrate, a quite pleasing combination, oddly enough. The break in the programme had come at exactly the right time; Lloyd had heard his voice echo round the entire area when he had appealed for witnesses over the PA system. He could get used to that—maybe he would be a DJ on local radio when he retired.

The ones who thought they might have seen something of interest were being interviewed in the church; Roman Catholic, of course. No way that C of E adherents would have kept their church going in an area like this. Tom Finch was over there now, sorting the wheat from the chaff, appropriately enough.

They had so far found five cartridges in the underpass, from a semiautomatic pistol of some sort, but no pistol. They would be searching the park tomorrow.

Lloyd walked along the underpass to where Drummond's body was slumped against a buttress in a kneeling position, facing the wall. It was bloody and bullet-ridden, and it smacked of an execution to Lloyd. It was right at the other end of the underpass from the bonfire, almost at its exit into the park. That was where Drummond's mobile had been found, broadcasting Handel to the emergency services. He could have realized he was in danger, dialled 999, and then dropped it as he ran away from his pursuer, only to be followed into the underpass.

Lloyd walked up the ramp to the railing-enclosed parkland, crisscrossed with paths, its once formal flower beds and lawns being kept down, rather than up, by the Council. No shortage of trees and bushes, which probably looked after themselves, and into which the murderer could have thrown an entire arsenal of weapons. The odd bench and shelter. It was open all year round, twenty-four hours a day. It had a large paved area which had originally been for a bandstand; now, it had the occasional car parked on it. And it might have had a car parked on it tonight, Lloyd thought, but no one would have seen it. Which was, of course, what the murderer would be counting on.

He went back down into the underpass, and found that the lights and the SOCOs had arrived with commendable speed. He watched as the lights came on, as everyone got busy, while he considered the possibilities.

People who would have cheerfully murdered Colin Drummond, form an orderly queue, he thought. It would stretch from one end of the underpass to the other. All of his victims, save the one he murdered, and all of their husbands, brothers, fathers . . . an awful lot of people might have wanted to send Drummond off to join the great minority. Boyfriends, sisters, mothers, widowers . . . flatmates. Bobbie Chalmers. She was interesting, because she could very easily get hold of a gun.

And, of course, police officers could, especially if they were corrupt in the first place, get hold of guns. He had to bear Case's theory in mind to some extent; it might not have been Drummond who was pulling the strings in an attempt to incriminate Judy, but an ex-colleague of hers who had been manipulating Drummond. If they were both out to get Judy for different reasons, this could be the result of a falling-out of thieves. So, yes, he would bear in mind that an ex-Malworth police officer might well have killed Drummond. But for the moment, Bobbie Chalmers was his favourite, as a working hypothesis.

The emergency call had been made at three minutes past nine; the emergency services had arrived at nine-fifteen, still not knowing what they were looking for. The body had been found at nine twenty-five, the phone two minutes later. It was the uniforms who had found him, but at least Case couldn't complain about their efficiency. It had, of course, been sheer luck. A lone officer had thought he'd better check the underpass. Still, the CID had a lot to live up to on this one.

"Guv?" Tom came along the underpass towards him. "I've got someone over there who saw a woman going into the underpass at about nine o'clock," he said. "He noticed, because women hardly ever use it if they're alone, not after dark."

"Did we get a description? Could it have been one of his victims?"

"Well," said Tom. "I don't think so. Dark-haired, about five-seven, nicely dressed, thirties, respectable-looking. Mrs. Jarvis is fair-haired, Lucy Rogerson and Ginny Fredericks are too young—I don't think it could have been any of them."

"Could have been Bobbie Chalmers," Lloyd said. "She has more reason to want to kill Drummond than most."

Tom frowned. "She's blonde," he said.

"Not anymore."

"She's only about twenty-six," said Tom.

"Well? It was dark."

"Nicely dressed? She's a bit flashy for that description, isn't she, guv?"

"Nice is in the eye of the beholder," said Lloyd. "She has every motive in the world to want to shoot him, and I'm sure she can have access to a semiautomatic pistol if she chooses."

"That's why I'm having trouble with 'respectable-looking,' " said Tom. "I mean—that description sounds more like Judy than Bobbie Chalmers. With respect," he added, with a smile.

Tom had obviously been treated to Judy's opinion of their new Chief Superintendent. He was quite famous, apparently, though he had been merely a name to Lloyd, one he had heard floating around Bartonshire Constabulary for years. Matt Burbidge apparently knew him as Hard Case; Lloyd privately thought of him as Head Case. "Tom, can you hold the fort here?" he asked. "I'd like to talk to the Drummonds, find out if they know where Colin was going, what he was doing tonight."

"Sure, guv."

Colin's parents lived on the other side of the bypass, naturally, on the outskirts of Malworth, where the houses took up a great deal of room, and rarely had more than two occupants. The Drummonds looked so much older than when Lloyd had last seen them that he was quite shocked; it had only been two years. But they had seen their son tried for rape, and convicted. Custom had suffered; they had had to close the Malworth shop, and the Barton one had only just survived. Then the conviction had been overturned; now, their son was dead. Lloyd didn't suppose that he would have come out of that lot looking any less emotionally ravaged.

"I don't want to intrude," he said. "It's just that if we can get an idea of where Colin might have been going, it would help."

"He said he was meeting someone," said Mrs. Drummond.

"Meeting someone? Did he say who?"

"No." She wiped her nose, her eyes, with a paper handkerchief screwed into a ball so tight it could hardly be seen. "Someone rang him."

"When?" said Lloyd.

"I don't know. He didn't say."

"Did they ring here, or his mobile?"

"I don't know." She smiled tearfully. "He took that everywhere," she said. "It reminded me of when he was little and he had to take this spoon everywhere. Just an ordinary dessert spoon. But if we took him out anywhere, he had to have his spoon."

Lloyd nodded. Until now he had never thought of Drummond as having had a childhood. "Can you tell me what he said about this phone call?" he asked.

"He said someone had rung him saying that they had information on Rosa. That's the—the girl he was seeing."

"Yes," said Lloyd. "I know."

"And then he said, 'so I won't be in this evening,' and he left here about half past eight."

"Thank you," said Lloyd.

"He was very anxious to trace Rosa," she said. "She could prove that he didn't do those things. It's one thing—being acquitted—it's another being able to prove to people that you're innocent."

"Yes," said Lloyd.

"Do you—" She broke off, touched her nose with the tiny ball of paper, and tried again. "Do you think someone lured him with that?" she asked. "And killed him?"

Yes, he did rather. "I don't know, Mrs. Drummond," he said. "But rest assured, we will know more soon." And he left.

Mr. Drummond hadn't said a word.

When he got back, Freddie was just getting out of his car. He grinned at Lloyd. "I know I wanted you to get him," he said. "But a simple arrest would have done."

"Someone got him," Lloyd said, as they walked into the underpass to a backdrop of Roman candles and starbursts.

Freddie stopped walking. "Be honest, Lloyd," he said. "He threatened Judy. Off the record, this time of all times—do you honestly *care* who killed him?"

"I don't give a damn that he's dead," said Lloyd. "You can make as many jokes over this corpse as you like. But no one has the right to do that to anyone else, so of course I care who killed him."

Freddie shook his head. "You can be a sanctimonious so-and-so, do you know that?" he said good-humouredly.

Lloyd didn't think so. "If it's what it looks like," he said, "it's someone taking the law into his or her own hands, and exceeding even its powers."

"Yes, Lloyd." Freddie sighed, on the move again, anxious to get to the corpse as ever, as it came into view in a blaze of light, and he crouched down in the draughty, damp underpass to begin his examination, the legends "FU" in blue paint, and "FU2" in red paint on the wall behind him, a happy man.

In due course, Freddie said the body could go to the morgue; Lloyd sent a car for the Drummonds, so that formal identification could be made and details released to the press, who were already gathering as word got round.

¿

The caretakers left, and Matt shut and locked the back door. The block of shops and businesses were owned by some development company who employed caretakers; they worked until ten-thirty, and after that those of their tenants who felt the need for security made their own arrangements.

Matt was on duty now until the staff arrived at nine. He checked that the main door was double locked and bolted, that the lights were all out, that the internal doors were all locked, that the vaults were in order, that the cameras were operational, that he'd remembered to bring his sandwiches, and that the windows were secure.

Then he switched on the alarms, and Northstead Securities was guarded against fire, flood, and pestilence for another night.

ọ

"Well, you're not concussed, there's nothing broken, and there's no serious head injury," said the doctor, and smiled at her. "If we'd known that we wouldn't have seen you so quickly," he added. "You'd have had to wait your turn behind all the burnt hands."

Ginny smiled back. It wasn't easy, with her lip twice its normal size. She had been taken straight in; she had been given all sorts of tests and things. Her open eye ached, and her cheek was swollen up so much she could see it, and not much else.

"So I'm going to let you go home," he said. "But only if there's someone there to keep an eye on you."

She nodded. "Lennie," she said.

"Can I ask who Lennie is?"

"My husband."

He looked surprised, and finished stitching the cut on her forehead. She couldn't feel anything. He'd done it like the dentist does your teeth. He said it would hurt when it wore off. It might as well. Everything else did.

"There," he said.

"Will I have a scar?"

He wiggled his head about. "You will," he said, "I'm afraid. But it won't be a bad scar." He smiled again. "Interesting," he said. "That's what it'll be. About an inch long. It goes through your eyebrow, and the hair won't grow back, but you can use eyebrow pencil to cover it."

That didn't sound too bad. But she hadn't seen herself in a mirror yet, and she knew she didn't want to. She slid off the trolley. "Can I go, then?"

"Yes," he said. "I've given the police inspector a card—it just says what your husband should watch out for. You've taken a lot of nasty blows to the head, and these painkillers are quite strong. I thought it better to give it to her, in case you do get a bit groggy and forget. Is that all right? She said she'd be taking you home."

"Yeah."

"What happened to your throat?" he asked. "Another client?"

"Yeah."

"How old are you, Ginny?"

"Nineteen next month," she said.

He shook his head slightly. "You could do anything you wanted," he said. "You don't have to run these risks. Find yourself a less hazardous occupation."

Ginny didn't know what that meant, but she supposed it meant one where people didn't try to strangle you because they felt like it.

The doctor walked with her out to where Inspector Hill stood. "Here she is," he said. "As good as new."

"Hello, Inspector," said a nurse, who came along the corridor with a trolley wheeled by two porters. "We've got a suspected GBH here, if you're interested—he was found just round the corner on the pavement."

"No thanks," said Inspector Hill, smiling back. "You can go through the usual channels—I'm off-duty."

"Is this just a hobby, then?" asked the doctor, jerking his head at Ginny.

The inspector smiled, and they went out to her car. Ginny got to sit up in it this time. But she didn't get any peace.

"Right, Ginny," Judy said, as soon as they were on their way. "What happened to you?"

Ginny shrugged. "A punter," she lied.

"Where were you with this punter?"

"In the underpass."

"You're going to have to do better than that," said the inspector.

à

Stansfield had had its own Guy Fawkes celebrations, of course; the boating lake's bonfire was being damped down, the firework display long over. For the last hour people had been drifting off in ones and twos and small family parties, going home after the fun. Rob had been busy. But now only groups of teenagers hung around, looking to get into mischief, not taxis.

Rob drove on to the main road and turned right, up to the rank at the top of the hill, in the town centre. He pulled in behind the dozen or so cabs already there, waiting for the pubs to start emptying.

He wished he hadn't told Lennie about the gun. He had been peeved at being taken by surprise like that. He'd got slow since he'd left the army. It had annoyed him, someone like Lennie doing that to him, and he'd said it before he'd thought. Ginny had probably got a hiding for it, and it had been a stupid thing to do. He moved up the rank as the taxis peeled off. Roll on midnight, when he could relax and have a snooze.

He deserved it. He'd done a good night's work.

§

"One," said Judy. "You don't need to take customers down the underpass. Two, it was too early for that—the punters don't start coming until at least ten o'clock, and three, you wouldn't be wearing an old sweater and jogging pants if you'd been working." She glanced at her, at her poor, battered, swollen face, at the neat row of stitches through her eyebrow. "Did Colin Drummond do that to you?" she asked.

"No," said Ginny.

"It wasn't a punter, was it?"

"Yeah."

"Why would you be in the underpass with a punter?"

She shrugged. "Lennie's got me working the park again," she said. "They can't drive me back to the house—it would take too long with the traffic."

"What's wrong with the van? He's still got it. That's what you used to use."

Ginny went sullen on her. Judy had been driving faster going back than she had coming, but now she deliberately slowed down to give herself more time to talk to the girl without Lennie there.

"Ginny—will you tell me the truth about something if I promise I won't tell anyone else unless you say I can?"

It took Ginny a while to sort that out. She wasn't fond of compound sentences, and that one had been a bit of a facer, Judy realized.

"Depends," was the answer she finally came up with.

"OK. Did Colin Drummond really assault you in Hosier's Alley?"

The silence made her turn her head to see Ginny's one-eyed baleful stare.

"I thought you believed me!" she shouted.

"I do," said Judy, quickly.

"No, you don't! You're like all the rest. You're like that jury and the fucking judge! You're like Matt Burbidge and Rob Jarvis! I'm a whore, so I never got raped! I'm a whore so you can't take my word for anything! You're all the fucking same!"

Judy saw a lay-by, glanced in her mirror, and took the car into it. Ginny would do her damaged face a mischief, shouting like that.

"Ginny," she said, taking the little girl's hands. "I do believe you. I've always believed you."

"You're a fucking liar," she said huffily.

"It's the truth," said Judy. "I've never doubted you."

"Why'd you ask me, then?"

Judy sighed, shrugged. Because she couldn't honestly believe that her one-time colleagues could have used her like that; but they had, and she wasn't supposed to know, so she couldn't say that. "I can't tell you," she said.

"Why not?" asked Ginny.

The little girl's whole being was suspicious. But she hadn't taken her hands away from Judy's, so she hadn't entirely written her off as being just like all the rest. Judy decided that the truth was all that could be told in this situation. "I'd be grassing someone up," she said, with a smile.

Ginny's open eye grew less suspicious, more interested. "Yeah?" she said. "A cop?"

"A friend," said Judy. "And a cop. But I'm really sorry I asked you," she said. "Because I do believe you, and I'm very, very sorry about what happened to you that night."

Ginny shrugged. "Wasn't your fault," she said.

"No," said Judy. "It wasn't." She clasped the girl's hands more tightly. "Ginny, did Drummond do this to you, too? I saw him go into the underpass. Did I scare him off? Was he assaulting you?"

"I never saw him," she said. "I heard feet, though. I hid."

Judy had heard feet, too; right at the other end of the underpass as she had entered. She had been going to go back up, see if she could see where he was going from ground level, but she had heard a whimper, had thought an animal had been hurt by a firework. And found poor little Ginny.

"You mustn't be scared of him, Ginny. If he did that to you, we can deal with him."

"It wasn't Drummond," Ginny said. "It was a punter."

"All right," Judy said, admitting defeat, and took the car back out onto the road. Then she replayed in her head what Ginny had said to her when she was angry. She had said that she was like all the rest. She was just like Matt Burbidge, and just like Rob Jarvis. Rob Jarvis had a taxi.

"Is it Rob Jarvis that Lennie's working with, Ginny?" she asked.

"Yeah."

"How come?"

Silence.

"Come on, Ginny! I'm only being nosy."

Ginny, she found, had not been refusing to answer, but merely grappling with the concept of hypothesis, though she didn't know that was what she had been doing.

"Say you've got a deal with someone," she said. "Like—I'd give them something if Lennie could drive their cab, and get to keep some of what he takes on it—is that all right? I mean, is it against the law?"

Judy smiled. "It's quite legal," she said. "But if the something's what I think it is, then you should have made the deal, of course. Not Lennie."

"Yeah," she said.

Yeah, thought Judy. And listened as Ginny told her about the deal, more intrigued than ever by the strange liaison. The familiar injunction not to tell Lennie that she'd told her was appended.

Lennie was at the Transit in the alley when Judy drove up with

Ginny, quickly sliding the door shut when he saw her. The side door to the house stood open, and light flooded out.

"What the fuck's she doing here?" was Lennie's greeting to his wife.

Ginny's sweater was covered in blood, she had stitches, her face was swollen like a balloon, she had a cut lip and two black eyes, one of which was shut fast, and Lennie hadn't been in the least shocked to see her. Judy stared at him.

"She took me up the casualty," said Ginny.

Lennie? Surely not. He'd given Ginny hidings in his time, God knew, but this was vicious. And yet her insistence against all the evidence that it had been a punter meant she was covering up for someone, and who else would she ever cover up for but Lennie?

"I found her in the underpass," she said.

Lennie said nothing.

"Did you do that to her?"

"Mind your own business."

"Did he, Ginny?"

Ginny didn't speak.

If he had, it had to have been because of the search warrant. She must have got very close to something, and Lennie blamed Ginny for letting her in the day before, maybe, letting her see how they lived. Or maybe they'd even missed something. Something important enough to make him lose control of his temper. She looked at the Transit, at the doors that had been shut so quickly. "What have you got in there that you don't want me to see?" she asked.

"Get a search warrant, if you want to know," said Lennie.

Lennie knew his rights. You had to have further evidence to search the same place twice, and she hadn't actually had any in the first place. She saw Ginny wilt a little, and put her arm round her. "She should be inside," she said, and helped her down the alley and into the kitchen.

There were smears of what looked like blood on the stairs, and on the sparklingly clean work surface. A kitchen chair was overturned.

"What happened here?" Judy asked, when Lennie followed them in.

Lennie touched the tip of his nose. "Keep that out, copper," he said. "This is between her and me. You've brought her home, so you can piss off now, can't you?"

Ginny was already taking a damp cloth to work surfaces.

"Will you be all right?" she asked her.

"Yeah." She didn't seem scared.

Judy gave Lennie the card from the doctor. "It says on there what to watch for," she said. "There were several blows to the side of her head, which could have caused serious injury. The doctor doesn't think they did. If you're interested."

Lennie blinked a little, took the card.

Judy left, and realized that it was almost midnight; Lloyd probably wasn't expecting her for dinner anymore. She would ring him when she got home.

⸱

Lennie took the cloth out of Ginny's hand. "Don't do that," he said, and put his arms round her, rocking her like a baby. "I'm sorry, Ginny," he said. "I'm sorry, I'm sorry." He could feel tears in his eyes. "What did you tell her?" he asked.

"I said it was a punter. I said I was in the underpass with him. She didn't believe me, though."

"Good girl." He kissed the only bit of her poor face that looked as though it might not hurt. "You stick to that if anyone asks you again. Whatever they ask you, whatever they say—even if they don't believe you. You—stick to what you told her."

She nodded.

He looked at her, at the state she was in, and the tears fell. "I'm sorry," he said, again, and let her go, wiping the dampness from his face. "You should be in bed," he said. "Put your arm round me."

He lifted her up, carried her upstairs for the second time that day, laid her on the bed. He pulled off the jogging pants, and looked at the sweater. There was no way he could get it over her head without hurting her. "I'll have to cut this off," he said.

"No!" She looked up at him. "You like me in it," she said. "It'll wash, won't it?"

He nodded. He didn't want to upset her. "Well," he said. "Keep it on for now. Do you want a cup of tea?"

She tried to smile, God help her. "No," she said. "I'm fine."

He tucked her up, and waited with her until she slept, then went down and cleaned up the blood and straightened the kitchen, and made a pot of tea. He did take one up to her in case she was awake, but she was still asleep. He listened to her breathing, and felt her forehead, and decided that she really was just asleep. Then he came back down, lit a cigarette, and picked up his mug.

Tea spilled on the table as his body began to shake with sobs. Oh, God, what had he done?

Chapter Eleven

Saturday 6 November

R ob hooted again, but still nobody came out. Frowning, he switched off the engine and got out, knocking on the door. "Didn't you hear me hoot?" he asked, when Lennie finally opened it.

"I heard you. I was busy. And I'm not working today."

Lennie looked terrible. Bags under his eyes, his face pale. "What's wrong—some sort of bug?" asked Rob.

"Something like that," said Lennie. "Anyway, I'm not working, so—"

Rob wasn't listening to him. He was looking over his shoulder at Ginny, coming down the stair. "Jesus Christ," he said, under his breath, and looked at Lennie. "You didn't—" he began, and looked at Ginny again, who had only now made it to the foot of the stair. "That's not because of what I—" He shook his head. "Did you do that to her?" he asked, appalled.

"None of your business," said Lennie.

"It's my business if—" Rob lowered his voice. "It's my business if it's because of what I said. Jesus, Lennie—look at her!"

"You tried to strangle her," said Lennie.

"I was—" Rob began, then realized that he couldn't explain that to himself, never mind Lennie. He hadn't even thought about it until now. It had been because of seeing Drummond, he supposed. He hated having to go with a whore, and sometimes he hated her for having aroused him in the first place, hated her for knowing what Drummond had done to him. He was only with her because of Drummond, because Drummond had made him have to prove himself over and over again. With a cheap whore. And Drummond had just been in his cab. And . . . the two things had just overwhelmed him when she had brought out that gun. Guns are for killing, he'd thought, and he had wanted to kill, or possibly to die. He hadn't been sure which. He didn't know if he would have stopped, could have stopped. He had relied on Ginny's instinct for self-preservation kicking in long before it mattered, and it had. She was right: he hadn't known whether the safety catch was on or off, or if it even worked. He had played a game of Russian roulette. And maybe he had lost.

"I—I wasn't going to strangle her," he said. "I just wanted her to know that guns don't protect you all by themselves."

Ginny was sitting at the table, sipping tea with difficulty. Her face was bruised and battered and swollen—she had *stitches*. What kind of man could do that to a little girl that you could blow down with a puff of cigarette smoke?

"I think maybe our arrangement should end here," Rob said.

"Suits me," said Lennie, and he closed the door.

Rob drove home hardly aware of what he was doing, the busy Saturday traffic in Malworth hooting at him now and then as he lost concentration. It didn't matter; they expected taxi drivers to behave badly, to stray into their paths as they caught sight of a fare. He pulled up outside the house, and sat for a while in the cab before going in to face the inevitable discussion of what had been all over the news all morning. But Carole didn't say much; asked him if he'd heard that someone had killed Drummond, that was all. She was glad he was dead.

He didn't want the meal that Carole had made for him, but he ate it somehow. He wanted to be left alone. But she sat there, and he could feel that more discussion was about to be unleashed as soon as he had finished. And before he had time to get up, go upstairs, escape, she spoke.

"I wanted to go out last night," she said. "I wanted to drive the car."

He looked at her, his breath caught in his throat. She wouldn't even let him leave the car where she could see it, never mind drive it; she hadn't set foot in the garage for over two years. Surely she hadn't—

"I did it, Rob," she said. "I thought I couldn't, but I did. I went into the garage."

He looked away from her.

"Don't you think I'm owed an explanation?" she asked.

Ŷ

Judy had just finished breakfast when the eight o'clock news had come on. What she had heard had filled her with a mixture of shock, disbelief, apprehension, and frustration.

He was dead. He couldn't do that to any more women because he was dead. But he shouldn't be dead. Someone had bought themselves a whole load of trouble, and cheated her out of being able to lock the little bastard up again. Then she had heard the next bit. The "police would like to interview" bit. She had sat, her hand at her mouth, scarcely able to take it in.

Which was why she had had to get Lloyd out of the briefing, and why he was sitting opposite her, looking, as Tom Finch would say, gobsmacked. Just as she had stared at the radio.

"*You?*"

She nodded. "I'm afraid so," she said.

"What were you doing there?"

"Well," she said.

He closed his eyes. "Am I going to want to hear this?" he asked.

"It might be of some use," she said. "I went to see Ginny last night."

" 'Back at nine' is that?"

"Yes, well, that was always a bit optimistic. But I had a rather eventful evening. I did try to ring you when I got in."

She told him about her eventful evening, and realized as she did so that she was being interviewed. She knew his technique. He listened without comment to the witness's entire story, then went back over it, asking questions. It was odd, being on the receiving end of it. "I didn't think there was much point in trying to get an ambulance on Bonfire Night," she said. "I thought it would be quicker to take her myself. I took the car round the back of the high-rise and drove it right up to the underpass—she couldn't have walked any further than that. You should have seen the state she was in, Lloyd. They took her straight in when we got to casualty. But when I finally got her home . . ."

She told him about Lennie's reaction, about the van, and finished, feeling a little as though she had been giving a lecture. "She seemed to think she'd be all right with him," she said. "So I left her there. There wasn't much else I could do."

Lloyd nodded. "I'm not sure where to start," he said. "I've got two sets of questions, really. Witness questions, and what-the-hell-do-you-think-you're-playing-at questions." He ran his hand over the strip of hair. "Let's start with the witness questions," he said. "I suppose the first one has to be did you hear any gunshots in the underpass?"

"Lloyd, it was like the Battle of the Somme."

"Oh, yes. Of course. Stupid of me—that's why he or she chose Guy Fawkes night. So no one would notice the shots." He looked at her. "I don't know how to do this with you," he said, looking uncomfortable. "Did Drummond have time to beat Ginny like that before you got there?"

Judy shrugged. "How long does it take?" she asked. "If someone Drummond's size starts laying in to someone Ginny's size, it won't take long to do real damage. Yes, I think he had time to have done it. It didn't take him three minutes to walk through the underpass, did it? And I definitely saw him go in and I heard someone running out of the other end."

"But there's a good chance he never came out the other end," said Lloyd. "And I thought you thought Lennie had beaten Ginny up."

Judy sighed. "I've never known Lennie to be that violent," she said. "But then again, whatever happened seems to have happened in their kitchen, and he obviously already knew what state she was in." She shook her head. "It's possible my search rattled him, and he just lost control, or something."

"I don't know," said Lloyd. "Drummond rang you about unfinished business. If Ginny did set him up, maybe he went after her. And maybe she defended herself."

"Where would Ginny get a gun?" asked Judy. "And whose feet did I hear?"

"That's what's wrong," said Lloyd. "I can't interview you like I would any other witness—you ask questions. You argue."

"Sorry," said Judy. "I'll try not to."

"This is starting just like the Marilyn Taylor one," Lloyd said. "You get what sound like really good leads, and they fizzle out." He shook his head. "Well," he said, "since I can't seem to ask you proper witness questions, I'll move on. What the hell were you playing at, going to see Ginny?"

"I just wanted to ask her face to face about Drummond and Hosier's Alley," said Judy.

Lloyd shook his head wearily. "What you did was go to interview a victim in the rape enquiry from which you have been removed."

Judy bit her lip. "I honestly never gave it a thought," she said. "It's quite hard to remember that you're the subject of a complaint when you haven't done anything wrong. And it was just for my own satisfaction. I wanted to look her in the eye, and ask her."

"And did you?"

"Yes," said Judy. "Literally, bless her. Only one eye would open. And I have absolutely no doubt whatsoever that Drummond raped her." She thought about that. "So I think it's unlikely that he beat her up last night, really. I mean—either he would have sexually assaulted her again, or he wouldn't have assaulted her at all, I'd have thought. I think it must have been Lennie—and he definitely didn't want me to see what was in his van."

"Mm," said Lloyd. He leant his elbows on the desk, his face showing concern. "Judy," he said. "Be careful, please. I know it's only a matter of time before this investigation nonsense is over, but Case is . . . well . . . on your case. He thinks because you were at Malworth that you can't be trusted."

Judy sighed. "I just feel so—so frustrated," she said.

"It might not be for much longer," said Lloyd. "Presumably Bobbie Chalmers will tell the truth now."

Judy should have been pleased about that prospect, but she wasn't, not since her visit to Matt. "Meanwhile," she said, "is there anything being investigated by this police force that I can work on?"

"The burglaries," said Lloyd, with a grin. "I understand there was yet another one last night—and you might have got your wish. It was reported while it was in progress."

"Then why haven't we got the burglar?" asked Judy.

"It and the 999 came in almost simultaneously, so I understand that resources were stretched," said Lloyd. "You'll have to take it up with the uninformed branch. The detective branch had nothing to do with it." He smiled. "And there's a GBH," he said.

"Oh, yes," said Judy. "The GBH was brought in while I was in casualty with Ginny." She shook her head. "I've had enough blood and guts for one week," she said. "Bags I the burglary."

She left Lloyd's office, and found DC Marshall studying the report of last night's burglary. The burglar had unlocked the front door of the house, which had caused the solo police officer sent to the scene to open it when he routinely tried it on arrival. The pots, pans, cans of lager, etc., that the intruder had piled against the door had alerted him to someone's presence, and he had made his escape through the *back* door.

"Cunning stuff, eh, ma'am?" Marshall said.

"Did he see what the burglar got away in?" she asked. "A Transit van, by any chance?"

"Do you still think it was Lennie?"

"I saw him last night," she said. "He was very anxious that I didn't see what he had in his van. I think it was the proceeds of that burglary."

"No, ma'am, it wasn't. He got interrupted too soon. The stuff was all inside the back door, waiting to be loaded. But nothing was taken."

"What about the neighbours? Didn't any of them see anything?"

"No. Whoever rang us said that there was a light moving about inside and the people were on holiday. But he just hung up, and they all denied all knowledge. Did not wish to become involved."

"I don't blame them," said Judy. "Neither do I. Where was it?"

Marshall gave her the address, and she realized that she did want to be involved after all. They were friends of hers. She sent Marshall to the hospital to interview the GBH, and popped in on Lloyd on her way to the burglary.

"Alan Marshall says Lennie couldn't have had stuff from the burglary in his van, because nothing was taken," she said.

"I think I'll get Tom to pay a visit to the Fredericks's house," said Lloyd. "With a particular remit to have a look inside that van. It's probably got nothing to do with Drummond, but at least we might find out what it is." He got up. "And I'm off to my second post mortem in three days," he said.

Judy went to the burglary, where the neighbour who had been entrusted with the keys was trying to put things back where they belonged, now that she had been told there was no need to leave them piled up by the back door. "Thank goodness he didn't take anything," she said. "I would have felt terrible."

"It wouldn't have been your fault," Judy said.

"No, but you feel responsible," she said. "And . . . this is going to sound really silly, but you know the thing that really made me think how awful it must be to have strangers messing about with your things? He pulled the plug on Keith's serial."

Keith was like Lloyd; he watched things, recorded things, collected things on tapes. And the burglar had unplugged the video minutes after his programme had started.

"I know it sounds silly, when people lose all sorts of valuable things, or personal things, but I don't know, it just seemed so . . . unfair."

"It is unfair," said Judy. Lloyd was watching it, she was sure. He might have recorded it—she'd ask when she got a moment. But, she thought, she had better not tell him why she wanted to know; producing yet another friend he knew nothing about would not be wise. "You didn't see anyone hanging round—any vehicle you didn't recognize?" she asked.

"No, well—I was out most of the evening."

"You wouldn't know if Mary and Keith took a taxi to the station, by any chance?"

"Yes, I believe they did. I'm sure that's what she said they'd be doing. Because it had to come really early, and she was worried that it wouldn't turn up—if you know her, you know what she's like."

"Yes." Judy smiled. "You wouldn't know which firm?"

"No."

She was right about Lennie. She was sure she was. There had been a burglary on Tuesday night, too. The stuff might be kept in the van until he could shift it. If Ginny was telling the truth about being with a punter in the underpass, it could have been because Lennie's van wasn't available.

Marshall came back from the hospital not long after she had got back to the station.

"That was a short visit," she said.

"His name is Monty Evans, he is a local entrepreneur with a big house in Malworth, and interests in various fields. Like vice, dodgy finance, secondhand motors—he's got a record going back to his teens. It was a short visit."

Judy smiled. "And?"

"And he fell downstairs. I pointed out to him that he was found on a very flat pavement on a street which was entirely devoid of stairs. He says he has no recollection of how he got there, but that he does remember falling downstairs somewhere. He thinks he must have tried to get to casualty. Thus, he was found round the corner from the hospital."

"And what did the doctor say?"

"He said that his injuries were more or less consistent with falling downstairs. Or being beaten up. And that memory loss is only to be expected when you've been unconscious as long as he was. Or if you don't want to report a crime." He shrugged. "He said he was very lucky not to have been more seriously hurt, and to go away and stop bothering him, basically."

"Let's hope this keeps up," Judy said. "If everyone takes to refusing to report any crime, we can sit with our feet up, can't we?"

⟨

"The first shot killed him," said Freddie. "It was the one to the back of the head."

"How can you tell?"

"The muzzle was held close to, but not touching, his head," said Freddie. "There's tattooing—tiny lesions on the skin round the entry wound—and it's brown. That means he was alive when he received the wound. The other wounds have produced tattooing, but it's yellow—and that means they were inflicted postmortem. That's a simplification, but it's the case. There are six wounds in all."

"Six?" said Lloyd.

"Six. The other five are to the body."

"We've only found five cartridges. Could he have been killed somewhere else, dumped in the underpass, shot again to make it look as though he'd been killed there?"

"It's possible," said Freddie. "If he was moved very soon after death. Time of death is definitely around the nine o'clock mark."

Judy saw him go into the underpass at a minute to nine. So . . . perhaps he had walked along to the other end, emerged, found someone waiting for him with a gun. "The lab says that there was blood on the phone before the emergency call was made," said Lloyd.

The forensic lab would be working all weekend; people in high places wanted Drummond's murderer found, and quickly, in view of the speculation and rumour surrounding the whole business, and the national press coverage.

Lloyd thought about what Freddie had said. "I suppose he could have been shot in the park, tried to get help, staggered into—"

"No, he couldn't," said Freddie. "Colin Drummond was no longer with us the moment that bullet hit him. If there was blood on the phone when the call was made, it wasn't made by Colin Drummond. Unless it's someone else's blood, of course," he added. "And he made it before he was shot."

They would check that. It might be Ginny's. If he was beating her up, and she pulled out a gun, held it to his head . . . he could have used a bloody hand to key 999 in the hope that help would arrive before she pulled the trigger. So—what had Drummond been doing immediately prior to his being shot? "Are there any other marks on his body?" Lloyd asked.

Freddie looked up. "You mean consistent with his having raped and murdered someone two nights previously?" He shook his head. "I haven't found any foreign hairs, scratches, anything like that."

"No, I meant more recent marks. Fists? Had he been hitting anyone?"

"Not in such a way as to damage his hands," said Freddie.

But he wouldn't damage his hands. You wouldn't have to punch someone like Ginny too often in order to render her semiconscious.

"It seems Mr. Drummond is unwilling to leave us clues even to his own murder," said Freddie.

Lloyd took his leave, and went back to the station, where they now had a full printout of the calls made on Drummond's phone right up to the 999 call. Judy's number, several times. Stansfield police station, twice. The Ferrari, several times. Bobbie Chalmers's home number, once. The last call to Stansfield police station had been immediately before the 999. Had he been trying to talk to Judy again? He rang the switchboard, but no personal call had been received then. Anyone calling had probably gone on to the queuing system, the girl said. The line would have been busy. He put down the phone and saw Tom eagerly coming towards him along the corridor.

"Guv," he said. "You might have been right."

"I'm always right," said Lloyd.

"Oh, yes. I forgot."

Lloyd smiled. "What was I right about this time?"

"The cartridges? We got a print from one of them."

"Someone we know, I presume."

"Bobbie Chalmers." He grinned. "Was it just an inspired guess?" he asked.

"A guess," said Lloyd. "Hardly inspired. Think back to why we've got her prints, Tom. *And* Drummond raped her. And then he murdered Marilyn. I can think of no other single person with more motive." He stood up. "Let's go and talk to her," he said.

They hit the interminable wait for the bypass traffic. "There should be a roundabout or lights or something here," he complained. "How are people expected to make this journey every day, if they have to sit here like lemons for ten minutes?"

"I'm getting used to it," said Tom. "I sort of think of it as a ten-minute break. I'm thinking of bringing a flask and sandwiches in future."

Lloyd always seemed to be surrounded by philosophical people who took life as it came, and didn't get hot under the collar about things they could do nothing about. He hated it. He wanted them to get angry, like he did.

Bobbie looked pale and hurt, but Lloyd recognized the determined look, the touch of steel that was in her makeup, from last time round, as they sat round a table in the lounge bar. Her attire was more conservative than usual; the landlady had lent her clothes, because she couldn't face the flat. Nicely dressed, respectable-looking. It wasn't Judy who had been seen at all, thought Lloyd. His instant theory was coming good.

"Can you tell us where you were at nine o'clock last night?" he asked.

"Here. I was serving behind the bar."

Lloyd glanced at Tom. "All evening?" he asked her.

"Six in the evening until two in the morning."

"When do you have breaks?"

"I have fifteen minutes from eight until eight-fifteen, and an hour at ten o'clock. Then I work straight through. I was here at nine—you can ask any of the regulars."

"Do you own a semiautomatic pistol?" asked Tom.

"No."

"Your fingerprints were found on the cartridges ejected by the gun that was used to murder Colin Drummond," said Lloyd.

The tiniest of reactions. Barely noticeable.

"Do you have an explanation for that?" asked Tom.

Her auburn hair made her face look even paler, Lloyd thought. He thought he probably preferred her as a blonde.

"After—" She paused, as her composure left her for an instant, then started again. "After I was raped," she said, in her first acknowledgement of it in Lloyd's hearing, "I was given a pistol for protection. And about . . . two months ago, I met someone who—who knows nothing about my past. I want to break away from it, I want to make a fresh start. Part of that was giving the gun away."

"Who to?" asked Tom.

She looked at him, and shook her head, almost smiling. "I can't remember," she said.

"We could continue this at the station," said Tom.

They could, thought Lloyd. And this would be precisely what they would be continuing. Bobbie sitting there, unbending, Tom going red in the face with frustration. He smiled when he remembered that sometimes he was more philosophical than Tom. He rather liked a challenge—and Bobbie was just that. And he had got what he wanted from her once before with subterfuge; he wondered if he could do it again. Same trick, he decided. Magicians said that if a trick worked once it would again.

"I take it you are unable to corroborate her story," he said.

She frowned. "Whose story?"

Lloyd turned to Tom. "What's that little prostitute's name?" he asked. "The one Judy found beaten up in the underpass?"

"Ginny?" Bobbie asked, concerned. "Is she all right?"

Lloyd turned back to her. "No," he said. "She's not. She's had to have stitches in her forehead. She took several hard blows to the head—she's got two black eyes and severe bruising to the mouth and face— She's lucky her cheekbone wasn't broken."

"I knew he'd go after her! I heard them in here—they said she'd helped get him caught."

"Who?"

"Drummond, of course!"

"No—who did you hear?"

"Policemen. Just before his trial. They used to drink in here in those days."

"What did they say?"

"They were lucky they'd had Ginny in custody. If it hadn't been for her, they'd never have caught him—that sort of thing. And then at his trial, he said they'd set him up with her. I told her to be careful! I knew he'd go after her."

"When did you give her the gun?"

"The day those idiots let him go!" She looked at him, then her eyes darkened slightly as she realized what she had said. She gave a little rueful laugh. "You did that to me once before," she said, and shook her head at her own gullibility. "Ginny didn't tell you I gave her the gun, did she?"

"I didn't say she had," said Lloyd.

"No," she said.

"Do I take it that you are now going to tell the complaints investigation people the truth about what happened to you that night?" asked Lloyd.

She nodded. "I didn't want to get Inspector Hill into trouble," she said. "But after what he did to Marilyn—" Her hand went to her mouth, and she fought back tears. "I was frightened," she said angrily. "And if Ginny did kill him, then I think everyone should just be grateful to her!"

Back to Stansfield, to the station, and to lunch at the canteen, where he found Judy, unusually enough, and joined her. "Taken up eating?" he said.

"It's better than dying of boredom," she said. "I'm doing follow-up visits and preparing cases for the CPS."

"My first theory's bitten the dust," he said, as he started to eat his lunch. "Bobbie Chalmers was in full view of about fifty witnesses at the time of Drummond's demise. But," he added conversationally, "it seems that Ginny did have a gun."

"Ginny did? How?"

"Bobbie Chalmers gave her it, in case Drummond went after her. She thinks he did, and so do I. It was self-defence."

"He was shot in the back of the head," said Judy. "And I heard running feet. Did he run the entire length of the underpass before dying?"

Lloyd grinned. "No," he said. "According to Freddie, he did nothing whatever but die. Instantly. With the first shot."

"Shame."

"Judy!" said Lloyd, shocked.

"Sorry," she said. "But I wouldn't object to his having endured a little pain before he finally succumbed."

"Well, he didn't." He wished she wouldn't say things like that. "But *she* could have run the entire length of it before collapsing," he pointed out.

"So who did I hear? Anyway, whatever happened to Ginny happened in her own house, and Lennie knew all about it," she said. "Besides which, Ginny didn't set him up, so why would he be after her?"

Lloyd accepted that his second theory left a little to be desired, but she hadn't finished demolishing it. "And someone rang him saying they had information on Rosa," she said.

"Ginny knew Rosa," said Lloyd.

"Anyone who was at that trial knows that Drummond wanted to find Rosa—you don't actually have to *have* information to lure someone with the promise of it."

"All right," Lloyd said, smiling. "You can work on another little puzzle in your spare time. Why shoot someone during a firework display, and then broadcast the fact over the phone? For all the murderer knew there could have been a police car a hundred yards away. In the meantime—will you come and have your birthday dinner with me tonight?"

She looked a little guilty. "Yes," she said.

"Good." Lloyd saw Case advance across the floor with food. No. No, he wasn't coming this way, he mustn't. He hadn't had Judy to himself for days. He *was* coming this way. "Talk about anything but work," he muttered.

"You've not been watching *Time-Served* by any chance?" she said, instantly.

"Mind if I join you?"

"Not at all, sir," she said, smiling pleasantly.

"Yes, I have," Lloyd said, grateful as ever for her quick-wittedness. Tom didn't have that, though he did have other qualities. "It's pretty good, isn't it?" he went on, as Case sat down. Judy, he was sure, wouldn't have seen a moment of it; she had picked it because she knew he watched it.

"Only I missed this week's episode," she said, moving her own stuff over as Case arranged his various dishes on the table.

"Did you?" said Lloyd. "I'll take that, sir." He took the tray that Case was holding aloft as he looked round for somewhere to put it, and handed it to a passing canteen assistant with a winning smile. "That's a shame."

"I wondered if you'd recorded it," said Judy.

"What's that then?" said Case.

"A serial on BBC Two," said Lloyd. "Called *Time-Served*. Have you been watching it, sir?"

"No." He addressed himself to his meal.

"Sorry," Lloyd said to Judy. "I watched it when it was on—I can tell you, though, bring you up to date." He switched to what Judy called his literary Welsh, the accent he used to quote poetry, at her request, in circumstances rather more intimate than the ones they now enjoyed. It turned her on. He had the pleasure of watching her go a little pink as he began, and she realized what he was up to.

He enjoyed himself enormously. He was telling a story, which he loved to do, shutting Case right out, and sharing a very private moment with Judy all at the same time. He finished at precisely the same time as her lunch hour.

"Thanks," she said, getting up, smiling at him. "That was nearly as good as the real thing."

Touché, he thought, as he felt his own face flush slightly.

"If you'll excuse me," Judy said, and left.

Case pushed his plate away. "My office," he said.

Lloyd could think of few ways of spending his lunch hour that he would like less; like a sulky schoolboy, he walked one pace behind his boss all the way back, all the way up, and closed the door of Case's office when instructed, with an ill grace.

"Playing footsie with her in the canteen isn't a very smart move," Case said, sitting down, not inviting Lloyd to do the same.

"So you keep saying," said Lloyd. "How you can look at Judy and still believe all these ridiculous imaginings is beyond me."

"What's beyond you is seeing *past* how she looks. I'm not talking about someone who takes bribes and deals cocaine and has a villa on the Costa del Crime, Lloyd. I'm talking about cop turned crusader. More acceptable and more dangerous. Because you can't see them coming, you can't pick them out in a crowd. They do look like her. They are honest, and principled. But their principles get twisted, and their honesty is compromised."

Lloyd looked at him, frowning a little. "You rehearsed that," he said.

"Yes, I did. Because I realize that I offended you last night. If you've known her that long, then obviously it wasn't quite the way I saw it. But I still think you should back off while you can."

"I know why I'm so certain you're wrong," said Lloyd. "Why are you so certain you're right?"

"I hear things."

"On jungle drums? By holding a glass to the wall?"

Case smiled. "Perhaps the methods are a little primitive, but they work. I've got a mole."

"In the investigation team?"

"No. In the Mafia."

Lloyd's eyebrows shot up. "And they're saying Judy was involved?"

"No," said Case. "But they are saying that Drummond was fitted up—not just for the last one. For all of them."

"How can you rig a DNA test?"

"I don't know. But at the time, they believed that Drummond had raped these women, that they were just . . . speeding things up. Now, it seems, another candidate is emerging."

"One of their number?"

"I think he must be. I told you what I thought last night."

"Last night, you thought Bobbie Chalmers had never been raped at all," Lloyd reminded him.

"Yes, I accept that. I was wrong. But she has no more idea of who raped her than any of the others had."

"And who is this second candidate?"

"I don't know, and neither does my mole. They don't actually hold monthly meetings. He hears things, and he tells me. And if what he's hearing turns out to be the case, and Drummond did not carry out the rapes, then even you must come to the inescapable conclusion that he could not have given Inspector Hill that statement."

"If," said Lloyd. "You haven't met our pathologist, have you?"

"No," said Case, puzzled. "Not yet."

"He says that theories always come to grief," said Lloyd. "It's a good thing to bear in mind. Your one about Bobbie did, and so did mine. And your one about Judy will. You can depend upon it."

"Come!" shouted Case, as someone knocked on the door, only just getting the word out as the door opened. Lloyd didn't need to turn round.

"Excuse me, sir," said Tom. "Guv—we've checked Lennie Frederick's Transit, and we found blood. There had been an attempt to clean it up, but he'd missed a bit."

"You're sure it's blood?" asked Case.

"Lennie confirmed that it was blood, but refused to say how it had got there, sir. We've got forensic picking up the van. Lennie wasn't inclined to come voluntarily, so I arrested him on suspicion. He's being processed, and Ginny's in the interview room."

Lloyd frowned. "Ginny's here? Is she well enough?"

"No, I don't think so. I said we'd get a neighbour in to stay with her, but she wouldn't let us. She was coming with Lennie, she said. I couldn't really leave her there on her own—she can hardly walk. So she's here. And we do have to question her, guv. She's the one who was given the gun, and she's the one who got beaten up."

Lloyd turned to Case. "Do you want to be in on the interviews, sir?" he asked.

"Not yet," said Case. "If and when they get interesting."

Back downstairs, Lloyd took one look at Ginny, and closed the door of the interview room again. "Has the FME seen her?" he asked Tom.

"No, boss," he said. "Like I said, she's not under arrest—"

"Then get her! I want to know that she's fit to be interviewed— she doesn't look fit to be out of bed!"

Tom shot off to phone the FME. Lloyd sighed. He wasn't angry with Tom. He was angry with whoever had done that to Ginny Fredericks. He was angry with Case for listening to what a band of disillusioned, about-to-be-disgraced, and quite disgraceful police officers were saying, and presuming to judge Judy by it.

He wasn't going to interview Fredericks until he'd calmed down. If he did that to that little girl— Words failed him, even in his head. But . . . perhaps he didn't. He went through the CID room, and knocked on Judy's door, going in to find her filling in forms, and told her what Tom had found.

"New theory," he said. "Lennie Fredericks, who has told you that he knows nothing more about Rosa than her name, realizes once you've spoken to him that she is currency. He rings Drummond, says he has information."

Judy nodded, happy with that.

"But Drummond arrives at the Fredericks residence before the due time, and gets Ginny on her own—tries to beat information out of her that she perhaps doesn't even have. Lennie comes in and finds Drummond beating her up. He gets the gun and shoots him. In the back of the head." He looked at her, waiting for objections.

"Go on."

"Go on" meant that his theory was flawed, but had possibilities; Lloyd felt that he might be getting warmer. "They then transport him in the van to the far side of the underpass and dump him in there, shooting him again, several times, to make it look as though it had happened there. Hence, six bullet wounds, five cartridges at scene."

"Yes," she said.

"They then put distance between themselves and Drummond by running back along the underpass, towards home, abandoning the Transit until a later time. That way they could say it had been stolen, or whatever, if the need arose. They were leaving the underpass, heading for home, when they heard you coming, turned and ran in the opposite direction. Lennie made it, which accounts for the running feet, but Ginny was too badly injured, and collapsed, so you found her."

She nodded again, looking thoughtful.

"Meanwhile, Lennie, knowing that Ginny has collapsed, tries to get help for her by using Drummond's mobile phone. His own is out of order, remember? He dials 999, then heads back home in the Transit. Not hearing anything about Ginny, he is about to go to the hospital to make sure she got there, when you arrive with her. There are bloodstains in his van, so he closes the door before you can see in."

"Nice," said Judy. "Neat. Except that I saw Drummond go down there under his own steam."

"You saw someone in dark clothes and a crash helmet," said Lloyd.

"Who had just got off Drummond's bike," said Judy. "And who took his crash helmet off."

"He was a long way away by then. You were seeing him through heat haze and smoke from the bonfire. Perhaps you were mistaken."

"And perhaps it was his twin brother," said Judy. "But it makes more sense than your last one."

The FME said that if Ginny had no objection, then she could be interviewed. Lloyd sent her with a WPC, whom he tried to remember not to call WPCs, to have some lunch in the canteen first, and prepared to interview her husband.

*

Carole watched the news again. The underpass, the enormous bonfire, still smouldering even when the camera crews got there. The firemen, damping it down, the policemen looking through its ashes for the weapon, in case it had been thrown onto the fire.

Somehow it seemed more real, now that it had been sanctioned by the TV news. It was so neat. Edited, marshalled, explained in short sentences. Not a bit like life. But it made Drummond seem much more dead.

There was no emotion, as she watched Detective Chief Superintendent Case say that they were keeping an open mind as to the motive behind the murder; no elation, no relief, even. Colin Drummond was dead, and it was just another anxiety.

◊

Ginny was here somewhere; Lennie was worried about her. She wasn't well enough to be here.

"No comment," he said, to the question of why there was blood in his van.

"Drummond raped your wife, didn't he?" said Sergeant Finch.

"She wasn't my wife then," said Lennie. "I didn't even know her. Maybe if I had, I'd have wanted to kill him, but—" He shrugged. "I didn't," he said. "I didn't want to, and I didn't kill him. Is she all right?" he asked.

"As well as can be expected," said Finch.

She shouldn't be here. But give Finch his due, he hadn't meant for her to come; Ginny could sometimes just put her foot down. Even with him.

"Did he come after her again? Did *she* kill him?"

"I don't know who killed him."

"But your wife had a gun, hadn't she, Lennie?"

"I don't know," said Lennie.

"Someone gave her a gun. Last Friday."

"Did they?"

"Did she kill Drummond?"

"No."

"You just said you didn't know who'd killed him."

"I know she didn't."

"How?"

Lennie sighed. "No comment," he said.

He had gone back in to her this morning after Rob had gone, and had had to plead with her to let him cut the sweater off. He couldn't bear looking at it, and it had to have been uncomfortable. He'd promised to get her another one, just like it. Tears came into his eyes again, and he knocked them away.

"Something bothering you, Lennie?"

He didn't speak. The GP had come to see her then, once she had proper clothes on, thank God, or Lennie didn't know what the man would have thought of him. As it was he didn't think much.

"She should be in bed, Mr. Fredericks," he'd said. "It isn't just the injuries, you know, but the physical shock of having received such a beating." He was Asian, spoke very quickly and quietly. He blamed Lennie for letting her work as a prostitute. "She should be resting, quiet."

"She won't stay in bed," Lennie had said.

If the doctor was so bloody clever, he could come here and make her go home and go to bed, because neither he nor the police could.

Chief Inspector Lloyd wasn't saying much; even less than he was. He had just sat there, until now. Now he was walking round the room, reading the notices as though they hadn't been up there for months. And now, he spoke. "Where were you when that happened to Ginny?" he asked.

"I drive a cab. I was taking it back to the guy who does the night driving. Rob Jarvis."

"And while you were out someone came in and gave her that beating? How did that make you feel, Lennie?"

"How do you th—?" Lloyd turned as Lennie spoke, eyebrows raised, and Lennie realized what he had done. "That isn't what happened," he said. "Ginny was with a punter in the underpass."

"No comment," he said, to every question after that.

They left him after they'd had enough.

◊

Matt had lunch, packed a bag with stuff already folded, ready for the journey. He checked the house like he checked the bank. Doors, internal doors, windows. Gases. Lights. He checked his pockets. Wallet, travel documents, passport, maps, paper, pen, phrase book.

He threw the bag in the boot, got in, and drove off.

◊

"Virginia Fredericks," she said, when invited to do so for the tape. She was angry. Angry because they'd come in and said they wanted to look in Lennie's van and then they'd said there was blood in it and he had to go with them and it was her fault. It was all her fault. Why should Lennie get the blame?

"Now," said Chief Inspector Lloyd, "if at any time, you feel that you need to rest or to stop the interview altogether, you must say so. Do you understand? We won't carry on until you feel up to it."

"Yeah," she said.

"It's important that we know who did that to you," he said.

"A punter."

"What were you doing with a punter in the underpass?"

"What do you think I was bloody doing?"

"Why did he hit you?"

"He just turned nasty."

"For what reason?"

"They don't need a fucking reason!"

He smiled. "You know," he said, "Inspector Hill tells me that you went through almost a whole day in court without swearing once. Do you think you could pretend you're in court now?"

"Why should I?"

"Well," he said, "it's quicker, if you don't. Takes up less space on the tape. Saves money. Puts more bobbies on the beat. Prevents more crime. Brings down insurance premiums, brings down how much it costs to store things, therefore how much it costs to sell them, therefore how much it costs to buy them. Everyone would have more money. Just think," he said. "If this was a long enough interview, you could make Britain great again."

She smiled, despite herself.

"Now," he said. "Bobbie Chalmers gave you a gun, didn't she? Last Friday?"

"Yes." Lennie hadn't said she shouldn't tell them about that.

They asked who else knew she had the gun. Not Lennie, she said quickly. He thought she'd taken it back when he'd told her to. Rob Jarvis knew about it, she said, and she told them she had shown him it on Wednesday morning.

"Why?"

"He said Drummond might come after me, and I said I'd got protection. Showed him the gun when he didn't believe me. He told me how to use it."

"And where's the gun now?"

She shrugged. "I dunno," she said.

"Where did you keep it?"

"In a drawer in the room where I take the clients."

"Was that where you were assaulted?"

"I wasn't assaulted," she said, shaking her head. "Just beaten up."

"Oh, right." He smiled. "But it happened in the house, didn't it?"

"No."

"I think you or Lennie got the gun to stop it happening."

"No. It had gone by then anyway." She said she thought Rob had taken it.

Lennie had told her that he'd packed in driving his taxi, that she didn't have to do him in the mornings anymore. That was good, but she'd said how that meant that neither of them would be bringing in money for a while, not until her face mended. He'd said he'd think of something.

Chief Inspector Lloyd asked when she had last seen the gun, and she told him Thursday lunchtime. When did she know it was missing? Yesterday afternoon.

"So what makes you think Rob Jarvis took it?" asked Sergeant Finch. He was cute. He'd got curls, like a little boy.

"He was there yesterday morning," she said.

"Was he alone in the room at all?" asked Lloyd.

"Yeah. Just for a minute. He goes straight upstairs when he comes in."

"So he saw it on Wednesday morning, was alone in the room yesterday morning, and you noticed it was gone yesterday afternoon—is that right?"

"Yeah," she said, feeling her eye and her cheek beginning to throb at the same time as one another. She felt a bit sick.

"I think you could do with a rest," said Lloyd. "I'll send you in some tea and biscuits. Or would you rather have a glass of water?"

"Water," she said. "Can I take my painkillers?"

"Of course. Someone will take you home, if you want."

She shook her head. She didn't want to be there without Lennie.

"I think you should have a rest in our sick bay," said Lloyd. "We call it that—it's a tiny room with the same kind of bed as you get in the cells, but fewer people have thrown up on it."

Lloyd was quite nice really, like Inspector Hill. But the one with the curls was cute. Sergeant Finch. When Chief Inspector Lloyd put off the tape, she told him that. The Chief Inspector laughed, and Sergeant Finch went all red, right up to the roots of his curly hair.

Chapter Twelve

Carole heard Rob moving about upstairs, and she went up to him. She just wanted to talk, to tell him what she'd done. She had to tell him.

He was just putting on his dressing gown; he pulled it round his naked body when she came in, turned away, looking out of the window. She watched as he tied the belt. He was embarrassed because she had caught him without his clothes on.

The knocking on the door made them both jump. It was probably someone selling double-glazing or religion, and she wanted to talk to Rob.

An even louder knock, then the doorbell. "Police, Mr. Jarvis! Can you open the door, please?"

He walked past her, out of the room. She didn't go downstairs with him.

❡

Jarvis was in; the cab was there, and anyway, Lloyd had seen him at the bedroom window when he had pulled up. He was about to call through the letterbox again when he saw the figure through the fluted glass.

"DCI Lloyd, Stansfield CID, Mr. Jarvis," he said. "May I come in?"

"Yes," said Jarvis. "Is this about the girl that was murdered? I told DC Marshall—I didn't see anything. I haven't remembered anything that might help you."

"It's not exactly about that," said Lloyd. "Though we haven't ruled out a connection. It's about Colin Drummond."

"Oh," said Rob. "I do hope you don't expect me to be over-whelmed with grief."

"No, sir," said Lloyd. "But we have traced the gun used in his killing to a prostitute called Ginny Fredericks—I believe you know her?"

Jarvis nodded.

"She says you saw this gun, sir. On Wednesday morning—is that true?"

"Yes. She had it for protection from Drummond. I showed her how to use it. And if she used it to blow away that little shit, she deserves a medal." He walked to the window, looked out as he spoke.

"She says she thinks you must have taken it," said Lloyd. "That it went missing some time between Thursday lunchtime and yesterday afternoon, and that you were in the room alone for a few minutes yesterday morning."

Jarvis shook his head. "I didn't take it," he said.

"Would you say Mrs. Fredericks was a quick learner, sir?" asked Lloyd.

"What?"

"You show her how to use a gun on Wednesday, and by Friday she is carrying out an efficient instant killing. You served in Northern Ireland, I believe?"

Jarvis turned. "What's that got to do with it?" he asked.

"The style of the killing," Lloyd said. "It reminded me of a ter-rorist execution."

"Everyone's seen that a dozen times in films and documentaries,"

Jarvis said. "Even Ginny. Otherwise, how do *you* know what a terrorist execution looks like? Come to that," he went on, "I've only seen it that way."

Yes, all right, thought Lloyd. If I want my theories demolished, I've got an expert. I don't need amateurs horning in. "You were in your cab opposite Marilyn Taylor's flat on Wednesday night," he said. "You told DC Marshall that you had seen nothing, but I find that hard to believe, Mr. Jarvis, because someone left that block of flats at about quarter to eleven, and according to you, you were still across the road."

"I must have been looking the other way," said Jarvis. He went to the sideboard, took out a glass. He hadn't looked at Lloyd once.

"I don't think you were," Lloyd said. "I think you saw Drummond leave that block of flats, and I think you followed him, right into Stansfield. I think you saw him put something on the bonfire at the boating lake, and you went to check what it was. Someone saw a man by the bonfire, shouted at him, and watched him leave in a taxi, Mr. Jarvis. It was you, wasn't it?"

Jarvis gave a brief nod.

"Why didn't you tell the police what you'd found?"

"I just found a bag of clothes—it's not against the law to put things on bonfires. I didn't know he'd raped anyone, not then." He poured himself a whisky, and splashed soda into it.

"But you still didn't tell the police once you did know," said Lloyd.

"I just didn't think it would do my wife any good if we got involved with Drummond again," he said. "I'm sorry. I should have told your constable, but I just didn't need that sort of hassle."

"I think it might have been because you wanted him all to yourself," said Lloyd.

Jarvis frowned, shook his head. "Sorry," he said. "I don't know what you mean."

"You didn't want him arrested and tried—you wanted to kill him."

"Yes," said Jarvis, setting his drink down again, and looking straight at Lloyd for the first time. "Oh, yes, Chief Inspector, I wanted to kill him. I wanted to kill him the moment I saw my wife lying in hospital, and I've wanted to kill him ever since. Every time I see my wife take a bus, because she can't bring herself to use the car that's sitting in the garage. Every time I go up Lennie Fredericks's stairs and wait for his wife, every time I think what my life, my marriage was like before I had to do that. What *I* was like before. So yes, you're right. I wanted to kill him. But I didn't."

"In that case, perhaps you can tell me where you were at nine o'clock last night?"

"I don't know exactly. On the rank, cruising, taking a fare somewhere—working. I don't know exactly where I was at a particular time unless I have a booking. And I wasn't the only one who had access to that gun—Ginny does have other clients."

"You're the only one to whom she showed it, according to her," said Lloyd. "And her husband didn't know she still had it."

"Oh, yes, he did," said Jarvis. "Because I told him she still had it— why do you think he gave her that beating?"

Lloyd didn't think Lennie *had* given her the beating. But, like Judy said, who else would Ginny be protecting? "When did you tell him?" he asked.

"At about twenty past eight last night." Jarvis picked up his drink. "So if he says he knew nothing about it, he's lying, Chief Inspector. And you'd be better employed asking him these questions."

◊

Matt had hit the M25 at its worst possible time. Lorries, vans, and cars sat nose to tail, inching along for seconds at a time only to stop again. He looked anxiously at his watch. Four o'clock. He had thought he had left plenty of time, but if he couldn't move faster than this, he'd have to hang about in Dover, and that was the last thing he needed.

Ten minutes—ten *minutes* later, the traffic moved. Ten yards.

◊

She'd told them about the gun. So perhaps he could stop denying its existence, said Finch, and tell them when he last saw it. Lennie sighed, admitting the logic of that.

"On Friday, when she was given it."

"Which Friday?"

"Last Friday. A week ago yesterday. I told her to take it back where it came from."

"Why did you do that?"

Lennie shook his head. "I don't like guns," he said. "And I don't trust people who give them away. So I told her to take it back. And I thought she had until now. If she says she didn't . . ." He shrugged.

"So where do you think it is now?"

"How should I know?"

𝄑

"ABC Cabs were booked to take Mr. and Mrs. Gloucester to Stansfield railway station at ten past six on Wednesday the third of November," said Marshall, appearing in Judy's open doorway.

"I knew it," said Judy.

"Only thing is," said Marshall, in his unhurried, measured tones, "that wouldn't be Lennie's shout. He only gets the cab from nine o'clock in the morning."

Admittedly, Judy really couldn't see Lennie working at six o'clock in the morning, even if there was a possibility of ill-gotten gains as a result. Lennie was too indolent to put himself out to that extent.

"And if we're right," Marshall went on, "then the driver would have to get them talking, find out how long they were away for, and if the house was going to be empty, that sort of thing."

Judy smiled. "You think I've been looking at the wrong driver," she said. "Don't you?"

"I think it would be worth my giving Jarvis another visit," he said. "I mean—it's a weird setup, isn't it? Him choosing to drive at night?"

She agreed, and Marshall had been gone about five minutes when Lloyd came in, airing his latest theory. He, it transpired, had also just been to see Rob Jarvis, which visit had spawned theory number four.

"It was an IRA-type execution," he said. "Ginny says Jarvis had every opportunity to take the gun. God knows, he had reason to want to kill Drummond—he said so himself. He suddenly can't remember where he was at nine o'clock last night. He knows how to use a pistol. What reason could he possibly have for keeping quiet about seeing

Drummond dump those clothes, other than that he intended getting his own revenge on Drummond?"

"Well ..." said Judy. "We'll probably find that out when the owners come back from holiday."

"What?"

"Chances are he was burgling a house at the time," she said.

"You think *he's* the burglar?"

"Marshall does. I think he's right." She smiled sympathetically. "Sorry to dent another theory," she said.

Lloyd frowned. "That doesn't mean he didn't murder Drummond," he said.

"It does," said Judy. "The burglary happened at the same time—remember?"

Lloyd's face fell. The knock on her door was followed by Sandwell, who apologized for the interruption, explaining that the phone wasn't connected to the incident room yet. He wanted Lloyd to look at what he called "the publicity material" for the rape enquiry, amongst other things. As though poor Mrs. Ashman was some sort of pop star being promoted.

Lloyd went back out through the CID room, and detailed Tom to speak to Ginny. "Find out who else has been in that house who could have had access to the gun," he told him. "DC Marshall seems to have stolen Jarvis from us. And Lennie knew about the gun—Jarvis told him Ginny still had it. Check that out."

Her phone rang, and Judy was summoned to the presence; she went upstairs, knocked, and entered on the command, and then stood for some moments while Case marked things off in his apparently endless files, her back straight, her feet together, hands clasped loosely behind her back, at ease. Technically.

He looked up at her eventually. "How is your investigation of the burglaries going?" he asked.

"DC Marshall has gone to interview Jarvis," she said. "I expect he'll be making an arrest."

"Quick work, Inspector."

"Marshall did most of it, sir. I can't take the credit."

He nodded. "Chalmers has retracted her statement to the complaints investigation, and has admitted that she was raped that night," he said. "She has given the hospital permission to release her medical record as confirmation. You are no longer under investigation."

"Thank you, sir," said Judy, and took a deep breath. "And in that case I must tell you that Constable Burbidge had absented himself from duty and was not in the car with Constable Turner at the time of Bobbie Chalmers's rape." She paused, trying to gauge his reaction, but she couldn't. So she went on. "And a roll of adhesive bandage which should have been in the first-aid kit was discovered some time later to be missing. It was replaced the following morning. When asked to account for his absence from duty, Burbidge said that he was attempting to sort out a domestic crisis."

She was used to Lloyd, the volatile Lloyd, who would go off like a drop of nitroglycerine hitting the floor, or go quiet and be sarcastic and cutting, like acid spreading over it. Case did neither of these things.

"I presume you checked out this alibi?" he said.

"No, sir. The whereabouts of his wife and children are unknown to him, and my attempts to trace them have so far failed."

"You have made the attempt, then? I suppose that's something. When were you given this information, Inspector?"

"During my interviews with both Turner and Burbidge on Thursday the fourth of November," she said. "I was also told, and have since confirmed, that Burbidge had been working undercover at the farm where Lucy Rogerson was later raped."

Case flicked his pen backwards and forwards between his fingers, the only indication that he was a very angry man. But Judy knew one when she saw one, despite his still calm delivery. "And you withheld this information?" he said.

"I didn't consider it relevant, sir."

The pen stopped, and he pulled it into his fist. "This I must hear," he said. "Why didn't you consider it relevant?"

"I was interviewing Matt Burbidge because he had been seen in the vicinity of the flat where Marilyn Taylor was raped and murdered," she said. "I checked his alibi, which was confirmed, and I had no reason to doubt it. The rest did not seem to me to be relevant to my enquiries." She had been rehearsing this ever since Lloyd had made her realize that Bobbie would admit the rape now that Drummond was dead.

"Finch was with you, wasn't he?" he said. "Did he also regard the rest as irrelevant?"

"Sergeant Finch asked Burbidge to accompany us to the station to answer further questions. When he refused, Sergeant Finch was of the opinion that we should arrest him. I overruled him. It is entirely my responsibility."

"Too damn right, it's your responsibility," said Case. "You ignored vital evidence pointing to him as a suspect in the Chalmers rape. The man had no alibi, and refused to cooperate. It was your duty to arrest him, Inspector."

"On what grounds, sir? Bobbie Chalmers had stated quite categorically to me and my senior officer that she had never *been* raped. I had no reason to think that she would alter her stance. Therefore I had no grounds for arresting him, and I instructed my sergeant accordingly."

Case's eyes widened slightly.

"Now that I have learned that Bobbie has made an official complaint of rape, I have passed on the relevant information," Judy continued. "The lack of an alibi *is* only relevant once there's a crime to go with it. I don't believe that I've done anything wrong, sir."

The pen made a dull clicking noise as it was tapped against Case's bottom teeth, and he looked out of the window. The tapping stopped; he swung his chair round and looked up at her again. "Very clever, Inspector," he said. "Very clever. And I suppose you've got an answer for not passing on the information about the Rogerson girl?"

"Burbidge's connection with Lucy Rogerson has become relevant as we now have a live complaint of rape to investigate. Since it is similar in every detail to the other rapes committed at that time, presumably the reopened inquiry is no longer merely window dressing."

"Oh, no, you don't!" He threw the pen down. "You're not dragging me into this, Inspector."

"Into what, sir?"

"Oh, for God's sake, sit down, woman! And stop talking like a bloody computer!"

Judy sat down, taking out her cigarettes. "Do you mind?" she asked, lighting one without waiting for an answer, wishing her hand wasn't shaking. She wasn't used to sticking her neck out like this. She wasn't used to sailing quite so close to the wind. She needed a cigarette.

"Why are you shopping him now?" Case asked.

"I'm not shop—"

"You must think you can't keep the lid on this any longer," he said, talking through her. "That this way you can get out from under."

"I'm not shopping anyone!" Judy said angrily. "I don't have to get out from under anything!"

Case shook his head. "You're working to your own agenda, Inspector," he said. "Credit me with some intelligence."

Judy acknowledged the grain of truth in that with a slight nod. "I stretched the rules," she said. "Because Matt Burbidge didn't rape these women. Drummond did. I hoped I might be able to keep Matt out of it. But I can't, not now that Bobbie's admitted that she was raped."

Case reached over and took one of Judy's cigarettes out of the packet. "Give me your lighter," he said.

Judy watched him draw in smoke and release it in a calming blue stream.

"I ought to be reporting this entire conversation to the DCC," he said.

"Why aren't you?"

"Because I think you would win, like you did with Drummond's complaint about you. But I believe now more than ever that Drummond was fitted up for these rapes, and that his statement to you was a fake."

"Sir—" Judy began, but he held up a hand.

"Don't say anything, Inspector," he said. "When I get you, it's going to be on something you *can't* talk your way out of. You can go."

It was useless. He had her down as a double-dyed villain, and nothing was going to change his mind unless she could prove that Drummond was the rapist. She got up, picked up her cigarettes and lighter, then put them down again, and left his office. If she'd started the man smoking again, she could at least leave him the requisites. He was on the phone, demanding to know Lloyd's whereabouts, before she had closed the door.

၇

Carole had come downstairs once Lloyd had left, but whatever she had been going to tell him, she had obviously changed her mind. Rob drank his whisky and poured himself another.

"Don't drink too much," Carole said, as the doorbell rang again. "You don't want to get Breathalysed."

Right now, he wasn't sure he cared.

Carole got up to answer the door, and came in with DC Marshall in tow.

"I've already had a visit from your Chief Inspector," said Rob. "I've told him everything I know—including the bits I didn't tell you."

"Is that right, sir? That's very interesting, but . . . it's not why I'm here."

"Oh?" said Rob, feeling the adrenaline rising. "Why are you here?"

"I understand you took a Mr. and Mrs. Gloucester to Stansfield railway station at . . ."

Rob was barely listening. He had been waiting for this. He had thought that he would be stopped last night. Or picked up on the rank. He had thought when Lloyd came that it would be about the burglary; so had Carole. That was why she'd stayed upstairs. She hadn't wanted to see him getting arrested. But it hadn't been about the burglary. This was.

He was being asked about some of the other runs he'd done to stations and airports. He was being asked if he realized that all these people had been burgled while away on holiday, and that he was the only factor they had in common. He was being asked if Marshall might take a look round the house.

"I'd rather you didn't," he said.

Carole was looking stiff with worry.

"Do you garage your cab, Mr. Jarvis?"

"No," said Rob. "It's on the road twenty-four hours a day."

"But you do have a garage?"

Carole made a little sound; Marshall realized his faux pas. "I do beg your pardon, Mrs. Jarvis," he said. "I wasn't thinking. Might I take a look in there, Mr. Jarvis?"

Rob saw no reason to spin it out, especially in view of the effect it would have on Carole if he made Marshall go and get a search warrant. He took out his keys, and walked round with Marshall to the garage where the stuff from Tuesday night's burglary, the stuff Carole had seen when she opened the garage door, was sitting.

So Carole did see him being arrested. He told her not to worry. She would, of course.

§

"Do you feel up to answering some more questions?" asked the policewoman.

It was almost worth getting beaten senseless for all this, thought Ginny, as she stiffly got off the bed. She had been in the hands of the police more times than she could possibly count, and they had treated her like something they'd found on their shoes, mostly. Some of them were OK, like Inspector Hill. But most of them were like Lennie said.

"Yeah," she said, enjoying being the one who said what was what, for once. "All right."

Sergeant Finch was waiting for her, to take her to the interview room. They walked down a corridor, past offices with open doors. Typists, people listening to tapes with headphones on. And a big room, with a blackboard, and stuff pinned up on the walls. Chief Inspector Lloyd was in there with a tall man, and Ginny saw the poster they were pinning up of a girl standing at some sort of shop counter with a bottle of milk in her hand.

"What's she done?" she asked, as a grey-haired man pushed past them into the room.

Sergeant Finch stopped, and frowned. "Who?" he said.

"Lloyd!" the grey-haired man shouted. "A word. Now."

"Her," Ginny said, and pointed to the poster. "Rosa."

Chapter Thirteen

H e tried to maintain his old car as best he could, given his financial situation, but Matt always looked gratefully upon the emergency stopping lane as he went down the hill to the ferries at Dover. So far, the brakes had held out, and they did again today, as he drove towards the terminal, checking his watch yet again, hoping that something would delay the ferry's departure.

The white cliffs, which looked grey and a little dirty when you were close to them, towered over him as the lights of the ferries came into view, moving up and down fairly ominously on a choppy, dark sea, the P & O funnel visible. But as he arrived, he could see no lines of cars, moving or otherwise; he was halted, and had to watch helplessly as the gangway and the *Pride of Calais* parted company.

₹

Case had obviously found Ginny's revelation interesting enough to merit his presence at her interview, and to delay whatever he had been going to talk to Lloyd about.

"I'll lead," he'd told Lloyd brusquely as they had followed Ginny and Tom into the interview room, and now Ginny sat wide-eyed, unsure of why her innocent remark had caused such a stir.

"Do you recognize this woman?" asked Case.

"Yeah," she said. "It's Rosa, like I said."

"Chief Superintendent Case is showing Mrs. Fredericks a photograph of Mrs. Rachel Ashman," said Tom.

Ginny frowned at him. "It's not Mrs. Ashman," she said, shaking her head. "She got raped—she's the one who killed herself. This is Rosa."

Lloyd had the file in front of him. Rachel Olivia Selina Ashman. He had only been peripherally involved in the rape enquiry, because the first one had taken place in Stansfield. Had he been investigating, he liked to think that he would have got on to her initials. But Matt Burbidge had known her, and this photograph had been up on the wall in Malworth for almost two months during the enquiry. He couldn't *not* have seen it. Lloyd leant his elbows on the table, leaning his chin on clasped hands. He didn't like the turn things were taking.

"I don't understand," Ginny said.

Lloyd opened his mouth to explain, but Case had no time for that, and went briskly on to his next question.

"You told the court you saw her after she had been with Drummond," he said. "Did she speak to you?"

"Yeah."

Case sighed. "Well, what did she *say*, girl?"

Ginny looked at Lloyd. "He said I hadn't got to say," she said. "I don't want to get into trouble."

Lloyd frowned. "Who said?" he asked. The Malworth Mafia, he supposed. Matt Burbidge had visited Ginny; he had doubtless put pressure on her to keep quiet.

"Him in court. Drummond's lawyer. He said not to say what she said to me."

Ah. Lloyd smiled. "It's just in court that you can't say what someone has told you," he said. "You can tell us."

"Well," she said. "She came into the club going on about Lennie.

She was mad at him 'cos he'd clouted her for doing Drummond without a condom."

Lloyd closed his eyes, then opened them and looked at the little girl opposite, his mouth pressed to his hands. He could feel Case's eyes on him, could feel waves of discomfort coming from Tom, which was why he chose in these circumstances to look at Ginny, painful though it was to look at her battered face. Its expression was merely perplexed, as ever.

"She tried to get some off me, but I said no. So she said she was packing it in," said Ginny. "I thought she meant just for that night, but she never came back."

No, thought Lloyd. Because she had popped into the service station for some milk, and had been viciously raped. Her husband had said that she had been at home all night. Why? Because he knew what she had really been doing? He had had a fall from scaffolding in a building site, and he had not been employed through official channels. No tax, no insurance equalled no sick pay, no compensation. Living on the subsistence level of government handouts, he might have been prepared to let his wife do that in order to hang on to his home. But not necessarily. There was no reason to assume that he knew. They had had a small child, and he had been in no state to be left in charge of one. He could just have been covering for that, thinking that the social services might be let loose on him. His wife could have been deceiving him, too, about her evening employment, turned to in desperation, perhaps. In which case, did he need to know?

They would have to decide what to do about Mr. Ashman. But all that Lloyd had to worry about now was that Mrs. Ashman had been raped, and not necessarily by Drummond. Not anymore. And if Drummond had not raped these women, then he couldn't have given Judy that statement. Everyone knew that; no one said it.

But he *had* to have given her the statement, so it *had* to have been Drummond. And this was a coincidence? Lloyd didn't believe in coincidence. Not to this extent. He hadn't believed in any of the coincidences surrounding Drummond's arrest; he didn't believe in this one.

Nothing had been said for some time; Case seemed to be leaving the floor to him now.

"Ginny," he said. "The night Drummond was arrested for assaulting you, you had been at Malworth police station for a long time."

"Yeah."

"Did anyone speak to you while you were there?"

"No. They just put me in a cell and left me there. Then someone came and said I could go."

"Didn't that surprise you?"

"A bit."

"You weren't offered some sort of deal? Told they would let you go if you did them a favour?"

"Well, not at the *police station*," she said, in the tones of one who thought him a little simple. "In the park, they did. If you went with some of them they wouldn't nick you."

"Did PC Burbidge ever take advantage of you like that?" asked Case.

"No. He just nicked me."

It was a relief to know that they occasionally did what they were paid to do at Malworth, thought Lloyd. "I didn't really mean that," he said. "I meant did they ask you to do something else for them?"

She frowned, and then her eyes narrowed. "You mean did I set Drummond up for them!" she said, her voice rising. "Look—that sod raped me, and I'm fed up with people saying he didn't! He had a knife—he scared the shit out of me and he raped me! He fucking well *raped* me—all right?"

"You'll mind your language while you're in here," said Case.

"Aw, shut up!" said Ginny.

Lloyd smiled into his clasped hands. That's what he should have said, rather than going into a tirade against him. It was much more effective. And he saw what Judy meant about Ginny. Only real, honest-to-God resentment could produce that reaction.

"Anyway," Ginny went on. "He reckons he was only in the alley 'cos he stopped for a slash. How was anyone supposed to know he'd do that?"

Lloyd smiled openly this time. "Good point, Ginny," he said. They should have had Ginny prosecuting at Drummond's trial; she was sharper than Whitehouse, obviously.

It was Tom who remembered what he had intended asking Ginny in the first place. "Ginny," he said. "Can you tell us who was in your house, upstairs, between the time you showed Rob Jarvis the gun and the time you realised it was missing?"

"A regular Thursday lunchtime and Rob Jarvis yesterday morning."

"Who's the regular?"

"He works for the people we got the house from," she said.

"Was he alone in the room at all?"

"Yeah—when you came to the door asking which cab firm Lennie drove for."

"So—I can't think why he'd want to, but he could have taken the gun, couldn't he?"

She shook her head. "He was handcuffed to the bed," she said seriously.

Lloyd smiled happily. He thought he would like to spend his life interviewing Ginny.

"What about punters on Wednesday and Thursday evening?" asked Tom, still grinning.

"There was Matt Burbidge, and he wasn't really a punter. Lennie had me working out of the van at the park."

"Was he alone in the room?"

"No."

"Was anyone else besides you and Lennie upstairs alone, and *not* handcuffed to the bed?" Tom asked.

"Just Inspector Hill," she said. "When they were searching the house."

"Interview terminated, fifteen thirty-five hours," said Case. "Finch—take Mrs. Fredericks for a cup of tea—or something."

Tom, looking even more anxious than Ginny, shepherded her out of the room, and closed the door.

"I hope you're not going to say what I think you're going to say," said Lloyd.

"Oh, you don't know the half of it yet, Lloyd," said Case, opening the door and bellowing to a passing minion to get DC Marshall here on the double.

"As I see it," he said, taking out cigarettes, "four people had access to that gun. Lennie and Ginny Fredericks, Jarvis, and Inspector Hill. So let's start eliminating them, shall we?"

Lloyd wished Judy's name didn't keep cropping up in this enquiry. And why were they taking Ginny's word for it that the gun went missing at all?

Marshall arrived at the door, breathless, and still trying to swallow something. "You wanted me, sir?" he said to Case.

"Jarvis," Case said, lighting his cigarette. "What's happening with him?"

"He's been arrested for burglary, sir. We found the stuff from the last job in his garage, and he admitted it. He's not been processed yet, so I thought I'd grab a bite—"

"Fine," said Case. "Before you carry on with your meal, tell Finch to bring ex-Constable Matthew Burbidge in to help us with our enquiries into the rapes." He shut the door in Marshall's face, and turned to Lloyd.

"So now we're down to three," he said. "And one of them was seen entering the underpass where Drummond was shot dead, and she's beginning to look like she had a very good motive."

Lloyd didn't dignify that with a response, but he hadn't been expected to respond; Case carried on, and Lloyd listened with mounting dismay to what he was being told.

"Now do you accept that she's mixed up in this business?"

Lloyd shook his head. "No," he said. "No. She feels guilty about Matt Burbidge getting the sack—she was just trying to keep him out of it, as she said."

"Of course she was trying to keep him out of it," said Case, crushing the cigarette out in the tinfoil ashtray. "Matt Burbidge knew Rosa—he would have known that Drummond was a client of hers. And if he knew that Drummond had been with her earlier that evening, he would know that Drummond's—and only Drummond's—DNA would be found, if any was found at all. That's how you rig a DNA test."

"But how could he know that?" said Lloyd. "At that point there had only been one rape, and we had no reason to suppose the rapist didn't ejaculate like everyone else!"

"The rapist knew."

Lloyd's eyes grew wide. "Matt Burbidge?" he said. "Is that why you asked Ginny if he'd gone with her?"

"Yes. It might have shed some light, if we could have found out how he functioned. Why didn't he tell us who Rosa was?"

"It was Judy who *told* us he knew Rosa, so she was hardly covering up for him there!" said Lloyd. "And the fact that Drummond was with Mrs. Ashman earlier in the evening does not preclude his having raped her *later* in the evening."

"You're clutching at straws, man!"

Lloyd stood up, wishing, as ever, that he was taller, as he looked into the other man's eyes. "Drummond gave Judy that statement," he said slowly, a space between each word. "I know he did."

"How *can* you know?"

"Because she says so." Lloyd sat down again. "And that means that *he* raped those women," he went on. "No one else."

"Right now, who raped them is not our greatest concern," said Case. "Right *now*, who murdered Drummond himself is. Now—there's blood in Fredericks's van that he won't account for, and his wife admits having been in possession of the gun that killed him. If and when we find the gun, it may tell us more. And we had better find that sixth cartridge in their house, or I don't see how we can hang on to them."

He slammed the door on his way out, and Lloyd sat for a moment, staring at it as he thought. If Lennie or Ginny had killed Drummond, the obvious motive would be that he had come looking for

Ginny, beaten her up for helping set him up for his arrest, and that one of them had shot him. He'd like that scenario better if he even half believed it himself.

He was on his way to talk to Judy when he saw Tom coming along the corridor towards him.

"Sir?"

Tom never called him sir. Guv, boss—Lloyd, off-duty. Never sir. Lloyd knew he wasn't going to like whatever was coming. "What's happened now?" he asked.

"The DNA results were faxed through a little while ago," said Tom. "You wanted to see them as soon as they came in." He handed Lloyd the typewritten sheets, pointing to a marked paragraph. "That's the bottom line, sir," he said.

Lloyd read it, closed his eyes, read it again, and looked at his sergeant. "Thank you, Tom," he said. He patted him on the shoulder. "I know you must have tried to talk her out of it," he said.

"Sir," said Tom, unhappily.

"Look—press Ginny about this gun," said Lloyd. "I want to know if it really did go missing. We haven't found the other cartridge, have we?"

"No. Or the gun. They'll start looking for it again at first light."

Lloyd nodded, and took the stairs slowly, wearily, like an old man. He didn't wait to be told to come, he didn't allow Case his moment of pretending to work while someone waited to talk to him. He put the report down on the desk, on top of the file on which Case was working, right under his eyes.

Case read it in silence, then picked up the paper, and dropped it in his in tray. He looked up for the first time. "*That* shit, Lloyd," he said, pointing to it with his pen. "*That* fan."

⸮

"Yes," said Rob, smoothing out the skin under tired eyes. "That was one of mine. Tenerife, they went to." He yawned, massaged his temples.

Marshall smiled. "Is that how you remember them?" he asked. "By where they'd gone on holiday?"

"Yes. It's how I thought of them. Tuesday night's job, Tenerife. Saturday night's, Crete. Thursday night, the Lake District. It got quite hectic in the summer."

"I know," said Marshall, with feeling.

There was no way Rob could remember all the houses he'd done. He recognised the addresses when he heard them, though, and Marshall was going through every burgled house in Stansfield for the last six months. A lot of them were his, but not all. Marshall had to sort out which were his and which weren't. He hadn't, and wouldn't, give them the name of his fence, which Marshall had pointed out would not go down well when it came to court. But Rob really didn't care.

"Forty-two Lancaster Walk?"

"No. Not mine." It was a long, slow job. "Could I phone my wife?" he asked. "I'm entitled to a phone call."

"That's usually to inform someone that you're here," said Marshall. "Your wife already knows."

"Yes, but I didn't realize everything would take so long," said Rob. "I just want to tell her I'm all right—she'll be worried."

"Yes, all right," said Marshall. "Interview suspended . . ."

\?

Ginny had been fed again, and now she was back in an interview room. Sergeant Finch switched on the tape.

"Interview with Virginia Fredericks at eighteen twenty-five hours on the sixth of November," he said. "Officers present DS Finch and DC Richards." He sat down, and looked at her. "I must remind you that you are not under arrest, and are free to leave at any time. This interview is being taped. You do not have to say anything, but it may harm your defence if you do not mention when questioned something that you later rely on in court. Anything you do say may be given in evidence. You are entitled to free legal advice—"

"You said all that before," said Ginny.

"Yes," said Sergeant Finch. "We have to remind you now and then of your rights, or we get into trouble."

Ginny hadn't liked to say before, when Chief Inspector Lloyd was there, but she didn't mind asking Sergeant Finch. "What's it mean?" she asked.

Sergeant Finch sighed. "You were asked if you understood the caution, Ginny," he said. "You said you did."

"I *do* understand the caution," she said indignantly. "I just don't understand that."

He looked at the woman, and then at her. "That's the new caution," he said. "You've not been in a police station for a while, have you?"

"No. So what's it mean?"

"It means that if you end up in court, and you tell them something in your defence that you didn't tell us when you had the chance, they'll wonder why you didn't. And they might think it means you're guilty."

She frowned. "But I've not done anything," she said.

"Maybe not. But you're not telling us the truth, are you?"

"Yes," she said, not looking at him.

"You know what I think, Ginny?" he said. "I think you were beaten up in your own house, not in the underpass. Inspector Hill saw blood on the staircase in your kitchen. I think Drummond came to your house when Lennie wasn't there, and beat you up. I think you shot him. I don't think that the gun went missing at all."

"It did! I wouldn't have let him get me into this state if I'd had a gun, would I?" Ginny said.

"That's fair enough, Sarge," said DC Richards. "I wouldn't have, either, if all I had to do was go to—" She looked at Ginny. "Where did you keep it?" she asked.

"In the drawer," said Ginny. "The one where I keep the stuff for work. Condoms, and . . . you know. Stuff." She looked at Sergeant Finch. "Handcuffs and that," she said. It had made him smile last time. It didn't this time.

"Well, there you are, Sarge," DC Richards said to Sergeant Finch. "If it had been there, Ginny would just have gone and got it." She turned back to Ginny. "Wouldn't you?" she asked. "You'd have gone to the drawer and got the gun, told him to leave you alone or else. I would have. Anyone would."

"Yeah," Ginny said to Sergeant Finch. "See? It wasn't *there* anymore, so I couldn't. Rob Jarvis must've taken it."

Sergeant Finch nodded. "But you couldn't have gone to the drawer and got it if you had been in the underpass, could you, Ginny?" he said. "So it happened in the house. Didn't it?"

Oh, hell. Ginny nodded sullenly. "Yeah, all right," she said. "But it was still a punter. And the gun wasn't there."

"I think I'd better have a word with Lennie," said Sergeant Finch. "Interview suspended . . ."

♩

Carole had always known that this would be the real test. She had to do it. And it wasn't difficult. You just opened the door, drove in, switched off, got out, walked back out, remotely locked it, closed the door. Two minutes? Not even that.

She could do it. She had opened the garage door the other night, and she could do it tonight. She could take the car in there. But now as she addressed herself to the task, it was memories of what she had found in the garage that came back to her.

This place that had haunted her for over two years, that had represented the breakdown of her health, her job, her marriage, her life; this place that it had taken such strength of will simply to enter—this place was being used to store stolen goods. By her husband. Because he thought they'd be safe from discovery there. It had been like being raped again. Maybe worse.

She threw open the door, and looked at the garage, innocent of rapists and stolen goods. She drove the car in, and sat there for exactly one minute before she got out. Just to prove she could.

♩

"Why do you keep telling us lies, Lennie?" asked Finch.

Lennie, being fed at Her Majesty's expense, saving money on lighting, heating, petrol, thought that perhaps all in all he was in the best place, even if he did have to put up with being shunted backwards and forwards from the cells.

"Which lies, Mr. Finch?" he asked.

"Jarvis told Chief Inspector Lloyd that you knew all about the gun. He told you about it, told you Ginny still had it. Is that right?"

"No comment."

"He says you beat Ginny up because she hadn't taken it back when you'd told her to."

"No comment."

"I don't think you beat her up. I think you found Drummond beating her up. We know it didn't happen in the underpass. It happened in your house. I think you got the gun, and you shot him, and Ginny's covering up for you."

"No comment."

Finch suspended the interview again. Lennie was taken back to the cells.

ℓ

Judy had bought more cigarettes; she had smoked more in the last three days than she had in the last thirty. Lloyd was still with Case, and she couldn't leave without seeing him.

"Come in," she called, to the almost tentative knock on her door, surprised to see Tom. He didn't knock tentatively; he never waited to be asked in. "Are you still here?" she asked, seeing the empty CID room beyond him.

He nodded, pulled a chair over, and sat down. "Trying to get the truth out of Lenny and Ginny," he said. "But I've left them to stew for a bit. I saw you coming back—I wanted to talk to you. Have you seen Lloyd?"

"No. He's with Case."

"Have you seen the DNA results?"

"No," she said, surprised she hadn't been shown them. But, of course, she wasn't on the rape enquiry. "Oh, God, I hate not being involved in this!" she said, and looked at his face. "It wasn't Drummond's hair, I take it," she said.

"No."

"I suppose it was always too good to be true," she said. Case would just have to go on thinking she was corrupt; the last chance had gone of ever proving that Drummond was the rapist.

"It wasn't the boyfriend's, either," said Tom.

"No?" Judy shrugged. "Maybe Marilyn was two-timing him."

"I don't think so," said Tom. "The blood on Drummond's jeans," he went on. "They did manage to get a profile."

"Yes, well, that's not going to be much help. It's Matt Burbidge's blood."

"Yes," said Tom. "And that's the problem. Because it *is* a match for the hair on Marilyn's bed, Judy."

Judy stared at him. "That's not possible," she said.

"It is, Judy. I had to let Lloyd see it—I couldn't find you. I just—"

"It's not *possible*." Judy looked away, at her own reflection in the darkness beyond the window. Her shoulders sagged. "Have you arrested him?" she asked.

"He's done a runner. A neighbour saw him put a bag in the boot of his car and drive off."

Judy looked at Tom's reflection then, at his face, strained and serious and not at all like it usually was. "I don't believe this is happening," she said.

"We checked with the travel agents, found him eventually. He was booked on the Dover-Calais ferry. But he wasn't on it. Or—his car wasn't, at any rate. They found it parked at the terminal. We've got the Kent police—"

"Yes, all right!"

"I'm sorry, Jude."

She turned and looked at him properly. "It's not your fault," she said. "I made sure Case knew that."

"I know," he said.

"You really couldn't have arrested him, not then. And it was my interview—I chose not to pass on the information."

Tom nodded. "There's more," he said. "It gets worse. Ginny recog—" He broke off as Lloyd appeared in the open doorway.

"Could you leave us, Tom?" he said.

Tom looked anxiously at her, then got up slowly, and left, closing the door quietly behind him.

Lloyd looked at her, his eyes bright with anger, his face pale and set. "I think you'll find that what your loyal sergeant was about to tell you is that a short while ago, we learned that Rosa was none other than Rachel Ashman," he said quietly. "And that Drummond had had unprotected sex with her earlier that evening, which is why his DNA was found."

Judy stared at him, her mouth opening slightly. "Mrs. Ashman?" she repeated, idiotically. "Rosa?"

"Does that surprise you? I certainly hope it does."

Judy nodded, her mind racing. "Has anyone told her husband?" she asked.

"We are still debating the ethics of that, if ethics mean much to you," said Lloyd.

Judy barely noticed the insult. "But Matt Burbidge must have known who she was," she said. "That photograph of her in the service station was up on the wall of—"

"Yes," he said. "He must."

Oh, God. Judy took a deep breath. "Look, Lloyd—I agree that it now looks as if—in theory—Matt could have carried out the rapes, and made it look as though Drummond had committed them. But he didn't."

"There's no theory about it, Judy! I assume Tom's told you about the DNA."

"There has to be a mistake! He was with Ginny when Marilyn was raped."

"He was with her until ten-twenty or so," said Lloyd. "He was seen at the underpass minutes later—that's a stone's throw from Marilyn's flat. He could have doubled back—it looks as though he must have doubled back. The DNA makes it slightly more than a theory, don't you think?"

"But it's—"

"I'll tell you a theory, Judy," he went on. "In theory, you could have seen that gun on your first visit to Ginny Fredericks, and taken it during your fruitless search of the Fredericks's premises two days later. In theory, you could have lured Drummond to the underpass by saying you had information on Rosa, and shot him dead in order that he ceased to be a threat to you. That's what Case believes, and who can blame him? A witness saw you at the scene of the crime moments before it happened. You were the first person we were looking for! And someone rang Stansfield police station immediately before dialling nine-double-nine."

"Why would I ring Stansfield?" asked Judy, mystified.

"To establish some sort of alibi, to talk to me—who knows? But you changed your mind, or found yourself on the queuing system, and gave up."

"So why would I ring 999?"

"You would ring 999 to get help for Ginny, who had run away from her violent husband, and whom you practically fell over. Then you decided that taking her to hospital yourself would give you a sort of an alibi. Better than nothing."

Judy nodded. "And is that what you believe?" she asked.

"No. I think Drummond beat up Ginny, Lennie discovered them, and shot him. And you'd better hope I can prove it," he said. "Because you're the only other candidate!" He looked at her, his head shaking. "How could you do this to me?" he asked. "How could you *do* this to me, Judy?"

"I haven't done anything to you!"

"No," he said. "Nothing at all. Three days after the event, you finally get round to telling us that Burbidge wasn't in the car when Bobbie Chalmers was raped? That the bandage was missing? That he has no alibi whatsoever? That he knew Lucy Rogerson, knew that farm? You kept me in the dark, you put Tom in a very invidious position—why, Judy?"

Tom had put her in an invidious position. Loyalty cut both ways. Tom understood that. "You know why," she said. "I told Case why. Drummond gave me that statement!"

"Did he?"

Judy felt as though she had received a physical punch.

"I have spent the last four days defending you on just that point," Lloyd went on. "Defending your integrity, your honesty, your honour, even! And now I don't know who or what I was defending. I don't *know* you, Judy!"

She picked up her cigarettes, matches, put them in her bag, took out her keys, locked up her desk.

"You can't walk out."

"Watch me." She picked up her jacket, and opened the door, walking quickly through the empty CID room.

"Judy—I didn't—"

She closed the door, kept on walking, down the corridor, out of the back door, into the car park. And her new car started at the first time of asking and took her home much faster than the law allowed, along the dual carriageway, onto the new bypass, down into Malworth. Along High Street. She parked outside the greengrocers, and let herself in, and upstairs. Into the flat, over to the phone.

She found his card, dialled the number.

"I'm sorry, I'm not available to take your call at the moment . . ."

She listened to the message, waited for the tone.

"I think I need a good lawyer," she said. "Tonight."

Chapter Fourteen

Lloyd sat at his desk, looking at, but not seeing, the papers in front of him. He hadn't meant it. He hadn't meant it. Judy would rather he had accused her of murdering the man than of falsifying a statement.

His wildest dreams could just about accommodate her having killed Colin Drummond. Deciding after what had happened to Marilyn Taylor that enough was enough, taking the gun, going after him, making sure he never raped or murdered again. But she wouldn't have lured him to his death, wouldn't have shot him in the back of the head, wouldn't have let Ginny or Lennie or anyone else come under suspicion. If ever Judy was going to take the law into her own hands, she would do it with a flourish. And everyone would know it. It would be an honest murder.

He *couldn't* imagine her falsifying a statement, not in any kind of scenario his mind could conjure up. Dishonesty wasn't in her makeup. He knew that, so why had he said it? To hurt her. And like Lennie might have done with Ginny, this time he had gone over the top.

He had told Tom to keep working on Lennie and Ginny, but Tom had said he thought the gun really had gone missing. Ginny wasn't a convincing liar, he'd said. And she was pretty convincing about the gun. And if it really had been stolen before Lennie even knew she hadn't taken it back as instructed, then three of Case's four people were eliminated, leaving Judy.

But then . . . there weren't only four people who had access to the gun, he thought. Jarvis may have been burgling a house, but his wife hadn't. And if Jarvis took the gun home, then she could have found it. She had as much motive as he had.

Lloyd headed out once again for the Jarvis house.

ò

He must be getting near the end now.

"Seventeen Epstein Drive," said Marshall.

"That was last night's," Rob said. "A time-share in Spain." He looked at Marshall. "You still don't know, do you?" he said.

"What's that, Mr. Jarvis?" said Marshall, ticking off the address.

"Well," said Rob, almost enjoying this now that it had finally happened, "I was hiding, not to put too fine a point on it, in the garden of the first house up the side road when your guy was talking to the people across the street."

The house was on a corner plot, with a gate on to the road running up the side. He had parked right outside the gate, not unnaturally.

"He was bound to search the gardens, and I'd be crouching down behind someone's forsythia when he did, so—I took a chance when he had his back turned."

Marshall was listing the stuff he'd taken from the houses he'd done while he spoke.

"I went back to the cab," he said. "Your officer spoke to me."

Marshall's head shot up.

"He was very polite," Rob went on. "I assured him I had seen nothing suspicious."

Marshall didn't look pleased.

"But I thought it was one thing fooling him—it would be another story when the CID got to hear about it. I mean, I was the only person at the scene, and I had transport parked at the gate. I was expecting a visit from you hourly," Rob said. "But I guess he didn't bother telling you."

"Interview terminated eighteen fifty-two hours," said Marshall. "I will remove these tapes, Mr. Jarvis. You should sign both—"

Someone was in for a rollicking, thought Rob, as Marshall's manner grew positively brisk with annoyance.

ò

Ginny was being asked question after question. Lennie always said just to say no comment, but she wasn't good at that. And no matter how many times she answered, Sergeant Finch would ask again and again.

"Who gave you the beating, Ginny?"

"A punter."

"How did you end up in the underpass?"

"I—I ran away."

"From the punter."

"Yes!"

"How? How did you get away from him?"

"Lennie came—" She stopped, flustered. She hated Sergeant Finch. "No comment," she said, and then remembered that she could tell them to stop the interview altogether. So she did.

ò

More police. Carole had lost count. It was as bad as— She switched her memory off instantly, just like she had done before. Nothing had changed.

"DCI Lloyd, Stansfield CID," he said.

That was the one who'd come in between DC Marshall's visits. She'd heard him tell Rob.

"Can you tell me where you were at nine o'clock yesterday evening?" he asked, as they went into the sitting room.

"In Malworth."

He nodded. "Anywhere near the bonfire?"

"Yes, since you ask. Why?"

"Colin Drummond was killed in the underpass at nine o'clock

yesterday evening," he said. "The underpass, as you may know, was also near the bonfire. Would you know anything about Mr. Drummond's death, Mrs. Jarvis?"

"No—only what I've seen on the news."

She sat down. "Please," she said, indicating a seat, but he didn't sit.

"He was shot with a pistol that may have gone missing from the house of a Mr. and Mrs. Fredericks," he said. "Do you know anything about that?"

"No."

"Which? That they had a pistol, or that it had gone missing?"

"Neither."

"Your husband knew about it," he said.

He was walking round, looking at the pictures she had on the wall. From her better days, when she could buy prints simply because she liked them, and hadn't had to count the pennies. He would think they'd been bought with money from the burglaries. She was still trying to come to terms with that. All that stuff in the garage. She had said that they ought to get window locks, when a burglary seemed to be being reported every week, in the summer. "Good idea," Rob had said. And all the time . . .

"I said, your husband knew about it."

"I didn't know about it."

"Mrs. Fredericks thinks your husband took it," he said. "Have you seen a pistol in his possession? Or anywhere that he might keep such a thing?"

"No. And I wouldn't have the first idea where he would keep such a thing," she said.

"Were you at the firework display when the emergency vehicles arrived?"

"I saw them, but I wasn't actually at the bonfire," she said. "I was visiting a friend in the area. We watched from a balcony."

"Could I have the name of your friend?"

Almost exactly the same words. She was doing it to him again. She was sending the police round to Steve again, because of Drummond, again. "His name is Stephen Morgan," she said.

His eyebrows lifted very slightly.

"Yes," she said. "That is who I was with before I was raped. I've no doubt you're having to go through the files again. I'm sure his name is fresh in your memory."

"Yes," he said. "It is."

"I—I didn't carry on seeing him," she said, defending herself. "I tried, I swear to God, I tried to make my marriage work again."

"Mrs. Jarvis, it really is no business of mine—"

"You can't know! You can't know what it was like!" She was crying now, pouring out to this total stranger all the helplessness, all the disappointment, all the frustration, all the guilt.

He came and sat beside her on the sofa, his arm round her shoulders, trying to calm her, but she wouldn't, she couldn't stop. She hadn't been able to talk to anyone, not even Steve. It would have been a betrayal. But this man—he didn't know Rob, he had no stake in her life or his. He could listen. Someone had to listen.

"And when . . . when I realized he was seeing Ginny twice a week, I thought that meant he could live a normal life with someone else, but he wouldn't—he just . . . he said we were married until death parted us."

"Is he a religious man?" asked Lloyd.

"No!" she said. "No. I would have understood if he was, but he's not. He's just obsessed! Truly. It's like an illness—it is an illness. He thinks Drummond's waiting for us to split up, that he'll know that he caused it, that he made Rob—" She wiped her face, her nose. "He was burgling houses to make ends meet!" she cried. "Because he wouldn't sleep with me, and he wouldn't let me go into the spare room, even! He worked at night, even though he was earning next to nothing, so that he could pretend that it was just circumstances. Because he slept in the mornings, and I worked in the afternoon, and he was out again in the evening—that was why we didn't have sex! Not because he couldn't—" She made a real effort to calm down.

"Then I started seeing Steve again," she said. "And I knew that I still wanted to be with him—we still wanted to be together. I tried to tell Rob I wanted to leave, but—" She shook her head. "Last time, he said he'd kill me sooner," she said. And she told him about last night, about the terrible trauma of simply opening her garage door, of the discovery that the garage was being used to store other people's domestic goods, of how that felt almost like being raped all over again. She was sure he would think her melodramatic, but that was how it had felt.

"Anyway. That's where I was. Steve's."

"Thank you," he said, getting up. "I will have to check with him," he added gently.

"I know," she said.

Just like last time.

ọ̀

"You came home and found Ginny being beaten up, didn't you, Lennie?"

"No comment."

"She very nearly told us," said Finch. "But she stopped herself in time."

Poor kid. This was wearing him down. He didn't know how Ginny could possibly withstand it, the state she was in. But she must be doing all right. Not for much longer, maybe.

"You've told her to tell us lies, Lennie. Why?"

"No comment."

But Finch didn't give up very easily, and Lennie was getting more fed up with saying no comment than he was with hearing it. Now, he was being asked for the millionth time who had beaten Ginny up.

He looked at Finch, trying to gauge how much he knew, how much was guesswork, how much Ginny had let slip. "She was with a punter," he said, tiredly. "He beat her up."

"We don't buy that, Lennie. Why would she protect a punter who did that to her? Why wouldn't she give us a description? Why would she be seeing a punter you knew nothing about?"

"No comment."

ọ̀

Matt had been picked up in the bar, while he waited for the first ferry he'd been able to switch to.

Now he sat in the back of a police car with a silent constable for company, and another at the wheel, going the opposite way round the M25, still choked with traffic.

They didn't dare speak, these two, in case they inadvertently asked him a pertinent question, and started the time clock ticking. They had arrested him, and they had to be careful if they didn't want Stansfield CID breathing fire. He had never paid much attention to the Police and Criminal Evidence Act when he had been on their side of the fence—no one at Malworth had—but he knew its provisions, and they knew he did.

He would get his eight hours free from questioning. And then he'd be ready for the bastards.

؟

Judy poured the last drops of one bottle of wine into her glass, and went to the fridge for another, topping up her glass with it.

She couldn't remember ever having done this before. It had taken until now to take hold. But now, things did seem to have softer edges, even life, which had never been such a bitch. She had regretted ringing Hotshot as soon as she'd done it; she had rung back, wishing there was an erase button on telephones. She had told him to disregard her previous message. And then she had set about getting drunk.

Lloyd hadn't rung, hadn't done anything. She lit a cigarette as her doorbell rang. They didn't have modern things like door phones in these old flats. Just a row of bell pushes. Lloyd? she wondered, as she went out, and made her way carefully downstairs. No. He'd have used his key. Unless he was throwing his hat in first. But that wasn't like Lloyd. Maybe he didn't want to come in. Maybe he'd come to give her back her keys. She wouldn't blame him if he had. She opened the door.

"Hotshot," she said, relieved, disappointed, confused, embarrassed, but not surprised.

"I found a message on my answering machine," he said.

"I rang back," she said. "I told you to forget it."

"I didn't listen to any more messages after that one," he said, with a smile. "Can I come in?"

"Isn't it a little unethical?"

"I don't think so," he said. "Unless it offends your ethics, of course."

"I don't have any, apparently."

"Good—that makes everything much simpler."

She let him in, and went past him up the stair. "This way," she said.

He followed her into the flat, and closed the door. She saw him looking at the wine bottles, and at her. "Do you want a glass?" she asked.

"Well, I think someone had better join you."

She found a glass and knelt by the coffee table to pour him some wine, spilling a little, which she brushed away with her hand.

"Cheers," he said, sitting down.

She sat on the floor. It seemed easier than getting up again. "Why did you invite yourself to lunch with me?" she asked.

He smiled. "Because I fancy you," he said.

"Oh, sure—and that's why you tried to get me suspended?"

He frowned. "Oh," he said. "Drummond—he went through with it, then? I didn't act for him. I didn't believe a word of it."

Judy drank some more wine. "I thought what you believed didn't matter?"

"It doesn't. Not when I'm defending him. Providing he gives me no reason to disbelieve him. But I don't have to represent him if I think he's a lying little sod, so I didn't."

Judy smiled. "Good," she said, and then felt her lip tremble, and the tears come back.

"Hey, come on," he said, and joined her on the floor, putting his arm round her. "What's happened?"

"I . . . I'm probably going to be charged with falsifying a statement, and neglect of duty, and murder," she said.

"Nothing serious, then?" He smiled. "That's good." He leant back, his elbow on the sofa. You didn't think of barristers sitting on the floor, not when you saw them in court with their wigs and gowns and everything. "I think you'd better tell me, don't you?" he said.

She told him. Everything. About the Malworth Mafia using Ginny as bait. About trying to keep Matt out of it, about Case believing she was *part* of the Malworth Mafia, everything. When she had finished, she drained her glass of wine, and poured them both more.

Hotshot said nothing for a minute or so, then nodded slightly. "I couldn't better your defence of the neglect of duty charge," he said. "I think if we went in for a hairsplitting contest, it would have to be a tiebreak."

Judy smiled, a little reluctantly. Everything was pleasantly hazy now, including Hotshot. It all seemed like some sort of game. It wasn't real. It was only a story.

"I doubt if they'll proceed on that," he said, and took a sip of wine. "Now—falsifying a statement. That's a bit more tricky."

"I didn't," she said. "I swear to you, I didn't."

"But it looks as though you must have."

"So you think I did?"

"No. I just said it *looks* as though you must have. I can think of circumstances in which Drummond could have given you that statement even though he didn't actually carry out the rape."

Judy shook her head. "No—no, don't try saying he was just making it up from what he'd been told and all that," she said, putting down her glass, the better to use her hands, which she felt obliged to do, since she was aware that her voice wasn't really working all that well. She could think quite clearly; speaking clearly was the problem. "Bobbie's was different, all right? It was different. She had carbon monoxide poisoning. *She* knew how she got it, *I* knew how she got it—and Drummond knew how she got it. He told me. Told me about the exhaust pumping into her face, making her gag, the little bastard—he told me!" She pressed her steepled fingers to her lips, her eyes closed, as angry now as she had been when he had told her.

"He could have told you that if he had *watched* the rape," said Harper quietly.

Judy opened her eyes, lifted her head. "Watched it?" she said. "You're the one who went on about coincidences!"

"Which weren't coincidences at all, on either side, according to you," said Harper. "That poor little girl was the rope in a tug-of-war between Drummond and the Malworth Mafia."

"Oh, right," said Judy. "They weren't coincidences—so this one's OK, even though it's the size of Texas?" She seemed to have developed a lisp, and to be condemned to choosing words with esses in them. "Someone hero-worships a rapist, dresses like him, behaves like him, and then has the sheer good fortune of seeing his idol at *work?*"

"Would it be such a coincidence? They had exactly the same MO—watched people in parked cars. There aren't that many people these days who do their courting in parked cars. Their paths were pretty well bound to cross sooner or later—the wonder is they hadn't crossed before, if you ask me."

"Drummond would have told you that!" she said angrily. "It would explain how he could give such a detailed statement! He'd have *told* you!"

"Would he? He would have told me that he saw a policeman carrying out a rape? A rape that wasn't even reported? A policeman who was ostensibly on duty?" He shook his head. "We don't know what went on that night," he said. "We only have the word of two discredited police officers, who have lied and lied again! He was scared, Judy—just like he said. He told me as much as he dared. And he would never have dared tell me that."

Judy stared at him, then looked away. She took out a cigarette, lit it, inhaled smoke. My God. Oh, my God. They were both at the football ground. They had both followed her, each unaware of the other's presence in the thick fog. Matt . . . and Drummond. Matt had raped her, Drummond had watched. And when Matt had left her there, Drummond had stayed and continued to watch until Bobbie had got herself together enough to get back into her car and drive off. Then he had bombed off on his bike, arriving at the police car in the speed trap a minute after Matt. And Matt— Oh, God. Drummond had said something. Something—Matt knew, knew he'd been seen. That was why he had hit him, and Harper was right—they had no idea what else they had said or done to him.

She had got it all wrong. She drank some more wine. She had got it *all wrong*. "How?" she said. "How could I have got it so wrong?"

"I take it that you are the only police officer in the history of organized policing ever to have been wrong?" said Hotshot.

Judy pulled a face.

"Oh, I see! It's just the first time in your own personal career that you have been wrong."

"It's not that," said Judy.

"Well, forgive me for thinking it might be, in view of the look on your face. So, you were wrong. Don't you think you should be a bit more worried about being suspected of murder?"

She shook her head.

"Why not?"

"Because I didn't murder him," she said. It seemed simple enough to her.

"Oh, yes. And we all know if you didn't do it . . ."

"You've nothing to worry about, sir," Judy said, remembering what Lloyd had said. "Which means I'm almost certainly guilty."

"Should I understand that?" said Hotshot.

"No." She looked a little unsteadily at him. "Look—I don't care if they think I killed him."

"You'll care if you find yourself doing twenty years in Holloway," he said.

"Yes—yes, right. Yes. But—I . . . well, I can't see it coming to that, right? I mean—it might. But I'll cross that—" She couldn't remember what you called them. "You know," she said.

"Bridge when you come to it," said Hotshot. "Are you thinking of drinking any more?"

"I might," said Judy. "But I have come to this particular bridge. I was wrong. And . . . and instinct's my . . . thing, do you see?"

Hotshot shook his head.

"Well—Lloyd's is puzzles. He can spot what's wrong with a story, a situation. He calls them little puzzles. Like—why did Marilyn not lock herself in the loo?" She hadn't really given that the thought she had said she would. She had been too busy. "And Tom, he sees things."

"So will you, soon," muttered Hotshot.

"I mean he observes things. Not just sees. Sounds, smells—he notices things. You know. What time someone bought a packet of cigarettes—how many are left in it. Whether they could really have smoked seventeen cigarettes in ten minutes—that sort of thing."

"I'm sure he's a veritable Sherlock Holmes." He smiled.

"Well, you can make fun. But if—if your job is sorting out other people's messes, you have to go about it somehow. My way's instinct. For instance, I saw you in court, and I thought you were a smoothie lawyer with no scruples, and then I met you, and—" She smiled. "I *knew* you were," she said, with a shrug.

He laughed. "I sort out other people's messes," he said. "What's my line of attack?"

"Words. Listening to what people say. Properly. Like . . ." She thought for a moment, trying to find an example. "Like Merrill saying he said 'if' Drummond had raped those women he could prove it. And you said Drummond might not have noticed the word 'if.' " She looked up at him. "And Merrill might not have said it," she said. "He was very God-fearing and upright, but I don't . . . I don't think he was very principled."

"No," said Hotshot. "I don't think he was. But he did say 'if,' as it happens. For the record."

"See? You didn't say he hadn't. But you even made *him* think he hadn't, because he knew he hadn't been playing it straight, and he wasn't sure. That's your thing."

"Don't you think perhaps everyone's got a thing?"

Judy shrugged. "Probably," she said.

"And don't you think that there have been actors who could have made you believe they were rapists?"

"Sure."

"Acting was Drummond's thing," he said. "He did it all the time. He did it without thinking. The bewildered innocent. The not-very-bright inadequate. The sharp-as-a-tack wide boy. The rapist?"

"Mm," she said.

"And everyone meets their Waterloo," he said. "I might be sharp with words, but little Ginny left me with egg on my face more than once, and she can't even read and write."

Judy laughed.

"That's better," he said.

"Do you think she really did help to set him up?" she asked, still finding that impossible to believe.

"No," he said. "Not necessarily. He did hero-worship the rapist, remember. And he had had a master class. Wanted to prove himself, perhaps—possibly was even encouraged to prove himself, to make the Mafia's task easier. I think he attempted to carry out a copycat rape on you, and when that failed, the Malworth Mafia offered Ginny up to him. He took the bait, and they had him where they wanted him."

Yes. Yes, that made sense. At least she hadn't been wrong about Ginny. Judy leant back against the armchair. "Let's talk about something else," she said.

Chapter Fifteen

s Ginny all right?" Lennie asked, after he had been given a break for a much needed cup of tea and a cigarette, and the interview was under way again.

"No," said Finch. "She's tired. Not very well. She won't tell us what happened, because you've told her not to. So you had better give us some answers if you want her out of here. Who beat her up?"

"I did," said Lennie, making his mind up. If he kept saying no comment, they would be here all night.

"Why?"

"Jarvis told you. Because she told me she'd taken that gun back. I gave her a hiding for lying to me." He sat back. "OK?"

"A *hiding*?" said Finch. "Inspector Hill had to take her to hospital! She needed stitches! That was a beating, Lennie."

"Yeah, well . . . I lost it. She ran away, and after a bit I went looking for her in the Transit. I'd just got back when she got home from casualty. That's when Inspector Hill saw me."

Finch shook his head. "That doesn't explain the blood in the Transit," he said.

"She tried to shut herself in there—I went in after her."

"You do know we're having that blood analysed," said Finch.

"Yeah, well. It's Ginny's."

"She'll confirm this, will she?"

Lennie shook his head. "No way," he said. "Not until I say she can."

"I'm not sure that's good enough, Lennie," said Finch.

◊

Rob was being given his belongings back, signing even more bits of paper, being asked if he understood that he had been bailed to appear at Stansfield Magistrates' Court on Monday morning.

"Will I go to jail?" he asked.

"Well, not on Monday," said the sergeant. "Providing you turn up."

"No—I mean . . . eventually. Will I go to jail?"

"Couldn't say."

He wished they had kept him in custody. He had thought that they would; burglary was a serious crime. But they said that they only did that for violent crime, or where they thought the person might not turn up at court. He wished he looked a little more disreputable.

He would take the taxi out. Sleep on the rank.

◊

"Did Drummond come to the house while Lennie was out?"

"No." Ginny's face throbbed now that the painkillers were wearing off, and she wasn't allowed to take any more for another hour. The cut over her eyebrow was hurting.

"Did anyone come to the house?"

"No."

"What about the punter?"

She frowned. "What punter?" she asked.

"The one that beat you up! Have you forgotten him so soon?"

She was getting confused. Lennie said just to say no comment, and they'd soon get tired of asking questions.

"No comment," she said.

"It wasn't a punter, was it, Ginny?" Sergeant Finch looked at her, worried. "Ginny—we might have to arrest you if you won't tell us the truth."

"I've not done anything!" She sat back, and looked down. "I get beaten up, and I'm the one that gets arrested," she said.

"You've not been arrested yet. Did Lennie give you the beating?"

"No!" she said, her head shooting up so fast the pain made her dizzy. "No! Lennie would never hurt me like that—never!"

"He says he did."

Ginny stared at him. What was she supposed to say now? Lennie couldn't have said that. Sergeant Finch must be trying it on.

"You're a liar," she said.

"He said he gave you a hiding because you hadn't taken the gun back."

No. He never said that. Ginny shook her head. No matter what they say, tell them it was a punter. That was what Lennie had said. That's what she should do. "It was a punter," she said, tiredly, desperately. "It was a punter."

Finch sighed. "Interview terminated twenty fifty-two hours," he said, and switched off the tape. "Come on, Ginny—I think you need a proper rest."

ọ

Matt was put in a cell. He sat on the bed and listened to his fellow detainees yelling and banging and throwing up. Saturday night in the cells—it made him feel quite at home. Better than Saturday night in some froggie B & B, if you asked him. Ex-job, he got some perks. They'd even gone out for fish and chips for him. Wouldn't have got that in La Belle France.

They had made good time in the end; once they were clear of the traffic the lads had used their initiative, and their flashing light. It was nine o'clock. If no one had seen him by ten, he could be pretty sure he'd get left alone until morning.

It bothered him to know that chalked up outside his cell would be the words *Burbidge—rape*. But other than that, he wasn't sure he gave a stuff anymore.

ọ

Nothing had changed. He had come home, told her he would be in court on Monday, and then gone out with the cab. He was taking it all so calmly, as if this happened to him every day. She thought of burglars, if not as people with striped jerseys and bags marked swag, then as something quite close to that. Not Rob. And yet he had gone into other people's houses, and taken what didn't belong to him. He had used the garage, of all places, to store his ill-gotten gains. He blamed Drummond. But Drummond was dead, and nothing had changed.

She didn't know if she could cope with this. But then, she thought, she had coped with being raped. She had coped with making herself go back into the garage. She had coped with what she had found there. She had coped with Rob being arrested. This was just one more hurdle. She had got this far; she couldn't cave in now.

He just kept saying everything would be all right. She couldn't imagine everything ever being all right again. And she wondered how poor Steve was getting on now that she had set the police on him again.

ᵒ

"Stephen Morgan?"

"Yes," said the man who had answered the door two-thirds of the way up the Parkside high-rise. "Can I help you?"

"Oxygen would go down quite well," puffed Lloyd. "Your lift's out of order. DCI Lloyd, Stansfield CID." He showed him his card while trying not to look as though he were gasping for air.

"You'd better come in."

Lloyd gratefully sat down, and waited a moment before attempting to speak.

"It's a bugger, isn't it?" said Morgan. "It'll probably be on again before you go. It's kids—they jam it. Someone'll find whatever it is and unjam it."

Lloyd was very glad he hadn't come to arrest the man. It would have been very embarrassing. "Right," he said, when he felt that his breath had been sufficiently restored. "I believe you know a Mrs. Carole Jarvis?"

"Yes—is she all right?" he asked, alarmed.

"Oh, yes, yes. I would just like confirmation of when you saw her last, that's all."

"Is she missing?"

"No. She's perfectly all right, and at home." Lloyd frowned. "Why are you so worried that something might have happened to her?" he asked.

"Oh . . . no reason. A visit from the police—you know."

"I would just like to know when you saw her last."

"Yesterday."

"At what time?"

"Oh, now . . . let me see. I know she was here at nine, when the fireworks started—see." He pointed to the window. "We had a terrific view from the balcony here. There have to be some compensations, I suppose."

"Nine," said Lloyd, distrusting anyone who could produce an alibi for the very moment of death.

"Well, she came a few minutes before that. She only stayed for the first display, so she was here altogether . . . twenty, twenty-five minutes?"

Lloyd wandered over to the window. He doubted if a man-eating tiger would get him out on that balcony. He could see the lights of Malworth proper beyond the darkness that was the park. Closer to, he could see the orange streetlights shine down on the little cobbled streets and alleys where Ginny and Lennie lived. Down beneath him, lit by the windows of the high-rise, the huge charred circle which was all that remained of the Malworth bonfire.

The rapist hadn't been able to dump his clothes there because of the vigilantes, so he had gone into Stansfield. Rob Jarvis had watched him dump them there, on Stansfield's bonfire. He had assumed that it was Drummond, but one man on a motorbike looked very much like another, as Lloyd had pointed out to Judy.

But did Matt Burbidge have a motorbike? Could he get away with not getting to work until after eleven? He was on his own; perhaps he could. And yet, hadn't Finch said that there were caretakers there until ten-thirty, when the security firm took over? They would have to be spoken to, obviously.

He had thought for a few furious and bewildered moments this evening that he had let Judy's obsession with Drummond get to him. Now, he wondered if it wasn't Case's obsession with Burbidge that had got to him; that they should all truly be keeping open minds.

"Chief Inspector?"

Lloyd turned. "Oh!" he said. "I do beg your pardon. It's been a very long day. I was . . ." He made circular movements with his hands. ". . . working out the geography," he said.

"It's easier in daylight."

"I imagine so. Mr. Morgan—it occurs to me that Mrs. Jarvis was unlikely to have come here purely to watch the first half of a firework display."

Morgan sat down heavily. "No," he said. "She came to stay. I wouldn't let her."

Lloyd raised his eyebrows.

"I want to be with her just as much as she wants to be with me," he said. "More, probably. If that dreadful thing hadn't happened, I doubt if I would have had a look-in once her husband was back. But it did happen, and it changed him, not her. I didn't want her to be anywhere he knew to look. I think we have to plan this—move somewhere he can't find her. I think he could be dangerous. He's threatened to kill her now. That's why I was worried about her."

Lloyd nodded. Well, Mr. Jarvis might be taking care of that problem himself. He couldn't do much to her banged up in the Scrubs, as Finch would doubtless have pointed out, had he been here.

"Anyway—I suppose Carole is bound to be a suspect," he said. "It is Drummond's murder that you're investigating, isn't it?"

Lloyd had perfected a facial expression that seemed like a response and could mean anything at all.

"But she was here. And I had some friends here who *did* come to watch the firework display. They'll vouch for the fact that she was here from just before nine until about twenty past—and that she didn't shin down the drainpipe and murder Drummond. I dropped her off home at nine thirty-five or so."

"Dropped her off?" said Lloyd. "Wasn't she in her own car?"

"No. She came by cab." He found a sheet of paper on his comfortingly untidy desk, and scribbled on it.

That was odd, thought Lloyd, absently taking the paper.

"The addresses of the people who were here," Morgan said.

"Oh—yes. Thank you, Mr. Morgan. You've been most helpful."

The lift graciously allowed him to descend; he tried not to breathe through his nose—not to breathe at all, come to that. He was not at all sure he wouldn't have preferred the stair. Back at the station, he was told that the search of the Fredericks residence was complete: no cartridge had been found. He released Lennie, thus giving him back responsibility for the unwell and unhappy Ginny, and decided that Matt Burbidge could wait until tomorrow. He had fences to mend.

§

They had talked about themselves, mostly. And a lot about Lloyd, a little about Michael, Judy's ex. A little about his ex, with whom he still had a friendly relationship. A little about Freddie. Now, a silence had fallen, but it wasn't uncomfortable.

Judy liked Hotshot. He always seemed to be faintly amused; he didn't take anything much very seriously, except his job. That was why he and his wife had split up, he said. He didn't think he was cut out for a serious relationship; he liked to take things as they came, and leave them when he wanted to. There was something calming, something soothing about that; it was very undemanding, unthreatening. And it seemed to her that he was a very good man to have around when you were in trouble; he didn't make matters worse by getting into a state about it.

"If I am charged with murder, will you defend me?" she asked.

"No," he said.

"Why not?"

He smiled. "I think you know why not," he said.

Judy looked at him, and smiled back. She picked up the bottle, and held it enquiringly over his glass.

"It depends," he said.

"On what?"

"On whether or not I'm driving."

She thought about it; thought about the sheer relief that a cheerful, uncomplicated liaison, free from emotional entanglements, would bring. She thought about it, then put the bottle down again, a little reluctantly.

"Pity," he said. "It could be fun."

"I'm sure it would be," said Judy. "We could make all these jokes about sliding down barristers and watching briefs."

He smiled. "But you think that sex should be some sort of a commitment?"

"No," said Judy. "I don't, really. Not even when I'm sober." She poured the wine into her own glass. "But I know a man who does," she said. "And that's very important to me."

"Then why are you ringing up near total strangers and inviting them to bed with you?" Hotshot enquired, still smiling.

"I did not invite you to bed."

"Yes, you did."

"All right—yes, I did," Judy conceded. "But I cancelled the invitation."

"I didn't get that far along the tape."

"Yes, you did."

He laughed. "And I thought I was on a promise," he said.

"I'm sorry," said Judy. "I shouldn't have rung you—I was hurt, and angry, and—well, I shouldn't have rung." She looked back into the kind, amused grey eyes that looked into hers. "Look—I've messed everything up," she said. "My job's on the line. Maybe so's my freedom, for all I know. But if it's not there already, my relationship with Lloyd's not joining them."

"Even though he makes you hurt and angry?" Hotshot's eyes were still amused.

"He only does that because I make *him* hurt and angry," said Judy.

"Sounds like a wonderful relationship."

"It is."

"Good."

Hotshot managed to get up from the carpet gracefully; Judy wasn't even going to try without assistance.

"Why on earth don't you marry the man?" he asked, holding out his hand and helping her to her feet.

Judy might have answered, had the door not opened, and Lloyd appeared. She and Hotshot were holding *hands*. Still, if her mental coin had landed the other way, it could have been a great deal worse.

"I'm sorry," he said coldly. "I didn't realize you were entertaining."

"I'm not," said Judy. "I'm quite drunk, but I'm not in the least entertaining. Lloyd, this is—" She looked at him, and giggled. "I don't know your first name," she said.

"James," he said.

"This is James Harper, and James, this is Lloyd. I do know his first name, but I'm not allowed to tell you it."

"How do you do?" said Hotshot, admirably bearing up to Lloyd's less than friendly handshake. "I've heard a lot about you."

"Don't let me break anything up," said Lloyd.

"I was just leaving," said Hotshot, smiling, picking up his jacket, making for the door.

Judy went with him. "Thank you," she said. "I think I did need a good lawyer. You cheered me up."

"You're welcome. And I'm sure it won't come to it, but if you do really need a good . . . well, I can give you the name of a very good lawyer. It's the same as mine—he's my father."

"The other Harper," Judy said. "I'll bear that in mind." She closed the door.

"What was he doing here?" demanded Lloyd.

Judy smiled. "Giving me advice," she said.

"It didn't look like that," said Lloyd. "And how much have you had to drink?"

Judy focused on the wine bottles. "He had about a glassful, I suppose," she said. "I had the rest." She squinted at them. "There's still some in one of them if you want a glass," she said. "And you're right—it very nearly *wasn't* like that." She knew she was only saying this because she'd had far too much to drink, but she was going to tell him anyway. "I came this close," she said, holding her finger and thumb a millimetre apart.

"I hope you didn't deny yourself on my account," he said, picking up a newspaper, pretending to be terribly interested in something that had just happened to catch his eye.

"No," said Judy. "I didn't."

He looked up.

"There was no self-denial involved," she said. "It wasn't him I wanted. It was you."

"Why?" asked Lloyd. "He's twenty years younger than I am, he's handsome, got all his hair—he's rich and successful. You seem to like him."

Judy nodded, then giggled again. "But he was ten years old when we met," she said.

Lloyd put down the paper, and his arms were round her, and he wasn't walking out on her, or yelling at her, or demanding an account of the entire evening. He was saying he was sorry for what he'd said, that he had never thought for one moment that she had done any such thing, that he could have cut his tongue out—

She held a finger to his lips, and she told him *she* was sorry. About everything. Hotshot, everything. She had been wrong—Hotshot had explained about how Drummond could have given her that statement, and she had been wrong, and now they were in this awful mess, and it was all her fault. And she was sorry about everything else. She *had* been shutting him out, but she hadn't honestly meant to, it was just that she was afraid to let go of what she had in case what she got wasn't what she wanted, so he was in a different compartment. In a way.

Lloyd shook his head slightly. "I think I got most of that," he said. "Are you aware that your speech is slurred and your breath smells of alcohol, madam?"

"I'm drunk," she said.

"No!"

"Do you want to know what Hotshot's advice was?" she asked. "He thinks I should marry you. So do I."

"Well, you did say you probably would."

"Definitely," she said, definitely. "I'm sorry, Lloyd. I'm sorry I've messed you about for so long."

"Are you remorseful enough—or drunk enough—to put a date on this definite marriage?" he asked.

She nodded. "When you retire," she said.

He smiled. "Well, that's something to look forward to when I'm drawing the old-age pension," he said. "Just another fifteen years to go."

"No! When you retire from the job."

He laughed. "That could be next month," he said. "Especially if you get done for murder."

"Then I'll marry you next month," she said. "Will you marry me? If I'm being done for murder?"

"Yes," he said. "And I'll tell you what I'll do for you—and I don't do this for all my customers—I'll let you reconsider your proposal when you're sober."

"I'll say the same when I'm sober."

"Good. Now, I'm going to make you something to eat."

Judy sat down on the sofa, her knees a little stiff from her evening on the floor. Lloyd always fed her when things got a bit emotional. She could hear him busying himself in her kitchen; he would find things to make into a proper meal. She never could. Funny—she would have thought he'd have been huffy for days about finding her with Hotshot, but he had taken it in his stride.

She was starving, she realized, when a mixed grill and chips made its appearance.

"Not exactly what I had in mind for the birthday meal," he said. "But I expect you'll like it better anyway."

She sobered up enough as she ate for him to bring her up to date with work, at her request. His latest theory had bloomed and died before she had even had a chance to vet it.

"But it's another little puzzle," he said. "Isn't it? Why would she make what was an immense effort to make herself go into the garage, and then not use her car? I mean, I know she had a thing about it as well, but the garage was the big thing. Once she'd done that—why would she stick at the car?"

"Wouldn't start," said Judy. "Or . . . she needed Dutch courage to get in there, and thought she'd get done if she drove it." She thought for a moment. "Or maybe seeing all the stolen stuff made her feel shaky—she hadn't driven for two years, didn't want to risk it. She—"

"All right," said Lloyd. "It isn't a puzzle at all. End of work session."

Judy smiled, and kissed him. He made coffee, they moved to the sofa, and things got quite exciting. Then she remembered she hadn't taken her pill, and had to find her handbag, and then had to turn it out to find the packet, and it was while she was doing this that Lennie's scornful appraisal of street girls came into her mind. They think if they're on the pill, they're laughing. They'd all be HIV positive in five minutes.

She stopped with the pill halfway to her lips. That was Drummond, she thought. It was Drummond that Rosa thought couldn't make her pregnant. And she had said he couldn't *make* her pregnant, not that she couldn't *get* pregnant. It had nothing to do with her being on the pill.

"What's wrong?" said Lloyd.

She swallowed the pill. "Nothing," she said.

Light was beginning to dawn. But it could wait. The work session was over.

Chapter Sixteen

Sunday 7 November

Rob was signalling, approaching the turnoff for Parkside, before he remembered.

He took the right, carrying the acute turn on like you could in London cabs, so that he was facing the other way, a manoeuvre only possible here at this time on a Sunday morning, when there was no commercial traffic, and the Sunday drivers were still tucking into their bacon and eggs.

He pulled out onto the bypass again, and drove back through Malworth, on to Stansfield, and home. No more Lennie. No more Ginny. No more break-ins.

Today was the first day of the rest of his life.

ф

Lloyd had unilaterally reinstated Judy to the two enquiries from which she had been barred; Case didn't know yet, and Lloyd was well past caring what he did or said when he found out.

He hadn't told her, couldn't if he'd wanted to, how he had felt when he had walked in on her and Harper. The feeling had been, quite simply, indescribable. His worst fears realized. And he knew his subsequent reaction had puzzled her, for he had a tendency— perhaps even a marked tendency—towards jealousy where she was concerned. He put up with Freddie flirting with her, just. He had hated it when she had still been married to Michael. He had regarded with deep suspicion the men with whom she inevitably worked until he had satisfied himself that they had no designs on her, and that she wasn't interested in them. And last night, there she had been, obviously very relaxed, to put a kind construction on her condition, holding hands with someone he didn't even know she had met.

But she had had a straight choice, and she had chosen him. He had won the gold medal, and wealthy, handsome, debonair, charming Hotshot Harper had come puffing in for the silver. She may have been uncharacteristically squiffy, but Lloyd had been as high as a kite. And he had discovered that he sometimes did like the company of drunken police officers.

And now, complete with hangover, she was pursuing enquiries of her own with Ginny, and he was facing Matt Burbidge across the table in the interview room. He hadn't been able to run a motorbike to earth, but his chat with the caretakers had been interesting; if Matt hadn't turned up by half past ten, they had said, they just left; he had a key to the back door. He hadn't arrived by ten-thirty on Friday night, but this was not unusual. So, motorbikes apart, he could have raped and murdered Marilyn Taylor. But Lloyd started off with Rosa.

"You must have known as soon as you saw that security camera still that Mrs. Ashman was the prostitute whom you knew as Rosa," he said. "Long before you were suspended, long before Drummond ever mentioned her."

"Yes."

"Why didn't you tell anyone that?"

"I did," said Burbidge. "It's a long story."

"Tell me it," said Lloyd, sitting back. "I've got all the time in the world."

"All right," said Burbidge. "When I was on the beat in Parkside, I nicked those whores every time I could. I don't approve of it. Never have. Carrying on like that where decent people are trying to bring up kids. But I was told not to arrest Rosa, so I didn't."

"Who told you not to arrest her?"

"It doesn't matter. But when I saw that security camera photograph, I went back to this person, told him. He said to forget it, but I didn't think that was right. So I told DCI Merrill, who was in charge of the rape enquiry. Told him she was working the Ferrari under the name of Rosa. Turned out he already knew that. And he didn't want it broadcast."

Ginny had told them about the police taking advantage. That in itself hadn't surprised him; he just hadn't thought of Merrill as being one of the ones she meant. "Who's the other person who knew?" he asked. "The one who told you not to arrest her?"

"Oh, no—you're not getting names from me. The investigation team have tried that once or twice. I've only given them one name. Your girlfriend's."

"I take it you're referring to DI Hill?" said Lloyd, getting up, stretching a little. Feeling a slight twinge of back pain. "Are you saying she knew?"

"Not about Rosa. But she's involved."

Suddenly, things got a lot clearer for Lloyd. "You're DCS Case's mole, aren't you?" he said.

Burbidge nodded. "I was keeping him informed," he said. "Until your girlfriend decided to stitch me up, too. Now he's not sure he can trust me. You have to admire her style, don't you? She gets rid of me and Barry, makes herself look true blue with the top brass, gets herself airlifted out of Malworth, then gets all the glory in a murder enquiry. Then when things get sticky, she turns the tables on me, making out I raped the Chalmers woman. I knew what the bitch was up to when she came round asking questions— Why do you think I was on my way to France?"

Lloyd frowned. "Why were you on your way to France?" he asked.

"To talk to my wife's parents! Tell them that I had to see her, that she had to make contact. That I needed her to confirm that I was with her that night, not raping anyone!"

"Wouldn't a phone call have done?"

"Do you think I haven't tried? They hang up!"

"What have you done to upset them all so much?"

"Mind your own business."

"And Marilyn Taylor's rape and murder? Is DI Hill stitching you up for that, too?" asked Lloyd.

"Of course she is."

"And how is she supposed to have done that?" he asked.

"The blood on Drummond's jeans matches the hair found on Taylor's bed. Well, I know it isn't my hair, so it can't be my blood, can it? Anyway—I didn't cut myself that badly. I doubt if I even got any blood on his jeans."

"So whose is it? It isn't Drummond's."

"It must be the real rapist's blood, mustn't it?"

"And how would it get on Drummond's jeans?"

"Because she put it there!"

Lloyd laughed. "DI Hill had nothing whatsoever to do with Drummond's jeans," he said. "She never even saw them, never mind handled them."

"No, but her mate did, didn't he? Finch? They know who the rapist is, and they're covering up. They've been covering up all along."

Lloyd felt much more philosophical about all the accusations swirling about Judy's head now that he realized that Bartonshire Constabulary wasn't really alive with mutterings about Judy's alleged corruption; it was the concoction of one very bitter man and one misogynistic anachronism, which was one of the things he was proudest of having called Case during their little tête-à-tête about Judy.

He sighed, shook his head. "You know your trouble, Burbidge?" he said. "You and your friends at Malworth were conspiring to pervert the course of justice for so long that you think everyone's doing it."

"She is, that's for certain."

"No," said Lloyd. "She's not." He tapped his temple. "That's all in your mind, Burbidge," he said. "And if the blood on Drummond's jeans isn't yours, that's easily confirmed. Let us have a sample of blood."

"No. You can't charge me with that girl's murder, not on what you've got. And even if you do, no jury's going to convict me because the blood on someone else's jeans matches evidence found at the scene. You can say I refused to give you a sample, but it won't do you any good. I was never anywhere near that flat, or that girl—and no one's going to frame me for it."

Lloyd smiled. "You're out of touch, Burbidge," he said. "I can oblige you to submit to a sample of saliva being taken. Didn't you know?"

Burbidge stared at him.

Lloyd sat back, folded his arms, and examined Burbidge for some moments. "And I can't think of any reason why you wouldn't cooperate unless it is your blood," he said. "Therefore I will so oblige you."

Burbidge sighed, ran a hand over his unshaven face, and looked at the tape recorder. "Put that off," he said. "And I'll tell you."

Lloyd reached over, stopped the tape. "It's off," he said. "But you are still under caution, and I will give anything you say in evidence if it's pertinent to this enquiry."

Burbidge nodded. "Fair enough," he said.

¿

DI Hill looked a bit pale, Ginny thought. She hadn't seen her yesterday—maybe she'd been sick. Lennie had gone out the minute she'd arrived, saying he'd be back in an hour, if the inspector could stay that long.

"I don't need a baby-sitter," she had said, but DI Hill had said she didn't mind staying.

"I'm not going to fall over now," Ginny said. She felt better today. Her face still ached, but her eye didn't feel so bad, and at least it was sort of open now.

"Forty-eight hours you've to be watched, it says on that card," said DI Hill. "And you should really be in bed."

"I don't want to be in bed. I spend half my life in bed."

That made the inspector laugh. "Speaking about that," she said. "Tell me about Rosa."

"I didn't know she was that Mrs. Ashman."

"I know. Tell me what you did know about her."

Ginny shrugged. There wasn't a lot to tell. She had come in to the Ferrari one night with Lennie, and then she had started coming most nights. She hadn't had many punters. Drummond was her only regular. And of course that DCI from Malworth, but he never paid her for it, so she didn't make much money. Ginny hadn't been surprised when she had packed it in.

"The night she packed it in," said the inspector, "she spoke to you. What did she say?"

"I told them yesterday. She was mad at Lennie for smacking her. Do you want a cup of tea or something?"

"I'll make it," the inspector said, and got up and put the kettle on. "What exactly did she say, Ginny?" she asked, and sat down at the table again. "Tell me everything she said."

"She said he'd hit her for doing Drummond without a condom. She thought it was stupid, because it wasn't like he could get her pregnant."

The inspector was leaning forward slightly. "Why couldn't he?" she asked.

"That's what I said. And she said he couldn't come while he was doing it. He had to, like, come out and do it himself, or he just lost it."

DI Hill sat back, smiling. "Are you saying that he suffered a sexual dysfunction whereby seminal emission during coitus could not be achieved?" she said. "That self-stimulation was his only alternative to loss of penile erection?"

Ginny stared at her. "You what?" she said, getting up automatically when the kettle boiled, so used to making Lennie endless cups of tea that she could have done it in her sleep.

"Did you hear them going on like that in court?" she asked.

"Oh, yeah. I didn't know what they were on about." Ginny made tea, brought it to the table, got two mugs. "Is it important?"

"Well, it's done wonders for my hangover," she said.

"Is that what's up with you?" said Ginny. "I was wondering." She frowned as she got the milk and sugar. "What's it mean, then? All that stuff about sexual thing?"

"It means," the inspector said, "that he couldn't come while he was doing it."

"Why didn't they just say that?"

She smiled. "I don't know," she said.

"Should I have said? In court?"

DI Hill shook her head. "They wouldn't have let you," she said. "You're not allowed to tell them what Rosa told you."

"Oh, yeah. But I can tell you. Mr. Lloyd said."

"Yes. Did she say anything else?"

Ginny poured the tea. "Not really. She was telling me about him—we were having a laugh about it. She said she reckoned he'd been wanking off for so long he couldn't do it any other way. We thought he'd gone, but he hadn't. He was playing one of the machines. And he walked out, all red in the face. Served him right."

The inspector had gone serious again. "He heard you and Rosa laughing about him?" she said.

"Yeah."

"Did Rosa leave straightaway?"

"No, she stayed and had a drink. There wasn't much doing—I wasn't working, either. She was a good laugh. She went about eleven, I think, because one of my—" Ginny broke off. She hadn't worked it out, not until now. "He followed her, didn't he?" she said. "Because we were laughing about him? He followed her, and—" She didn't finish the sentence. "She was a good laugh," she said.

The inspector leant close again. "Ginny—did he attack you again? Did he do that to you?"

"No!"

"Listen—if you tell us exactly what happened, and how it happened, it could be self-defence. Even if Lennie shot him. Even though you tried to cover it up. But you must tell us now, Ginny. You must tell us now."

"It had nothing to do with Drummond!"

"Then who beat you up? Lennie didn't—I don't care what he says."

"It was a punter."

The inspector sighed, and picked up her tea. "You make a good cup of tea, Ginny," she said.

She should. She got enough practice.

◊

Matt had told Lloyd about going to work undercover on the farm, about living and working there for a month. About seeing Lucy every day, and talking to her. She had flirted with him. She wasn't interested in the young lads—it was very flattering. He was forty. She was seventeen. And she—well, she didn't want some teenage boy mauling her; she wanted someone with a bit of savvy, someone . . . like him. He had had an affair with her. He had been the first. People would say he'd seduced her, but it hadn't been like that. She had . . . chosen him. To initiate her into the ways of the world.

He didn't say all that to Lloyd. But he tried to explain that he hadn't seduced her. Not really. He had carried on seeing her after he'd left the farm. And he had been with her, in the barn, that evening. He had left her, had walked down the track towards the road, where his car was. He had seen Drummond, only obviously he didn't know who he was at the time. He had been checking something on the bike. Matt had noticed the registration, the way policemen did, automatically.

And that night, when he had come on duty, he had discovered that moments after he had left her, Lucy had been raped. Just like the other two. The first woman had said that it was someone on a motorbike.

"You knew who it must have been, and you kept quiet about it?" said Lloyd incredulously.

Matt nodded. "Yeah," he said. Lloyd would have done the same in his position. Anyone would. "I had no excuse for being at that farm! Isabelle was already suspicious because I kept going out—I'd started seeing Lucy when I was there on duty! I'd have lost everything if I'd said."

"You did lose everything," said Lloyd. He wasn't looking at Matt;

he was looking out of the high window in the interview room, almost on tiptoe, as though there was something really interesting going on out there, and he was bored with the conversation.

"Only because your lady friend couldn't keep her mouth shut," Matt said.

Lloyd shook his head. "You blame Judy? Have you tried looking in the mirror?"

"The only thing I don't blame her for is my wife walking out on me," said Matt. "That was Drummond's fault. She'd followed me— she knew I was going to the farm. She thought it was Lucy's mother I was seeing until Lucy got raped and Mick Rogerson told us that she'd been with someone just before, but she wouldn't say who he was."

Lloyd turned from the window, frowning. "He told you that?"

"Yes, well. He's a mate of mine. I worked there before I joined the police. His father had the farm then. He and I were best mates."

"And you seduced his daughter?"

"No! She came on to me! She'd been away at school. I hadn't seen her for a couple of years. She was . . . grown up. It wasn't my fault. Why should I get landed because someone raped her? I went to see her after, and—explained the situation."

"You put pressure on her to keep quiet about you?" Lloyd looked horrified, just like Isabelle had.

My God, Matt had just told him that his lady friend was framing him for murder, and he'd taken that in his stride. But everyone had to make a fuss about what he'd done.

"Not pressure. Just—you know."

"She was seventeen," Lloyd said. "She had just been brutally raped. And all you could think of was saving your own skin?"

"You sound just like Isabelle! That's why she left me. But what was the point of my name coming into it? What good would it have done?"

Lloyd still looked like Isabelle had done. Matt gave up. "And that night, I tried to stop her leaving, but I couldn't," he went on. "I got back to the car, we saw a bike pass us, and we gave chase. When I saw who it was I tried to get him on something, anything. Anything that would give the rape enquiry a chance to get their hands on him. A blood sample. If he was drunk, we could get a blood sample. But he wasn't drunk. We couldn't hold him. So I—I just . . ." He looked at Lloyd. "I would have killed him," he said. "If Barry hadn't got me off him, I would have killed him. My wife had just walked out on me because of him."

Lloyd didn't speak.

"So I told some of the lads that he'd said he was the rapist. And I told them about Rosa. And that if she'd been working the night she was raped, then there was a fifty-fifty chance they'd get something on her that pointed to Drummond, because she didn't have all that many customers. They said they would get him. I was suspended, and the next thing I knew he was under arrest for raping one of the other girls at the Ferrari. I heard later that they'd arranged for that to happen. I had nothing to do with that."

"Highly commendable." Lloyd sat down.

"Now I don't believe he was the rapist," said Matt.

"Who else could have raped Lucy?" asked Lloyd. "You saw him."

Matt shook his head. "Maybe he *was* just a Peeping Tom," he said. "Watching us."

"And maybe you raped her, and Drummond wasn't there at all."

"No. I didn't rape Lucy, I didn't rape Chalmers, and I didn't rape and murder Marilyn Taylor. It isn't my blood on Drummond's jeans—it can't be, not if it matches anything you found at the scene, because I was never there." Lloyd would have to believe it, sooner or later. Matt had raped no one. And someone was stitching him up. "But if you get a DNA sample from me," he went on, "it'll match up with the unidentified one from Lucy, and then everyone will know about that."

"We don't publish the results," Lloyd said.

"No? Maybe not, not if I was an ordinary member of the public. But I'm not. I'm an ex-cop. It would get round in no time flat."

Lloyd didn't seem too bothered about that "Someone rang Drummond, saying they could tell him about Rosa," he said. "Was that you?"

"No."

"You went to see Ginny—did you take a gun from her?"

"No."

"Didn't you still want to kill Drummond?"

"No." No. He'd rather hoped that Drummond would have a go at Judy Hill again, but he thought it politic not to say that to Lloyd, if there was a chance of getting out of this without too much damage to his reputation. At the moment, he was the man who had had a go at a rapist, and been sacked for it; if they found out the rest, he'd be the man who was knocking off a seventeen-year-old kid when he should have been working, the man who walked away from her and left her to a rapist, the man who got her to cover up for him.

"Where were you at nine o'clock on Friday night?"

"I was getting the car ready for France. I was filling her up, and—" Matt remembered, and pulled out his wallet. "Look," he said, pushing a receipt across the desk to Lloyd. "I paid for my petrol at one minute to nine."

Lloyd looked at the receipt, and raised his eyebrows. "I could commit a murder at four o'clock in the morning of the twenty-seventh of February in the year two thousand and fifty, if one of the receipts I once got was used as evidence," he said.

"It's a petrol station—it's got cameras, like they all have. I'll be on there, with the time and the date. You can check."

"I will. And you're giving us a saliva sample, like it or not."

Q

Carole doggedly prepared Sunday lunch; Rob was in bed.

Lennie didn't have the cab; Rob said he'd ended their arrangement. He'd have to, Carole supposed, if he was going to prison. She supposed he might—he had burgled an awful lot of houses. Stephen had said they must wait and see what was going to happen before they did anything. She must carry on as though nothing had happened.

So she was making Sunday lunch. Just as though nothing had happened.

What else could she do?

Q

"Thanks," said Lennie.

"You're welcome," said Inspector Hill. "She's a lot better today."

"Yes."

He closed the door and looked at Ginny. She was, he supposed, a lot better. She didn't look ill, not like she had yesterday. But she still looked battered, and he would never forgive himself for that.

"Where've you been?" she asked.

He took a breath, and said the three words as though they might poison the air by being spoken. "The Job Centre," he muttered.

She frowned. "It's Sunday."

"Yeah, well—they've got cards in the window. I just thought I'd—you know—have a look."

He hadn't even understood half of them. "Must be conversant with . . ." seemed to consist purely of things he'd never heard of, mostly initials. Anyway, he had a record; most people wouldn't look at him even if he could work a computer, which he supposed was what you had to be conversant with, and he couldn't. Ginny had got one in her job lot of goodies from the Co-op, and it just sat there.

But maybe he could get a real job as a cabby. He'd liked it, driving around, talking to people. And he could still do the odd deal on the fare, if he was careful not to get caught. They didn't all own their own cabs. He'd ring round, tomorrow.

They'd be all right, he told Ginny. He'd get something.

§

All that stuff in Lennie's house still bothered Judy; Marshall said he had asked Jarvis if Lennie was in on the burglaries and had been given an unequivocal and heartfelt no. But that wasn't top of her agenda at the moment; she went back to the station anxious to talk to Lloyd, who wasn't, of course, in his office, and went to her own office through an empty CID room. She looked in vain for aspirin, and decided that her head wasn't bad enough anymore to merit a run to the supermarket chemist.

Her door was knocked on and opened in his more usual fashion by Tom. "They've found the gun, guv," he said.

"Good," said Judy. "Has it gone to forensics?"

"Yes, but there's something else."

Judy sighed. "Lloyd's right," she said. "Every lead we get is followed by a but. But what?"

"The sixth cartridge had jammed in the mechanism. So there's no reason to suppose that he wasn't killed where he was found."

Judy was uncomfortably aware that the missing cartridge had been the only thing that stood between her and real, helping-with-enquiries suspicion; she could practically feel Case licking his pencil and turning to a new page in his pocketbook.

"Do you know where Lloyd is?" she asked Tom as he was leaving.

"Out checking Matt Burbidge's alibi."

"Another theory? Great."

Lloyd came in as she spoke, and Tom left. "Another alibi," he said. "Burbidge was filling up with petrol when Drummond was murdered. Another theory stillborn."

Judy looked at him glumly. "The best theory I've heard yet is the one where I did it," she said. "But—Ginny made me feel a lot better." She told him about Rosa's more down-to-earth description of Drummond's dysfunction.

Lloyd listened, nodding.

"And when he heard Rosa laughing about him with Ginny, he waited for her to leave, followed her," she went on. "Then when he was charged, he found out that she wasn't called Rosa at all—she was known as Mrs. Rachel Ashman, and no one knew she had been working as a prostitute. And since he'd been with her earlier, he could see a way of getting the DNA evidence discounted."

"But he couldn't admit to knowing that Rosa and Mrs. Ashman were the same person," Lloyd said thoughtfully. "So he insisted that all the victims had to give evidence so he could 'recognize' her when she went into the witness box."

"Quite," said Judy, sighing as she realized what must have happened next. "And when Mrs. Ashman knew who had been charged, she knew that would happen."

"Do you think she knew it was Drummond who had raped her?"

Judy shrugged. "Maybe," she said. "Maybe not. But what she did know was that he'd tell the court that she worked as a prostitute, that he'd been with her earlier that evening. Everyone would find out what she had been doing. Her husband would find out." She looked away. "And she killed herself sooner than let that happen," she said.

"Which rather foiled young Mr. Drummond's plan," said Lloyd.

Judy looked back at him. "That was why he had to bring his visits to Rosa out into the open," she said. "He had to say she existed, or no one would ever make the connection. And he had to have a reason for wanting her found—so he said that she would prove that he functioned quite normally. She wasn't in a position to contradict him, was she?"

"But he overestimated Malworth's devotion to duty," said Lloyd. "And *he* wasn't in a position to prompt them without incriminating himself."

A little silence fell; it was Lloyd who broke it.

"But once he was out," he said slowly, "and it was over—why was he still so keen to meet someone who had information about Rosa?"

"He still wanted the connection made," said Judy. "By someone other than him. He wasn't satisfied with the DNA evidence being given too much weight—he wanted it discounted. He wanted the compensation to increase, and the press and TV to give him even more airtime. Poor innocent Colin, mistaken for a rapist. How much do you suppose his story would have been worth?"

Lloyd nodded. "I'm sure you're right," he said, sitting on her desk. "But what Rosa said to Ginny isn't evidence. And even if you could prove that Drummond was sexually dysfunctional, it wouldn't prove he'd raped anyone. And he didn't rape Marilyn, did he? It wasn't *his* hair we found." He looked thoughtful. "Do you think Burbidge is bitter enough about it all to have done that to Marilyn in the hope that Drummond would get the blame?"

Judy decided it was time to give him a look.

"It's possible!"

"He might be bitter enough," she said. "He isn't stupid enough. Did you get a saliva sample?"

"Yes," said Lloyd, and told her about his interview with Matt.

"Very gallant," said Judy. "But I don't think he raped anyone, Lloyd. Drummond did. He raped them all." She looked at him. "Would you hang on to the sample?" she asked. "Just for a little while? In case we can prove some other way that he didn't rape Marilyn Taylor?"

Lloyd shrugged. "Why not?" he said. "But I don't see how it can be anyone else's blood on the jeans. Burbidge was the only person who had physical contact with Drummond that night—it has to be his blood."

Judy had stopped listening. How could she have lost sight of her original aim? And Lloyd's little puzzle? And her own little puzzle, never voiced. The open drawer in that neat, tidy room. She had thought that Drummond might have been looking for something, but he hadn't. Marilyn had.

"He isn't the only person who had contact with Drummond that night," she said.

"Who else?" said Lloyd, frowning, getting off her desk. "Baz? I suppose we've only ever had their word for it that Baz didn't hit him, and only his word for it about where *he* was when Bobbie was raped. That might be why he was so keen to point the finger at Matt. If he—"

"Not Baz," she said, interrupting him. "Bobbie."

Lloyd sat down. "But I thought we were looking for whoever raped and murdered Marilyn," he said.

She shook her head. "You asked the question," she said. "Why didn't she lock herself in the bathroom?"

"Why didn't she?"

"Because she wanted to get to the bedroom, that's why. Because that's where she thought the gun was. In the drawer—it was open, remember? She went to get the gun, but it wasn't there anymore, was it, so he overpowered her."

Lloyd shook his head, still looking slightly puzzled. "And?" he said.

"And I thought she had been raped and murdered on her own bed. Only it wasn't her own bed, was it? It was Bobbie's gun. It was Bobbie's room."

"It was Bobbie's bed," said Lloyd. "It's Bobbie's hair."

"Yes," said Judy. "And it's Bobbie's blood on Drummond's jeans—that's why they match."

Lloyd sat back, nodding. Then they were on their way to the Ferrari, and Bobbie, still flintily coping with grief.

She hadn't been back to the flat at all; she had had no idea that Marilyn had been anywhere other than her own room. She confirmed that her bedroom was the last door on the left along the corridor, and that she had indeed kept the gun in the top drawer of her bedside cabinet. It hadn't occurred to her to tell Marilyn she'd given it away; she hadn't thought that Marilyn would care what she'd done with it. She would give them samples of anything they liked, if it would prove that Drummond was the rapist. Even if he was dead. It would be a sort of full stop to it all.

"One puzzle's been cleared up," said Lloyd, as they got back into his car. "The rest will get much easier—you'll see."

Judy certainly hoped so, in view of her less than secure position. Her prospects seemed even less bright when they got back to the station to find DCS Case apparently waiting for them on the doorstep, like an irate father waiting up for his daughter.

"Just on my way to HQ," he said. He looked at her. "I owe you these," he said, giving her twenty cigarettes, and her lighter. "And an apology," he added, in the manner of one who didn't make them too often.

"Don't apologize too soon," said Judy. "I'm still in the frame for murder."

"I don't care if you *murdered* the bugger," he said. "And I owe you this, Lloyd." He tossed a penny to him as he spoke.

Lloyd caught it. "Thank you," he said, unsmiling.

He refused to tell her what that was all about, as Case walked off to his Range Rover, but she would get it out of him. Sooner or later.

Once they actually got inside the building, Tom had news for them. More negative news, as ever. "It isn't Drummond's blood in the Transit," he said. "They want to know if they're to give it back to the owner, or what."

"Oh, why not?" said Lloyd, frustrated at every turn. He sat down on Marshall's desk. It made a change from hers, thought Judy. It was a mystery to her why he didn't just sit in chairs. "Maybe it is Ginny's. Maybe he did beat her up in there."

"You don't believe that," said Judy.

"No, but if it isn't her blood and it isn't Drummond's blood, who the hell's is it?" he demanded.

Judy had had enough of blood, and said so. "I seem to have spent my every waking moment discussing blood, asking people for blood, analysing blood, mopping up blood—I wasn't cut out for all this blood. I even sent you to the GBH," she said to Marshall. "Because I was sick of the sight of—" Her eyes widened. Hangovers sharpened her faculties, it seemed.

"What did you say Mr. Evans did for a living?" she asked.

Chapter Seventeen

I know whose blood's in your Transit," said Inspector Hill. He had known, really, that he would never get away with it. Lennie stood to one side. "Then you'd better come in," he said.

Ginny was in the sitting room, watching television. Lennie closed the connecting door.

"His name's Monty Evans."

Lennie invited her to sit down, and offered her a cigarette; she smoked. He'd liked that about her when he'd found out. She might be the only police officer in the known universe that he actually liked. "I didn't know him by any name," he said.

"You're not still saying he was a punter, are you? Because he's got girls of his own working the streets in Malworth, so I don't—"

"Don't I know it," said Lennie. "Only I was too stupid—" He broke off, feeling the tears hot behind his eyes again. He cried every time he thought of that brute with Ginny. Every time. He wiped his eye with the heel of his hand. "I'm an amateur," he said. "Rosa,

Ginny. Just, you know. Keeping an eye out for them. Making sure no one but me takes advantage of them," he added, in an attempt at a joke. "I'm not in that league. Don't want to be."

"Are you going to tell me about it?"

Lennie looked round the kitchen, every surface gleaming, everything put away where it belonged. He'd been very careful to tidy up after he'd made Ginny something to eat.

"We moved in here six months ago," he said. "And about three weeks later, I come home to find some guys unloading a three piece suite, taking it in here. I said they'd got the wrong address, but they showed me the docket, and said there was loads more in the van. It was from the Co-op. Everything. Television, video, rugs, tables, lamps, computer games—you name it."

Inspector Hill leant over and tapped her ash into his ashtray. Lennie put it in the centre of the table.

"So I told them it would have to go back—we couldn't pay for it. Paid for, they said. Gave me all these receipts. I asked Ginny what was going on, and it turned out she'd met some bloke in the Ferrari, told him about her new house, and he'd said that he could lend her the money to furnish it."

"Oh."

"Yeah," said Lennie. "Oh. And I was going to get the furniture taken back, pay him off, only—I couldn't." He drew on his cigarette, and looked away from the brown eyes that watched him so closely. "She was happy," he said. "I'd never seen her look really happy. I mean—you know how she lived. You know what sort of background she had. I couldn't take it away from her."

"And you couldn't keep up the payments?"

"It was all right to start with. Then things got a bit tight, but I got this deal with the cab—God knows how Jarvis survives, because he's got no idea. I made a lot of money with that cab, one way or the other. But things got slow again—they do. And I stopped paying other things. The phone got cut off last week—the electric and gas'll be next. But I still couldn't meet the payments. And I went to him, expecting threats and God knows what, but he says not to worry. Pay him when I've got it. All the more interest for him. Didn't lean on me . . . just let it drift. And so did I. I'd pay him when things picked up, I thought."

The inspector nodded slowly. "He was selling the debts, wasn't he?" she said.

"I know that now. But I'm an amateur, like I said. People think I know all the angles, but I'm—" He sighed. "I just don't get involved in things where people get their heads broken," he said. "Then on Wednesday, I picked up this guy. Flash suit, cigar, muscles. He'd bought the debt, and he wanted to make an example of someone."

He told her of his desperate attempts to raise the cash by Friday, about his reprieve, about his dream punter. He assumed it was off the record; he didn't care much if it wasn't. "I owe you a thank-you for searching this place," he said. "If you hadn't, I'd have got my money, and gone to meet him. And then sat outside his house like a berk while he was—" He drew in his breath, held it for a moment, released it. "As it was, he'd only just started, and look what he did to her. It was because I'd told him what she did. He saw where he could make an example of me and get rid of the competition all at the same time."

"What happened?"

"When I came in he was at the top of the stair with her. He—he was hanging on to her, smashing his fist into her face—I grabbed a chair, and ran up. I sort of fended him off with it, told Ginny to run. Hide. I didn't think I could hold him too long—I thought he might go after her, and I couldn't even call your lot, because the bloody phone was—" He wiped the tears. "I don't expect you to believe this," he said. "But he pushed the chair away, lunged at me—and he fell downstairs. His head was cracked open. I thought he was dead. I didn't know what to do." He had just sat on the stair and looked at him. He might still have been there, if someone hadn't knocked on the door, frightened him into action. "In the end, I got the Transit right up to the door, and I managed to get him in there. I was going to dump him, but he was still breathing. So I drove him to casualty, pushed him out in a side street. Then I got home and started trying to clean up the van—that's when you brought Ginny home." He looked bleakly at her. "Is he dead?" he asked.

"No," she said. "And he's confirmed that he fell down stairs—can't remember where. Memory loss. Very common, apparently."

Lennie felt as though a huge rock had rolled off his shoulders. "I'm not going to be arrested?" he said.

"No. He might sue you for damages, but . . ." She smiled.

Lennie was almost laughing with relief. "I thought he'd die. I thought I was going to get done for murder."

"Ginny could have him charged with grievous bodily harm," she said. "That's a possible five years. Why don't you pay him a visit, and see if he's prepared to swap that for what you owe him?"

Lennie's eyes widened with surprise. "Are you supposed to say that sort of thing?" he asked.

"No, I don't suppose I am. But I'm quite sure Ginny would rather have her furniture than have to give evidence in court again."

She was OK, DI Hill. Ginny was right. Not *all* cops were bastards.

*

"You can go," said the custody sergeant.

Matt got off the bunk, and saw Lloyd. The sergeant left, and Matt looked warily at his visitor, who blocked the cell door. "Come to duff me up for being rude about your girlfriend, have you?" he asked.

"No," said Lloyd. "I've come to tell you that we will not, in all probability, have to use your saliva sample. It will be destroyed within five days of confirmation of what we now believe to be the case. You may witness its d—"

"Yeah, yeah. I'll trust you. Thanks."

"It's not me you should be thanking," said Lloyd. "It's Judy."

"Well, I've got her to thank for everything else, so maybe she owed me."

Lloyd's face grew dark, his eyes bright. "She owed you nothing," he said. "She came within an ace of losing her own job trying to keep you out of this."

"Pity she didn't." Matt walked out, went to the desk, and went through the process of being unarrested. "Thank you, my man," he said, as the custody sergeant gave him his belongings. He signed for them with a flourish.

Lloyd escorted him to the door, and spoke quietly in his ear. "You," he said, "are a worthless, sad little man. I wouldn't have done you a favour if my life had depended on it. But if it gets you off Judy's conscience, then it was worth it."

Conscience? Matt doubted that she had one.

⸬

Lloyd was joined by Judy in the canteen, but then she just toyed with her food.

"What's wrong?" he asked. "I thought you'd be pleased. You've got your rapist, Marshall's got his burglar, Burbidge gets to keep his grubby little secret, and even when you get it wrong, you get it right. You stopped Ginny ending up in intensive care. Not bad for a couple of days' work."

"And you're left with your murderer," Judy said. "You'd better arrest me, because I don't see how anyone else could have done it."

"But in a few days you'll have proof that Drummond raped Bobbie," Lloyd said. "Your motive's gone."

"No," she said. "It hasn't."

No. Now that he thought about it, it hadn't. The only way she had ever been going to prove that Drummond had raped Bobbie was if Bobbie told the truth. And the only way Bobbie had ever been going to tell the truth was if the threat was removed. And someone had removed it.

"Lennie was manhandling Evans into his Transit," she said. "Jarvis was burgling a house. Matt Burbidge was paying for petrol. Carole Jarvis was with her boyfriend and sundry others. Only one other person had access to that gun and could have used it. It's obvious, Holmes," she said. "I did it."

"You've missed out Ginny," he said.

"Ginny was semiconscious."

Lloyd nodded, ate, thought, ate some more, then aired his absolutely final theory. "It has to have been Lennie," he said. "He did know the gun was still there, that Ginny had never taken it back.

He took it, earlier in the day. Arranged to meet Drummond. And killed him *before* he got home."

"Why?"

"Because he raped Ginny."

"Mm."

"Ginny was beaten up by Evans, and the reason she knew the gun had gone is because she went to get it—that's why she ran upstairs. But it wasn't there. He fell, and she ran away from him, hid in the underpass, Lennie found her, and rang us on Drummond's phone— he might have been ringing you, so you'd get help for her—he trusts you. He found himself on the queuing system, and rang 999 instead, before running away. That's what you heard."

She didn't look convinced.

He pushed his half-eaten pudding away. He really ought to think about a diet. You didn't want to put on weight if you had a dodgy back. And he didn't want to be fat and bald and have a bad back with men like Harper lusting after Judy.

"Come on," he said, "Let's pay Mr. and Mrs. Fredericks another visit."

The Sunday traffic was building up now; the cars with roof-racks piled high with bicycles and dinghies and other things with which he was blessedly unfamiliar. He tried to take the wait at the turnoff like a man, but he was soon muttering.

When they finally made it to Parkside, Ginny was on her own.

"Where's Lennie?" asked Judy. "I thought he was supposed to be keeping an eye on you?"

"I'm all right!" protested Ginny. "He said he had to visit someone in hospital." She looked puzzled. "I didn't think he knew anyone in hospital," she said.

Lennie going hospital visiting was indeed a difficult concept to grasp. Lloyd was aware of only one person recently connected with Lennie who was in hospital. He detected Judy's hand in Lennie's sudden concern for the sick, and chose to ignore the whole thing.

He sat down at the kitchen table, and motioned to Ginny to do the same. "When this man attacked you," he said, his voice very deep, very Welsh, and very stern, "what did you do?" Ginny seemed totally unmoved by stern Welshmen with deep voices, so he decided to abandon that.

"What Lennie said. I ran. I just ran—I didn't even think where I was going. The park, I suppose. I feel safe there. You can hide in the bushes."

This last was offered as advice; Lloyd thought he might take it. It would be nice, now and then, to hide in the bushes.

"Before Lennie came in, if he came in," he said.

She frowned. "I ran upstairs. I thought if I could get to the bathroom, I could lock myself in."

Lloyd could hardly fault that reasoning. "You didn't run into your room to get the gun?"

"No!" She turned to look at Judy, who was standing by the door, just out of her line of vision. "I thought this was all finished," she said. "It had gone by then."

"How do you know?" asked Lloyd.

Ginny turned back, and looked at him almost pityingly. "It wasn't there," she said. "So it must have gone."

Lloyd nodded. "But how did you know?" he tried again. "If you didn't look for it?"

"I already knew. It was in the drawer with my work things," she said. "I had a punter that afternoon. I had to get a new pack of condoms out. And the gun wasn't there."

"You had a customer? On Friday? Besides Jarvis?"

"Yeah. In the afternoon."

"Why didn't you tell us that?"

"Because you only asked me about ones who could have taken the gun. He couldn't have. I knew it was gone before he came upstairs."

Lloyd nodded slowly. "And . . . this punter. Was that before or after Inspector Hill had searched your house?"

"Before," she said promptly.

Lloyd heaved a huge sigh of relief and looked at Judy, who was looking similarly relieved. He turned back to Ginny. "Why did you say Inspector Hill could have taken the gun?" he asked.

"I never said that!" said Ginny, aghast at the very thought. She twisted round to Judy. "I never!" she said. "Honest—I never!"

Lloyd thought hard about the interview. "But when Sergeant Finch asked you if anyone else could have got it, you said, 'Just Inspector Hill, when they were searching the house'—didn't you?"

Ginny shook her head, frowning, thinking, then nodded. "Yeah," she said. "Yeah, I said that. But he didn't ask who could have got the gun. He said had anyone else been upstairs and not handcuffed to the bed. And she *had* been upstairs," she said earnestly. "And she wasn't handcuffed to the bed."

Lloyd smiled broadly, trying, unsuccessfully, to ignore the image that had sprung inevitably to his mind. No, he thought. She'd never stand for it. Would she? He looked at her, saw her trying desperately not to laugh, so as not to offend the deadly serious Ginny. You never knew. She might, he thought, on a good night with a fair wind. But where in the world could they get hold of handcuffs?

"I was just trying to get away from him," Ginny went on. "But he got me at the top of the stairs. Lennie came in and got him off me."

He left Ginny with great reluctance. He really did want to spend his life interviewing her. He envied Lennie.

"There you are," he said to Judy, as he drove off. "The gun was there after your first visit and gone before your second."

"Mm."

Lloyd heaved a great, melodramatic sigh. "Now what?" he said.

"You've just proved that no one murdered him," she said. "Now, that would suit me down to the ground, but I've a feeling you would rather catch whoever did it."

Well, yes. He had given Freddie a lecture on the subject. And, indeed, people couldn't go around doing that sort of thing willy-nilly. But once in a while . . . ?

Maybe not. "All right," he said. "Do your thing."

"What thing?"

"The little puzzles," he said.

"The little puzzles are your thing," she said.

"But you list them in chronological order—I know you do. So go through all the little puzzles about any of the people who could have got hold of the gun."

He now waited for a break in the traffic to allow him to escape from Parkside. Judy was turning pages in her notebook, and almost broke her neck when he shot out into the first available space in a most un-Lloyd-like fashion. Serve her right. She was always doing it to him.

"Right," she said, as they drove through the quietness of a Mal-worth Sunday, restored to it by the all-too-successful bypass. In an old town like this, it was almost the way driving used to be, when he was a child, and anyone with a car was godlike, majestically sweeping past, their gleaming chariots stirring up faint clouds of dust on the underused roads. "Why did Rob Jarvis team up with Lennie, of all people?" she asked.

"Ginny."

"Yes, but if he'd got an honest partner to drive during the day, he could have afforded the going rate for Ginny, and still had a profit to show for it," Judy said. "So why Lennie? He knew he was being ripped off—he told Marshall he knew."

Lloyd thought. Jarvis was a burglar, without form. Lennie was someone who had tried his hand at a lot of things, all illegal, until quite recently, and would doubtless be doing so again any minute. "Fall guy?" he suggested.

"But he didn't even try to use him as a fall guy, did he? I mean—if Lennie had keys to the garage, he didn't say he had."

"He couldn't, really, though, could he? He had the taxi that night, not Lennie. He didn't bargain for someone calling the police while he was on the premises."

"True." She ticked it off. "Why use Bonfire Night as a cover, and then ring nine-double-nine?"

"All right," said Lloyd, sweeping out onto the dual carriageway, giving that some thought. "It wasn't the murderer who rang nine hundred and ninety-nine. It was a passerby who didn't want to get involved."

"Why did this passerby ring Stansfield first?"

Stansfield looked very pretty at this time of year. It wasn't by any stretch of the imagination a picturesque town—all housing estates and neighbourhood shops with flat roofs. But in spring and autumn, its woodland setting and its planted roundabouts came into their own. The parkland round the boating lake was a wonderful mix of greens and browns, with great orange splashes, and deep red tinges. Yellow leaves were just beginning to lose their grip on the trees, carpeting the grass beneath them.

He signalled left, and tried not to look at the town centre, about which he had bad dreams. He didn't know who had designed it in the first place; he hadn't thought much of it then. But now . . .

"I don't know," he said. "I can't think of any reason. I thought it might be Drummond himself, trying to ring you, but the lab says no. The blood was on the phone before those digits were pressed. Who knows police station numbers?"

"Police officers."

"Apart from police officers."

"Informers?"

"Neighbourhood Watch," said Lloyd.

"Solicitors."

"We've got a taxi-driver-cum-burglar, a petty villain, a secretary or whatever Mrs. Jarvis is, and a copper turned security man."

"And a police officer," said Judy.

Lloyd ignored her. "I like the last one best," he said. He thought hard to try to produce a reason for anyone at all ringing Stansfield, especially Matt Burbidge, but he couldn't. "No," he said. "Still no answer. Next."

"Why didn't Mrs. Jarvis use her car?" said Judy.

Lloyd turned left and left again into the police station car park, and squeezed the car into his space. He switched off, and looked at Judy. "I thought that one had so many possible answers it didn't constitute a puzzle," he said, getting out.

"It has," said Judy, as they walked towards the building. "But maybe we should find out what sort of car she drives. Drove. Whatever. Maybe she did take it—maybe someone saw it at the scene."

"And maybe all Mr. Morgan's friends are part of a conspiracy?" Lloyd grinned, and held the door open for her. "You're getting worse than me."

In the CID room, Marshall blinked a little, gathering his thoughts slowly, like he did everything else, as he was asked the question. "I don't know," he said, at last. "I didn't see her car. I can find out for you, sir."

"No, that's all right." Lloyd sat on his desk. "You didn't see it?" he repeated. "Was the taxi in the garage?"

"No. It was on the road outside the house. There wasn't a car in the garage. Just all the stolen goods."

"Was there a car outside, in the courtyard of the garages? Or outside the house, where the taxi was?"

"No. No, because I was the only car there when I parked, besides the taxi. And there was nothing parked outside the garages."

"And both Mr. and Mrs. Jarvis were there?"

"Yes," said Marshall.

"Then where was her car, Constable Marshall? The car that sits in her garage while she takes the bus?"

"Sorry, sir?"

"Nothing." Lloyd got off Marshall's desk, went into Judy's office, and sat on her desk, facing her as she followed him in. "She wouldn't have been able to drive it if it wasn't there," he said. "Would she?"

"But who could have taken it? The only likely candidate is her husband, and he was driving his taxi—he couldn't drive two cars at once."

No. Lloyd tried hard to think of even the wildest scenario that could include Burbidge getting his hands on Mrs. Jarvis's car, but it defeated him. "Lennie hasn't taken to stealing cars, has he?" he asked.

Judy laughed. "That would be too much like hard work," she said. "Besides, Mrs. Jarvis wouldn't have had to gather up her courage to open the door—it would have been open."

Lloyd turned to look at her as she sat down, and shrugged. "I don't think Mrs. Jarvis's car can have anything to do with it," he said. "Lenny must have taken the gun. Ginny must still be covering for him."

"Why would Ginny keep me out of jail rather than Lennie?" asked

Judy. "She thinks the world of him. If it was a toss-up between me and Lennie, there would be no contest. She would have said she only missed the gun after I'd been there. Like a shot."

"But she doesn't know it's a toss-up between you and Lennie. She thought she was putting the blame on Rob Jarvis."

Judy nodded. "She wasn't to know Jarvis was pulling the plug on Keith's serial at the very moment Drummond got a bullet in his head," she said.

Lloyd stared at her. "Who's Keith?" he asked.

She looked up. "Oh, Lloyd—he's just the husband of a couple who lived next door to Michael and me. Please—don't start thinking I'm throwing myself at every—"

"No, no," he said, holding up his hands as though he was stopping traffic. "No—I mean, is that why you wanted to know if I'd recorded it?"

She looked a little guilty. "Yes," she said. "And I didn't want to say that I had more friends you didn't know ab—"

"Judy," he said. "What you were doing at nine o'clock on Friday night may be a matter for speculation, but not what I was doing. And I can assure you, I wasn't watching television."

She frowned. "*Did* you tape it, then?" she asked.

He made a loud, impatient noise. "You're sounding just like Ginny!" he said. "No, I didn't tape it. It wasn't *on* on Friday night! It's on *Wednesday* nights!"

Lloyd had been defending Judy's honour at nine o'clock on Friday. He had been in the act of placing a bet with Detective Chief Superintendent Case on that honour when they had heard about Drummond's murder.

And he'd won his bet. But that had been betting on a certainty—no fun at all. This was much better than that. For once, *he* had the answers to the little puzzles. Even the anonymous Neighbourhood Watch call to Stansfield police station.

He stood up, and looked out of Judy's window at the town centre, bathed in autumn sunshine, along what used to be a street but which was now a pedestrian walkway strewn with strange things for children to play on, people to sit on, potted plants, the odd tree, and a great deal of windblown litter, up to where the taxis formed a U at the top. The taxi rank; one of the places Rob Jarvis had thought he might have been at nine o'clock on Friday night.

But he had been burgling a house, hadn't he?

♀

"Did you see your friend?" asked Ginny, curled up on the sofa, not watching a programme about dragonflies. She switched off the TV as Lennie came and sat beside her.

"Yes," he said, smiling, putting his arm round her.

"Is he all right?" She assumed it was a he.

"He's going to be fine," said Lennie. "And so are we." He took his arm away, and felt in his back pocket for his wallet, taking out a twenty-pound note and a five-pound note. "That's our capital," he said. "But the debt's been paid off, Ginny. He won't be back."

"How could you pay him all that money?"

"It doesn't matter. It's settled. This'll buy food for a bit. And there are some jobs around. Casual work. On the demolition round here, and stuff like that."

Ginny smiled. "You don't know how to do anything," she said.

"I know how to do this." His hand slipped inside her shirt, and his fingertip brushed her breast. He put his arm back round her again, and she leant back, her eyes closed, enjoying the gentle tickling.

"I wish I could kiss you," he said.

"You can."

"It'll hurt."

She shook her head, and felt his mouth gently touch her bruised lips.

"I love you," he said.

"I know," she said.

♀

Carole Jarvis opened the door, and smiled nervously at Chief Inspector Lloyd. He had a woman with him; he introduced her as Detective Inspector Hill. She was attractive. Well dressed. Somehow she never thought of policewomen as looking like that. She thought of them in uniform, and looking a bit butch. Stereotyping. Like her burglar with his bag marked swag. But burglars looked like Rob, and policewomen looked like her.

"Mr. Lloyd. Do come in. I—that is—Steve . . . Stephen said he'd given you the names and addresses of the people at his flat that night—I'm sure they'll—"

"That's quite all right, Mrs. Jarvis," he said. "It's actually Mr. Jarvis we've come to see."

Yes. He had eaten his Sunday lunch. He hadn't wanted it; she could see that. But he had eaten it.

"Is he at home? I noticed his taxi was outside, so I thought . . ."

"He—he's doing some work on my car, I think," she said. "He keeps it in good order—just in case I want to—" She held the back of her hand to her mouth. "He . . . he'll be in the garage, I expect," she said. "If you want to speak to—"

She closed the door on them. They could find him. Maybe he really was mending her car, but there had been nothing wrong with it when she had driven it. After he'd rung her up from the police station, told her to take it back to the garage, to put it away, just in case anyone had seen him drive away from the park. He didn't want it seen.

She had known, as soon as she had heard about Drummond, why her car had been gone from the garage; why all she had seen when she had opened the door had been someone else's property, neatly stacked along the wall of her private hell. She had made him tell her.

And when the interview about the burglaries had taken such a long time, he had had to ask her to take the car back. It was parked in a street off Epstein Drive. She had picked it up, driven it back. He had come home eventually, and he should have been glad that it had worked, that he was free of Drummond forever, and no one any the wiser.

But he had just taken the cab out. Nothing had changed. Nothing at all. And he had known that it wasn't going to work from the moment he had pulled the trigger. And she knew why he had gone to the garage, why she mustn't stop him. He couldn't go on like that; he had wanted to die ever since it had happened, ever since Drummond had raped him.

It had been a long time since he'd gone; it must all be over. But she hadn't been able to go and see. She couldn't have brought herself to open that door. Not again. She had been so relieved to see Chief Inspector Lloyd.

She would ring Steve. Once they had found him. He would understand why she hadn't stopped him.

è

Judy was having her birthday meal at last. Candlelight and Lloyd's seduction table lamp were all that lit the room, and the tension between them had gone at last. They had talked, as they had a perverse tendency to do in their most intimate moments, about work.

Judy had automatically pulled the hose from the exhaust pipe as soon as Lloyd had opened the garage door, but it had been too late; Drummond had claimed what she hoped and prayed was his final victim. But there was no guarantee of that.

They had pieced it together. Jarvis had teamed up with Lennie, had allowed Lennie to rob him blind, to use his cab for immoral purposes, to do what he liked with it, in return for two things: Ginny, and someone to blame when his luck ran out.

But then Drummond had come home, and Ginny had shown him the gun. Jarvis had been a soldier, and a gun was a quick and efficient way of bringing about Drummond's destruction; the seed had been sown, and he hadn't wanted Lennie to take the blame for the burglaries anymore, because they were going to give him his alibi.

That night, Wednesday night, he burgled Keith's house. He unlocked the front door, left pots and pans piled up against it. At a few minutes after nine, he unplugged the video, the television, everything he would usually steal, and piled it up at the back door, left it unlocked, and went back to his cab driving.

If the burglary had been discovered before the firework display that was to mask the sound of the shots, then perhaps the murder would not have happened when it had. But it would have happened, of that Judy was certain.

Jarvis had driven to Malworth, to pick up his fare, the one who had eventually decided to stay the night. And he had seen Drummond leave the block of flats opposite, followed him, watched him dumping clothes in a less jealously guarded bonfire than the symbolic Parkside Regeneration bonfire. If he had had any doubts about carrying out his plan, then surely what he must have heard on the early morning news had made the decision for him.

On Friday morning he went to Ginny, and took the gun in the moments when he was alone in the room. Then he rang Colin Drummond, promised him the information that everyone present at the trial knew he most wanted, arranged to meet him at nine o'clock in the underpass. Some time in the afternoon, while she was at work, he drove his wife's car to a street close to the semiburgled house. At twenty to nine that evening, he left his cab outside number seventeen Epstein Drive, and ran to his wife's car. He drove back to Malworth, left the car in the desolate and deserted park, an hour before the two or three street girls gathered, and went into the underpass to wait for Drummond.

Drummond had been on time; Judy had seen him. He had walked along the underpass to, as Lloyd had said all along, his terrorist-style death, passing the barely conscious and terrified Ginny, who had pressed herself into the shadows at the sound of his footsteps. Jarvis had carried out the execution, taken Drummond's mobile phone and had gone back up the banking to his car. Judy had heard his running feet just before she had found Ginny. He had made what Lloyd called his Neighbourhood Watch call first; he had rung Stansfield police station and reported that he could see a light moving around in seventeen Epstein Drive, whose owners, he knew, were on holiday. Then he had hung up, and had keyed three nines and thrown the phone down in the open space, so that Handel's music booming over from the bonfire would alert the emergency operator as to where the emergency was, and everyone would know exactly *when* Drummond had died.

He had thrown the gun into the bushes, had got back into his wife's car, and had driven through Malworth's deserted streets back to Stansfield, back to the street close to Epstein Drive, and had left the car. He had watched from a safe distance, then had made himself known to the constable attending the burglary, got into his cab, and driven away. Sooner or later, they would get him for the burglary.

And, as far as Jarvis ever knew, it had worked. He didn't know that Keith had been recording something; he didn't know that Lloyd's taste in television programmes had found him out. When he had shut himself up in that garage to end it all, it was in the belief that he had been successful, that he had done what he had had to do. But it hadn't made him well again.

Judy was glad they had got there too late; sometimes, you just had to let sick people take their own way out.

Lloyd touched her glass with his; she smiled. The candlelight flickered, casting dancing light in Lloyd's blue eyes.

He put his glass down. "Sooner or later," he said, marginally adjusting the position of the pepper grinder, "they're going to drop the Chief from Chief Supers and Chief Inspectors."

"I know," said Judy.

"So Case will be a Superintendent, and you and I will both be inspectors."

She nodded.

"And they probably won't need two CID inspectors. And Bell's a long way off retiring, so they won't be needing any other kind of inspector, either. And . . . chances are, I'll have to take early retirement."

"Yes," she said. "You'll get a lump sum as well as your pension, won't you?"

"Yes," he said. "Why do you ask?"

"Oh," she said. "I was just thinking that it would be just what you'd want, really. To start married life."

He took her hand and kissed it. "How much of that wine have you had?" he asked, his lips brushing her skin as he spoke.

"One sip."

He clasped his fingers in hers, and they held hands tightly for a long moment before he let her go, his face grave.

"Your handcuffs or mine?" he asked.

About the Author

A native of Argyll, Scotland, JILL McGOWN has lived in Corby, England, since she was ten. She wrote her first novel, A *Perfect Match*, in 1983, and others have followed, including *Gone to Her Death, Murder at the Old Vicarage, Murder Movie, Murder . . . Now and Then, The Murders of Mrs. Austin and Mrs. Beale, The Other Woman* and A *Shred of Evidence*.